WRECKAGE

By

J.D. PRATT

&

ANDREW WOLFENDON

ISBN 10: 1944083236
ISBN 13: 978-1-944083-23-6

CHAPTER 1

Ever see that old beer commercial, "Life doesn't get any better than this"?

That's what I'm afraid of.

August 23, 2017

If I wasn't feeling bleak *before* entering Gauthier's Shop 'n Go, I am certainly getting the job done by the time I arrive at the Buddee's Hot Dog Flavored Potato Chips display and double back toward the Build-It-Ur-Self Nacho Station. Gauthier's is one of those discount food marts seemingly designed for one purpose only: to crush the human soul. It doesn't sell a single product that a self-respecting, mentally healthy individual—not that I fit into either of those categories—would consume at gunpoint.

Cereal it is. I grab a box of store-brand Reese's Puffs, pay the sullen cashier with the nose pimple big enough to be mapped by Hubble, and make for the exit, flushing like a shoplifter.

Cold cereal, dinner of champions.

After scoring some off-season lager to pair with my candy-flavored corn balls, I cruise past the tire and exhaust shops of south Wentworth and park in front of my tired and exhausted *house*. Well, my *parents'* tired and exhausted house; the place I grew up in. Legally it is mine now—I inherited it when Mom died last year and have been living alone there since—but I've made zero effort to claim it as my own.

May I just say, nothing makes a thirty-eight-year-old feel more chipper about his life management skills than going to sleep every night in the same bedroom where he deflowered his first Victoria's Secret catalog.

I am, in case you haven't picked up on it, battling depression.

Well... *battling* is a strong word. The truth is, the fight went out of me ages ago. That's what most people who've never been depressed don't realize: the fight is the first thing to go.

I sit curbside in my vintage Hyundai, staring at the peach-colored, vinyl-sided bungalow and its twenty years of deferred maintenance—waiting, I guess, for it to transform into a sparkling seaside villa in France. When that doesn't happen, I step out of the car and let my feet start their programmed death-march toward the sagging front steps.

"Hey, douche-weed," says Clyde Gilchrist, my optimistically muscle-shirt-wearing neighbor, approaching me from his side of our scraggly dividing hedge. The man has a gift for crafting a conversation opener. "Can you do me a favor? Next time you decide to throw a bag of empties in my backyard, can you at least aim for the—?"

I cut him off with a flip of the hand. I've never, in fact, thrown anything into his yard—except disdain—but I'm not in the mood for Clyde Gilchrist this fine evening. I jam my key in the door and slip inside. The odor of last night's Kung Pao Shrimp greets my nose as—

A hard object clubs my Adam's apple. Feels like a flesh-covered pipe. My cereal box leaps from my hand, and my bottled beer and car keys crash to the floor. My feet try valiantly to continue their forward march as my neck is jerked backwards with a sickening crack of cartilage.

The hard object is a forearm. A muscled humanoid has me in a chokehold from behind. I can feel his biceps twitching and his hot breath in my hair.

My unseen assailant whips my body around in a smooth one-eighty and drags me backwards through the house, face up. I cannot breathe, and my eyes feel as if they're about to pop their sockets. My feet flail, trying to gain purchase on the bare floor.

What the hell is happening here? Why?

I'm a second-rate computer game artist. I don't own anything worth stealing—a casual glance around the house would tell you that—and I've masterfully engineered my life to be of no real consequence to anyone. Ergo, whoever this guy is, he has the wrong person. The wrong house. The wrong information.

Wrong, wrong, wrong. On every count.

I hope I can convince *him* of that. Whoever he is.

If only I could pull some air into my lungs.

As he jerks my body into the kitchen, I take absurd note of the black cobwebs dotting the ceiling. I haven't looked up in years, I realize.

The man's gym-forged arm forces me down into a kitchen chair, set in the middle of the floor, directly below the ceiling light, interrogation style. He releases the pressure on my neck just enough for me to gulp some air.

Standing in front of my parents' 1970s Kenmore electric is a second man, smallish in stature, maybe five-seven or so. He's wearing a Star Wars storm trooper mask. The jaw section has been cut away to expose his real mouth. Perhaps so he can speak and be heard more clearly? A well-trimmed reddish beard rims a set of small, even teeth.

The man wears latex surgical gloves and holds in his hands—almost comically, it seems at first—a branch-cutting tool, the type with two long handles and short, curved scissor-blades.

The pipe-hard arm maintains its lock grip as Storm Trooper addresses me in a soft, precise, and rather high-pitched voice that comes off as *almost*—but not quite—prissy. "This tool," he says, holding up the instrument, "is called a lopper. Did you know that? This particular model is a long-handled, high-torque, bypass lopper. It can snip an inch-thick branch off a green tree as easily as slicing cake."

Storm Trooper lays the lopper on the kitchen table and picks up an iPad. He holds the tablet device about a foot from my face, waits till my freaked-out eyes focus on it, and then taps it awake with a latex-covered finger.

On the viewing screen is a video, cued up and ready to roll. Its frozen image is that of a fifty-year-old man strapped into a metal garden chair, his arms and wrists duct-taped to the chair's tubular arms. The man's hands have been left free to move.

Storm Trooper taps the Play icon.

Trooper's own recorded voice issues from the iPad's speaker. He's standing just off screen in the video. "I'll ask this question once and once only," Troop's high voice says to the taped-up man on screen. "Who knows about this besides the woman?"

Video-guy in the chair replies, "I haven't said a word to—"

Before he can finish his sentence, the open blades of the lopper lunge into view like a snapping turtle's jaws. They hook the man's left pinkie and ring finger into their curved bite and lop them off cleanly. A plastic bag is snapped around the man's hand. He lets out a keening *eeeee-eeeee-eeeee* of raw agony, as blood streams into the bag and sweat pours from his face. He shouts in the voice of a man whose spinal cord is on fire, "Clarence Woodcock! Clarence Woodcock! Clarence Woodcock! Clarence Woodcock!"

My stomach twists like a wrung dishrag. Storm Trooper shuts off the video, puts down the iPad, and picks up the lopper once again.

"I hope that video was instructive," he says in his almost-but-not-quite-prissy manner. "The way we work is this: I give orders, you follow them without a moment's hesitation. Thus, you avoid the lopper. Are we abundantly clear on that?"

I nod. Yes. Abundantly.

"My partner is going to release your neck now. You are to remain seated while he straps you into the chair. Clear?"

Again, I nod. My list of alternatives does not stretch from sea to shining sea.

Chokehold-man wordlessly pats me down and pulls my phone from my pants pocket. He wraps a band of rubbery, self-sticking fabric around my chest and upper arms several times, fastening me to the chair-back. He does the same to bind my rear and thighs to the seat.

"Before we begin," Trooper says—begin *what?*—"let me explain something that I hope will put this situation in perspective and enlist your cooperation." Trooper Dan has my undiluted attention. "If you've seen many crime thrillers on TV, you may be thinking that because I am wearing this mask, I do not wish for you to see my face. Which, in turn, you might assume means you have a chance of sauntering away from this encounter."

I do not want to hear whatever comes out of his mouth next.

"That is a faulty assumption. I wear the mask only out of an excess of caution. You *are* going to die today, Mr. Carroll. I get no joy out of telling you that, but I don't define the job parameters."

Adrenaline rips through every synapse of my nervous system. Not only does this guy know my name— my hopes of this being a case of mistaken identity have fizzled like spilt champagne—but also, he intends to kill me. My heart and lungs pump in triple-time.

"To employ a tired cliché," says the masked man, "we can do this two ways..."

He pauses. I become aware of a detail I failed to take in before. The kitchen floor is covered with a sheet of clear plastic, *Dexter*-style. Not a hopeful sign for the protagonist, as a rule of thumb. "Option A—cooperation—is better for all concerned, believe me when I say that, but we will revert to option B without qualm. Option B, needless to say, brings the lopper into play. A testicle sliced in half is a memorable experience, I'm told." His high, even voice has an almost hypnotic quality. "So... choose an option, Mr. Carroll."

Does he actually expect me to choose aloud? Apparently, he does.

"Option A," I say flatly.

"The only choice, really. Still, it's surprising how often option B becomes necessary. Let's begin."

He lays the lopper down again and reaches into a paper bag on the table. His latex-gloved hands emerge holding three items: a plastic bottle of Svedka vodka—my brand, yippee—and two brown plastic prescription vials.

"This is a process I understand you're familiar with from past experience," he says. How could he possibly know I OD'd on vodka and pills half a year ago? "As you know, it's a no muss/no fuss procedure. Pleasant, almost. Though last time you tried it, you didn't get the job done, did you? Today we're going to bypass the 'cry for help' stage and go straight for DOA."

He hands me one of the vials. "Your instructions are to take *all* the pills in both containers, wash them down with the vodka, and then continue drinking the vodka until you are rendered... non-functional. Then, bim bam bom, it's all over and we leave you to rest in peace."

I stare at the vial in my hand, knowing I have no choice but to obey the man, but trying to prolong the moment before my fate is sealed. That's when I register the soft *clack-clack* of my computer keyboard from the adjacent den—my "office." Chokehold guy hasn't left the kitchen, so that means there's a third member of this rogue Jehovah's Witness cell.

What have I, Finnian Carroll, low-level computer artist and general life failure, done to merit a three-man criminal operation?

And what do they think they're going to find on my computer? The missing Snowden files? Yet, pathetically, a sense of violated privacy wells up.

"You're not going to find anything useful there," I shout toward the den.

"Oh, we know exactly what's on your computer, Mr. Carroll," says Troop. "Trust me. Come on, swallow the pills."

I pour the contents of vial number one into my palm. Cute little rectangular prisms. Xanax. Close to a hundred twenty of them. My own prescription, as confirmed by the name "Finnian Carroll" on the label. I filled it just two days ago.

I review my options. One tactic might be to fling the pills, scatter them across two rooms. Buy myself some time. Would that result in lopper discipline? Probably not. If these guys are going to all this effort to stage my death as a suicide, the lopper is probably a bluff.

Wasn't a bluff for the guy in the video, though.

"The pills, Mr. Carroll." Trooper-man eyes me through the mask, waits precisely two seconds, then turns and reaches for the lopper.

"I'm doing it!"

My hand, filled with pills, flies to my mouth—Chokehold has left my forearms free to do the deed. A few pills miss their target; the majority score a hit. Trooper hands me the vodka. "Drink."

I take an obedient swig, working the pills down my throat. I swig again. Storm Trooper takes the vodka from me and hands me the second vial of pills. These I recognize too. Diazepam—generic Valium. A script I filled but never used. Ninety blue pills, a three-month supply. Ten-milligrammers. I dump about half of them into my mouth. Troop hands me the vodka to wash them down. I glug away.

I eat the remainder of the pills and wash them down too.

Now it's just a matter of waiting for the results to come in. So to speak.

Well, this is what I wanted, right?

God, what have I just done?

CHAPTER 2

"**D**rink up, Mr. Carroll," says Storm Trooper, strutting back into the room.

He has left me alone with Chokehold for a long while, to give the pills time to work their magic and so that he can confer around my computer with thug number three. Choke has been nudging my arm periodically, and I've been taking measured sips of vodka, but now Trooper Dan seems eager to step up the pace of my demise.

"Hurry, hurry, faster," he says, rapping the Svedka bottle with his latexed knuckles. "We don't have all day. Things to do, Mr. Carroll, things to do."

Things to do.

For some reason, these three simple words snap me out of the fog of numbness I've slipped into. I will never, ever, ever have another *thing to do*. My thing-doing days are behind me. This stark reality blows through me like a polar wind.

No! I will never dab paint on another canvas. I will never smile at another pretty woman in a summer dress. I will never drink another pint of Arrogant Bastard Ale on the outdoor deck of Pete's Lagoon on Musqasset Island with my best friend Miles.

I will never again *set foot* on Musqasset Island, the only place on Earth where I was ever genuinely happy-ish. I will never again sit on the rocks at Mussel Cove with Jeannie, watching the seals bob in the waves, laughing myself sick.

I will never again make love to Jeannie. (Full disclosure, that customer left the barber shop years ago.)

My thoughts cluster surprisingly around Jeannie, whom I haven't seen in four years. Why did I let her go so easily? Why didn't I fight for her? What trivial principle had I been trying to prove? My soul for a do-over! Until this moment, I didn't even realize I wanted one.

A hot blade of longing stabs my heart. Longing for the life I once held in my hands and failed to embrace, longing for the life I will never have.

Suddenly all my "struggles" of the past year—the half-assed suicide attempt, the endless search for "the right therapist," the maudlin boozing—unmask themselves as nothing but drama. Posturing. I realize I haven't *really* been struggling with depression; I've seen what a monster *real* depression can be. No, I've been struggling with disillusionment. Clinical disappointment.

What a child, what an ungrateful tool.

Troop taps the vodka bottle again. I drink.

I mentally replay all the decisions and circumstances that brought me to this place and see the truth of my recent life with the crystalline insight of the soon-to-be-dead.

About four years ago, I left my beloved Musqasset Island to move back home to despicable Wentworth, Massachusetts, from whence I hail. Outwardly, I made the move to care for my mother who had Stage IV bladder cancer, but really, I was just escaping a situation on the island that was too taxing for my poor, pain-averse psyche to handle. The six months Mom was given to live turned into three years, which I "endured" with demonstrated valor, secretly grateful for the excuse it gave me not to make affirmative choices in my own life.

Then, about a year ago, Mom died, and I slipped into a downward spiral—well, *further* downward. Not because I was traumatized by her death, but because, upon being stripped of my "noble caregiver" role, I was suddenly confronted with a life bereft of purpose. Storm Trooper dismissed my previous suicide attempt as a cry for help. I hate to admit it, but he's right. And not just about the overdose itself, about all of it. All my drama and self-flagellating.

A fully shaped realization bubbles up from the depths of my awareness like a beach ball that's been stuffed under black water: I do not want to die.

Do not. Do not. Do not. Do not. Do not.

I want to live. I desperately, passionately, whole-heartedly want to live. No more screwing around. I have been cured of "suicidal ideation" for life. I want another crack at this thing.

True, I have a belly full of pills and am strapped to a chair under the glaring eye of a psycho killer, but a strong instinct rises up within me: my time's not up yet. Can't be.

But what are my options here? *Think.* Try to talk my way out of it? Beg for sympathy? Not a chance. Bargain?

"What do you guys want?" I venture, my words slurring a tad. "What can I give you?"

Trooper Dan, his eyes obscured by the helmet mask, leans over me and whispers, "What we want, Mr. Carroll, is for you to die so we can get to Applebee's before happy hour ends. Sláinte!"

He waits till I take an obedient swig of vodka and then backs away.

The keyboard in the den starts clacking again. "Whatever you're looking for on my computer, I'll tell you where to find it. Then you can be on your way and let me call 911. I haven't seen your faces."

Trooper Dan doesn't even dignify that one with a response.

What other options do I have? Only one, really. Make them think I'm already dead. Well, not dead. Faking dead is impossible when you're under a magnifying glass, as I am. But maybe I *can* fake unconscious-to-the-point-of-no-return.

If I can convince them I'm down for the count before I actually am, maybe they'll leave while I'm still alive and I can call 911. It's not much, but it's all I've got.

"Drink," says Storm Trooper.

I take another swig of booze and begin mapping out my strategy. If I'm going to sell the ultimate possum ploy—and survive it—I need to keep a mental edge. Not easy to do when you've just swallowed two hundred benzos and you're pounding straight vodka. My challenge will be to outrace the real effects of the drugs with my faked performance. Piece of cake. Ha.

How much time do I have? I still feel reasonably clearheaded, but it's hard to judge. I try reciting the alphabet backwards in my mind, the old mental acuity trick. Z... W... X... Y... Nope. A screw-up right out of the starting gate.

Crap, I'm already mentally compromised. I probably have fifteen minutes, tops, before I sink into the chemical stupor that will end my life.

That means I have, at most, *ten* minutes to convince my captors I have slipped into terminal unconsciousness.

The tug of gravity yanks at my chin. Real sleep is hooking its line in me. I need to do something, fast. Something unexpected.

Instinct takes over. When Storm Trooper taps the vodka bottle again, I burst into a fit of laughter so sudden and authentic, it takes *me* by surprise almost as much as it does Troop. I laugh till I'm gasping for air.

"I'll bite. What's so funny, Mr. Carroll?"

"You! With your little mask and your 'lopper.' Taking yourself so seriously." I'm skating on thin ice to mock this guy, but I want him to think I'm losing it, throwing caution to the wind. "And the funny part is..." I break into whoops of laughter again. "The funny part is... We're on the same side! We both want this loser dead. Hoo-wah, so let's do this thaing!"

With a big, forced smile on my face, I steer the bottle toward my mouth and take a long swig, staring defiantly at Troop. I want him to think I've not only *surrendered* to my fate but am welcoming it with open arms.

I begin taking manic gulps, watching the bottle's fill-line go down. I'm well past sloshed by now, but my "second awareness"—something I learned to harness years ago during my meditating period—has kicked in. A deeper part of me remains detached and watchful. I need to ride that part. Zen my way through the chemical haze.

A burp escapes my belly. With a mock-serious face, I pronounce, "Hints of sweetness with a pleasingly yeasty body and peppery finish." I dissolve into fits of giggles again.

Storm Trooper's red-bearded mouth curls into a tiny smile below his mask. "Might as well go out laughing, eh, Mr. Carroll?"

"With a whimper, not a bang." I toast him with the bottle. "I mean with a bang, not a wimple. Ha, ha, wimple!"

I sit up rod-straight, pretending I just remembered something urgent. Breathing fast and hard, I say, "I guh go. I guh go."

As if trying to make a frantic burst for the door, I push off with my right leg, causing the chair to topple to the left.

My head hits the plastic-sheeted floor and bounces hard. The vodka bottle clunks to the floor. My eyes roll up in their sockets, and my eyelids shut.

I am officially down for the count. Win or lose.

Silence reigns as my captors and I remain motionless.

I can hear their breathing. Studying me for signs of consciousness.

I am turnip, watch me vedge.

Time flattens into eternity. Not a word from my captors. Not a twitch from me.

One of the men crouches, his knee cartilage cracking, and flicks my cheek. I don't react.

More wordless breathing.

A hand shakes my shoulder. I let my body wobble liquidly and allow my breathing to become labored and ragged. I don't know how long I lie there, strapped to the chair. Clock time no longer exists.

My whole brain blinks off, like a faulty light bulb, then blinks back on again. Shit. I am minutes away from real and permanent turnip-hood.

Spearmint-scented breath warms my cheek as one of the men moves his face within inches of mine. What is he going to do, kiss me? ...Is he?

"That was an inspiring performance, Mr. Carroll," Troop whispers in my ear. My heart flops like a dying fish. "But you don't fool me. I know you're fully conscious. And so here is what's going to happen. I'm going to position the lopper blades on your nose."

Sharp metal brushes my nose-skin on either side. My Zen state retreats. I must summon all my willpower not to flinch.

"When I count to three, you will open your eyes. If you fail to do so, I will lop the nose off your face. One..."

Troop is only testing me. I'm betting my nose on it.

"Two... Three..."

Troop pauses for a moment and does nothing.

I do nothing.

The lopper tightens ever so slowly against my nose. I do not throw my eyes open and beg for mercy. I, rutabaga.

The blades halt before breaking the skin. They stay poised in that position, pinching my nose flesh, for what seems like a month.

And then, the blades retreat. Trooper withdraws the lopper and stands, his cartilage crunching again.

"He's gone," he says to his partner. "If not, he would have cracked." My heart leaps with crazy hope.

Chokehold whips the plastic sheet out from under me like a magician doing the tablecloth trick. He starts cutting the strapping material with a knife. Yes! They're getting ready to leave. And if this is to look like a suicide, they can't leave me strapped to a chair.

Choke whisks the chair away, letting my limp muscles spread onto the floor.

"All set here," he reports to Troop. His first spoken words. What's that accent? No "r" in "here." Boston? Brooklyn?

"Good," says Trooper Dan in his high, almost-prissy voice. Then he utters the words that crush my hope like a sat-on birthday cake. "We'll give it another ten minutes to be sure he doesn't puke or pull any surprises, then we're out of here."

Ten minutes? No way can I hold onto consciousness that long.

Barely five seconds later, my brain blinks off again. Gone. Over and out.

The opening bars of Schubert's "Ave Maria" ring out in an angelic soprano. For a moment I think I've died and gone to Catholic-school heaven. Then I realize it's a ring tone, waking me up. Storm Trooper exits the room to take the call in private.

Twenty seconds later he returns. "Time to go," he says to his partners. "Let's do a quick clean-up, grab our stuff, then we're out of here. Bim bam bom."

Chokehold loudly bunches up the plastic sheeting. Three sets of footsteps clomp off through the house, one heavy, one light, one medium. The three bears. Someone clangs a bucket into the laundry room sink, fills it, and starts cleaning up the spilled beer and broken glass in the entry hall with a broom and mop.

Faster, I silently urge the men as my brain fights to avoid blinking out again. The next time it blinks will be the last. My chances of walking out of here are dimming by the minute.

The downstairs toilet flushes. I hear the mop being rinsed and returned to its place.

Faster.

Several quiet seconds pass. What's happening?

A cold finger of spilled vodka touches my arm, nearly making me jump.

"Finis. Let him die in peace," says Troop. And with that, the three home invaders exit by the back door.

I wait till I hear the muted sounds of car doors closing and a vehicle driving away before opening my eyes.

I try to sit up and find my body now weighs a pleasant five hundred pounds. After three failed attempts, I heft myself to a sitting position, then grab the edge of the table and hoist myself to a stand. All my strength is needed.

The empty pill vials. Somehow, I muster the presence of mind to stick them in my pocket so the ER staff—if I can make it to a hospital—will know what I OD'd on. The mad puppeteer beneath the floor is still pulling my limbs down with all his might.

Call 911. But where's my cellphone? Chokehold took it. I'll need to get to a neighbor's phone.

I lumber toward the front of the house, feeling as if I have twenty-pound weights strapped to my ankles.

My heavy footfalls on the old wooden floorboards jiggle the mouse on my computer desk, and the screen awakens.

A Microsoft Word document pops open, snaring my attention even through the mental fog. I haven't used Word in over a week.

I stare fuzzily at the screen. I need to get medical help—*now*—but I also need to know what these guys were looking for on my computer. And what they found.

Stepping closer to the desk, I try to read the title of the document, but the letters are swimming around and doubling up in my vision.

I force my vision to lock in on the document's heading. In bold sixteen-point font, it reads, "Finnian Carroll's Absolutely Final (This Time I Mean It) and Incontestable Suicide Note and Last Confession."

What? Sounds like something I would write, but...

But I *didn't* write it. Of that I am certain, even in my massively compromised state.

Damn. Those guys weren't trying to take something *from* my computer, they were planting something *on* it.

I try to read the body of the note, in smaller font, but I can't get my eyes to work in synch. The letters dance apart and bunch together like ants at a barn dance. I can only make out isolated phrases. Still, the few chunks of text I *can* pick up, in those floating bits and pieces, suggest something horrifying and impossible.

A wave of nausea overtakes me. My knees buckle, and I drop to the floor.

The hard wood feels like bliss. I want to sleep—for a long, long time. I come perilously close to giving up the fight, but then an unsuspected reserve of mental toughness kicks in and forces me to my feet again.

I stagger heavily to the front door, then out onto the porch. My feet tramp down the front steps, across the sidewalk and into the street.

No neighbors in sight. A yellow step-van with a cartoon face painted on it bears down on me from the upper end of Bell Street.

I plunge to my knees and use the last of my strength to throw my arms up for help.

CHAPTER 3

"**T**his release-form states you are leaving the hospital against the advice of the treatment team," the social worker says in a voice so slow she must be going for comedy.

"Understood," I reply, my knee dancing a fevered jig. I'm sitting in the day room of Saint Dymphna's, the psych ward of Calvary Mercy Hospital, signing my discharge papers.

"Before you sign the release, Mr. Carroll," labors the social worker, "please read this document and initial it." She hands me an information page detailing the perils of the particular cocktail of benzodiazepines and alcohol I ingested (I vaguely recall the ER doctor referring to it as "the full Whitney Houston"). It includes confusion, dizziness, brain damage, hallucinations, and that grande dame of side effects, death.

Roger that. I need no convincing that my overdose was a bad idea. After getting my stomach pumped in the ER, receiving activated charcoal treatment, and undergoing sixteen hours of vital-sign management under glaring fluorescent lights, I'm all set on that.

Following my medical treatment, I was shipped, FedEx Express, to the psych ward upstairs. Having stayed there once before, I knew the ropes a bit. Rope number one: when you come in on a "voluntary," you cannot be held for more than seventy-two hours without a commitment. Technically, my admission was voluntary, so the first thing I did, after sleeping almost twenty-four hours straight, was sign a "three-day note."

And now I intend to honor it. I don't need suicide counseling, and I don't need protection. From myself, anyhow. What I need is to go home, stat, make sure I still have a job, and try to figure out what the hell happened at my house last Friday.

I sign the papers.

The social worker hands me a large manila envelope containing my wallet and belt. "Mr. Carroll... May I call you Finnian?" *Not a lecture, please. I didn't pack a lunch.* "This is your second stay with us. When patients come back a third time, the staff starts to refer to them as 'regulars.' Don't become a regular."

"I won't." I mean it too.

Despite the circumstances, I feel more alive than I have in years.

✶✶✶

I've only been away five days, but as I step from the cab, my parents' place looks alien to me—shrunken, dark, angular. I try the front door. Unlocked. Handy, since I don't have my keys.

I step into the entry hall, flinching involuntarily. No attacker grabs me by the throat. Still, the silence feels fraught.

"Hello?" I shout. Hidden assailants, as we all know, are rendered defenseless by the shouted hello. Needless to say, no one responds.

I do a quick walk-through of both floors to see what traces my "visitors" left behind. Did they sack the place? Steal anything? I make a pass through my upstairs bedroom, which I'm still treating as temporary quarters, after four years. It's a disaster, but in the customary way.

I check my mom's room, which, since her death, I've been using mostly as storage space for stuff I don't want to deal with. Nothing's been moved.

The bathroom also seems undisturbed, but the stranger I see in the mirror gives me a jump. My normally thin anatomy looks almost skeletal—drawn cheeks, sunken eyes. The ice-blue irises that occasionally draw a second glance from passing females have a slightly manic glow, framed by the dark of my untrimmed hair and six-day stubble. Yikes. No one hiding in the shower, though.

It isn't till I step into the kitchen, downstairs, that a chill sweeps across my skin. All the kitchen chairs are arrayed neatly around the table—not the way we left them—and there is no trace of the vodka bottle. No spilled booze on the floor, no stray pills.

This can mean only one thing. Trooper Dan and his buddies returned to the scene of the crime. Finding no body, they cleaned up the "suicide" traces. Why, I don't know. But one thing's for sure: the bad guys know I'm still on the sunny side of the grass.

Therefore, I am unsafe in this house.

My keys are splayed on the kitchen counter where I always leave them, along with my banged-up phone. The phone is a surprise. I figured, for some reason, my assailants would have kept it or destroyed it. Why? Suddenly I'm The Man Who Knew Too Much?

I turn the phone on. No recent activity except a few missed calls and a text from work. I'll give my boss a call in a minute.

My computer. I've been saving that for last.

I step warily into the den where my workstation is set up and roll the mouse to awaken my Mac. Only my desktop wallpaper (a painting I did of Fish Pier on Musqasset Island) appears on the screen. No suicide note. *Where the hell did it go?*

My captors must have deleted it when they returned to the scene. I sit in my eighty-dollar HomeGoods office chair and open Word. Moving the cursor to the File menu, I select Open Recent. A blank list pops up. Someone has cleared the Recent files list. Not I. Clicking the Trash icon to look for the deleted document, I note the Trash has been emptied. Again, not by me.

What other ways are there to find a recently created and deleted document? I click All My Files, arrange them in order of date. Nothing on the date of my assault. I check the folder where AutoRecovery files go. No joy. Maybe my drug-addled mind dreamt the note up.

My anxiety is mounting. If Trooper and company came back here at some point—and obviously they did—they're no doubt aware I was hospitalized and probably also know I've been discharged. They might be planning to swing by for a visit.

They might be here already. It's not out of the question.

I listen again. Nothing.

Still, I'd better get out of here, pronto. But go where and do what?

Wait. Better TCB first. Call work. Check my emails. And find that file. But hurry.

I work for a computer game company in Cambridge, creating artwork for animated adventure games for the iPad. It's an okay gig, though miles from my former dream of becoming a museum-level oil painter. Being a puzzle-minded guy, I pitch in on the game designs too.

I'm a 1099er, not a salaried staffer. The pay is tragic, but the freedom agrees with me. I show up at the office once or twice a week for meetings. Most days, I patch in from home.

I call Rajam, my boss, and tell her sorry, sorry, I've been dealing with a medical emergency, but I'll make up the work later. She says fine and she hopes I'm blah-dee-blah.

I consider calling the police, but what would I tell them? My visitors left no traces, and I can't identify them except to say that one of them had a reddish beard and small, even teeth. But of course, the larger issue is that until I know what happened to that "suicide note"—and until I read its full contents—I don't feel too jazzed about bringing in the cops.

I check my emails. There are several from the programming and design teams at work. They can wait. I also find one from my sister Angela, saying she's worried about me. The hospital must have called her. Her name was listed as next of kin.

Angie lives in Wentworth too. She helped me with Mom duties whenever she, Ange, was sober. Unfortunately, that wasn't all too frequently, and she and I haven't talked a lot since Mom went to her big Parish Bingo Night in the sky. Complicating matters is the fact that Mom bequeathed the house to me, not Angie, which is a touchy spot between us. I briefly consider asking Ange if I can stay at her apartment for a couple of days, but I don't want to put her in danger, and I *really* don't want to deal with her drinking.

I need to find that deleted suicide note before I leave. Supposedly it's hard to fully delete a file from a computer; it can almost always be recovered. But I have no idea how. For a guy who works in a technical field, I am astoundingly low-tech.

A muffled thump issues from somewhere behind me. I freeze. Squirrel or assassin? My urgency to vacate the premises shoots into the red zone.

I run upstairs to my bedroom, dig out a backpack, and throw in a few haphazard changes of clothes, some toiletries, a couple of books, and a phone charger. Grabbing my all-weather jacket, I dash out to the car, leaving the computer behind.

CHAPTER 4

I pace the floor of my sad single standard at the Oak Crest Motel (nary an oak to be glimpsed), trying to ignore the thick smell of bleach—I hope it's bleach—in the air. I chose this place because of its off-the-beaten-path location and rear parking lot. I don't want my car to be seen from the road.

I haven't come up with a plan beyond "house bad, motel good." The anxiety in my chest feels like a physical mass. I long to talk to someone I trust but tragically have no one to call. Angie, whom I love dearly, is probably hammered to the nines by this hour and, alas, is also physically incapable of listening. I don't want to argue about the house either.

There was a time I would have called my friend Miles in a situation like this. He's a pretty good listener, or at least pretends to be. But we had a "cooling off," shall we say, when I left the island, and he and I have some ground to cover first.

Besides, if that note said what I thought it said, my relationship with Miles has just taken on a troublesome new twist. I still have a few other friends on Musqasset, but we don't really have "chat on the phone" relationships.

Besides, I'd rather they thought I was painting in a loft in Bruges.

That damnable suicide note is eating at my mind. There should be some trace of it that can be reconstructed. I regret having left my iMac behind. I wish I could tool with it right now. With darkness approaching, though, I don't feel safe going home to get it.

If only I had some way to tap into my computer remotely. I've never bothered to hook it up to the Cloud. I rack my brain to come up with a solution, but low blood sugar has turned my skull into an ever-tightening vise. I've got to put something in the ol' Twinkie-hole.

✶✶✶

I'm sitting at the bar at J.B.'s Pub, a rural roadhouse with poor self-esteem and a truly frightening jukebox lineup, scarfing down a Cowboy Burger and watching a cornball old movie starring George Segal and a fresh-out-of-acting-school Denzel Washington. It's called *Carbon Copy*. Each time the title comes up, my gut tickles, but I can't figure why.

Then, mid-burger-bite, it hits me. There's an online service called CarbonCopy—it provides remote backup of personal computer files. I have it on my iMac, courtesy of Rajam; its icon sits there in the upper corner of my screen.

My skin prickles with excitement. CarbonCopy makes daily backups of your files and archives them. That means even if my home invaders eliminated all traces of the suicide note from my computer when they returned to my house, there's a chance a copy exists on my backup. And I can access my backup from any computer.

My burger loses its scant appeal. I need to get into my CarbonCopy account. That means getting my hands on a computer. My phone won't do. Technically, it's an Internet portal, but it's a Barney Rubble iPhone with a tiny screen, all scratched up. I need to use a real computer. Where can I find one at seven forty-five on a Wednesday evening?

Do Internet cafés still exist? I google "cyber café" and find there is, indeed, a brew-house in nearby Haverhill that rents computer time. It's open till eleven and only a few miles away.

I slap a twenty on the bar and head out the door to saddle up my trusty Hyundai. Yee-ha.

Brew Moon is a wannabe-hipster joint that suffers from a pronounced dearth of hipsters. Other than the requisitely goateed and eyebrow-impaled barista, who crafts my iced Vietnamese Cà Phê Dá with studied indifference— ten bucks says his name is Bennett or Django—the rest of the tiny night crowd is woefully unhip and borderline desperate-looking. All but one of the computer stations are available. I pay for my Cà Phê Dá, which comes with a free hour of computer time, and settle into a Mac station in the darkest corner of the room.

I google CarbonCopy and go directly to its website. I'm able to access my account and view the mirror image of my home hard drive. After a bit of clicking around, I learn that CarbonCopy lets you restore any folder to an earlier version by date.

I do the restoration process for August 23, the date of my home invasion. Can't believe my eyes—at the top of the AutoRecovery folder is a Word file created on that date. I double-click on the auto-generated filename and hold my breath.

Holy crap. There it is: a document with the heading, "Finnian Carroll's Absolutely Final (This Time I Mean It) and Incontestable Suicide Note and Last Confession." With my brain now free of toxic chemicals, I can read the text easily. I wish I couldn't.

> *Friends, Romans, Countrymen,*
>
> *I, Finnian Carroll, have opted to "put in for early reincarnation," i.e., terminate this failed attempt at an earthly existence. I do this because I can no longer come up with a defensible reason to crawl out of bed each morning. Thus have I swallowed a large quantity of the very pills intended to keep me alive, along with enough vodka to kill a Russian game programmer (or at least get him mildly buzzed). I apologize to whoever discovers the "results" of my actions—hope it wasn't too grisly a scene (unless it was you, Clyde Gilchrist, then I hope it was straight out of* Battle Royale*).*
>
> *They say confession is good for the soul. I hope that's true, because my soul is going to need all the help it can get.*

The tone then takes a less smarmy turn.

> *Eighteen years ago, on May 12, 1999, the night of my college graduation, I made a lethal mistake, which I failed to atone for.*

I stand up and walk away from the computer, blowing air from my cheeks. I'm starting to hyperventilate. I need to calm down. Taking a slow breath from my diaphragm, I sit back down and continue reading.

> *That night, I went to a graduation party at a professor's farmhouse in Bridgefield, Mass. There was a lot of drinking. Late in the evening, a close friend and I went outside to share a goodbye toast in private.*
>
> *Somehow, we'd gotten our hands on an expensive bottle of Glenmalloch single malt scotch. We passed it back and forth, sitting by a stream behind the house, talking and reminiscing. I had never drunk scotch before and had little experience with hard liquor in general. I did not realize how drunk I was getting (not an excuse, just an explanation).*
>
> *I left the patry*—my eyes note the misspelling—*alone. Foolishly and regrettably, I got behind the wheel of my car, taking the scotch bottle with me.*
>
> *As I was driving home—on the "back roads"—I dozed off at the wheel and almost struck the stone wall bordering the Dempsey Bridge. I jammed on*

the brakes, making a loud squeal, and went into a panic. What if the noise attracted attention? I'd had way too much to drink and was carrying an open container of alcohol. I had to get rid of the bottle.

What I did next was an honest mistake, but the costliest one of my life. I threw the half-full bottle over the bridge. I won't describe the consequences of my action here, but for those interested in knowing...

Here the note provides a link, presumably to a news article (the name *bostonglobe* is embedded in the URL).

Where I erred, morally speaking, was not so much in making the initial mistake but in failing to own it once I realized what I'd done.

I have regretted my actions every day since, and it's not an overstatement to say they have ruined my life. I deeply apologize to all those whose lives I have affected.

Until next life,
Finnian Carroll

I feel like there's a blowgun dart in my neck. This note is a flat-out impossibility. Shock waves bombard me, and I can't make sense of my world. I wobble to my feet. If I don't get some air, I'm going to pass out, right on the floor of Brew Moon.

CHAPTER 5

I hang an "In Use" tag on the monitor and tell Barista General Django I'll be back. Punching the door open, I stumble out into the chill night air.

My legs are on autopilot. I jam my hands into my pockets and pound my bootheels up Washington Street, past the sleepy pubs and closed thrift shops. Without conscious intent, I'm heading toward the bridge over the Merrimack River.

Questions tumble in my head like clothes in a dryer. Logic can't get traction in my brain. There are so many disturbing elements to the note, I have trouble putting them in order of enormity. First and foremost, it contains facts *no one could possibly know about*. No one on the entire planet but me. No one. Then there are other details only Miles and I would know. But also, there are crucial facts that are flat-out wrong or omitted. Why? How? Either someone is lying or doesn't know the whole story.

Who could possibly have learned these private and unknowable truths? And why are they making a move now, after eighteen silent years? And, oh yes—don't want to overlook this trifling detail—why do they want me dead because of it?

Of course, the biggest question of all—and the one I must answer before this evening is over—is, *What actually, factually happened after the bottle was thrown that night?* My entire adult life has been an exercise in stuffing that jack into its box. But tonight, when I get back to that computer at Brew Moon, the jack will be sprung, baring its grinning teeth. I will learn the facts. At long last. I am both terrified and relieved.

I arrive at the Comeau Bridge and gaze down at the rushing black Merrimack far below. I reflect that if a certain glass bottle had landed in these waters all those years ago, as intended, the worst crime committed would have been littering.

The flowing water has a hypnotic effect. I allow myself to be carried back to a night I spend as little time thinking about as possible.

✶✶✶

May 12, 1999. Miles and I did indeed go to a party, at a farmhouse in the rural section of Bridgefield, where a sociology professor we knew co-ran a small organic farm.

The Godwin College graduation had taken place that afternoon, and I was now a certified Bachelor of Arts. Stand back, world. Godwin, a small private college in blue-blooded Bridgefield, Massachusetts, catered largely to upmarket students who didn't make the Ivy League cut but wanted to go to a school that looked the part. About two-thirds of its students were residents who lived in the dorms or college apartments. A third were local commuters. Townies. Like me. I lived in Wentworth, the neighboring blue-collar city, with my parents, and never could have afforded Godwin if not for a full scholarship.

I drove Miles and his live-in girlfriend Beth to the party that night. They were planning to return the next day to Miles's home state of Connecticut, there to take up their rightful places in the world of privilege-by-birthright that I knew only from behind a glass wall. This was to be our final night together as college friends.

Jeannie, my unofficial girlfriend, came to the party too but tellingly did not come with me. We were already starting to do the emotional mitosis necessitated by our career choices: she had taken a job in Quebec and I was heading to grad school at RISD—Rhode Island School of Design. Jeannie and I were planning to have our grand goodbye the following weekend.

The beer was flowing freely, but I was trying to be temperate. I knew I'd be driving later and the local constabulary would be out in force on this celebratory night.

May 12th was a gorgeous spring evening, strident with frog song, that seemed to stretch on forever. There was a pass-the-guitar session around a fire pit, and I yowled out a couple of Cohen tunes. There were sloppy toasts and long goodbye hugs and tearful reminiscences.

Toward the waning part of the evening, I managed to get Miles alone for a private goodbye. Miles Sutcliffe was my best friend. We came from different worlds, but we had bonded at a level I'm not sure I understand even today. I was working-class all the way, deeply self-conscious and insecure. Miles was cool and self-assured, *from old Connecticut money (though the bulk of the family money had taken its show on the road a generation or two earlier, leaving mostly old Connecticut attitude).*

Our friendship grew from the fact that we both loved to talk endlessly about topics no one else was remotely interested in—Castaneda, game theory, obscure Monty Python sketches. We tended to drive other people away with the fervor and exclusivity of our conversations.

Miles was a handsome SOB, with a smile that made estrogen boil. For the first three years of college, he had an endless, overlapping stream of gorgeous, brainy, and cool girlfriends. In fact, I can't remember a single girl—except Jeannie—who ever spurned his advances. It wasn't till senior year that he became exclusive with Beth, who, oddly enough, was the "plainest" looking girl he'd ever dated, as well as one of the least imaginative. Well, maybe not so odd when you realized how much her dad was worth.

The dudes loved Miles too. Yep, all the preppy boys and girls genuflected at the altar of Miles Sutcliffe. And because I was his friend, and a reasonably funny guy, I got to nibble at some of his social crumbs. But when push came to shove, most of his friends regarded me as little more than smart-assed white trash. Fun to have around in a group setting—a capuchin monkey in a bellhop cap—but not invite-on-the-ski-trip material.

Here's the thing about that miserable bottle of scotch: I bought it for Miles as a gift, and I didn't drive with it in my hands, as the note claimed. ...And I was not the one who tossed it off a bridge.

About eleven o'clock that evening, I went looking for Miles and found him embroiled in a flirt session with a pair of comely female underclassmen.

"Sutcliffe," I said, holding up two heavy-bottomed whiskey glasses I'd appropriated from the house. "Come with me, I want to give you something."

"A kiss? You can do that here," he said. "Everybody knows." The gals laughed. It was an open joke that certain members of the male student body opined that Miles and I were gay because of our constant and enthusiastic companionship.

I wiggled the whiskey glasses like fishing lures and started down the path to the stream behind the farmhouse. Miles followed. When we got to the banks of the brook, I surprised him with the bottle I'd hidden in the riot of early spring growth. It was the Glenmalloch, his dad's favorite single-malt. This was the sixteen-year stuff, and it came in a special, limited edition, decanter bottle, rectangular-shaped and made of heavy glass. It had set me back eighty-something bucks. I was proud of it.

"I want to have a private toast with you," I said, "and I want to do it with a man's drink, not something from a red Solo cup."

I handed Miles the bottle. He responded with an overly hard hug that told me he was already pretty toasted. He uncorked the bottle expertly and poured us each a finger. We clinked our glasses and drank. To my uncultured tongue, the stuff tasted like Listerine. But Miles, as in so many other things, was light years ahead of me, tastewise. He rolled the nectar around on his tongue, savoring the texture and flavor.

"That's whisky as God intended it," he proclaimed. "Blended scotch ought to be used for soaking machine parts." A ridiculously pompous statement for a 21-year-old but the kind of thing Miles could get away with.

I was soon to learn that Miles, who was always judicious in his consumption of beer and wine, was powerless under the spell of single malt. Over the next hour or so, as we swapped memories and promises by lantern light, he swigged from the bottle like it was a hiker's canteen. His speech got sloppier as his tongue got looser.

Miles was typically a guarded guy beneath his cool exterior. He liked to have fun but not too much of it. He talked like an anarchist but was careful never to do anything that might besmirch the family name.

Not tonight, though. Tonight, he was throwing off the moorings. Sharing his family scandals with me, offering scathing analyses of all our friends. "What's the over-under on when Timmons gives up the hetero act and starts begging for bratwurst in his bun?" Whoa. My window of opportunity for getting Miles home conscious was slipping shut.

"Wait here, brother. I'm gonna go find Beth."

I took a walk around the property, looking for Beth amongst the lingering partygoers, but she was nowhere to be found. I didn't want to leave without her. Someone finally told me, "She left with Fitzy and Deb, like an hour ago." Beth often became impatient with Miles and me as a duo, so it didn't surprise me she'd found her own way home.

I packed Miles into the car. I was clear-headed enough for driving, but still, I did have more than trace quantities *of alcohol in my system, so I stuck to the back roads on my way to Miles's apartment. Miles clung to the Glenmalloch and continued to hit it like it was Dr. Pepper.*

We hadn't driven more than a mile or two when he let out a wounded-animal wail and buried his face in his hands.

I found a place to pull over at the edge of the state park. There, Miles proceeded to have what I can only call a breakdown. He threw himself on the ground, chest-down, and blurted out all the fears and doubts he'd been stuffing inside for years. Fears about his future. Fears about the expectations hung on him by his family and himself. Fears about his upcoming marriage to Beth. "I want what you have with Jeannie. I want to be an artist and a vagabond like you. You're so lucky. You can live the life you choose. Love whoever you want."

I think I offered him some thin counsel, but he was too drunk to hear it. Just as well. He finally staggered to his feet, wrung out, and stumbled back to the car.

After driving another mile or so, I spotted a police car parked in the shadows on a wooded section of Carlisle Road. Watching for speeders and drunks. My heart revved.

"Shit," I said to Miles, "The bottle." Massachusetts law forbade "open containers" of alcohol in moving vehicles.

As I drove out of the woods onto an open stretch of road, I kept my eyes glued to the rear-view mirror, certain the cop would be tailing us any minute. I didn't notice we were going over a bridge, but Miles evidently did.

Before my brain could register what he was doing, he rolled his window down. He slurred the words, "My apology to the river gods," and then his window went back up. My eyes were still riveted to the rear-view mirror, watching for the cop.

A moment later, we were passing a carved wooden sign with a crucifix on it when I heard—or thought I heard—a series of sounds that didn't make immediate sense to me.

"Miles? Did you hear that?"

"Hear what?" he said, his head wobbling precariously.

I glanced at Miles's lap and noticed it was empty.

"What did you do with the bottle?"

"Tossed it in the Merrimack," he said. "Ba-bye."

It was then I noticed headlights following us at a distance.

"Shit, Miles, that's the cop. What if he saw you throw it?" I didn't think the cop could have seen anything; he wasn't behind us at the time, but still...

"Jeez, I was jus' try'na help."

"We're screwed, man."

I drove a little farther, hewing to the speed limit, and the headlights continued to follow us. And then the dreaded thing happened. Blue lights. My heart hammering, I looked for a place to pull over. That was when I noticed another bridge up ahead of us on Carlisle Road.

My body must have put two and two together before my conscious mind did, because a wave of nausea rose from my gut. "Oh no, Miles," I said. "This is the bridge over the Merrimack. This is the bridge over the Merrimack."

I pulled the car over as the full weight of the realization sunk in.

If this was the bridge over the Merrimack, that meant only one thing: the previous bridge had been the bridge over route 495.

Oh no. Oh shit. The sounds I'd heard—or thought I'd heard—when we were passing the crucifix now made damning sense. They were the sounds of squealing brakes, shattering glass, and smashing metal.

The blue lights loomed larger in my mirror. Life as I knew it was about to end.

But instead of pulling to a stop behind me, the police car turned on its siren, did a quick three-point turn, and sped off in the direction from which it had come.

I should have been massively relieved that the cop was rushing off to deal with an emergency but was only sickened by the implications. "Miles," I said, gathering my strength to tell him what I now knew. "You didn't throw the bottle into the river, you threw it onto the highway."

But as I turned to look at Miles, he was passed out, stone cold.

CHAPTER 6

I stare, spellbound, at the rushing black water below. There's no question what my next move must be, though I long for an excuse to stall.

I drag myself back to Brew Moon, giving Django the Brave a little nod as I enter. He fails to acknowledge my existence with even a microscopic facial twitch.

Jumping back onto the rented computer, I pull up my "suicide" note and stare at that hypertext link on it, ripe with odious promise. I click the link before I can change my mind. The elderly iMac churns arthritically.

Moments later, a Boston Globe news article from 1999 appears on my rented screen: "Police Investigate Fatal Three-Car Collision in Bridgefield."

No, no, no.

I want to throw up. I want to run away. I want to drink something infinitely stronger than a Cà Phê Dá.

I can't believe what I'm reading, yet the words strike home with the fatedness of cancer after a thirty-year smoking binge.

A fatal accident occurred at 1:21 a.m. Sunday on Route 495 South near the Carlisle Road exit in Bridgefield, say police. According to an eyewitness, a 1987 Chevrolet El

Camino driven by Edgar Goslin of Wentworth lost control "for no apparent reason" and veered into the passing lane where it collided with a 1998 Ford Aerostar occupied by Paul and Laurice Abelsen and—please no—their two-year-old daughter. The Abelsens' vehicle veered off the highway, rolled over and struck a tree, where Goslin's car struck it a second time, crushing the roof of the Abelsen's vehicle and the front end of Goslin's car. All three members of the Abelsen family were pronounced dead on arrival at Wentworth General Hospital. Goslin is listed in critical condition with multiple undisclosed injuries. Police have not ruled out alcohol as a factor and are continuing to investigate.

I read the words again. Then again. And again.

Nausea reaches right down into my soul.

Thinking back to that night long ago, I revisit the fateful decision I made. After the cop sped off, I drove away, letting Miles remain unconscious. I remember convincing myself I probably hadn't heard those crashing noises. And if I had, the accident probably wasn't as bad as it sounded. And if it was, then Miles's tossed bottle probably had nothing to do with it. And even if the worst possibility was true—that Miles had inadvertently caused a serious accident—what good could come of bringing that to light? It was his graduation night. He was about to embark on an exciting new life. Why kneecap his destiny? Whom would it help, really, to assign blame? The cops had the situation handled.

And anyway, I probably hadn't heard anything. Right?

The day after graduation, though, I shocked my parents by announcing I had changed my mind about going to grad school in Providence. I wanted to take a year off to think about it. I'd decided, instead, to accept an invitation from a couple of college classmates to drive to California with them and hang loose for a while. Seek my fortune—by way of minimum wage—in the Land of Milk and Honey.

My folks tried to reason with me, but my mind was made up.

I busied myself on May 13, 1999, packing duffel bags, returning library books, selling my old Chevy at a used car lot open on Sundays, and saying goodbye to Jeannie a week earlier than planned. I studiously avoided looking at newspapers and televisions—if nothing was confirmed, then as far as I knew, no accident had happened. And then, on the morning of May 14, I jumped into a thirteen-year-old Aries K-car with two stoners from Godwin I didn't even like and headed for the Golden West.

I didn't return to Massachusetts for five years.

My attention snaps back to my Brew Moon environs. I study the suicide note on the computer screen again, mystified by both its accuracies and its inaccuracies, and dumbfounded as to its purpose. Who wrote it and why *now*?

I log into my Gmail account, copy the text of the note into an email, and send it to myself, verifying it arrived intact.

I do the same with the Globe article.

Twenty minutes later, I'm lying on my bed at the Oak Crest Motel, drinking a beer, staring at the cracked ceiling, and listening to the rattle and hum of the in-name-only air conditioner. My mind wants to spin out of control. I don't have the slightest idea how to process the events of the past few days, and I have no clue what I'm going to do when I wake up in the morning. Or any morning thereafter, for that matter.

It's ten-thirty at night, and I know what I *want* to do: call Miles. I have an almost physical urge to share the burden of what I've just learned. But the hour is late. And besides, I can't just dump those ancient deaths on him now.

Do I even have a *right* to dump them on him? After all these years? To throw such a crowbar into the machinery of his carefully executed life? The man is a partner in one of New England's finest law firms, for God's sake, and a state senator. What possible good could come of sharing this information? It would either ruin his career or destroy his peace of mind. Or both.

No. My time to speak was eighteen years ago, when I heard—or did I?—that distant sound of smashing glass and metal. Not now.

On the other hand, do I have any right *not* to tell him? Who appointed *me* Truth Fairy? Does he not have a fundamental right to know something of such vital import to his life?

That is the question.

I turn on my phone, play a little gem-matching game for a while, trying to numb my brain. It doesn't work. I look at the time again. Ten forty-three.

Screw it. I lose the battle. I won't *call* Miles, but I'll text him, see if he's still up. *Long time, brother,* I type.

Sorry for the radio silence. Hope all's well. Didn't want to phone this late and invoke the wrath of Beth, but if you're awake, so am I.

Less than a minute after I hit Send, my phone rings. Miles. The instant I slide the answer icon, a flat voice says, "So you didn't die in a freak circus accident."

"Is there any other kind of circus accident?" I deadpan back.

"Man, it's great to hear your voice."

"Yours too."

A pause ensues. We both know there are fissures to be mended, but, by silent accord, we agree to save the harder conversation for later. We are both happy to be reconnecting.

We spend the next few minutes playing catch-up. What am I up to these days? (I spin the living crap out of that one.) How's Miles's four-star career going? How are Beth and the kids? When the grace period for codswallop expires, Miles says, "But I'm guessing you didn't call after all this time just to find out if Kelsey made the freshmen soccer team."

He's right. But of course, I can't tell him what really prompted my call. Not by phone. No, if that conversation is ever going to take place—and that's a very large *if*—it will need to happen face-to-face.

I suddenly realize there's a deeper, truer reason I've called him: I miss my friend, and I long for his voice and comfort. "I'm scared to death, Miles." I blurt out the story of the home invasion, the attempted forced suicide, and the later clean-up of the evidence. The only part I omit is the suicide note, because that would lead us into complicated terrain. The whole time I'm talking, Miles is silent, but I can feel his listening presence like a ship's beacon.

When I'm done, he asks me to hang on. He puts me on hold for a couple of minutes, then returns and pronounces, "Here's what you are going to do. First, get some sleep. Mainline some Nyquil if necessary. Set your alarm for five a.m. When you wake up, you will drive directly to New Harbor, where you will get on the ten o'clock ferry to Musqasset."

Yes, Miles owns a summer home on my beloved Musqasset Island—a place he didn't even know existed until I browbeat him into visiting me there—and I am living in my parents' den of depression in Wentworth, Mass. How that perversion of fortune came about is a subject for later discussion.

"Beth and I and the kids are out on the island for the Labor Day weekend," he says. "You are going to stay with us. You will be safe here, and you and I will figure out exactly what is happening and what to do next."

"I'm sure Beth would love that."

"I already talked to her, and she thinks it's a great idea. She'll be thrilled to see you. Listen to me, Finn: it's important you get on the morning ferry."

"Why?"

"You *do* watch the news, don't you?" Actually, I've been a smidge preoccupied. "That tropical storm off the coast? It's huge. The morning ferry may be the last one leaving the mainland for a couple of days. Tell me you understand, and you're going to do what I say."

Why is he talking to me like I'm seven?

"I don't know, Miles. I haven't been back to the island since Jeannie and I..." No need to finish my sentence. "I'd have to think about it."

"Okay, then, think. I'll give you ten minutes."

He hangs up.

Go to Musqasset Island? Me? Tomorrow? I last set eyes on the place four years ago. Jeannie and I had just broken up for the second and final time. Changes were taking place on the island—Miles was in the thick of them—and the place just didn't feel right to me anymore. My mom's health problems gave me a handy excuse to return to Wentworth. So, one morning, I just quietly packed my bags, stepped aboard the ferry, and closed the door on the "Island Artist" chapter of my life. The end.

But not a day has passed that I haven't thought about Musqasset. As I close my eyes right now, I can hear the screeching of the gulls and the rumble of the lobster boats. I can see the seals basking like drunken cruise-ship passengers on Table Rock. I can feel the welcoming warmth of Pete's Lagoon, The Mermaid Café, Mary's Lunch.

And the light. Oh God, the light. There's a reason Musqasset attracts painters from all over the world. Everywhere you focus your eyes, from the tightest close-up to the grandest panorama, you see an oil painting—a tiny flower peeking out of the lichen, a lobster trap in the tall grass, the lighthouse silhouetted against a translucent sea. It's an artist's wet dream.

Leaving was agony. But the wounds have healed, the breaks have mended. And I know I can't go back.

Maybe for a few days, though. Arrive unannounced, hole up at Miles's place.

The idea makes sense, under the circumstances. For one thing, I'm not safe here in Wentworth. For another, I have no freaking clue what my next move is. It would do me enormous good to spend some time in a safe place with old friends. Step back from my predicament, think and strategize a bit.

Then, of course, there's the fact that I may need to have a serious conversation with Miles.

Momentum starts to build. If I slipped out of here in the pre-dawn hours, I could make it to New Harbor by eight or eight-thirty. Be out on Musqasset before noon. The brewing ocean storm gives me added incentive. By the time my assailants could pick up my trail, they won't be *able* to follow me, at least for a couple of days. The ferry will be down. I'll be safely unreachable, several leagues out to sea.

The logic seems ironclad.

But ultimately, it's not logic that moves my decision needle. It's the fact that I *feel* safe on Musqasset. It is still home to me. Deep down, I've been longing for an excuse to return there. If only for a visit.

Miles calls back.

"I'll see you in the morning," I tell him.

I lie back on the lumpy motel mattress and let my mind roam to the suicide note again. Of all the many disturbing, unanswered questions it raises, the one that will gnaw at my sleep the most is this: Why and how does the note sound exactly like something I would write—from its feeble attempts at gallows humor, to its linguistic style, to its specificity of details (like the Clyde Gilchrist reference), to its misspelling of the word "party" as "patry," a habitual typo of mine?

How could any other person have captured *me* so perfectly?

I'm scared about the places this question wants to take me. And I wonder if there's a deeper reason I don't want to get the police involved in this. Or talk to Miles about it.

CHAPTER 7

I'm up and dressed by four forty-five. I wouldn't have been able to sleep even if the motel mattress *wasn't* made of dead rodents, so I figure I'll hit the highway early.

As I throw my few belongings into my backpack and do a final room check, I can't tell if I'm excited or terrified. Maybe there's no difference. But one thing is certain: I feel more alive than I have in years. Being almost murdered has done wonders for my state of mind. Can't say I recommend it for everyone, but still.

As I slip out into the predawn darkness of the Oak Crest's unlit parking lot, a brisk morning breeze salutes me. Must be the western edge of that ocean storm. It smells of the sea, even this far inland. It smells of adventure too, if I'm being honest.

I consider driving back to the house and grabbing my iMac, but I'm worried the house is being staked out. Better not. I jump into my car and head north.

Route 95 is deserted at this hour; most of the trip I see no one behind me for more than a quarter of a mile. Same deal when I switch onto 295. No cars come near me, except to pass. Still, I take a couple of side trips onto the surface roads just to be sure I don't have a tail on me. And to gas and coffee up.

As I exit onto Route 1, the main coastal road, my confidence remains high that I'm alone and unfollowed.

I find a market in Damariscotta that's open early and buy some freshly baked crusty bread, a couple of bottles of half-decent wine, and the makings of a pasta puttanesca and a Caesar salad. I don't want to show up empty-handed at Miles's, and I know grocery options are sparse on the island.

It's seven fifty when I arrive in New Harbor, plenty early for the ten o'clock ferry. I park in the grassy field designated for long-term parking, open the car door, and pull the swirling ocean air into my lungs. Ah, that smell stirs my blood. I think on a cellular level I can still remember my ancestral sea-dwelling days. I probably had a nice lungfish family that loved me.

Trombly's Boat Tours and Ferry provides ferry service to "The Three Ms"—Monhegan, Matinicus, and Musqasset, a triangle of inhabited Maine islands more than ten miles off the coast. Musqasset, roughly equidistant from the other two and farther east—thirteen miles from the mainland—is a "walking" island. Some of the residents and businesspeople own vehicles, but the ferry is for pedestrians only.

As I approach the office of Trombly's, furious white-caps streak the Gulf of Maine, and billowing masses of gray crowd the eastern sky. I hope the morning ferry run is still on. If so, it's going to be a two-Dramaminer. Good thing I wore a weatherproof jacket.

Inside the ferry office, there's an atmosphere of controlled frenzy. An early crowd of gabbing, raingear-clad passengers has already formed. Phones are ringing, keyboards are clacking, and outside the back door, deckhands are bucket-brigading suitcases and boxes of groceries onto the docked boat. On a big TV screen tuned to a local weather station, the announcer talks about twenty-to-twenty-five-foot waves and winds off the coast gusting to forty-five knots, getting worse over the next thirty-six hours.

It suddenly hits me, dumbass that I am, that I should have called ahead to buy my ticket. Mainland living has made me soft in the head.

I recognize the woman at the ticket counter from past years of ferry usage, but she looks too harried for *hey-how-are-you*s. "Is the ten o'clock going to run?"

She fires off her reply by rote, "Captain hasn't made the final call yet. It ain't the ride out he's worried about, it's the ride back. He'll let everyone know in ten or fifteen."

"Can I buy a ticket anyway?"

"Sold out, my friend."

My incompetence knows no bounds.

"I can put you on the waitlist. Dozen people ahead of you, though."

Of course. Folks are scrambling to get out to the island before the storm shuts everything down. I should have known. Such an idiot.

"Hold on—your name's Carroll, right?" she says. "Finnian?" Nice to be remembered. "Didn't you buy a ticket online?"

"I wish."

"Looks like someone bought one for ya."

Miles. Bless his anal-retentive soul. I gratefully take my ticket and buy a travel pack of Dramamine. Two pills go down the hatch without water.

Backpack and shopping bag in hand, I wander out onto the dock to await the captain's verdict. The air feels more like late October than early September. I zip my jacket up to my neck.

Standing on the dock is like slipping into a pair of well-worn flipflops. Time was, I'd set up my easel here a few times a week. Did quick acrylic miniatures of the scenery and the weather for twenty-five bucks a pop. Tourist fodder. Yup, I was *that* guy.

I notice a couple of geezers—island guys—standing near me. They're bemoaning the impending loss of business over Labor Day weekend due to the storm. Sometimes when I'm romanticizing life on Musqasset, I forget how brutal it can be for the shop and B&B owners.

The outdoor loudspeaker crackles at last, and the ticket woman's voice bullhorns, "Attention, please. The ten o'clock *will* be running. But it'll be a delayed departure. Boarding starts in one hour." Immediately a line forms at the roped-off gangway. What's the rush, folks? We're all in the same boat. Literally.

✦✦✦

As I board the *Finny Business*—yes, tragically (on several levels), that is the ferryboat's name—I feel a thrill of excitement about seeing Musqasset again, even under less-than-optimal circumstances.

"Hey, Mr. Carroll," shouts a smiling deckhand, about 17 or 18, hurrying by with a rope and bucket. He looks familiar, but I can't quite place him. "Preston Davis," he supplies.

"Of course! Preston! Hey man, look at you. I'll catch up with you when you're not busy." I gave Preston painting lessons when he was still a pudgy kid. Now he's grown into a handsome young seaman with scruffy whiskers. Better brace myself for more changes.

The ferry has an upper and a lower deck. The lower deck offers both indoor and outdoor seating, but I opt for a spot on the open upper level. It'll be less crowded up there, with the weather as it is, and I want to be alone.

I climb the steps, hearing the familiar clang of my shoes on the metal grating. I find an open deck table in the rear corner and claim it with my shopping bag and backpack.

The boat is already dipping like a tilt-a-whirl car, though we're still docked, and the wind is whipping my hair, but I feel incongruously calm and even-keeled. The sludge of depression that has been gumming up my life for years seems completely absent. I find I can move and breathe with unaccustomed ease.

I'm glad I made this decision. I do feel a bit awkward about descending on Miles's family—especially Beth, whom I've always suspected enjoys my company about as much as she enjoys a nice root canal—but I intend to stay out of everyone's way. Their house is huge, and if I can't find a quiet corner to read in, there are a few people I wouldn't mind dropping in on.

Which brings me to a topic I've been strategically avoiding. Jeannie. She still lives on the island. It was "her" place before I moved there, and it seemed only right that it revert to her after we broke up.

That was one of the reasons I left. Musqasset is a small community. Fewer than a hundred people live there year-round. Socially, things can get a bit "close."

I've heard she had a child with my replacement dude. I don't know if he's still on the scene—my replacement— and frankly I don't much care to find out.

Do I want to see Jeannie? Well, she's only the most beautiful woman I've ever laid eyes on. No exaggeration. So, on a selfish, testosterone-driven level, of course I want to see her. Do I think it's a good idea? Not even fractionally. I'm sure we're both over the breakup and would behave politely toward each other. But I'm certainly not her favorite human on Earth, and I don't want to rock the boat of her new life—or, worse, discover I lack any rocking power.

Besides, I've got enough on my plate. Why pile on?

The captain's voice comes over the P.A. "Okay, folks, we're ready to shove off. Waters are pretty choppy, as you've probably noticed." He proceeds to give half-joking instructions on what to do if you need to barf, which, of course, instantly makes me want to barf. Then he blasts the earsplitting horn. The folks on the dock wave goodbye.

We're off. Like dirty skivvies, as my dad used to say.

I try to read a book, but the ceaseless pitching of the boat, combined with my inner turbulence, makes concentration impossible. A coffee would perhaps be therapeutic.

Leaving my bags to mark my spot at the table, I head for the downstairs snack bar. The cabin is jammed with gabbing passengers, some drinking coffee, some hoisting pre-noon Pabsts and Sutter Home singles, yo ho ho. The choppy waters have everyone laughing a bit harder than strictly necessary. I move to the end of the customer line and take my place.

It suddenly hits me how zonked I am from lack of sleep. I plant my feet wide apart for balance and let my eyelids drift shut. The chattering voices meld together in my mind and become the echoey "rhubarb" of a movie mob. The sound has a soporific effect, and I'm soon getting drowsy on my feet.

I think I do doze off for a few seconds, despite the boat's rocking.

Something snaps me to attention—three syllables, leaping out of the random noise of the crowd behind me: "Bim bam bom."

Nope, not possible. My impulse is to whip my head around, but I force my gaze to stay trained on the Harpoon Ale sign on the wall.

My legs go numb as I shuffle forward with the wobbly-legged snack line.

No way Trooper Dan could be on this boat. I left Wentworth in the dead of night, from an obscure flea-bag motel where I paid with cash, and there were no cars near me on the road.

And yet, "bim bam bom." Who says that? And did I even hear it? The voice I *think* I heard was in the same upper range as Trooper Dan's. But I might have drifted into a REM state and dreamt it. Or maybe my stressed-out brain distorted some like-sounding syllables.

What are some phrases in English that are phonetically similar to "bim bam bom"? Cue *Jeopardy* theme music. Answer: none.

Still, Trooper Dan can't be on this boat—*can't* be.

But what if he is?

Then two things are true. One, he's watching me like a cat. Two, he's not wearing his Storm Trooper mask. I have no idea what he actually looks like, except he has a short reddish beard and small, even teeth. Nor do I know his cohorts' faces—never saw them—or whether they are traveling with him today.

I don't want to look as if I've become suspicious, so I force myself to stay in line and buy the coffee I no longer want. When I get the lidded Styrofoam cup in hand, I stroll back through the crowd, exchanging "friendly" glances with the faces I encounter—a couple of teen-age boys, the two geezers from the dock, a trio of husky women with enough teeth for two...

I wander out onto the exterior deck and stroll around the perimeter, nodding greetings at my fellow passengers. Studying their faces. I encounter only one reddish beard, but it's long and attached to a tall, gaunt guy with Coke-bottle glasses. Anyway, Trooper Dan might have shaved his beard by now, or dyed it.

I go back upstairs and repeat the same procedure, walking around the whole upper deck wearing my rendition of a friendly face. I spot only one *possible* Troop candidate leaning on the rail, smoking an e-cigarette, looking out at the water—a guy about five-seven or so, trim of build—but his lips seem a bit too dark, his beard too wispy. I think I'll know my guy when I see him, and no bells are ringing. Not loudly anyway.

I return to my spot at the rear table and look around with "casual" interest. Only two new parties have moved into the vicinity since I left. One is a couple in their sixties with puffy pale-blue winter jackets and lots of camera equipment, the other is what appears to be a family of three: a husband and wife in their upper forties and an adult daughter in her twenties. They look vigorously Maine-ish in their fishermen's hats and L.L.Bean rainwear.

I ask myself, being strictly logical, which scenario is more likely: that a stranger uttered the phrase "bim bam bom" or that Trooper Dan is actually on the boat? I must give odds to the former, though I'm not bullish on the wager.

I try to banish fear from my mind and return to my book. But as the boat churns over the endless hills of water, I begin to feel that every person who glances in my direction wants to murder me. Maybe that's because we're all feeling pretty seasick. The ceaseless rise and fall of the *Finny Business* has put a dark look in everyone's eyes.

The watched feeling grows stronger by the minute, though I have no concrete reason to give it credence. The only passengers facing my way are the old photographer couple and the L.L.Bean family. The latter are in their own world. Daughter is asleep with her head on Dad's shoulder. Dad is willing himself to sleep with a crunched frown on his face. Mom, an intriguing shade of green not theoretically attainable by mammals, is trying to read a Kindle.

Several other passengers have begun milling about, though. E-cigarette guy turns and looks in my direction a couple of times. Am I imagining things or does he shoot a meaningful glance at a guy sitting on the opposite side of the deck—a bigger man wearing a slate-grey slicker with a hood?

If Trooper Dan *is* on board, I must find a way to force his hand and make him reveal himself. The prospect of being stuck on a small island with a psycho like him—with no means of escape, possibly for several days—is unthinkable.

So how can I flush him out? *What would I do if I were a character in one of the adventure games I work on for a living?* This is a mental trick I sometimes use to kick-start my creativity. Thinking like a game character, I come up with an idea. A ridiculous one, admittedly, but when has that ever stopped me?

I pick up my phone and locate VoxFox, a digital recorder app I use for work meetings. I open it and hit Record. Then, inviting attention, I go digging loudly in my grocery bag as if hunting for something. What I'm really doing is sliding my phone into the paper bag containing the crusty bread and bunching the bread bag closed.

Next, I dig in my backpack and pretend to find what I'm looking for: my notebook. I lean back and look around the deck conspicuously. I try to convey the impression that I'm getting *juuuust* a tad suspicious about being followed. I jot a couple of notes as if documenting my suspicions. As I do this, I make eye contact with every male who looks my way, as if to say, *I see you. And I'm making notes.* I'm actually writing random observations, but I hope to pique the curiosity of Trooper Dan, if he's here. I carry on with this façade for a while, then pretend I'm struck with nausea. I stand up, holding my belly.

I "surreptitiously"—but obviously—hide the notebook in the grocery bag, atop the crusty bread, and cover it with groceries. Then I lay my jacket over the bag and head for the stairs.

Here's my thinking: if I'm being watched, my watcher is going to wonder what the hell I've been writing—i.e., am I on to him? By going to the bathroom for a sick visit, I am offering him a grand opportunity to go digging for my notes. There's a long waiting line for the bathroom, so he can safely assume I'll be away from my stuff for a while.

And if he goes through my bag, aha, my phone will record him. This may not tell me *who* my stalker is, but it will at least confirm my suspicion that I'm being eyeballed.

As I said, a ridiculous idea. Still.

I go downstairs and take my place in the long line for the unisex toilet. At one point I turn and see L.L.Bean daughter waiting behind me. She's cute—*really* cute—despite the current pallor of her skin. We exchange playful glances, but the tang of fresh bile in the air, our mutual nausea, and our age difference preclude any serious flirting.

The guy in the slate-grey slicker—actually, I'd use *Davy's* Grey if I were going to paint it; slate with a tinge of green—strides by, casting a hooded glance in my direction.

Checking to see if I'm still away from my stuff? I finally make it into the bathroom—gad, what a horror show, we shall never speak of it—and then go hang out in the snack bar area for a while.

At last, I go back upstairs and reclaim my spot at the rear corner table. I'm careful not to open my grocery bag for a while. Playin' it cool. When it feels natural to do so, I remove the rain jacket from the top of the bag, reach inside, and slip the phone into my sleeve. Pretending to pull it from my pocket, I make a show of flipping through some menu screens and plugging in earphones. I lean back in my seat, tapping my hand in idle rhythm, as if listening to music.

What I'm really doing, of course, is playing the audio recording I've just made.

For the first few minutes of the recorded session, I hear nothing but a hiss and a low rumble: the churning ocean and the boat engine.

Then something puts me on high alert.

A paper-rustling sound comes through the earphones, and a voice says, "You stay on that side." The tone is sickeningly familiar—high-pitched and almost prissy—but I can't be sure. One thing is certain, though. If this guy is talking to someone, he's not traveling alone.

Rifling noises drown out whatever is said next. Then, just above a whisper: "Here it is." It's him. I'm certain of it. Trooper Effing Dan. Nausea surges through me. I stand up, turn around, and step to the rear deck-rail for fear my face will betray the horror I'm feeling.

"Doesn't seem to go in order," comes a second recorded voice, a deeper one, with a heavy Boston—Brooklyn?—accent. Chokehold. Must be talking about my written notes.

"Here's some stuff, dated today," says the Trooper voice. There's a fifteen-second pause before he says in his high tone, "It's nothing. Just pencil scratchings. He's clueless."

I hear the grocery bag being repacked, then a cloth zipper opening. My backpack? "Oh look," says Troop in an aww-isn't-that-cute voice, "he bought a round-trip ticket. Optimistic little fella."

Recorded Chokehold laughs as if this is the funniest joke he's heard since the last time he bashed a skull with a baseball bat, and then the two men clomp away.

I shut off the recording. I don't want to turn around until I've regained my composure, so I remain standing at the back railing staring out at the water. As I watch the wake of the boat melt into the rolling waves, I feel I'm watching my entire past slip away behind me.

Only the present remains.

The terrible, poisoned present, in which I am exquisitely screwed.

I do have one possible advantage, though. I know these jagholes are following me. But *they don't know that I know.*

CHAPTER 8

The sight of Musqasset's domed silhouette on the horizon does not lift my spirits as it has in the past. I feel like a baby mouse about to be set loose in a snake terrarium.

Several concerns vie for attention in my fear-hijacked brain. First and foremost, I need to make sure Miles does not meet me at the dock. I mustn't lead a psychopath brigade to my friend's home. Staying at Miles's is officially off the itinerary. I text him: *If you were planning to meet me at the ferry, don't. I'll explain later. Hate to sound cryptic, but DO NOT come to the ferry. IMPORTANT.*

Miles texts back a minute later: *Roger that, but I WILL want an explanation ASAP.*

My second concern is that I must find a way to ditch my pursuers as soon as I set foot on the island. I must do this (a) without knowing who they are or what they look like and (b) without betraying that I know I'm being watched.

Third—and this is the biggie—I've got to figure out a way to get back on this boat for its return trip. The ferry never docks on Musqasset overnight. It always returns to the mainland, so it *will* be going back to New Harbor today, regardless of weather, and I need to be on it.

As if reading my thoughts, the ferry captain comes on the P.A. "Ahhhhh, listen folks, we'll be doing a quick turnaround. I doubt we have any day-trippers on board today, but if you know anyone who has a ticket on the four o'clock back to New Harbor, tell 'em we'll be heading back early, as close to one-thirty as possible. It's twelve-thirty now."

Normally the ferry stays on the island for four-plus hours, giving the day-trippers time to poke around the shops and grab some lunch. Not today.

The stepped-up schedule means I have less than an hour to figure out how to get back on the ferry without being followed by Trooper Dan and company. Working in my favor is the fact they don't know I'm on to them. The last thing they'll be expecting is for me to turn around and get right back on the ferry I just arrived on.

So goes my theory.

The crew has a tough time docking the *Finny Business* because of the rough waters, but they finally manage to lock the gangplank in place. It's pumping up and down like a bellows as the passengers disembark. Dang, I never got a chance to talk to Preston Davis. Oh well, he's busy assisting seaweed-colored passengers anyway.

Anxious as I am to get off the boat, I stick to the rear of the exiting crowd. I want to be a watch*er*, not a watch*ee*, see if my pursuers reveal themselves in any way.

It's been storming on the island already. Everything's soaked, and some sizable debris has blown about. But the rain, if not the wind, has stopped for now.

Parked near the dock—here's a ritual that hasn't changed—are transport vehicles for the major inns, waiting to pick up arriving guests and their baggage. The Sea Grass Inn and The Hotel Saint-Étienne, the two upscale hotels, deploy passenger vans with cargo racks on top. Harbor House and Musqasset House, the lower-priced places, send out pickup trucks for their guests. You just climb into the truck bed along with your bags. Guests renting private houses or staying at the smaller B&Bs can take Dorna Caskie's electric-cart shuttle or just walk to their destinations. It's not a big island.

Economic stratification, let me say briefly, is not a subtle thing on Musqasset. The two upscale inns, along with some high-end B&Bs, are located on the western side of the island, called The Meadows. That's where the pricey private homes, higher-end art galleries, and a wannabe-gourmet bistro are also located.

Clustered around the middle of the southern bay, where the ferry docks, is "the village," a small collection of tourist shops and galleries, a few restaurants, a grocery and supply store, a donut shop/post office, three or four B&Bs, a tavern, and Musqasset House and Harbor House.

The eastern side of the bay, a district called Greyhook, belongs mainly to the working people—lobstermen, bartenders, tradespeople. Greyhook hosts a few small apartment buildings and rooming houses where the summer help—mostly young exchange workers from Eastern

Europe—stay, two to a room. There's also a bar there that serves cheap(er) drinks for the lobstermen and blue-collar folks. You won't get killed for wandering into The Rusty Anchor unaccompanied by a local, but you might get seriously glared at.

The central and northern part of the island consists largely of wilderness and hiking trails, along with a network of houses with attached art studios and galleries, called Studio Row, where many of the island's famous and semi-famous artists live and work. It's a major attraction for tourists with cash to burn.

Trooper and his entourage must have made lodging arrangements. I wonder which part of the island they're heading to. Perhaps they'll wait to see where I go first. In that case, maybe I can trick them into revealing themselves. After debarking the ferry, I hang around the dock, waiting for the foot traffic to disperse. I'm deliberately stalling before choosing a vehicle.

The van for the Sea Grass Inn takes off with its three guest-couples. A minute later the St. Étienne's van departs, carrying two families and a dowager queen type who is grasping her hat as if she's already regretting coming to a place so barbaric as to have weather.

E-cigarette guy is standing with the bigger guy in the Davy's Grey slicker, near The Dockside, a snack and souvenir shop. So, these guys *do* know each other. Noted. I climb onto the back of Musqasset House's truck to see what move they'll make.

Sure enough, a minute later, the two guys casually climb aboard the Musqasset House truck too. My heart pounds.

I wait till the driver yells, "Musqasset House," then pretend to notice I'm on the wrong vehicle. I jump off and climb aboard the Harbor House truck, where the old photographer couple and four or five other guests nestle amongst the luggage.

My bet is that e-cigarette guy and Davy Grey will switch trucks too.

They don't. The L.L.Bean family and a chunky guy in a Patriots sweatshirt come rushing out of The Dockside and are the last to board my truck before it starts off with a shout of "Harbor House."

Our truck follows the Musqasset House truck for a while. When we slow down to allow some pedestrians in oversized rain gear to cross the street, I grab my bags and jump off.

I scoot down a narrow alley between Hook Me Up, a fishing gear shop, and I Scream, a goth-themed ice cream joint I'm shocked to see is still in business. The shops and houses lining the bay are built on pilings, like docks. Ducking beneath their floors, I make my way along the waterfront to an overgrown yard a few buildings away. I crouch among the reeds.

With little time to act, I again try to think like a game designer. If I were devising a puzzle for an adventure game, what would be a good strategy for sneaking back onto the ferry?

A water drop slaps my face. Then another. Damn. Looks like the rain that's been on break has decided to clock in again.

But wait, maybe that's my answer. Rain. Maybe the way to get back on the ferry unnoticed is to hide in plain sight. Cover myself in some serious Maine raingear, with a big hood that shades my face. I don't think anyone sells that kind of gear on the island, though, and I don't have time to shop around.

Where can I get my hands on some?

Billy Staves. He has—or had, anyway—one of the few year-round homes in the village proper. Billy's a lobsterman. He and I were Scrabble buddies back in the day. We'd meet for a beer and a match on the porch of Harbor House two or three times a week in the summer. He kicked my ass on a fairly aggressive schedule. His partner, Dennis, sold lobster and crab rolls from a tiny sandwich shop attached to their house. Jeannie and I had them over for dinner once or twice, and I always helped Billy put up his traps for winter.

I hustle out to Island Avenue and make my way toward Billy's. After walking a hundred yards or so, I see a hand-painted sandwich board just past Black's Emporium, "Lobster Rolls. Crab Rolls. The Island's Best," with an arrow pointing to the right. Still there. Yay.

Dennis's sandwich counter sits on the back side of the building, facing the bay, so I cut through the alley between Black's Emporium and Billy's place, stash my bags in the open space beneath Black's, and approach the food counter from the ocean side. Damn—normally there's a wide, rocky beach here, even at high tide. Storm waves now cover most of it.

Dennis, a hefty, ruddy man with a curly, graying beard and suspenders, is perched behind the counter reading the *New York Times*. Not a lot of customers on a day like this. But he's open anyway, as are most of the food vendors, because the vacationers stuck here still need to eat.

"Look what the catamaran dragged in," he says, in a not particularly jovial manner.

"How've you been, Dennis?"

"Can't complain since they closed the complaints department." He puts an audible period at the end. Okay, I'm not in the mood for small talk, either, but I wonder why the cold reception. Dennis and I always got along well. Trying to elicit a little more chattiness from him, I say, "Hey, is it true what I heard about you and Billy?"

He dutifully holds up his hand to show a gold band around his thick ring finger. "Ayuh, the great state of Maine now recognizes us as a jointly taxable entity."

"Wow, that's amazing. Congratulations. Hey, I'm having sort of a storm-related emergency. Is Billy around?"

He shakes his head no and snorts. "Still out on the boat battening down the whatevers as much as possible. Obviously, he can't dock at Fish Pier anymore." Staring at me in a vaguely accusing way, he adds, "But I guess you know that."

I don't. I have no idea what's been happening with the Fish Pier situation since I vacated the island. It was getting ugly at the time I left, though, and I'm guessing it's gotten uglier since.

"Ayuh," Dennis continues, "he has to anchor out in the bay now and row in."

I don't have time to wait for Billy's return. "I really need to get my hands on some rain gear, Dennis, just to borrow for a bit. Long story, but it's kind of urgent."

"He's got his good gear out on the boat with him today," Dennis says, "but..." He looks me up and down and sighs. "I guess you can look through his old stuff if you want."

Dennis silently leads me through the house and points into a closet, where two or three retired rain outfits lie folded under a box of Christmas decorations. One of the suits, liberally patched with duct tape, is exactly what I'm looking for. Safety-orange in color, it's a two-piece Acadia-style affair, with pants and a spacious hooded jacket. The hood has a visor on top and a high collar that covers the lower part of the face. Perfect for traveling incognito.

I thank Dennis and duck under Black's to put on the rain suit. That task complete, I still have my travel bags to deal with. They'll give my identity away if I carry them openly. I head for Musqasset Mercantile, a grocery and supply store a little farther east on Island Ave.

The rain has picked up and is whipping sideways in waves, so my full-body raingear looks fitting as I trudge down the main drag. No one's out on the streets anyway, though I do get a "Hey, Billy" from a t-shirt shop worker in her doorway. Guess she recognizes Billy's duct-taped rainsuit.

I enter the Mercantile, where the clerk behind the counter is Barbara DeCamp. I once did a painting of her cat and helped her clean out her tool shed after her husband died. I don't identify myself as I buy a box of Glad Lawn & Leaf bags and a packaged sandwich, and she doesn't greet me by name. Just rings me up and says, "Nice weather for lobstas." Good. The disguise is working.

I go back under Black's and inhale the sandwich. Then I fetch my shopping bag and backpack—the surf is getting wilder by the minute—and place them inside a black trash bag to conceal them. According to my phone, I've still got twenty-five minutes till the ferry leaves. My plan is to be the last passenger to board, which means I've got a bit of time to kill.

A singularly bad idea oozes from the three-pound chimp-steak in my skull: dare I try to get a glimpse of Jeannie? It would be a shame to come all this way and not even take a peek. And hey, she won't recognize me in this ridiculous hooded getup.

Jeannie's house—*our* old house—is up near Studio Row. I don't have time to make it there and back. But I wonder if she still tends bar at Pete's Lagoon. That was where I ran into her, about nine years back, for the first time since college, and where, upon seeing her face behind the bar, my life's path took a sharp left. She worked at Pete's the whole time I lived with her on the island, so I'm betting she still does. Maybe she's on duty now.

And what if she is? Do I really want to load up my brain's hard drive with fresh images of Jeannie to hijack my dreams and ruin my nights?

I pace back and forth between Billy's and Black's, trash bag over my shoulder like a demented Santa Claus, debating whether to try to see her. I actually say aloud to myself, "Don't be a frigging idiot. Don't be a frigging idiot."

As if such an existential choice were mine to make.

Pete's Lagoon perches on the bay on the eastern edge of the village, near the western side of Greyhook. It's a bustling bar and eatery that attracts a mix of people from all over the island—tourists, artists, boat captains, shopkeepers, even some of the "landed gentry" from The Meadows. If there's a default gathering spot on Musqasset, it is Pete's. I was known to murder the house guitar there of an odd Thursday evening and to muck in as a bartender occasionally.

No one's on the outdoor deck of Pete's today except a diehard gull, and the indoor crowd seems thin too. No chance of blending.

Oh well, don't over-think it. Leaving my trash bag on the deck, I step up to the front door and go inside. I stride through the place, looking purposeful but staying hooded. I get another "Hi, Billy," which I don't correct. I make a circuit of the whole bar, upper and lower level. A seascape of mine still hangs over the fireplace. Cool. Jeannie's not behind the bar, though, unless she's put on eighty pounds and become an African American male. Maybe she doesn't work here anymore.

As I'm looping back toward the exit, the Daily Specials board catches my eye: Jeannie's printing, in chalk, no doubt about it. Her words too. The Bos'n Burger, today's special, has the write-up: "We start with a dead boatswain, grind and grill him to perfection, then inexplicably add slaw and a store-bought bun. Fries mandatory."

Pete used to get furious when she did these goofy negative menu write-ups, but then they became a thing. People would come in just to read the Specials board. Bet they still do.

Smiling to myself, I'm about to head out the door when I hear it. That laugh.

Oh, man.

I peer into the kitchen and there she is. Facing away, one-quarter view. Wild hair partially civilized by a clasp, swan neck, bone-thin wrists, dancing hands. She's towering over a couple of younger waitresses who look delightedly scandalized by the story she's telling. My feet are nailed to the floor.

I know I can't continue staring like this—Jeannie has an unerring stare-detector—but I can't pull my eyes away. Sure enough, she turns.

She looks right at me, though I'm sure my face is well-hidden in the flaps and shadows of the rain suit's headpiece. She lets her gaze linger for a couple of beats, then turns back to her coworkers.

I can't get out the door fast enough.

✷✷✷

Five minutes till the ferry leaves. Time to make my move.

I march down Island Avenue in my Billy Staves costume, toting the trash bag, and turn left toward the dock. My ticket is in my pocket, ready to whip out. I plan to wait till the boat crew starts pulling up the gangplank and then dash on board at the last second, allowing no one to follow me.

As I'm walking past the old bait shack across from The Dockside, a hand shoots out and pulls me in.

CHAPTER 9

I haven't been in a fistfight since high school, but auto-pilot kicks in. I start throwing punches at the shadowy figure grasping my arm. He's a husky guy, but I land a couple of jabs and hooks.

"Whoa! Whoa! Easy there, pal," he whisper-shouts.

It's dark in the windowless bait shack, but I can see there's a second guy in here too. Both men wear hooded rain jackets. I escape the grasp of dude number one, but before I can lunge out the door, dude number two bear-hugs me from behind.

It takes me several seconds to register his voice. "Finn! Finn! Calm down. Finnian. Whoa."

He waits till I stop struggling, then spins me by the shoulders to face him.

"Miles! What the hell?"

"Yeah, Finn, pretty much my words exactly."

"What are you doing here?" I ask.

"Um, let's see, I invited you out to the island, remember? You're going to be a guest at my house."

"I told you to stay away from the dock. I said I'd be in touch."

"Yeah, well, I was already *at* the dock when you texted, so I stuck around. I didn't like the tone of that text. Not one bit."

"I told you I'd explain things later, Miles, and I will. But not right now. I've got to get back on that ferry. You need to trust me on that."

I pull away from Miles, but the bigger guy steps in front of the door.

"No one's going anywhere just yet, Mr. Carroll," he says in a polite don't-test-me tone.

"Finn, this is Jim," says Miles. "He's with the Maine state police."

"What?"

"Relax. He's not on duty. He's just a friend who's on the island for the holiday weekend. After hearing that stuff you were saying on the phone last night, then seeing that text, I was... I don't know, Finn. I felt I should give him a call."

Jim holds up a pair of binoculars. "We've been watching you since you got off the boat, Mr. Carroll," he declares, as if this fact alone should explain Miles's concerns.

I open my mouth to defend myself, but no words come.

"What we're going to do," says Miles in the capable, persuasive voice that must have won his law firm many a client, "is give you a few minutes to settle down, and then Jim is going to drive us to my—"

"No, Miles, sorry. That's not what we're going to do. We can't go to your house because that will put you, Beth, and the kids in danger. Those guys who tried to kill me? They *followed me out to the island*, and they will find me at your house."

The two men stare at me like cigar store Indians.

"If you don't believe me..." I dig out my phone and fumble open the VoxFox app. In my agitated state, I can't remember how to play a recording. I can't even find a recording *to* play. Where does the stupid program store its files? "I'll play it for you later."

I edge toward the door of the bait shack, saying, "I wish we could have spent some time together. I love you, man, and I'm grateful for the invite. But I *need* to get on that ferryboat now. I'll call you as soon as I get things sorted out."

I burst for the door, but again Jim blocks my way. The two men move in on me gently but firmly, sandwiching me between their bodies and caging me in with their arms. No one says a word. It's an awkward tableau, to say the least.

The ferry horn blares its farewell note.

The lid is on the snake terrarium.

"Beth, look who's here!" Miles calls out as I follow him into his kitchen. He's carrying my backpack and shopping bag.

Beth comes running in from another room with a squeal and a lit-up smile and practically leaps into my arms for a hug. "Finn! Oh my God! I can't believe you made it out here in this weather!"

Her enthusiasm throws me. Maybe absence does make the heart grow fonder.

"Kelsey, Dylan, come say hi to Uncle Finn."

I'm not really the kids' uncle, we just say that, but I am Kelsey's godfather. Kelsey prances into the kitchen, smiling through braces, a fourteen-year-old foal who's all leg and almost a foot taller than the last time I saw her. We do the lean-in hug. Dylan, who must be twelve now, backs out of a room down the hall, doing a robot shuffle and holding an Xbox controller. He robo-waves at me.

"Uncle Finn's had a long trip," announces Miles. "I'm going to show him his room, let him rest for a while, and we'll see him at dinner."

Oh, okay, nice to have my schedule worked out. I'm terrified my presence will endanger Miles and his family, but Miles believes everything is fine and "We all just need to chill." And so, I have allowed his version of reality, as usual, to trump mine.

He escorts me to a preposterously inviting guest bedroom in the rear of the first floor, landward side. It has a hideaway TV, motorized curtains, and a full attached bathroom with heated floor and whirlpool bath. There are more pillows in here than in Martha Stewart's fever dreams.

"Why don't you take a warm shower," says Miles, "then maybe nap for a few hours or whatever will help you chill. Later on, we'll have a glass of wine with Beth before dinner and catch up. After dinner, you and I will find someplace where we can... talk."

Miles has a way of making suggestions that are actually edicts. "I *might* do that," I say, just to assert some autonomy—an old dance of ours—"or I might take a walk into the village."

"Why don't you just make yourself comfortable here?"

"Are there bars on the windows I should know about?"

"Yes," he shoots back in a Peter Lorre voice, rubbing his hands together, "you are our very *special* guest, heh-heh. All we ask is that you never look in the basement, heh-heh." He laughs and starts to head off but then turns to me with an earnest expression. "Finn, I need to put this out there, so there's no... dishonesty between us. Your sister Angie called me five or six months ago, when you were in the hospital after that..." He doesn't need to say it: pill overdose. The first one. "I didn't call you because I wasn't sure you'd want me to know. The point is, I'm aware you've had some... issues of late. And I just want to tell you, there's no judgment from me. You're safe and loved here and... that's all. We'll talk later."

He leaves, closing the door before I can reply. Another Miles habit. I love the man, but sometimes I want to jump up and down on his face with hard shoes.

I flop onto the bed. It's stupidly comfortable, as I knew it would be. I'm sure the mattress cost more than my used car. *Damn. So, Miles and Angie chatted after my first fling with pills and booze.* That certainly puts a fresh spin on things.

The situation at hand suddenly becomes Poland-Spring-clear to me. Miles doesn't believe a word I've told him. Not about the bad men in my home, not about being followed on the ferry, not about the danger I'm in here on Musqasset. He thinks I'm three scallops short of a fisherman's platter. He believes my recent brush with death was exactly what it appeared to be on the surface—another suicide attempt—and that I made up the bad-guy story, either because I'm embarrassed to admit the truth or because I'm flat-out barmy.

I need to convince Miles I'm telling the truth. Because if he doesn't believe me about the danger I'm in, he won't believe his family's in danger. And I can't stay in this house.

Luckily, I do have that digital recording from the boat.

Or do I? I check the app on my aging phone again, confident I simply overlooked the location of the recording in my earlier anxiety. But there's only one place the file could be stored: under "Recordings." And that whole screen is blank.

✶✶✶

During dinner, I try to deflect the conversational focus from myself. First, Beth talks about some New Age-y webinar she's involved with called *The Power of Words*. It sounds a bit cultish and full of daffy metaphysics to me, but she seems to take it seriously. And then I manage to get Miles talking about himself, never an arduous task. As he tells me about his recent career exploits that led to his winning a seat in the Maine state senate, I begin to feel steadily queasier.

Why? Well, first a bit of background:

When Miles was fresh out of law school, Beth's dad, a big Northeast real estate developer with his finger in many pies, pulled some strings to get Miles into the top-echelon law firm where Miles is now a partner. Miles chose to specialize in real estate and environmental law. Over the years, he did the legal work for several projects Beth's dad was involved in—a PGA golf course, a resort hotel, a riverfront shopping complex. Helped him get around some pesky environmental speed bumps. I've often chided Miles for being Beth's dad's lackey and for betraying all the values he stood for in college.

But in the years since he last saw me, Miles explains over dinner, he has started working his way back onto the green side of the fence. A few years ago, over his partners' objections, he decided to represent the Penobscot Indians, on a pro bono basis, in a case involving a new power plant on the Penobscot River. "Long story short, our litigators prevailed in court. The story got some positive press. Made the firm look like a company with a conscience."

"Since then," adds Beth, "he's taken the lead on a couple of other big pro bono cases. He saved an area near the Appalachian Trail from development. He also got the laws changed around noise pollution in Maine's state parks."

"It's a win/win/win," as Miles describes it. "The firm gets some positive press, the environment gets some protection, and I get my face in the papers as the Champion of Worthy Causes." Meanwhile, Miles explains, he continues to work behind the scenes for his high-end developer clients. Gotta pay the bills, after all.

The publicity he got from the pro bono wins allowed him to samba into the seat for Maine state Senate District 29. And he now has his eyes on bigger prizes. He leans over the table, lowering his voice to conspiratorial level.

"There's a situation shaping up, knock on wood, that could—*could*—land me in Washington."

"Holy crap," I say, duly awed. It makes sense, though. With his movie-star looks, graying temples, and easy charm, the political possibilities are endless.

"Maybe we should wait till we know more about that before saying anything else," Beth chastises him with a smile.

The whole time Miles has been talking, my belly has been turning to lead, and not from the pasta. What's making me queasy? Well, I already knew Miles was enjoying a lucrative law career and making strides in the political arena, but hearing this latest development—and seeing his family's faces light up as he alludes to it—has brought my dilemma into bold relief.

What am I to do with the terrible facts I learned last night?

After we clear the dinner dishes, Beth pours Miles and me a brandy and says, "You two probably want some alone time. I've got some journaling to catch up on for *The Power of Words*. But maybe we can all do something fun tomorrow." We say our goodnights, and Beth departs.

I had hoped Miles and I could go somewhere outside the house to talk, but rain is whipping the windows like strands of wet seaweed. We're not going anywhere.

I'm hoping Trooper Dan has gone to ground as well.

Miles suggests a move to the study—yes, he has a "study," which he refers to without a shred of self-consciousness. And so, we stand up and do something I never thought I'd be able to say I did in my lifetime: repair to the study for a brandy.

CHAPTER 10

Miles parks his brandy on the oak mini-bar and says, "I think I'm going to have something else instead." He stoops and reaches under the counter, and I know with alarming certainty what his hand will be holding when he rises.

He does not disappoint. Glenmalloch single malt.

Fate? Karma? Cosmic joke?

He sets the bottle down on the mini-bar, where it proclaims itself like a telegram from beyond the grave.

"How 'bout you?" he asks.

"Think I'll stick with the brandy."

Gazing at the Glenmalloch bottle, my head begins to swim, and I feel as if I'm standing on the ledge of a skyscraper. But then I realize the bottle is offering me a precious opening.

I pick it up and blow a laugh out my nose, pretending the embossed black-and-gold label has just now jarred a memory loose. "Do you remember our college graduation night?"

"Oh God," says Miles, shaking his head. "Parts of it. Without a doubt *the* drunkest I have ever been in my life. An epic cringe-fest, from start to finish."

"Do you remember the Glenmalloch?"

"Duh. You gave me that beautiful bottle as a gift. It was even better than this twelve-year stuff, right? Came in a special bottle. It must have cost you a fortune. And I, like an ass, proceeded to swig it like it was PBR. Got completely trashed."

"I think you had stuff you wanted... *needed* to get off your chest. Do you remember how we got home that night?"

"I know we left without Beth. I caught endless grief for that. I have these strange memories of being out in the woods somewhere, thrashing on the ground. So drunk. I remember you standing there patiently, trying to get me back in the car. I woke up on my sofa the next afternoon with one shoe on and... a *hospital wristband*. What the hell was that all about?"

I have a question of my own to ask first. "Do you remember the cop? On Carlisle Road?"

"Oh God, I'm not sure. You and I got pulled over a few times in those days."

"Yes, we did." I pause heavily—he knows why. "But on *that* night, we saw a cop at a speed trap on Carlisle Road. Remember? We thought he was going to follow us, so we had to get rid of the bottle."

"No! No! Tell me we did not toss a bottle of sixteen-year-old Glenmalloch on the side of the road. Please, I'm begging you, Finn."

I shrug a what-can-I-say.

He groans through clenched teeth. "I always hoped you kept that bottle and drank the rest of it yourself. Maybe had a nice goodbye toast with Jeannie. I certainly proved myself unworthy of it." He looks me in the eye and shakes his head in disbelief.

Gazing into Miles's eyes, I am positive he's recalling that night for the first time in eighteen years. This reaffirms what I already knew: Miles has zero memory of throwing that bottle and zero knowledge of what happened in the aftermath. I was sure about it already, but I still had to ask. Why my certainty? Because Miles passed out so coldly that night, I had to take him to the ER, where he was treated for alcohol poisoning. So yeah, he was about as conscious as a bowling trophy by the time the cop's blue lights came on. And even if he somehow managed to awaken trace cellular memories of what went down on Carlisle Road that night, Miles is quite literally the last person on Earth who'd want to awaken that long-sleeping dog and start the police asking new questions about it. He has nothing to gain, everything to lose. He was *not* the source of the private knowledge in that suicide note.

So, who was? And where does that leave me?

My only path forward with Miles becomes clear. I plop myself into a brushed-leather armchair, clap my hands to my thighs, and fix him with a gaze. "I need to be straight with you, bro."

"Okay," he says, intrigued by my shift in tone. "Fire away." He sits in the armchair facing mine.

"I think you invited me out here under false pretenses."

He probes my eyes to see if I'm messing with him. "What do you mean?"

"I didn't know you had talked to Angie back in March."

"I'm sorry, Finn." He works to hold my gaze. "But that changes things... how?"

"Oh, come on, Miles. It changes everything. For starters, you know I swallowed some booze and pills and got hospitalized once before. I'm sure you heard Angie's amateur diagnosis of me, too. But see, *I didn't know* you knew that stuff when we spoke last night. So, crazy me, when I was telling you about that shitstorm in my parents' kitchen, I thought I was talking to a friend who was believing every word I—"

"Finn, I do believe—"

"Shh, Miles. ...A friend who was believing, *literally*, every word I was saying and wanted to help me because—"

"I do want to help you."

"But you want to help me in the my-poor-friend's-out-of-his-gourd way. And I thought you wanted to help me in the my-friend's-in-danger-and-we're-going-to-get-to-the-bottom-of-it way."

"I want to help you in whatever way you need or want help."

"I appreciate that, Miles, but tell me honestly: when I was describing my run-in with those thugs, did you believe that really happened or did you think it was just a psychological breakdown and another suicide attempt?"

Imagine the face of a hooked trout. That's what I'm looking at now.

"What does... 'really' even mean?" he stammers. "What we *call* reality is just a series of neurological events. If *you* believe what happened was real, then it *was* real. To you."

"Let's skip the adventures in neuro-epistemology tonight. I just want to know what game we're playing, you and I, as friends. Do you believe me, factually, or not?"

"Finn..." The man is squirming as if an electric eel has crawled up his boxer-briefs.

"You can say it; I already know the answer. I just need to hear it from your mouth."

"Okay—do I have doubts about a trio of psycho-pathic hit men trying to make you commit suicide for no apparent reason? And that they've followed you here to Musqasset? Finn, I mean, jeez. Step back and look at this objectively. You just got out of a psych hospital *yesterday*, for crying out loud. I'm sorry, man. This is killing me to say..."

"It's okay, Miles. It's okay." It's time to let the trout off the hook. "For what it's worth, I think you may be right. ...And I think your instincts were spot-on too. Inviting me out to the island—getting me away from everything—was the right call. In just the few hours I've had to myself this afternoon, I've already started having *my own* doubts about what happened. The shrink told me hallucinations and delusions are a common effect of the chemical combo I took. So, I'm starting to think it's possible I concocted the whole thing in my mind, as a way of—"

"I hear you," says Miles. "No judgment here, just friendship."

"Here's what I propose," I say. "Let's stick to the 'treatment plan.' I'll stay here as we agreed, get as much R and R as I can. Probably spend a lot of time alone, if that's okay. In a couple of days, when this storm has blown over, so to speak, we'll... reassess."

Miles's relief is palpable. "I think that's a brilliant idea."

He stands and takes my brandy away, as if suddenly realizing that giving me booze might not have been the greatest idea since the inclined plane. He offers to make me a cup of herbal tea and bring it to my room. I accept, agreeing that an early bedtime is a capital idea, old chap.

✦✦✦

I sit in the guest bedroom, sipping my warm tea and watching the rain lash the window. I dread going out in the storm, which I'll need to do before long.

You see, that stuff I told Miles about believing myself to be delusional was grade-A cow manure. Over the course of the evening, I have come to see a couple of things with 20/20 vision. One, Miles believes I've had a nervous breakdown. Period. Therefore, he is not going to take precautions against the danger I'm in. Therefore, he and his family remain at risk.

And two, the only way to make him believe me would be to tell him everything. Show him the suicide note. Show him the Boston Globe article. Tell him what he did on that long-ago night. And I can't do that. I can't derail this man's life and career.

Not now. Probably not ever.

No, it seems I will need to bear that burden alone and pay whatever price it exacts. And that is probably as it should be. *My* guilt, after all, is far greater than Miles's.

Isn't it? Miles has no idea what he did; *I'm* the one who made a conscious decision to keep a secret on that terrible night. I'm the one who fled the scene.

Best for Miles and his family if I remain a delusional nutjob in their eyes.

And so here is my plan. I will wait until the house has been asleep for an hour or so. Then I will borrow a flashlight, a gallon of water, a blanket, and a few Clif Bars. I'll sneak out of the house, taking my belongings with me, and find a shelter on the island where I can hide out until the storm is over. I don't care if it's a tool shed or a moldy old boathouse. Once the ferry is running, I will board it. And the moment it docks in New Harbor, I will seek police protection, even if that means telling them the tawdry tale of the scotch bottle and taking the full blame for it.

By the way, no, there is no police department on Musqasset. We share one part-time peace officer with Monhegan, and he's stuck on the other island till the storm passes. We have no jail or protective custody facilities either.

***

My chin bobs off my chest, and I pull in a ragged snore. I must have dozed off—my tea has gone cold, and rain is no longer pelting the window. The wind is still howling, but the windowpane has dried a bit.

Was it a sound that jarred me from sleep? I freeze and listen.

Seconds pass, and I hear it again. A pebble tick on the window glass. Really?

No way. No one has seen me on the island, except Dennis. And he doesn't know where I'm staying.

That suggests only one possibility. My bowels tighten. Seconds pass. Another tick.

I look out through the glass, but a rhododendron bush blocks most of the view, and the darkness beyond it is inky.

I throw on my jacket and sock-foot my way through the sleeping house. I pull a butcher knife from a rack in the kitchen and locate my shoes in the mudroom. Grabbing one of the flashlights hanging near the door, I step out into the gusting wind.

It's pitch dark outside, as it always is at night on Musqasset. The island doesn't have streetlights. In fact, it still shuts off its entire power supply at eleven o'clock every night. The only buildings that have electricity after eleven are those with generators or battery backup. And even they don't use outdoor lighting. No one does on Musqasset. Nighttime is nighttime here. If you go for a walk at night, you bring a flashlight.

I tiptoe toward the blackness of the back yard, not wanting to turn my flashlight on and reveal myself until I know what I'm dealing with. The idea that my Wentworth stalkers would *invite* me to my doom by pebbling my window like a high-school suitor seems nutzoid, and yet here I am, bait taken.

As I'm rounding the rear corner of the house, feeling my way along the rhododendron, a flashlight ignites ten feet away, bottom-lighting a face in a hooded jacket.

CHAPTER 11

"**S**o, Finnian Carroll," says the hooded figure, "you walk right into Pete's and out again without so much as a hi-how-ah-ya?"

Jeannie.

"How'd you know that was me?" I slide the butcher knife into my jacket pocket and turn on my flashlight.

"Come on, Finn, this is Musqasset," Jeannie replies.

She's right, of course. A secret on Musqasset Island has the same odds of survival as dignity at a Renaissance fair. That's why I knew I couldn't stay on the island after we broke up; I would never be able to establish my own boundaries.

"Besides," she adds, "raincoat can't hide a vibe."

I scan my brain's hard drive for something witty and disarming to say. File not found. I have thought for years about what I would say to Jeannie if I ever saw her again, and now my skull is an empty jar.

She aims her flashlight at my face like an inquisitor's lamp. "What in the Jumping Jack Crap are you *doing* here, Finn?"

Never one to beat around the bush, Ms. Jean Eileen Gallagher.

The wind howls, accentuating my silence. I can't very well blurt out the whole truth, so I just say, "Miles invited me out for the holiday weekend."

"You two are talking again?"

"We were never 'not talking'; we just hadn't spoken in a while."

"Wow, there's a Finnism, sure and true."

"Something came up yesterday. I called him, we talked, he invited me out to the island. It was all very spur-of-the-moment."

"That's why I didn't even merit a heads-up?"

She shines the flashlight on my face again, then aims it into the wind-whipped bushes. She strikes off down a trail that leads out of the yard. I guess I'm meant to follow. You never know with Jeannie.

"I wasn't necessarily planning to contact you," I say, hustling to keep up with her long-legged stride. "I wasn't sure you'd want to see me or what your situation was."

She marches forward into the low, scrub-pine brush that blankets the shore properties here in The Meadows. We walk in silence for almost a minute. "My situation— the part that's any of your business—is: I'm still pissed at you. The way you left here sucked. No goodbye, no working phone number. You even killed your Facebook page and email address. Not cool, Finn, not cool. There were things that needed to be said."

"I could have handled things better."

We take a hard left curve through the twisting scrub, lighting the narrow trail with our flashlights. I feel myself getting sucked into an old dynamic. Jeannie would say or do something thoughtless or mean or downright wrong, and I would react badly to it. Then we'd spend an hour hyper-analyzing *my* poor reaction while overlooking her original transgression. In the case of our breakup, Jeannie pulled the big A. She had an affair. Now here we are, stuck on what a jerk *I* was for leaving the way I did. Suddenly I'm not feeling so wistful about the Jeannie days.

We come to a fork in the trail and stop short. Do I hear footsteps following us, a dozen yards behind?

No, just a shore bird scurrying through the brush. I think.

"A lot of changes since you left," she says in a reproachful tone much like the one Dennis laid on me. She shines her light down the right-hand path, the one that leads to Fish Pier. Or used to. "You need to see something."

We walk in silence through the gnarly pine for a minute or two, following our light-beams closer to the water. When we get to the inlet between The Meadows and the village, where Fish Pier stood last I knew, Jean shines her light on a hanging wooden sign I've never seen before. Twisting in the wind, it reads *Marina and Yacht Club at The Meadows.*

"Has Miles given you the grand tour yet?"

I make a *pfft* sound.

"Didn't think so. Brace yourself."

She sweeps her light-beam around the inlet, revealing a huge network of newly constructed private docks where the old fishermen's pier once stood. Yes, Fish Pier is *gone.* I haul in a breath. Pausing for dramatic effect, she raises the light above the docks to reveal a massive complex of retail buildings. It looks so *wrong* here, my visual cortex actually tries to reject the image. It includes a pretentious-looking restaurant with outdoor tables called Haar; two or three art galleries; a specialty wine, cheese, and pâté shop (North Atlantic Charcutiers); and, holy crap, an upscale hotel by the name of—gag me with a marlin lure—Kaiyo. There's also a marine repair shop and a dockable gas station, complete with a precious, country-store-styled convenience shop where Fish Pier's ice-making machinery once stood.

"What *is* this?"

"Don't look at *me*," she says. "Miles and his crowd *own* this end of the island now. They just dock their frickin' Catalinas and stroll right up to a restaurant or hotel, or take a golf cart to their schmillion-dollar homes, without ever having to sully themselves amongst the commoners."

"God, this is not what this thing was supposed to be."

"Ya *think*?" She shines her light in my face again and clucks at my incredulity.

"Miles's proposal—the one I supported—was nothing like this. You know that. It was a good idea. It would have *helped* the fishermen. It would have helped the *island*."

"Yeah, well, things went off the rails, as you well know."

"Yeah, but not to this extent. Man. How'd they push this monstrosity through?"

"The shit show just got worse and worse after you left."

After Miles bought his place here, he became a mover and shaker on Musqasset, much to my chagrin. He and some investment partners came up with a plan for a modest-sized yacht club and marina complex that originally included rehabbing and maintaining the old Fish Pier in perpetuity, not hauling it away on a salvage barge.

Fish Pier, you must understand, was the heart of Musqasset's fishing and lobstering trade. The heart of Musqasset itself. Islanders and guests would fish off the end of it, and all the fishing boats used to dock and unload their catches there. The pier itself was public property, but for decades a guy named Bo Baines ran a private outfit at the base of it called the Seafood Exchange. He bought the fish and lobsters from the local fishermen at the end of each day, then carted the whole haul to the mainland and sold it at a modest profit. It was a good arrangement for everyone. It meant the fishermen didn't have to lug their individual catches all the way to Boothbay Harbor or Port Clyde, so they were able to shave hours off their workdays. Bo sold gas too, and supplied the boats with ice, and was known to fix a bent propeller shaft or two.

But for years, Fish Pier had been falling into disrepair, and no one could agree on who was supposed to pay for the renovation. That was where Miles's development plan came in. Yes, it included a new yacht club and marina, which rubbed a lot of island people the wrong way, but it also provided funds for a complete overhaul of Fish Pier and for its ongoing maintenance. Under the plan, the new developers would own the Seafood Exchange, but Bo Baines would continue to run it. Though many locals griped about the change to the "character" of the island, to me it seemed like a win/win. Not only would Fish Pier get a badly needed rehab, but the town would also get a huge tax windfall, which it could use to build a new schoolhouse, hire a full-time police officer, upgrade the electric grid, and more.

"What happened?" I ask Jeannie.

"You saw the beginning of the end. Once everyone in town got a giant chubby for all that new tax and tourist money, the parade of amendments started. Let's add this, let's change that. Right after you left, Miles and his boys came back to the approvals board, claiming the slump in the local fishing industry had changed their 'projections for that part of the revenue stream.'"

"I was still here when that happened."

"Well, next they brought in some new 'tourism trend charts' showing the island could support a bigger retail complex than originally thought. They just wore the opposition down with dollars and promises." She looks at the buildings, and I can tell she's seeing old Fish Pier in her mind's eye. "A lot of people view them as saviors, though. The new schoolhouse has already been built, courtesy of the new tax funds. The island's hiring a full-time cop next spring."

"But not everyone is thrilled, I'm guessing."

She shines her flashlight on her unsmiling face.

Pivoting on her heel, she heads back up the trail that led us here. We walk without talking for a while, hearing only the changing notes of the wind. And... wait, is that the sound of footsteps behind us again? I stop. "Shh. Did you hear that?"

Jeannie strides on.

Eventually she turns onto an uphill trail leading to the north edge of the island. We hike for a bit longer, then ascend Lighthouse Hill to the top, passing the lighthouse on our right. Next, we work our way down the steep cliff-side trail that descends to Table Rock, lighting the slippery path with our flashlights.

Table Rock is a flat, slightly raked, slate-rock structure on the water's edge, where The Shipwreck, an island landmark, resides.

"Lots of other changes happening," Jeannie says. "Ready?"

She stops in her tracks when we're still twenty yards above sea level and shines her light down ahead of us. Massive storm waves are crashing on Table Rock, and something looks off to my eyes.

"The Shipwreck," I say. "It moved."

"It's mov*ing*. I think this storm is going to take it out to sea."

What? The thought chills me to the marrow. I sink my butt onto a rock. Jeannie sits beside me. In the light of our flashlight beams, we watch the giant waves crash, mesmerized by the spectacle.

The Shipwreck has been a Musqasset icon for decades, as well as the subject of a bajillion oil paintings, including a few of my own. The story is that in the late 1930s a mailboat named the *K.C. Mokler* ran aground here in a storm at sea, and its rusting metal hull has remained dry-docked on Table Rock ever since.

The Shipwreck holds a boatload of history for Jeannie and me. It was our designated place for bad behavior. During the day it belonged to the tourists, but at night it was ours. Whenever we felt like smoking a joint, or drinking some Chartreuse, or being sexually... *resourceful*, we'd end up at The Shipwreck. You could climb up on top of it or go inside the hull, depending on the weather—and your inclinations. The risk of getting caught added an edge of danger to our activities. And in keeping with the theme of the landmark, we were usually pretty well wrecked whenever we found ourselves there.

"I quit drinking," says Jeannie, as if tapping into my thought-stream.

"Wow, really?" Sometimes my font of eloquence is positively bottomless.

"Over three and half years ago now." She watches another wave crash on The Shipwreck, then adds, "Not that I owe you an explanation, but... I'm not the way I *was* anymore. I just thought you should know that."

As a statement, it couldn't be vaguer, but we both know what she means. I won't say Jeannie was promiscuous—that's not accurate—but she had issues with monogamy and was not willing to give up her sexual autonomy for anyone, including me. There were men who preceded me, whom she quietly continued to see from time to time even after she and I were an item. Her belief in her entitlement to these ongoing assignations was built on some obscure moral foundation I was never allowed to glimpse in full.

The men weren't island guys; she didn't want that kind of entanglement. Rather, they came by sea. One was a ship's captain, another had a yacht so big it couldn't dock in the harbor. (I prayed that wasn't a metaphor.)

She shielded these encounters from me, and I sensed that if I were ever to insist we confront them openly, I would lose her. So, I didn't. But this "pattern" of hers—and my utter ineptitude at dealing with it—formed the fault line in our relationship that eventually led to the quake that undid us.

"You coming back here was a mistake," she declares.

I don't reply at first. Instead, I watch the tide assault Table Rock. A monster wave crashes, spraying us from below. When it hauls itself back out to sea, I hear the deep cetacean groan of submerged metal dragging on rock. It's a sound that ices my skin. The *K.C. Mokler* inches closer to the Atlantic.

Still gawking at the historic drama unfolding below, I ask, "Why do you say that?"

I turn to look at Jean. She is gone.

CHAPTER 12

As I'm passing the lighthouse on my way back to Miles's, the wind carries a sound to my ear. A seashell crunching in the dirt. Jeannie? I turn my head and see nothing, but that's unsurprising on this starless night. I don't want to shine my light on whoever it might be, because if it's just a local, that would be a breach of island etiquette. And if it's someone trolling for trouble with me, I'm not eager to light that fuse.

I shut off my flashlight and step up my pace, hoping I can navigate the route back to Miles's house in the dark without breaking my fool neck.

Not twenty feet later, my foot snags on a vine, and I go sprawling. So much for hope. I rise, listening sharply. Only the whistling and howling of the wind. But my gut tells me I'm not alone out here.

I reach into my jacket to see if my phone is there. It is. I don't know whom I'd call for help or how they'd find me out here, but still, the phone feels comfortingly warm in my pocket.

I walk on, my eyes adjusting to the absence of flashlight, and come to a familiar fork where the scrub pine starts to turn into real woods. The righthand trail is a pretty direct route back to Miles's house, but if I take it I'll run the risk of leading my possible pursuer there. The lefthand trail is longer and twistier but will lead me into the village, the island's most "public" place. Which way to go?

A flood of light hits me from behind.

Like an idiot, I turn.

About a hundred feet behind me, three bright lamps throw their beams at my face. Flashlights. Strong ones. All three shut off at once. Island courtesy or am I being messed with?

Being a cup-half-empty guy, I put my chips on the latter.

I scurry down the lefthand path, the one that leads to the village, at the briskest pace I can manage without using my light. With each step, my nerve-strings tighten.

I go a hundred feet. Two hundred. The wind whipping the trees is loud enough to mask the sound of any footsteps behind me, but I can *feel* a presence gaining on me. The knife is still in my pocket, but do I have the will to use it? My fingers grope for its handle. Goosebumps tickle my back. Nervousness starts to give way to panic.

I spot a tiny, overgrown path snaking off to the left, through a stand of pine. If memory serves, it leads to an old, abandoned property. I ditch the main path, hoping my detour isn't picked up.

Blindly, I pick my way through the water-laden spruce needles pressing in from both sides of the narrow footpath. I get a face-full of wet spider web and step in a squishy, bitter-smelling fungus. I'm trying to move as quietly as possible, but the path is riddled with sticks that snap and vine runners that snag my shoes.

Up ahead, about twenty-five yards or so, I sense a clearing in the trees. I head toward it, letting the old scratch-mark of a trail guide my feet.

I dare not turn on my light, but I can make out a curved shape in the dark clearing. I think it's a rotting, upside-down dory I recall from old island excursions.

Instinct tells me to hide under the dory, though I'm not sure why. If someone follows me this far, they'll surely look under it. But instinct wins. I lift the port side of the boat, allowing for any resident fauna to disperse, then duck beneath its bowed gunwale.

The trapped air stinks of wet, decaying wood, but the hull is bowl-shaped and deep enough for me to sit up a bit. Resisting the temptation to turn on the flashlight and scope out the ecosystem I've just barged in on, I remain still, letting my heart rate reset.

Time dissolves. Sitting there in the almost perfect darkness, my senses—and perhaps my imagination too—shift into overdrive. I'm almost certain I hear stealthy footfalls below the sound of the wind. Someone creeping into the clearing? *More than one* someone. I think I hear a "shh," though it might be just the wind catching a pinecone or a curled leaf.

A twig cracks.

Something flutters. Fabric flapping in the wind?

A sixth sense—or maybe a fusion of my conventional five—tells me several human beings are standing stock still in a semi-circle around the flipped dory. Why aren't they moving? Speaking? Why aren't they looking under the boat? Every nerve and muscle in my body is at DEFCON 1.

I suddenly feel absurdly certain my phone is going to ring, but I don't want to make the move to shut it off, afraid the slightest rustle of Gore-Tex will give me away.

Minutes pass. I remain motionless.

Something raps on the hull. I almost scream but realize it's just the rain starting up again. Within seconds, it starts to whoosh down harder.

I hear—or *sense*, rather—the people moving away.

I can't stand the tension any longer. I heave the boat-edge upward, let out a lunatic yell, and charge out from beneath the dory. Slashing at the air with the knife, I shine the light around, screaming like a crazed baboon.

No one is here.

I sweep the light around the clearing. Vacant.

I stand in place, panting, for a minute or two.

Starting back toward the main trail, I'm about to write the whole thing off as pure imagination when a cold, wet object slaps me in the forehead. It falls to the ground with a flabby thud. When I see what it is, my head goes woozy.

A dead mackerel. A three-inch thorn has been jammed through one eye and out the other. A message. From Trooper Dan and friends?

How they found me so easily in the dark, I have no idea, but one thing is certain: they could have confronted me, or done whatever, but chose not to. Why, who knows? Maybe they're just toying with me, like a cat with a mouse, or maybe the reasons run deeper.

Terror takes a bite of me.

Think I'll *run* to the village. Keeping my flashlight on, I book it back down the brambly side-path, turn left onto the main trail, and run, full speed, till I reach the dirt road leading to the village. Then, what the hey, good children, I run some more.

Standing in the center of the village, hauling air into my lungs, I feel both safer and more exposed. The shops are closed, of course, and the lights are all off. Rain and wind are the only sounds. I shine my flashlight back in the direction I came from and see no sign of pursuit from the woods.

Maybe no one was following me. Maybe I cooked up the whole thing. The presence I detected in the clearing? Raccoons stalking one another for a fish. Sure, why not? I scared them away and they… ran up a tree, dropping their fishy prize on the way up. And it struck my head. The thorn through the mackerel's eye? An accident of the forest. Could happen.

And yet the thought of going back to Miles's, collecting my belongings, and then prowling around the island some more, in the dark and rain, looking for some possum-infested boathouse to hide out in for the next day or two, feels like a terrifying prospect. I'm exhausted, nerve-fried, soaking wet, and freezing.

Neither the island nor my own mind feels like a safe place right now.

What I really want to do is sneak back into Miles's house, go to sleep in that soft, warm, dry, stupidly comfy bed, and take a fresh look at everything tomorrow.

Maybe that's what I'll do.

CHAPTER 13

I awaken at nine, hours past my usual rising time, and sit on the edge of the bed, feeling oddly rested and recharged. My situation hasn't changed, but something has shifted inside me, can't explain why. Inner resources that have been walled off for ages suddenly seem accessible. Like there might even be some fight in me.

I replay last night in my mind. Despite the danger I'm in, the foremost thing on my mind is Jeannie. I won't say it was "good" to see her—binary terms like good and bad don't apply where Jeannie is concerned—but it was illuminating. A truth I've been denying for years has become as plain as the taste of oyster cracker a la carte: I'm still in love with her. I was in love with her in college but too thick to know it. I fell in love with her again when I ran into her on Musqasset Island several years later, and I am in love with her now. I know, I know: love and a five-dollar bill will buy you a tall Americano. I'm sure Jeannie is not even "available." And even if she were, it's colossally unlikely she would subject herself to another go-round with the likes of me.

Still, it's good to know my own truth, for better or worse, and to name it. Maybe *that's* what has shifted in me. Truth is power, maybe that's really so.

I think back on my experience in the woods. A night's sleep has not convinced me the threat was imaginary. Quite the contrary. I feel doubly certain there *were* men in that clearing. Trooper Dan was toying with me. The dead fish was intended for me, and its meaning seems clear: *You're dead, but at the time and place of* our *choosing.*

Maybe we'll see about that.

I open the window curtains, using the remote on the nightstand. Motorized curtains—whatever you say, Miles.

The rain has returned. With attitude. I switch on the bedroom TV and surf for a weather report. Here's one—a live broadcast of a yellow-slickered imbecile with a mic standing on a sea wall as waves crash behind him. "The storm system's forward progress has been stalled by a high-pressure zone," he shouts over the wind, "and it's 'parked' below Nova Scotia and spinning like a top. That means we can expect high seas to continue for coastal Maine and the islands through much of the holiday weekend, along with intermittent rain and—as you can see!—strong winds."

I'm not getting off this island till Sunday or Monday.

So be it. I refuse to spend that time feeling trapped and afraid. It's time to *do* something. *What*, I haven't the remotest idea. But something.

I find my jeans folded on the dresser, along with yesterday's shirt. Some early riser has thoughtfully washed and dried them for me. Dang. That means Miles and Beth know I was out last night. Guess I'll have to explain that.

★★★

Dressed and as groomed as I get, I venture out of the guest room. Wending my way toward the kitchen, I notice Miles at the table, talking to someone in whispered tones. I pause before entering the room, trying to glimpse the other party.

Miles spots me and shouts, "He's conscious!"

"Let's not make rash pronouncements." I step onto the imported, handmade tile floor of the kitchen.

"Finn, you remember Jim." I do indeed. The off-duty statie.

"Hey there," says Jim, standing for a handshake. "Don't punch me this time," he adds, doing a mock flinch. Ha, so funny. Jim is tall and broad, and I swear his head has a permanent groove around it from twenty years of wearing a state policeman's hat. "You've got a pretty fair right hook for an artist."

"Finn grew up in Wentworth, Mass," says Miles, as if that explains everything. Jim laughs heartily.

There's a bit too much forced bonhomie in the air. I wonder why. Then I notice the butcher knife sitting in the middle of the kitchen table. Crap, I forgot to return it to the rack last night. Miles or Beth must have found it in my room, along with my wet clothes. I nod at it. "I assume you're planning to ask me about that. Mind if I grab some caffeine first?"

Miles throws his palms open as if to say *this isn't a locked ward*.

Armed with my small-batch-roasted, single-origin, fair-trade Guatemalan coffee, I join the men at the table, and we make a couple of fizzling attempts at small talk. The Sox, the storm. Then Miles gets down to business. "So... seems you were 'oot and aboot' last night."

"I didn't realize I was under house arrest." I lean back, folding my arms. I'm in no mood to be treated like a mental patient this morning.

Miles snorts dismissively. "You're our guest. Obviously, you're free to come and go as you please, but I thought we had agreed on a basic script."

"Yeah, well, the writers and I got to chatting last night."

No one laughs. I tell him about seeing Jeannie.

He winces as if a crab just pinched his scrotum. "Do you think that was wise?"

"It wasn't a date. I didn't plan it."

"Oh really? You just happened to bump into her after turning in for the night in my house? I thought the whole idea was for you to relax and stay emotionally calm. I can't imagine seeing Jeannie was an emotionally calming experience."

"It wasn't. She took me to see the new Disney World over at Fish Pier. Wow, Miles."

"That's a topic for another time," he says. "Right now, let's keep the focus on you.

"Kaiyo? North Atlantic Charcutiers? No wonder you want to keep the focus on me."

"See? This is exactly my point. This is what Jeannie does. She stirs things up. She stirs *people* up. She's a one-woman wrecking crew..."

"*She's* a wrecking crew? Seriously?"

"...and I don't think seeing her is particularly wise, given your current—"

"Whoa there, gents," interrupts Jim. "I'm less concerned about who's dating who than I am about *this*." He picks up the butcher knife and twirls it weightily in his hands. "Can I ask why you felt the need to arm yourself with a weapon last night, Mr. Carroll?"

I think my decision was more than justifiable, given the circumstances, but I don't feel Jim Hat-Head is owed an explanation. "Can I ask why you're here, Jim? Not to be rude."

He ignores my question. "You see, Miles here was under the impression that you'd given up on this... *notion* that you were being chased across the Gulf of Maine by crazed psycho killers. But then you sneak out of the house late at night with a sharp knife, and we don't know what to think."

"It's not your job to think about it, Jim."

"Well, now, that might not necessarily be true. From a law enforcement perspective, the question arises as to whether a person might be a danger to himself and others. And with your recent—extremely recent—psychiatric history..."

"What's the bottom line here, guys?"

Working in tandem, the two of them trot out a proposal they obviously hatched before I awoke. They would like me to "see" a woman on the island they think can help me. A counselor. Welly well, so Musqasset has its own shrink now; *that's* miles past overdue.

I stand up. I've had about enough of this. The only reason I copped an insanity plea last night was to placate Miles so I could sneak out of his house and vanish. Now my exit will need to occur in plain sight. Time is short, and I have a rather serious problem to solve.

✳✳✳

"Thanks for the invite," I say to Miles as I step back into the kitchen, wearing my rain jacket and carrying my full backpack. "But I can't stay here. I shouldn't have come in the first place." I make a move toward the door, and Jim's strong fingers clamp my upper arm. "Jim, you have about two seconds to remove your hand."

"You want to think very carefully about your next words and actions, Mr. Carroll."

"Or what, Jim? You have no authority to hold me. I haven't been charged with a crime, and I'm not under psychiatric commitment."

"That could change."

"The state of Maine requires a blue paper"—an involuntary commitment—"to hold someone against their will," I tell him. "And I'm pretty sure it needs to be signed by a psychiatrist, not a licensed social worker who sells Herbalife on the side."

"In special circumstances, such as a storm like this, Mr. Carroll, if there's a clear and present risk, I can get a blue paper approved by phone on an emergency basis."

I suspect he's bluffing and tug my arm to test that theory. He lets go.

Theory supported. I push my way outside and march down the walkway that leads away from Miles's house. I barely notice the rain stippling my face with hard pellets.

Miles charges out the door behind me, throwing a raincoat on.

"Finn!" he shouts. "Stop! Damn it, I am *ordering* you to stop."

Ordering me? That's a new one. I keep walking. Miles catches up but stays two paces behind me.

"Classic Finn. Charging off on some internal goose-chase instead of facing reality."

The wrong thing for him to say at this juncture. I wheel about and face him, my neck flushing with heat. "*Me* face reality? You don't know jack, Miles! And you never have. You live in your little world of..." I stop myself.

"Say it. Come on, get it off your chest."

I have something on my chest, all right, but it's not what he thinks.

"Come on, Finn. Say what's on your mind. Because it's been poisoning our friendship since freshman year of—"

"Friendship? Is that what you call this? 'Cause that's not what it feels like right now."

I walk onward, my shoe soles slapping the mud. Miles follows, pulling at his rain visor.

"Back off, Miles. I need a *real* friend today, not a social worker, not a cop, not a—"

"Then convince me!"

"Of what?"

"That you're not out of your freakin' mind!"

My gait falters, but I don't stop. "I'm afraid I can't do that."

"Then let me get you some help and together we'll—"

"I can't do it because I would have to tell you things... that I'm not able to say."

"What are you talking about?" He draws abreast of me and clasps my jacket sleeve. Rain pours down like judgment on both of us. "Finn. What the hell are you talking about?"

Before cooler heads can prevail, I blurt out, "I didn't tell you the whole story of what happened to me because I didn't want to burden you with it. I was... protecting you. As usual."

I reach the road and keep walking. Miles stays glued to me, step for step, awaiting more. "There's a reason those men came to my house," I say. I turn and notice Jim following us, several yards behind. I lower my volume. "And it has everything to do with you."

What am I hearing from my own mouth? Only yesterday I swore I would never share my awful secret with Miles. But now it seems the only path forward.

"Me?" says Miles. "You'd better explain yourself, Finn."

"I can't."

"You have to."

"I can't!"

But we both know there's no stopping this train now.

CHAPTER 14

Miles and I sit side by side on a pew in the island's tiny non-denominational chapel. I didn't want to talk at his house, or in a public restaurant, or outside in the driving rain. There's no one else using the chapel on this rainy Friday morning, and the setting feels oddly fitting for the confessional work at hand. Jim has wisely left us alone.

"Those guys at my house?" I say, hushing for no good reason. "That really happened. Not just in my mind. I'm not crazy, Miles. Someone tried to kill me. When they left me for dead, *this* was showing on my computer." I pull up the suicide note on my phone.

Miles reads the text, his face a stone sculpture.

"But *you* wrote this, right?" he asks.

"No. I know it sounds like my words, but no I didn't."

If Miles wants to challenge me on this point, he doesn't. "It says you were alone in the car that night."

"Right. Why would *I* write that? Or some of this other crap?"

"Okay, so what's this big incident that's being alluded to? What's all the drama and guilt about?"

"People died, that's what."

"Died? What do you mean?"

"That Glenmalloch bottle? We didn't toss it on the roadside." I pause before delivering the *coup de grace*, knowing that what I tell him next can never be taken back. Doubt rears its head again. What right do I have to dump this ancient baggage on him? To torpedo his career and family life? His actions that night were careless, not evil. He has no real moral stain. Not yet, anyway. Not till he knows.

I suddenly see another avenue, a way to tell him *almost* the entire truth by changing one detail. In this way, all the major implications will remain the same, but Miles can be spared the guilty hand.

"We needed to get rid of the bottle," I say, weaving my new version of the story. "We were driving over route 495, but... you told me it was the Merrimack. You were drunk, you didn't know. I grabbed the bottle from your hand and threw it over the bridge without thinking. It was only when we got to the next bridge that I realized we'd made a mistake. I had thrown the bottle onto the highway, not in the river."

Miles tenses, waiting for more.

"I thought I heard crashing sounds from below," I continue, "but I wasn't sure. You had passed out by that point, and I couldn't wake you, couldn't talk to you about it. I didn't know what to do. So, I just drove off, told myself it was nothing."

"And...?"

"It wasn't nothing." I show him the old Globe article about the accident that I emailed myself. As he reads it, his face drains of blood, and his breath becomes shallow and audible.

"Jesus, Finn," he says, unconsciously pressing his palms together like praying hands. "How long have you known about these deaths?" Suddenly I'm not crazy anymore.

"Only since Thursday, only since I clicked the link in that 'suicide' note. The day after graduation, I avoided reading the papers or watching the news. Then I left for California."

"Jesus, Finn," he repeats. "Jesus." A sheen of perspiration has blossomed on his forehead.

"Now do you believe me? Now do you see why someone might be upset enough to want to hurt me? Now do you see why I can't be staying at your house?"

But Miles doesn't seem to hear me. He stands up and walks out of the church with his mouth hanging open and a benumbed look in his eyes. I start to follow him, but he warns me off with a sweep of his hand.

I've rented a room at Harbor House—to distance myself from Miles's home and family. Ordinarily, there would be no vacancies on Musqasset on a holiday weekend, but the storm has prompted numerous cancellations. I asked JJ, the manager, for a quiet room away from other guests, and he put me in 313, in the back corner of the third floor, with no one occupying the next two rooms.

I'm under no illusion that I'm safe here, though. If Trooper Dan and company were able to find me in the pitch dark last night, in a storm, on a wooded trail unfamiliar to them, then I assume, going out on a limb, they can find me in a public inn. But what can they do about it? That's what I'm pondering as I sit on the edge of the bed, biting at a hangnail. Would these guys really dare make a move on me here, in this creaky old inn where noise carries like electric current? Or in any public spot on the island?

Or will they need to isolate me somewhere, far from the madding crowd?

But they had their perfect opportunity last night in the woods, and they didn't act on it. Why? No frigging clue. I have no idea who these guys are or what their agenda is.

A knock at the door interrupts my ruminations.

Suicidally, I turn the knob and peek out.

Miles. He pushes into the room, carrying a laptop.

"Let's assume everything you said is true," he announces without preamble. "Who could possibly know about that night, and why would they care?"

What has caused this sudden shift of attitude? Miles plunks his computer down on the room's small desk, tosses his rain jacket onto the bed, and rolls up his sleeves as if he's ready to work. "Let's start by reviewing what we know for sure," he says. "See where that leads us." His energy is all business.

Fine, I'm in.

We convert my room into a makeshift "war room," moving the desk into the middle of the floor and stealing an extra chair from down the hallway.

We're in agreement that my only real hope of thwarting my purported stalkers is to figure out who they are and what they want. We know the odds of solving this puzzle from the remote location of Musqasset Island, in a storm, on a holiday weekend, with two rank amateurs at the helm, are slim, to put it wildly optimistically. But slim beats nonexistent.

"Before we go any further with this," says Miles, booting up his computer, "I want to state something 'for the record.'" Oh joy. "I'm choosing to believe you, and I want to help you, but... here's my dilemma. Now that I know what happened that night, I can't unknow it. And the more information we unearth, the harder it's going to be to pretend I can. What I'm trying to say is, in my career position, I can't be guilty of covering up... misdeeds."

"Don't worry about me, Miles. I'm prepared to accept complete responsibility for my actions at the appropriate time." It's true. I am.

"Are you sure?"

I nod. He nods. We lock eyes across the table for several seconds.

"Then let's proceed."

I go to turn on my voice-recorder app to capture our conversation—a habit of mine from work meetings—but before I touch the phone, it "wakes up" as if a text or call has come in. Nothing appears on the screen, though. Whatever message was snaking through the ether, trying to find me, has been swallowed by the storm. I tap "record" on the VoxFox app.

117

"The first question we need to ask," says Miles, "is who besides you and me could possibly know about your connection to that accident? No one else was there." He leans back, flaring his palms out. "Possibility number one: you or I told someone. Since I had nothing to tell until now, that kind of eliminates me." Miles drills his eyes into mine, doing his lawyer thing. "Over the course of the last eighteen years, have you told *anyone* what happened in that car? Anyone at all?"

Easy answer. "No."

"Are you sure? Anyone? Under *any* circumstances? Think. A confession to a priest..." Right. "A night in a bar... pillow talk with Jeannie or someone else?"

"Nope, absolutely not. I'm a hundred percent sure."

"Ever write about it in a journal or diary someone could have read?" I shake my head. "Or mention it to a shrink in a hospital, or a therapist?"

"No, Miles. I told you: I couldn't even admit it to *myself.* I moved to the far end of the continent just so I wouldn't have to know if there'd even *been* an accident."

"So, we didn't start the fire. Possibility number two…" He does a courtroom pause. "There was an eye-witness. Someone saw what happened, maybe got your license plate number."

Given the conditions that night—dark road, late hour, unpopulated location—we rule out the possibility of a random observer.

"Which leaves the cop, then," says Miles.

"Hmm, right. Here's the thing, though. I was watching for him like a hawk. My eyes were glued to the rear-view mirror at the time that I"—I almost say "you"—"threw the bottle. He wasn't behind us yet. ...Besides, if the cop saw me throw it, why wouldn't he have followed up? Why wait eighteen years to come after me, and why get thugs involved? Doesn't make sense."

"No, it doesn't. Which brings us to possibility number three. If neither of us told anyone, and there were no witnesses, including the cop, then someone pieced something together from evidence found at the accident scene."

"And the only possible evidence was the bottle itself. If they could somehow trace that."

"Right."

"But wouldn't it have shattered into a million pieces?" I ask.

"Maybe, maybe not. It was a thick bottle, as I recall."

An idea lightbulb switches on over Miles's head—almost literally, I swear—and he types "Glenmalloch" into the Google search box. He hits the search button. Nothing happens.

"Damn," he says. The Internet, it seems, has chosen this moment to desert us. "This place has satellite," Miles says by way of explanation. "We'll try again later."

Internet service on Musqasset is a crapshoot even on a sunny day in June. The concept of broadband is like time travel here. Video streaming is a joke. Satellite Internet is a common choice—that's what Harbor House uses—but its reliability varies, especially in bad weather. Quite a few residents still have dial-up, believe it or not, and many people use their cellphone service for Web access, but cell reception is trash outside the village, where the only cell "tower" (an eight-foot pole) is located. Even email can be spotty. Texting is probably the most dependable means of communication, but texts can show up at random times, or not at all.

"Okay," Miles continues, "Let's stipulate, for now, that someone has connected you to the accident—they obviously have, we're just not sure how. So, what's the next most obvious question?"

"Why would they want to kill me? 'Motive,' as they say on *Law & Order.* And why wait eighteen fricking years?"

"Let's look at motive first. Why would someone want you dead? Not for any apparent gain, it seems. There was no attempt to blackmail you or make demands. Right? Someone just wanted you deleted from the census report."

"So that would point to what? Vengeance or 'justice,' I suppose. Someone has a vendetta and wants me to pay for my... crime."

"Possibly." Miles thinks for a moment. "Or maybe you're perceived as a threat to someone. Are you?"

"Not unless bad computer-game art is a malign force to be reckoned with."

"*Do* you have any enemies, though, Finn?"

"I can think of a few people who might want to cross me off their Christmas card lists, but not off the *planet.* And even if they did, why stage my death to look like a suicide?"

"Um, so there wouldn't be a murder investigation." Duh. "Plus, the fake suicide note comes in handy if someone wants the world to know you threw the bottle. It's a flat-out confession."

"True." I'm still confounded by the fact that the suicide note sounded exactly like me, but I don't want to get into that right now. "Again, though, why wait eighteen years?"

Miles mines the air for answers. "Without knowing who's responsible, we'll never figure that part out. Let's stay with the who. Someone wanted justice... revenge?... for themselves or a loved one. So, who were the parties involved?"

We scan the newspaper article, and Miles types the names on the laptop:

Paul Abelsen
Laurice Abelsen
Ashley Abelsen
Edgar Goslin

Seeing the names in stark black letters brings home the fact that real human beings died that night in 1999. People who will never have children or grandchildren or taste another spoonful of strawberry ice cream. I feel a burn of shame and grief.

Miles, sensing my thoughts, says gently, "You didn't know, Finn."

"Because I didn't *want* to know. Because I avoided knowing."

Miles waits a respectful beat, then says, "The Abelsens—we need to talk bluntly about this—all died. But they might have friends or relatives who are seeking payback. Edgar Goslin was hospitalized with serious injuries. If he survived, he might have a score to settle."

"So, task number one," I say, "is to find out whatever we can about the Abelsens and Edgar Goslin. And that pricey bottle of scotch."

"All without a working Internet," grumbles Miles. No sooner does he say this than the results of his "Glenmalloch" search pop up on Google. "Back in business—for the moment anyway."

Miles clicks on the URL for Glenmalloch.com. The website assembles itself in piecemeal fashion. It's a hi-res site replete with polished wood grains and vessels of gleaming amber liquid. Miles finds a section called "Special Release Malts." It shows a pictorial history of all the unique whiskies the company has released in recent decades. Scrolling through the years, Miles freezes when he sees a product released in 1999 called Single Barrel 16, Anniversary Edition—"a premium Islay-style whisky matured in a single aging cask and offered in a hand-numbered, decanter-style bottle to honor the distillery's 150th anniversary."

The photo hits me like a slap in the face: a squared decanter with a heavy glass cork-stopper and a shockingly familiar black-and-gold embossed label.

"That's it," I say. Unnecessarily. "That's the bottle."

Miles nods, almost hypnotically. "Look how thick that glass is. If this bottle hit a car windshield, it might have left pieces big enough to identify."

Wow, a mere twenty minutes into our lame-ass "investigation," and we may have already found a pivotal piece of the puzzle. We stare dumbly at the screen.

"So how would someone trace it back to me?" I ask, even as my mind is supplying possible answers.

"Two ways I can think of," says Miles. "Fingerprints, for one. Either of our prints, or both, could have been on any part of the bottle." He blows out a shaky breath. "Have you ever been fingerprinted?"

"Not that I recall," I say, "though I came close once." I cast him a leaden glance. There was an incident during our sophomore year of college that we both look back upon with shame—for different reasons.

Miles and I had been at our friend Doc's apartment, watching Green Bay kick New England's ass on Monday Night Football. We'd had a few beers. Miles was driving me home in his van when we spotted blue lights behind us. He panicked, to put it mildly.

"Oh my God, Finn," he shrieked, "what are we going to do?" He started blubbering like a schoolkid, "I'm screwed, I'm screwed, I'm totally screwed."

I was appalled. This was the first time I'd seen Miles without the social mask, the first time I realized that behind his polished exterior there lived a terrified child.

"My life will be over if I get charged with DUI," he said. "Over! My father will kill me. I'll never go to law school. My grandparents will freak. ...You've got to switch seats with me."

He stopped the van and, without awaiting my answer, dove to the floor and climbed toward the passenger seat, as I, like an idiot, scrambled into the driver's seat. We pulled off the switcheroo—thanks to the curtains covering the van's rear windows—but I was taken to the police station, where I submitted to a blood test. I was finally released, no fingerprints taken, but it was a close call. Not one of our proudest moments.

"You?" I ask. "Ever fingerprinted?"

"I don't think so. No."

"The only other way to connect the bottle to me, then—assuming they could piece enough of it together to identify the brand—would be to trace the purchase somehow, right?"

"Right. Ordinarily, that would be almost impossible, but this was no Johnny Walker Red. This was sixteen-year Glenmalloch, numbered label. Do you remember where you bought it?"

I think back for a moment but oddly have no memory of purchasing the bottle. I shake my head no. Maybe it'll come to me later.

"There were only a couple of liquor stores in the Bridgefield area that would have carried a product like this," says Miles. "That bottle probably sold for close to a hundred dollars."

"It did, believe me," I say. "I wanted it to be memorable." Yay, score one for me on that front.

"How many bottles like this do you suppose were sold in our area within a week or two before the incident?"

The answer is plain. A handful at best.

Maybe only one.

CHAPTER 15

We're still staring at the web photo of the old Glenmalloch bottle when a bone-jarring crack of thunder splits the air above us. The lamp in the room loses power, and we go dark. We've lost the Internet signal again too. And I can't get online with my phone.

We're instantly back in the 1920s.

Miles's phone rings. He answers, listens, and says, "I'm on my way."

"Beth," he explains to me. "The generator didn't kick on."

He stands and puts his rain jacket on. Guess we're finished. There's not much more "detective" work we can do without Wi-Fi anyway. He gives me a light goodbye hug, but I catch his eyes scanning me like a doctor evaluating a head-trauma patient. He tells me to call him later and vamooses.

I'm left alone in my newly rented room.

My *tiny, isolated, powerless* rented room.

I wonder how long we'll be without juice. Minutes? Hours? Days?

Even though it's late morning, it's surprisingly dark in the old inn without lamplight and under this dense cloud cover.

With no Internet to focus on, my mind hurtles back to the danger I'm in. I have no idea who my stalkers are, where they're staying, what they want, or how insane they are. I don't know whether they're surveilling me 24/7 or not. The idea that I can somehow learn these things by digging up facts on an ancient scotch bottle suddenly seems like magical thinking of the looniest order.

To complicate matters, my mind, ridiculously and unproductively, keeps gravitating to Jeannie. *Does she really have a kid? Is she still with that clown who—*

Stop.

I wander downstairs to the lobby to snag a candle lantern from JJ. The L.L.Bean family is sitting around a coffee table, playing a board game near the fireplace. The daughter gives me a little finger-wave. Damn, she's *more* than cute. Under different circumstances, I might...

Enough. Stick to the task at hand.

Which is what?

✳✳✳

Back in my candlelit room, I'm staring out the window at the village below, trying to figure out my next move. A man in a dark raincoat—hard to tell its exact color—is standing near the donut shop/post office. He seems to be staring up at my window. I reflexively draw back.

A moment later I look again. The figure is gone.

A woman bustles by, carrying a floppy handbag that reminds me of one my sister Angie owns. Angie. *Call Angie!* Of course! Angie works at the city clerk's office in Wentworth, and she can find out anything about anyone.

Luckily, my phone is still working as a telephone, if not as an Internet portal. I ring Angie's work number and manage to catch her at her desk.

"Hey Ange, it's me."

"Oh, Finn. Hi. Listen, I'm sorry I haven't been up to see you yet, but I—"

Up to see me? Crap, she thinks I'm still in the hospital. "Um, I'm not at Saint D's anymore."

Short pause. "What? What do you mean?"

"I discharged myself."

Another pause. "Do you think that was wise?"

"I'm on Musqasset right now, Ange. It's a long story, and I might lose phone service any minute. Listen, I was hoping you could help me with something. I need some information on a couple of people in the Wentworth area. I'll explain why when we have more time."

"Okaaay..." she says, not exactly blasting me off my feet with enthusiasm.

I recap the 1999 newspaper account of the accident and tell her the kind of info I'm looking for—who the Abelsens were, any known friends and relatives, who Goslin is or was, what became of him, and so forth.

Angie is quiet for several long seconds. "What goaded you into digging for this information, Finn?"

What *goaded* me? Oddly phrased question. "I'll explain later. I'm afraid of losing my signal, and I've got more calls to make. Can you do me this favor? Ange?"

"I'll... see what I can find out," she finally offers. "If you think that's a good idea. But you *will* need to tell me what you're up to. I'm worried about you, Finn."

I thank her, asking her to email me—and Miles—whatever results she finds, and hang up. *Why the guarded attitude?*

Because Ange is nuts, that's why.

I'll let her do some digging into Goslin and the Abelsens, though.

Meanwhile, I'll try to focus on the scotch bottle—that rare and highly traceable scotch bottle that seems to be the sole thread tying me to the accident—with my phone as my only tool. If only I could remember where I bought the damn bottle, there's a chance the owner of the store, or an employee, might recall someone asking questions about it all those years ago.

But I *can't* remember. And it *was* almost twenty years ago. The store that sold it probably doesn't even exist anymore, and if it does, what are my odds of reaching someone who worked there in 1999? Still, I need to try.

It takes me a moment to remember how phone numbers were disseminated in the pre-smartphone era. Phonebooks, oh yeah. I recall that the Musqasset library houses a large collection of them from all around New England.

★★★

Island Avenue is half underwater as I trudge the two hundred muddy yards to the library, getting tommy-gunned by the wind-blown rain. I have a strong sense of being watched; every window looks like an eye. The instant I step inside the one-room building and stomp the rain off my shoes, Lester Hughes, the octogenarian librarian, chimes, "So the rumor mill was right."

Fabulous—the *town librarian* has already heard I'm on the island. Hooray for keeping my presence on the downlow.

Lester shows me the corner of the room once reserved for phone books. It has been converted into The Story Nook, as the hideous fairytale mural attests. No more phone books. "So, what do people do if they need a phone number and the Internet is down?"

Lester shrugs and flashes his Titanium White dentures. "Call 411 and invest a buck."

I'm back in the rain, my eyes scanning every shadow for movement. I'm trying to wring my brain for memories of that ill-fated booze bottle, but my thoughts insist on flowing in one direction only: toward Jeannie. Let's face it, I *need* to talk to her one last time. Just to learn the facts and be done with it. Is she in a relationship? Married? A mom, as rumor has it? I never got the chance to ask her last night.

Maybe I should resolve this distraction once and for all, since I can't do any online work right now. I'd love to see her face to face, but I can't just show up at her front door asking questions. Especially if she's living with AssFace von TurdClown.

Nah, too intrusive. Too awkward. Too risky.

Seeing my old home on Fishermen's Court brings up a knot of mixed feelings I can't begin to unravel. I assume

Jeannie still owns the place—a tiny blue-gray cape with a fenced-in yard and an English garden in need of taming. Out back sits an oversized storage shed I turned into a small painting studio. The location of the house, fittingly enough, is just a jig's cast away from Studio Row, where the "legit" artists live. So near and yet so far.

One glance at the old shed/studio unleashes a torrent of memories—light-filled images of painting at my easel for hours, then catching a fish off the pier in the late afternoon and cooking it for Jeannie and me as we drank summer wine. Seems like there were hundreds such vintage days, but maybe there were only a few.

Dare I approach the door? My brain says no, but my feet don't get the memo.

Standing on Jeannie's stoop in the rain, I feel as if the eyes of the world are upon me. I don't want to bring any danger down on her. And what if ClownAss von TurdFace answers the door? I should have brought a bag of dog crap to light on fire.

Ignore that last remark.

I tap the cat-gargoyle knocker I gave Jean for Christmas six years ago—not that I'm counting. No response. I knock a bit more bravely. Nothing. The house feels unoccupied.

I should just beat it, but I can't resist the urge to take a quick look around. A plastic play castle in the overgrown yard tells me the child rumors are true. No obvious signs of a live-in male, though. No wheeling tool chests, no recycling-bags bulging with Bud empties.

Oh well, time to make my absence felt. I start toward the village and freeze mid-step. Standing in the middle of the road about two houses down, legs splayed, facing straight toward me, is a man in a Davy's Grey rain slicker. His face is shadowed by a large hood, but a salt-and-pepper beard climbs high on his cheekbones.

I'm paralyzed into inaction. I stare at the man. His unseen eyes stare back. Malevolence streams toward me like an electric beam. Or so it feels.

"Finnian Carroll," a man's voice shouts behind me. Shit. Boxed in.

I turn to see Andy Rusch, an old painting buddy, plodding toward me, smiling, in waders and a fireman's jacket. I toss him an awkward greeting before whipping my body around to face Davy Grey again. He's gone.

"I *heard* you were on the island," says Andy as he draws up beside me. (Is there a Sherpa on a Himalayan mountaintop who doesn't know I'm here?)

We shoot the breeze for a minute, but the rain and wind—and my anxiety level—put a damper on real conversation. Andy tells me he thinks Jeannie is working today, and then asks, with almost comical earnestness, "Is everything okay, Finn?"

"Any reason it shouldn't be?"

"'Course not," he says, but I don't love the fact that he waits a beat before saying it, or that his smile is so broad. "'Course not."

The walk to Pete's Lagoon takes several minutes, and I find myself looking over my shoulder every few strides. Halfway there, a TV set pops on in a nearby house. The power must be back, at least for now.

As I step into Pete's and shake off the rain, I experience one of the strongest déjà vu moments of my life, one that instantly purges my mind of Davy Grey. Jeannie is standing behind the bar cutting lemon wedges, her back to the house, and she turns to see who has entered. It's an eerie replay of the moment I walked into Pete's about nine years ago. On that day of yore, she spun and looked at me from that same spot. I hadn't seen her since college but had thought about her plenty. I was visiting the island with a painter friend who insisted I couldn't call myself a New England artist until I had painted Musqasset. Jeannie was about the last person in the galaxy I expected to find tending bar thirteen miles off the coast of Maine, but the instant I saw the twinkle in her eyes, I was hooked like a swordfish.

Today the twinkle isn't quite there, but it isn't *totally* absent either. Unless I'm misreading. Which I am known to do on rare occasion.

"I was wondering when you'd wash up on the rocks again," she says, in that dry-as-sandpaper tone of hers. "What can I get you?"

"Dazzle me." I claim a stool at the underpopulated bar.

She lifts an eyebrow, then turns and lets her hand flitter along the top shelf of the back bar. I am weirdly unsurprised when she reaches for—was there any other possibility?—the Glenmalloch. It's odd that an island bar would even stock such an obscure brand of scotch, and yet I'd have fallen off my barstool, literally, if she had chosen anything else.

She pours me a dram of the golden nectar.

"Is it hard?"

She takes my meaning—working in a bar when you don't drink anymore.

"Not really," she replies. "At least once a day, some drunken pinhead says or does something that reminds me just how fargin' glad I am to be sober."

We chat about the weather for a bit, for the usual avoidant reasons, but also because, in a storm like this, it's really the only topic.

"I went by the house," I finally say, amending it to "*your* house."

"You probably shouldn't do that, Finn." Her bantery tone has evaporated. She looks around, confirming there's no one within earshot. "Listen, I know *I* was the one who came to see *you* last night, but I hope I didn't do anything to imply that the door was in any way open between... you know..." Us. "Because that ship sailed, sank, ran aground, and washed back out to sea a long time ago." Jeez with the metaphors, Jeannie. "We both agree on that, right?"

Drown me in a chum bucket.

"Of course," I say. "No, I didn't get any other impression. I just... wanted to see how you were doing, how your life turned out."

"Turned out? Crikey, I hope it's still a work in progress."

As she goes back to slicing lemons, she gives me the sanitized, Cliff Notes version of her life since I do-si-doed. No, she didn't stay with AssTurd del ClownFace. Hallelujah. Yes, she has a daughter, Bree, who's spending the holiday on the mainland with Jean's sister. Bree will turn three next month. A quick bit of arithmetic dashes any hope she might be, well, a blood relative. Jeannie had one other brief relationship after TurdAss de la FaceClown, she says, and that was the one that prompted her day of reckoning with herself. Since then, she has lived dude-free and alcohol-free and has been putting all her attention on her daughter. She's finally taking her writing seriously too and has had two horror stories published. Wow, amazing what a little non-Finn time can do for a person.

And me? Oh, right, my turn. I try to put a charitable spin on my life of the last few years, essaying valiantly not to make it sound like, "After we split up, my life went rocketing down the crapper so fast you'd think it was fired from a bazooka," though I'm pretty sure that's what comes across anyway.

When I'm done with my awkward PR spiel, Jeannie leans on the bar, stares me in the face, and says, "So why'd you come back to the island, puffin boy? Real reason."

I order the fisherman's platter, hold the fisherman.

CHAPTER 16

Miles rings me as I'm finishing lunch and says he's coming to pick me up. He's suddenly getting Internet reception at the house, even though the storm is still raging. The rest of his family is at a holiday charity event at "the club," so we'll have the place to ourselves for a few hours. I'm still worried about the possibility of leading my stalkers to Miles's house, but a working Internet signal seems an opportunity too good to pass up.

I say goodbye to Jeannie and am about to leave when, to my surprise, the words, "When do you get off work tonight?" leap from my mouth.

She shoots me a suspicious look. *Why?*

"If I were to show up at your place around seven with a garlic, mushroom, and artichoke pizza from The Barnacle, would you slam the door in my face?"

"Not without grabbing the pizza first." The Barnacle makes seriously good pizza. "But I don't know if that's a wise idea, Finn."

"Just two friends sharing a bite," I say. "Unless you've got other plans."

She grabs a rag; suddenly the bar top needs wiping. When she's five feet away from me, she says, "I guess it wouldn't kill me to throw a salad together and stick a dessert in the oven." Jeannie *bakes* now too? Peace in the Middle East. "Just as long as we agree that..."

"Yeah, yeah. See you at seven?"

✶✶✶

The rain blows in sheets as Miles and I drive down partially flooded Island Avenue in his canvas-topped golf cart. I'm not thinking about ancient bottles of scotch and bad guys in Davy's Grey raincoats, as good sense dictates I should be. I'm thinking about dinner tonight. I'm both thrilled and terrified about spending time with Jean, but I also can't help feeling disheartened by her portrayal of our relationship. I couldn't have expected otherwise but still, "sailed, sank, ran aground, and washed back out to sea"?

The memory of her words triggers a thought. I ask Miles to drive up Lighthouse Road. We park at the top of the hill, and I walk to the seaward edge. I urge him to follow me down the path descending to Table Rock. Miles is reluctant to brave the rain-slickened rocks, but he eventually brings up the rear. We stop partway down and take in the scene below.

The Shipwreck—*our* Shipwreck, Jeannie's and mine—has shifted its angle again and worked its way closer to the edge of the great bed of slate. The whole bow of the *K.C. Mokler* is now jutting out over the water. The waves continue to assault it.

"Holy shit," says Miles Sutcliffe.

"A few years ago," I say, "if you'd asked me to name the two most iconic sights on Musqasset, I'd have said Fish Pier and The Shipwreck. Looks like they'll *both* be gone soon."

We exchange a look that encapsulates our entire history on the island.

Not long after I showed up on that painting excursion nine years ago and ran into Jeannie, I moved here. I loved the island for many reasons, not the least of which was that it was *my* discovery, *my* place. Not Miles's. Miles had barely even heard of Musqasset when I talked him into visiting me here a year or so later, even though Beth was a Maine native and the Sutcliffes had become full-time residents of the Vacation State. Miles's decision to buy a summer home on the island was based almost entirely on my relentless beleaguering.

And boy howdy, did he make me regret it. Where I saw beauty and balance and thriving community on Musqasset, he saw economic opportunity. Where I wanted to preserve the place like a lost Winslow Homer painting, he immediately set about trying to change it.

Miles turns and heads back up the trail. We make our way toward his electric cart, wet and winded from the climb. I ask him to let me drive. He knows where I'll be taking him, and he doesn't like it, but he flips me the go-ahead.

I might not make it off this island alive, but I refuse to go to my final fishing grounds without saying some things that have needed saying for years. Tonight with Jeannie and right now with Miles. Before he and I do another thing.

Miles sighs as I take the road to old Fish Pier, now marked with an elegantly understated sign, "Marina and Yacht Club at The Meadows."

I park the cart on a hillock overlooking his new marina complex. The white-capped ocean churns beyond it. Gazing down at the rain-soaked cluster of aggressively tasteful buildings that look as if they belong anywhere but here, I no longer feel the anger I felt last night but rather, a sad sort of resignation. About what? The inevitability of money winning every battle, I guess.

I don't feel a need to speak for a while, and neither does Miles.

I break the silence. "I said some hurtful things to you when I left the island, and I'm sorry. One of my many, many, many—did I mention many?—flaws is that I hold things in, and then when I finally blurt them out, I say more than I intend to. But you *do* understand why I felt betrayed by you?"

"This thing was never about you and me."

"It was *always* about you and me. At least to me it was."

"That's why you'll never be a businessman, Finn. You don't understand that business isn't personal."

"You don't understand that it *is*. Especially in a place like Musqasset. *I* invited you to this island. That's personal. *I* talked you into buying a house here. *I* introduced you to people here who could make things happen for you. That's personal. When you came up with your original development plan, I put *my* ass on the line to help you sell it to the locals. A lot of people hated the idea of a yacht club on Musqasset—hated it—but *I* opened their minds by pointing out how great it could be for Fish Pier. And for the fishermen. And the island."

"It was a good plan, Finn."

"Was. What happened?"

"Things change. I had partners. They wanted a surer return on their investment. They saw a better way to leverage the assets at hand."

"Assets at hand? Fish Pier wasn't just a chunk of planks and pilings. It had meaning to people. History. It was the heart of the island's economy."

"The *old* economy. Time marches on."

"It was the soul of the island, Miles. The anchor. The root system. Couldn't you see that? This is a working island, not some trust-fund babies' playground. Generations of islanders docked their fishing boats and lobster boats at that pier. Island kids caught their first fish there. Hundreds of artists painted it, in every light and every season. Fish Pier *was* Musqasset."

"I did fight for the pier, Finn. I know you don't believe that, but I did. But I was outnumbered and out-moneyed. The other partners didn't live here. They had no sentimentality about Fish Pier whatsoever. But I fought my damnedest for it."

"Did you give them the letters?" Before I left the island, I launched a letter-writing campaign to preserve the pier. I asked Miles to present the letters to his partners, and he took it as a personal attack.

He glares darkly at me. "I gave you my word, didn't I? The letters didn't matter. You don't know these people. I had no influence. I didn't have any real skin in the game, I was just the front man. I don't know how much money you imagine I have—Beth's the one with the real money in our marriage—but the *vast* majority of the financing came from people who gave not crap one about Musqasset tradition."

"Then why'd you throw in with people like that?"

"Not everything in my world is as pure and simple as it is in Finn World."

"Don't do that, Miles. Don't dismiss me as some kind of moral purist who doesn't live in reality. Can you not see the position you put me in? I was a newcomer myself, but there were people here who had grown to like and trust me. I leveraged that trust to help *you*. Can't you see that when you abandoned Fish Pier, you abandoned *me*? How could I stay on the island after that?"

"So, it's *my* fault you left the island? Breaking up with Jeannie had nothing to do with it?"

"Maybe we wouldn't have *broken* up if this thing hadn't put so much strain on our relationship."

"Oh wow, Finn. This is classic. You're actually blaming me for your break-up with Jeannie."

"I'm not. All I'm saying is your actions have consequences. Human consequences. Sometimes I wonder if you've ever really understood that." Again, I'm tempted to blurt out some things that must remain unsaid.

"Here's what I think," Miles says. "Much as I miss Fish Pier, I think this new complex is saving Musqasset's ass. Ten, twenty years from now, people will look back on this development as a turning point for Musqasset. A positive one. And Fish Pier will be a quaint bit of history."

"You don't get it."

"*You* don't. The future of Maine's coastal economy is tourism, not fishing. That's a fact. I'm sure when the printing press was invented, the people who ran Scribes R Us thought the sky was falling. Change sucks. Until the money starts rolling in."

"It's more complicated than that, Miles. And if you don't know that, you don't know Musqasset."

"See that flat rooftop over there?" He points. "You know what that is? A helipad. We threw it in as a gift to the island. People can now be safely medevacked to the mainland in an emergency. Two lives have been saved this season already."

I don't respond. We stare down at the rain-drenched marina complex, and I'm sure we're each seeing a wholly different scene. If I'd known what sort of atrocity this thing was going to morph into, the fight Miles and I had four years ago might have involved dueling pistols.

"I do recognize you stuck your neck out for me," Miles says at last. "And I am forever grateful for that... So, let's get back to the house and get to work."

I could dissect the subtext of his final remark— he's helping me because of what, a sense of duty? Obligation?—but at this point I don't feel like arguing anymore. I need an ally, and I'll take one any way I can get it.

As we're stepping into Miles's house, an email arrives on his phone with a jingle. Random delivery by the weather gods. It's from Angie. Good thing I asked her to cc Miles.

His phone caught the email, my antique piece of iCrap did not.

The email contains a Word attachment. Ange's message is, "Kinda concerned about why you want this information. Promise me we'll talk about it ASAP. Hope it helps you with whatever you're working through."

Working through? I guess she thinks I'm still in psychiatric crisis. Take a number in *that* line, sister.

"Can I get you anything to drink?" Miles calls from the kitchen as I pull up a chair at the desk in his oak-infested study.

"I'll take a beer, thanks."

"How 'bout Diet Coke or O.J.?"

"Just give me a freaking beer, Miles."

He brings two. I move aside Beth's *Power of Words Journal* to make some space on the desk. We print up two copies of Angie's Word file. Her write-up:

> *As you know, the Abelsens and Edgar Goslin were involved in a highway accident in the early hours of May 13, 1999. The Wentworth Tribune said the cause of the accident was under investigation.*
>
> *An article in the Trib several days later said the cops had found evidence that a glass container, possibly tossed from the Carlisle Road overpass, may have contributed to the accident.*
>
> *The accident victims:*
>
> *Paul and Laurice Abelsen were mega-boojie types who lived in Bridgefield. Paul grew up there. Went to Bridgefield Academy. Owned a startup software company. Father, Gary, is a Mr.*

*Moneybags. Started a scholarship & memorial 5K
run in his son's name. Also offered a fat reward
for information that would help in the accident
investigation.*

*Edgar Goslin suffered head and pelvic injuries.
Was hospitalized and unconscious for weeks.
After he came to, he told police—S2S—that
something had broken his windshield and caused
him to lose control of the car. Was wheelchair-
bound at first but then had some surgeries and
rehab, got his legs back. Arrest record—DWIs,
drunk-and-disorderlies...*

*That's the quickie version. I may be able to get
more, but first I would need to know where you're
headed with this. – Angie*

So, Miles and I were right about pieces of the bottle
being found. Yay, us. Any sense of self-congratulation is
dampened by the ominous implications.

There's something in the note that's bugging me too:
"S2S." Sorry to say? Why would Angie think the cause of
the accident would upset me? It does, of course, but why
would *she* think that? Ah well, time to dig into our work.

Angie's research gives us a good place to start. We
divvy up the workload along unspoken lines: Miles will
look into the Abelsens, as they seemed to dwell in his
socio-economic stratum. I will look into Edgar Goslin
because, well, he's a Wentworth bottom-feeder.

Miles decides to work upstairs, where he says the
Wi-Fi is better, so for the next hour or so, we split up
and put Google through the wringer. At around three,

we reconvene in the study to review our notes together. I turn on my VoxFox app to record our session.

Miles has learned that Gary Abelsen, Paul's father, was a bit of a crusader. At first, he praised the police and asked the public to come forward with information. Later, he ranted in op-ed pieces about how his family had been forsaken by the cops. A surprising new detail Miles has uncovered is that Paul and Laurice Abelsen had a second child who was not in the car with them that night—a boy named Theo, three years old at the time, who was later adopted by his paternal grandparents. My heart lightens a bit upon hearing this.

As for my research: Edgar Goslin, yeah, apparent douche. Wife/girlfriend has had multiple restraining orders on him. Arrests for drunk and disorderly, both before and after the accident. A "friend" set up a charity fund in his name to collect donations to help pay his medical expenses, but something fishy happened—the person was hiring hookers with the funds, something like that. Friends in low places.

"Interesting," I say, after we finish sharing notes. "Both of these guys—Abelsen's father and Goslin— might have major axes to grind about the accident, even all these years later."

"True. Abelsen lost his son, granddaughter, and daughter-in-law all at once."

Again, a wave of guilt washes over me like hot oil. Miles is right about one thing: when the storm is over, this crime will need to be owned.

"Another thing about Abelsen," I add. "He has money. Those guys who came to my house were pros, not local juvies. They worked for somebody, or so they said. It can't be cheap to hire professional hit men."

"Goslin, for his part, suffered long-term injuries in the accident," Miles says. "He seems like the type who might bear a longstanding grudge. Belligerent dude."

"Right. But a guy like him would want to do the revenge stuff himself, don't you think? My guess is he wouldn't hire professionals, even if he could afford to."

"You're assuming those guys really *were* hired."

"What do you mean?"

"They might have been lying about that. Maybe one of them was Goslin himself."

I hadn't thought of that.

"Possible," I grant. "Whoever wrote that 'suicide' note knew all about me, that's for sure. Including the fact that I was connected to that godforsaken bottle I wish I'd never laid eyes on."

"Right," says Miles, raking his cheek stubble. "How did Goslin—if it *was* him—link the bottle to you if the cops couldn't? And why wait eighteen years to act?"

"Back to that question again."

Miles leans back in his nine-hundred-dollar Herman Miller office chair, laces his hands behind his head, and stares at the ceiling (no cobwebs in *this* house).

At last, he sets his chair back down, stares at his phone and says, "I didn't want to go this route, but..." He punches a number. "Hi, Jim. Hey, I want to thank you again for your help, and, listen, I hate to do this, but I need to ask one more favor."

CHAPTER 17

Miles wraps up his call and turns to me. "Jim says he prefers the kind of thank-you that comes in a bottle. He likes the Louis Jadot Pinot Noir they carry at the marina."

"I'll treat," I say. "So...?"

"He says if the accident took place on an interstate highway—which it did—the Mass state police had jurisdiction. He knows some people within that bureau, so he might be able to find out some things. Might take him a minute, though."

"That's awesome, Miles. Meanwhile, I guess we keep looking into the scotch bottle ourselves, see what we can learn?" Miles shrugs agreement. "Someone knows it was me who bought that booze, so they must have learned it from the merchant who sold it to me. Right?"

I'm googling liquor stores in the Wentworth/Bridgefield area when the kitchen door jingles and Beth shouts, "Wipe your feet!" at the kids.

"I wasn't expecting them back so soon," Miles says, then calls out, "Finn and I are in the study, hon." Warning her I'm in the house. Subtle, bro.

Beth pops her head into the study, greets me with a way-big smile, and says to Miles, in a faux-casual tone, "I didn't know you guys were hanging here today." (Read: "I thought you'd agreed to keep Finn off the premises, *Honey*.")

Miles explains the Internet situation to her and asks how the club party was.

"Pretty small. No one's on the island this weekend. Even the Gustafsons didn't show. Tons of food, though." She shoots Miles a freighted look and says, "Can I steal you for a sec?"

I can tell she's trying to wangle some privacy—call me Sherlock—so I inform Miles I'm going to take a walk and buy that wine for Jim.

I strike off through the storm toward the new marina complex. When I get there, dripping wet, I suppress my gag reflex and enter North Atlantic Charcutiers. It's a pretty nice store, it pains me to admit. Hell of a lot better wine selection than the Mercantile—and they *dust* their bottles. Dandy-looking pheasant sausages too. I buy half a case of the pinot for Jim.

I arrive back at the house ten minutes later to find Miles in a frantic new gear. He's cleaning the study as if the Dalai Lama, the Pope, and Oprah are about to drop by for tea.

I ask him what's up.

"Nothing, I just have to deal with some stuff right now."

Message received. We can't continue our work anyway, what with Beth and the kids home, so I leave the wine for Jim, grab my phone, and tell Miles and Beth I'll see them later. They're heartbroken over my departure, I'm sure.

✶✶✶

The moment I enter my room at Harbor House, something seems off. I sense the dense proximity of other humans. I freeze in place for a moment. A floorboard creaks. Someone is nearby or has *just* departed the room, and the floor is resettling in their absence.

Another creak. It has a weightiness to it; a body, a present body, shifting its position. Seems to be originating from the supposedly unoccupied room next to mine. I grab the drinking glass from its doily on the dresser and put it up to the tongue-and-groove wood paneling. Yup, the ol' cup-to-the-wall trick. No technophobe I.

I hear a muffled baritone voice. Can't make out the words. A higher voice replies, also hushed and muffled. It's the voice of Trooper Dan, I'm sure of it.

Well, *sure* is overselling it. I listen again. Okay no, it's a woman's voice. One thing's for certain, though. There's a furtive vibe to the chitchat.

I look around my room. For a man who's feeling lethally endangered, I am alarmingly light on weaponry. I notice a wooden dowel, maybe fifteen inches long, standing inside the window casing, propping up the top window. Nice touch, JJ. I snag the dowel and, wielding it like a club, step out of my room.

The doorknob *two* doors down from mine rotates. That room should be unoccupied too! Out steps Daughter Bean, squinting like she just woke up from a nap.

Lordy, she is one agreeable-looking individual.

"Oh, hey," she says. "*Thought* I heard something." Her eyes go to the cylindrical piece of wood in my hand. "What are you doing, um, rolling pie crust?"

"Yes," I say without missing a beat, "but I prefer lard to butter. Do you have any?"

"Lard?" she deadpans, slapping her body in a couple of random spots. "Nope, all out. Might have some plumber's grease, though. If that'll work."

I laugh. I like this gal. She's funny and she's got the kind of Emily Blunt vibe that makes my chromosomes do backflips. I'm wishing there was a parallel me who wasn't in fear for his life and wasn't still in love with his ex who could spend this stormy holiday weekend trying to coax young Ms. Bean, of the Beans of Maine, into his private chambers.

"You have neighbors now," she says, referring to herself and her family. "Hope that's okay." She explains that her parents' room had a ceiling leak from the storm, so they asked to be moved. The two rooms next to mine were the only side-by-side ones available.

"Welcome to floor three," I say, "where the elite come to meet. And cheat. And... bleat?"

We chat for a minute, flirting with the edge of flirting, and I learn her name is Leah. I finally pull myself away from her gravity field, saying maybe I'll catch her for a drink later.

Back in my room, I realize, with a slap to the fore-head, that the hushed conversation I heard through the wall minutes ago was no doubt the sound of Leah's parents trying to have a little afternoon delight while their adult daughter napped in the next room.

Finn Carroll, ace detective.

Ah well, time to get back to work. I fish out the liquor-store phone numbers I jotted down at Miles's house and flop down on the bed to plan a "strategy." Ha.

The two booze vendors near Godwin College that might have carried that bottle—Bridgefield Package Shop and Academy Liquors—are still in business, according to my Google research. There's also an old standby in Wentworth, the Cordial Shoppe, that claims to have "the region's best selection of single malt scotches." So, what should I say when I call these places? I doubt any of them have sales records going back to 1999, or that they'd share them with me even if they did. I doubt I'll find any employees who were around back then, either.

My best tack might be to try to talk to the store own-ers themselves, find out if they owned their stores back in 1999, and if so, ask them whether they remember anyone, police or otherwise, questioning them about a bottle of Glenmalloch they sold.

The task would be easier if I could remember where I bought that damn bottle. The memory should be a clear one, but it isn't. True, it was eighteen years ago, but still, it's not every day you drop a C-note on a bottle of booze. I'm still drawing a blank, though.

I go to grab my phone, and that's when the odor hits me. That low-tide smell of rotting sea life. It's a common perfume on the island, one you become nose-blind to after a while. That's probably why I didn't notice it sooner. I sniff around the room. The windows are closed; maybe it's drifting up from the kitchen on the first floor. (If it's the Catch of the Day, the day must have been last Tuesday.) No, it has a nearer, and rawer, source.

I tear open the dresser drawers. Empty. I grab my backpack and unbuckle its flap.

A yelp flies from my throat. I drop the bag.

There's a dead fish inside it. Two-pound cod. About twenty-four unrefrigerated hours old. So someone *has* been in my room. I wheel about, pulse racing, fully expecting to be jumped. But no one is here.

A quirky thing about Harbor House: the room locks are the original, nineteenth century, skeleton-key type. Room keys are essentially ornamental, interchangeable with one another. Musqasset is an honor-system island, through and through. Anyone could've gotten in here.

I bend down and pull the fish out of my pack by its tail. A nail has been pushed through its head, eye to eye, just like the earlier thorn. A note is wrapped around the fish, written in Sharpie on brown paper. My heart does a drum solo as I read it: "Your next asshole."

Assuming the piscine gift is not meant to be a replacement anus for me, I'm guessing what the author *intended* to write was, "*You're* next—comma—Asshole."

The clumsy wordsmanship irks me. Trooper Dan is a verbally sophisticated fellow. This doesn't feel right coming from him. Also, what's the practical value in sending me threats like this? They just serve to make me angrier, more vigilant, more likely to seek help. Clearly the sender's intent is to make me squirm, not to play his cards skillfully.

Which, again, points to a vengeance motive. Something personal.

Trooper Dan and company, on the other hand, were cool and clinical in their approach. But maybe *that* was all an act. And what's the alternative theory? That *two separate* groups of psychopaths have followed me from Wentworth, Mass, to Musqasset Island, Maine, in the middle of a nor'easter? And the dead fish is from Group B?

Right.

I'm feeling confused and off-balance. Which is probably my stalkers' intention. I wander down the hall and knock on my new friend Leah's door.

She laughs when she sees what I'm carrying by the tail. "So, we've established it's *codfish* pie you're making." She notes my non-comedic aura. "Hey, what's up?"

"Don't mean to be nosy, but have you guys been in these rooms long?"

"Hour and a half, two hours. Why?"

"Did you hear anyone go into my room before you talked to me?"

"Just one person, like, ten minutes ago, but that was probably you."

It was. Crap. I go downstairs, still carrying the cod by the tail, and ask JJ if he's seen anyone unfamiliar in the building.

"No. Why? Something fishy going on?" Everyone's got a Netflix special.

I deposit the fish in the compost bin behind Harbor House, then come around to the front porch and plant myself on a rocking chair. Sitting out there in open view, I feel as if there's a sniper's laser dot on my forehead.

Again, the message my stalkers seem to be sending me is, *We can take you whenever we want, Sunny Jim, but we will do so at the time and place of our choosing.* In other words: *Finnian Carroll, you are powerless in this thing.*

I refuse to accept that. Though the dead cod has me duly alarmed, I am still feeling more energized than I have in years, and nowhere near ready to roll over. Screw these guys.

I return to my room with fresh resolve. As I grab my phone to start calling those liquor stores, I notice my battery level is oddly low. Then I realize why: that stupid VoxFox app is still running from when I was at Miles's. I forgot to shut it off.

Hello. That means I left the recorder running when I went to buy the wine for Jim. Intrigued, I stop the recording and press play. My earlier conversation with Miles plays back through the tiny speaker. I move the slider bar ahead until I locate the spot where Beth entered the scene and I excused myself to go buy the wine.

No sooner do I hear the recorded sound of the kitchen door jingling from my exit than the recorded voice of Beth says to Miles, *"So what have you two been up to here?"*

CHAPTER 18

There's an audio version of a voyeur; it's called an ecouterist. I feel every inch the ecouterist as I eavesdrop electronically on Miles and Beth's private conversation. But that's not quite enough to make me tap Stop.

What must have happened when I left to buy the wine was that Beth joined Miles in the study and sat right at the desk where I left my phone. Neither of them was aware that VoxFox was capturing their words in crisp digital clarity.

"I thought we had agreed it would be best to keep him away from the house," says the digitized voice of Beth, *"now that we know what state he's in."*

"We invited him out to the island, Beth," says Miles's voice. *"To our home. It was your idea. We can't just abandon him. We have some responsibility here."*

Beth's idea? Didn't see that one coming.

"I only suggested it," Beth replies, *"because I thought it was an olive branch you could offer. You didn't tell me he had just broken out of a psych hospital. I had to learn that from Jim."*

"He didn't 'break out.' He discharged himself, which is perfectly allowable. If the staff had thought he was a danger, they would have kept him under lock and key."

"But you do agree he's out of his freaking mind? Right? Jim certainly thinks so. Wandering around the island with a knife in the middle of the night."

"I agree he's having some mental challenges."

"So why are you encouraging him?"

"I'm not. I was just trying to help him figure out if there might be some... external triggers for his fears. Some real-world stuff that's been playing into his delusions."

"He's crazy. You can't fix crazy."

"But that doesn't mean there's no basis whatsoever for his—"

"Crazy, Miles."

"As a screen door on a submarine. No argument from me."

"And you think it's fine for him to be around the kids?"

"No. I don't. That's why I waited till you and the kids were gone. I thought you'd be at the club all afternoon. Finn understands the situation here. Notice how he made himself scarce the minute you guys showed up. He needs a friend right now, Beth."

"He needs a syringe. Loaded with Haldol."

This from a woman who just yesterday was explaining to me, with a perfectly straight face, how the words we say and think "with focused intention" can alter the nature of physical reality itself, thanks to *The Power of Words*. And yet *I'm* the crazy one. Okay.

"So, what exactly have you been doing for him 'as a friend'?" recorded Beth inquires.

"Just talking, you know, processing, helping him sort out a few things."

The voices pause, and I hear papers being shuffled about. The printout of Angie's write-up, no doubt. And our research notes. Eek.

"Jesus, Miles, what is this stuff? What the hell have you guys been doing?" I'm surprised by the heat of her concern. *"What the hell is this stuff?!"*

"Just, like I said, some online research I was helping him with. He can't get any Internet over at Harbor House, so I—"

"But what's all this garbage about some old car accident?"

"I don't know. He thinks he might have played some role in it. He thinks some people might be after him because of that."

"And you're helping him with this idea? Seriously, Miles? Is that wise? The man is having paranoid delusions. And you're feeding into them? Helping him cook up some ancient... what? Conspiracy theory? Revenge plot?"

"For the record, I don't believe he's actually being followed. I think it's his own guilt that's chasing him. Over something he thinks he did. And now some... circumstance has reawakened it. And he's feeling extremely vulnerable. Anyway, I thought if we could put to rest whatever was triggering his fears—"

"Oh really, Dr. Jung? And you've had this strategy approved by the American Psychiatric Association?"

"I'm not trying to play shrink, Beth. He's my friend."

"Well, sometimes I wish you would choose better friends."

"Meaning what?"

Three-second pause.

"I talked to Mom today," says Beth.

"And..."

"They're coming to the island."

"Your parents? When?"

"Sunday or Monday. As soon as weather permits."

"Ah, shit. Why?"

"Why do you think? They want to see the kids. And us. For the holiday. Daddy has some work stuff he wants to go over with you too. As usual."

Miles groans. *"I come out to the island to get away from all that."*

"Well, I couldn't just say no. So, they're coming. Deal with it. I think it's important right now—don't you?— that we make a good impression on them. The right *impression."*

Both Beth and Miles, going back to their college days, have always worked hard at cultivating a good image for their parents. I remember when Miles's parents would be coming to campus, he'd start preparing days in advance, as if for a military inspection. He and Beth are the same way as a couple. They worry a lot about what their parents think, especially Beth's.

My parents, conversely, were happy with me if I didn't torture dogs.

"Which means you can't be doing any of this *stuff,"* continues Beth. She rustles the papers. *"No Finn and his*

freakish delusions. No Finn sitting around here talking banana salad. No... Finn."

"Your folks have met Finn before. At our graduation, at Dylan's—"

"Exactly. That's why he can't be around! They don't get the Finn-friendship thing, Miles. They never have. Especially Daddy. Why don't we invite the Shapiros over on Labor Day? They're on the island now. They'll create the right... ambience."

"Whatever, Beth. Whatever you decide. But... despite what you've always insisted on believing, Finn is not the devil. Daft as a batfish, maybe, but not the devil."

"Ditch him."

With that, she leaves the room. I fast-forward through the rest of the recording. There's nothing more.

Jeez. Daft as a batfish. Ditch him.

At least I know where I stand with the Sutcliffes. I also know why Miles was so agitated when I came back from wine-shopping. Beth's dad is coming. Simon Fischer. Miles doesn't like to talk to me about the guy because I always taunt him for being Fischer's lapdog.

A blanket of sadness settles over me. I had thought perhaps Miles had changed his mind about me and believed I was on to something real. Turns out he's only been humoring me—he still thinks I've fallen off the zipline.

I try to dig into my liquor store inquiry, but my heart and mind are no longer in it. Besides, it's the Friday afternoon before Labor Day. People are just getting off work for the long weekend, and the liquor stores are hopping.

Employees have no time for nosy phone conversations about ancient history.

I stand on Fishermen's Court in the whipping wind and rain, steeling myself to knock on Jeannie's door. I'm holding a bottle of wine and a pizza box wrapped in a plastic bag and feeling dreadfully self-conscious. I don't want her to think I see this as a date.

Though I kinda do.

I'm also a tad embarrassed by the wine. She texted me to go ahead and bring some, insisting there was no need to abstain around her. I cheerfully obliged, and now I'm feeling selfish about that choice.

I suck it up and give the cat gargoyle knocker a rap.

Jeannie answers the door, wearing a burgundy-red top that offers a glimpse of cleavage. I must be mindful to do no more than glimpse. Which will be a monumental challenge. Did I mention Jeannie is the most beautiful woman on Earth? At least to my eyes. Her beauty comes perilously close to proving the existence of God.

Like garlic.

Allow me to explain. Just as it's impossible for me to conceive of the existence of the garlic plant without the concurrent existence of human taste buds, so perfectly designed to exalt its flavor, it is impossible for me to conceive of the existence of Jeannie's face without my eyes, so perfectly designed to exalt her beauty. Chaos theory withers with one glance at her lips.

So, yeah, what could possibly go wrong tonight?

Jeannie takes a sweeping look up and down the street and backs away from the door.

"That pizza better not be soggy," she says, her eyes sparkling like a distant galaxy.

Oy.

✶✶✶

We already covered the life basics at Pete's, so we're forced to dig a little deeper for our evening's warm-up banter. We talk about our mutual friends on the island—who's still here, who moved, who's boinking whom. The conversational flow isn't exactly effortless, as it once was, but it carries us through dinner. I, of course, want to know more about her daughter, and, of course, that's an easy subject for her. She asks me about my work as a computer artist, a good way to get me bloviating. She also asks me about my sister Angie. The two of them became friends through me but haven't talked much since Jeannie and I split up.

Jeannie has made a nice salad to go with the pizza and baked something deliciously gooey-looking for dessert. I'm impressed. She could not boil eggs when I lived with her; maybe it's a parenthood thing. There's something off about her mood, though. She seems tense, distracted. A couple of times I think I catch her glancing out the window watchfully. I *am* daft as a batfish, though, as you will recall.

After dinner, she says, "Why don't you get a fire going while I clean up in here a bit?"

Tasks completed, we settle in with our drinks, I with my wine on the loveseat, she with her tea on the sofa. We face each other in front of the fire. No place left to hide.

"I was a coward to leave the way I did," I say, when the timing feels ripe. "I was hurt, but that's no excuse. We had a lot to talk about. I owed you that."

"You didn't owe me much, Finn. I was a horrible mate and a horrible friend. I'm ashamed of how I acted. But yeah, I do wish we could have talked about it."

"Why him?" I ask, not accusingly but out of genuine curiosity. She knows exactly what I'm getting at. Jeannie, as I mentioned, carried on a handful of discreet dalliances with some rather exotic seafaring men during our time together. She kept these encounters infrequent and segregated from our home life, and she always stayed away from island men. Until Cliff.

Cliff was a native Musqasset fisherman whom I discovered she'd been seeing frequently—and *not* very discreetly—for months. Screwing in our house, to put it bluntly. Cliff was rugged, muscular, macho. Good-looking, yes, but about as bright and contemplative as a bucket of eye-bolts. So why pick *him* to steer our relationship into the rocks?

"He was the next logical step, I guess."

I know what *she* means too, without her needing to explain: I allowed her other indiscretions to go on unchecked until they had poisoned our union, so it was time to up the stakes. Force us to confront the issue, win or lose.

"I get that. A strange choice of partners, though."

"Not really, when you think about what was going on at the time. All that Fish Pier business. The infighting, the anger, the suspicion. And quite a bit of it was aimed at me."

"At you? I don't remember it that way."

"People questioned my loyalty. I brought you to the island, after all, and you brought Miles—the great destroyer of Fish Pier. That's how some people saw it."

"How could anyone lay the Fish Pier thing on *you*?"

"Come on, Finn, you know the rules here. If you weren't born on this island, you'll always be an outsider in some people's minds. I came here fourteen years ago. That's *yesterday* in island time. On the surface, people had adopted me, but they weren't totally sure where I stood—with the fishermen or with the moneymen."

"And so, when you slept with Cliff, you were..."

"Declaring my loyalties, I guess."

"Choosing the island. Over me. Over us."

"If it makes you feel any better, it didn't last. Cliff was a drunken loser. A week after you left, I was already wondering what I ever saw in him."

"But your thing with him got the job done."

Jeannie shrugs and tosses her hands up.

"Is Cliff...?"

"Bree's father? God no."

"You mentioned there was someone else after him."

"Let's not talk about that right now, okay?"

"Sure. Sorry."

Jeannie gives me a long, appraising look. "Why didn't you ever say anything, Finn?"

Again, I know what she means without her explaining. Why didn't I confront her about her sexual "detours"?

"I didn't think it was my right. You made it clear, from the start, that you had some 'arrangements' in your life that were your private business, and I wasn't to think I owned you in that way. I thought that was a condition of our relationship."

"In the beginning, maybe. When we were still in 'trial run' mode. I had a few good things going for myself, and, yeah, I didn't want to give them up for... 'light and transient causes.' But for the most part I was just… testing you. Didn't you know that?"

"Testing me? No, I didn't know. I always assumed if I forced the issue into the open and made you choose, you would have chosen your... 'independence' over me."

"Oh, Finn, you friggin' idiot." She gets up and tops off her teacup, flicking wary eyes out the window again, then returns to her seat. "*I* always assumed that because *you* didn't say anything, you were basically okay with the situation. I figured you wanted a relationship that was more 'roommates with benefits' than committed couple. I thought it gave you an easy out."

"That's what you thought? God no. I didn't want that."

"Then why didn't you fight for what you did want? Why didn't you fight for *me*?"

The trillion-dollar question.

CHAPTER 19

"**D**o you remember the first time we talked?" Jeannie says.

"Back in college?"

"We were at that party."

"At some dot-com clown's house in Ipswich."

"Right," she says. "And I was flirting with you. Everything was going great, and do you remember what happened next?"

"I'm sure you're going to exhume those blissfully buried memories."

"*Miles* came along and started making moves on me, and then I turned around and you were gone. You'd left. Without saying a word."

"I had already learned, when it came to women, never to compete with Miles. Miles always got the girl. Always."

"But I wasn't 'the girl,' I was me. And I wasn't interested in Miles, I was interested in you, thicko. *I* had to pursue *you* for the next three weeks, which was not something I was used to, believe me. Then, when we graduated, you just let me go. To Quebec. I would have changed my plans if you'd asked, but you didn't."

Her words, if true, are breaking news to me. "I never for a moment thought I had a serious chance with you, Jeannie. I mean, you were this wild, brilliant, tough, gorgeous rebel-goddess who every guy at Godwin wanted to sleep with, and I figured I was just a case of..."

"What? Romantic slumming?"

"Well, yeah." To me, this is a fact as obvious as barn-red acrylic paint.

"I ought to slap you in the face for that."

"Jeannie. Reality is reality. You've always been out of my league. You are literally *the* most beautiful woman I have ever laid eyes on. You know that, right? Not to mention the smartest, the funniest, the bravest, the most talented..."

Jeannie's eyes well with tears. "Oh, Finn," she says. "That's your whole problem right there. You don't believe you deserve good things, so you don't *claim* what's yours. ...And I don't think you ever will."

She gets up and starts moving dishes that don't need moving.

Taking the cue, I stand up and prepare to say my goodnights and goodbyes. But she surprises me by grabbing the bottle of wine and marching back into the living room. She pours me another glass, looks me in the eye, places her hand on my chest, and pushes me down onto the loveseat. It is a gesture she would employ, in our courting days, when she was fixing to have her sexual way with me, and it thrilled me to no end. But this time her intent is not amorous.

Instead, she flops down beside me on the loveseat and takes my hand. Again, this is not a romantic gesture but rather one that says *I require nothing less of you than consummate honesty.*

"You're going to tell me why you're here on Musqasset," she says.

✷✷✷

I spill the beans. I tell her everything that went down in my house the night the bad men showed up. I tell her about my stay in the hospital and the "suicide" note. I also explain my previous *real* suicide attempt (half-hearted though it was), my precarious mental state prior to the recent incident, and the fly-below-the-radar life-style I have adopted for the last four years.

Worst of all, I tell her about that doomful night after our college graduation party.

She takes it all in, betraying no judgment, seemingly accepting every detail.

Except one.

When I'm done telling the whole story, she cinches her brow and bites her lip. "So, *Miles* threw the bottle?"

"Yeah."

She faces forward on the loveseat, arms folded in contemplation.

"Why do you ask?" I inquire. She doesn't respond. "Jeannie? Why do you ask?"

"Can we stop there for tonight, Finn? That's a lot for one evening. I need to sleep. On all of this. Is that okay?"

"'Course."

Her reaction to that one detail of my story puzzles me, but I'm keen to make my getaway. Now that I've stripped myself naked before her, I don't want to see the diminished regard in her eyes.

It's nearly eleven anyway. The electricity will be shutting off on the island any minute. The unwritten code of lovers on Musqasset is that if you don't leave by lights-out, you're staying the night. The minutes before eleven can be an awkward time.

I stand and say goodbye in a way that feels final. Jean takes my face in her hands, then collapses against me in a tired hug. I bury my face in her hair—though I don't feel entitled to—then silently pluck my rain jacket from a chair and schlep to the door.

The instant I step outside, the island plunges into blackness. I hear Jeannie follow me out.

"Are you going to be safe?" she whispers.

"Probably not." Why start lying at this point in the proceedings?

"Then stay here. Sleep on the couch."

I grunt my refusal. The last place on Musqasset I would sleep tonight is Jeannie's house. Not because I don't want to but because I've put her in far too much danger already.

"You be careful, then," she says. "You be exceptionally careful, Finn Carroll."

I forgot to bring a flashlight along, a major blunder on Musqasset. I meant to buy one today. For some reason I don't ask Jeannie for one, and for some reason she doesn't offer. I start off down the road in the enveloping darkness. Jeannie patters a few steps after me.

"I'd have done anything you wanted," she says, aiming her voice at the night sky. I'm honestly not sure whether she's addressing God or me. "I was just waiting for you to ask."

I want to say, "Is it too late now?" but the words stick in my throat. Her door whispers shut. Musqasset darkness swallows both of us.

✶✶✶

The walk to Harbor House, along Bristol Road, takes six or seven minutes in broad daylight, but the going is slower in the black island night. Luckily, the rain has let up.

I've gone no farther than two kicks of a can when I hear shoe heels crunching in the muddy road-gravel behind me. Three or four pairs of feet. Moving as a unit. About ten or twelve yards back. This time there's no attempt at stealth. My followers *want* me to hear them.

They've been waiting for me outside Jeannie's. I should have expected this.

I stop. The footsteps stop.

I walk forward again. The footsteps walk forward.

I stop. The footsteps stop.

So that's the game we're playing? It's such a primitive scare tactic, it would almost be laughable... if it weren't so damned effective. Few fears are more deeply embedded in human DNA than that of being followed in the dark by an unseen enemy.

"Piss off, gentlemen," I say, trying to sound nonchalant.

No response.

I can't imagine they would really try to assault me, or worse, right here on this open road, in one of the most populated parts of the island. Even in the pitch dark. If I screamed for help, a dozen people would come running with flashlights. But still.

I walk again. The footsteps follow again.

I stop. *They* stop.

I take a stutter step just to catch them off guard. Then I peel off at a full sprint. Their flashlights turn on and light my back as the men take up pursuit. When I turn my head to look behind me, their lights go off again.

I grind to a stop in the gravelly dirt. My pursuers stop. They wait patiently in the dark, thirty feet behind me.

I stand there silently for a full minute. Two minutes. Can they hear my heart thumping?

I crouch in the roadway, wait some more.

I've got all night, lads.

If I just camp here indefinitely, how long will they stay back? At some point, will they get bored and make a move on me? What if I remain here till sunrise?

Despite my terror, I'm feeling an urge to engage them, to draw them into action and get this over with—whatever *this* is going to be. But my unarmed state makes that a foolish option. Why have I stepped out without a weapon?

I put on my gamer hat again. If I were a game character, how would I create some advantage in this situation? I almost laugh as I remember an actual puzzle from a game I helped design. I pat the dirt road around me and lay my hand on a nice, egg-sized stone the rain has laid bare. I stand, take my shoes off, and remove my socks. I insert one sock into the other to make a double layer, then drop the rock inside, creating a homemade blackjack. I slide my gritty feet back into my shoes and swing my new weapon around. It whishes, slicing the air.

Dang—this thing could do some serious damage. It's got a nice reach too.

Suddenly I don't feel quite so vulnerable. I'm guessing my pursuers have weapons of their own, but even so, if they try to come near me, they're going to have regrets.

"Got your lopper with you tonight?" I call out to them. "Why don't you bring it over here? I've got something for you too."

No response. No movement.

"Or do you only attack people who are drugged and strapped into chairs?"

Again, nothing.

I turn to start walking, and my foot slips on some more wet rocks. I've stumbled upon a cache of excellent throwing stones, loosened by the rain's erosion. I gather six or eight of them and stuff them into my pockets. If these guys continue to follow me, I'm going to start pelting them with rocks. I can sense their general location well enough that, even in the dark, I'm confident I can score some hits.

I start walking. *They* start walking.

I stop and turn around. They stop too. I'm about to hurl a rock in their direction when I freeze my arm. They haven't technically threatened or assaulted me yet. If I injure one of them, *I* might be guilty of criminal assault. I probably owe them a warning.

"Listen up. If you follow me one more step, I will consider that a threat. And I will defend myself. With rocks. I have a good throwing arm and you *will* get hurt. If you try to come near me, I've got a weapon I will use. With force. Consider yourself warned."

I turn back toward the road ahead and start walking again. I am gratified to note the men don't immediately follow. I've at least put a hiccup in their confidence.

They start walking again, but farther back now. Good. Still, I warned them not to follow at all. I stop, turn toward them, draw my arm back like a fastball pitcher's, and throw a rock as hard as I can. It sails in silence, then goes skittering and clacking down the dirt road. I'd better be careful not to bust someone's window.

No reaction from my pals.

I load another rock into my right hand, an angular one, and go into my windup. This time the rock whistles through the air and *thwhacks* one of their rain-jacketed bodies.

"Ahh! Shit!" cries a voice. Direct hit.

All at once, three flashlights turn on and the men start chasing me at a gallop. I run. Their lamps light the road for them, enabling them to run full throttle. But they also light the road for me, letting me keep pace ahead of them.

The men chase me till we're about twenty-five yards from the village, and then, as if on cue, they shut off their lights and melt into the night. Like they never existed.

The upstairs rear hallway of Harbor House is dimly lit by a rechargeable night-light. As I pass the room where

Mr. and Mrs. Bean—I probably should learn their real names—are staying, a faint glow illuminates the crack under their door. A laptop or a Kindle in use. For some reason, I take comfort in the presence of my new neighbors. I don't want to be alone tonight.

I raise my homemade blackjack as I unlock my door with my low-security skeleton key. The room is black. Reflexively, I flip the wall switch, knowing full well the electricity is off till morning. I have never felt more fear of a dark room. I know I left my stalkers outdoors, but still, I feel certain someone is hiding under the bed or behind the door.

My phone is on the dresser, where I left it charging. That is, it *should* be there.

I cross the room in one bound, grope for the phone, and find it. I quickly locate the flashlight app. It lights the small room like a crypt in a ghost-hunting show.

No one behind the door. No one under the bed. No one under the worktable.

No dead fish anywhere, at least that I can see—or smell.

I jam a wooden chair under the doorknob and allow myself to relax a bit. I take off my jacket and shoes and flop on the bed with my phone. I find a text message from Jeannie: *Be safe.* A well-intentioned, if utterly non-actionable, sentiment. There's an earlier text from Miles too: *Talked to Jim. We were right. Call me!* Right about what? Intriguing, but too late to call.

There's also a voicemail from Angie. It arrived just minutes ago. This one fills me with unaccountable dread. I tap the "play" arrow.

"Finn? It's me," says recorded Angie. She's drunk. Kind of like saying Yao Ming is tall.

"We need to talk. I don't understand what's going on. Why is everybody calling me? Why is everybody so interested in ancient history? What's going on? Call me." She mumbles something unintelligible, then says, "You're a good person, Finn. Don't let anyone tell you different. You're a good person. Call me."

Ange, over and out.

Hmm, strange. Who does she mean by "everybody"? Has she talked to someone besides me? About the accident? About something else from the past? I wonder who and what.

I punch Angie's number. Might as well get this over with; I know she's still up. Sodden as a mezcal worm but up. The call rings through and she picks up, but then the line goes dead. A moment later, a return call comes through from her. I slide the answer bar, but again the line goes dead. I try calling her again. Same thing.

The Musqasset phone gods are not going to cooperate tonight. Oh well, I tried. I'm about to fall asleep right there with my clothes on when the phone *bloops* the arrival of a text-message.

I look at the screen.

A single character. An emoji. Of a dead fish.

Before I can identify who the sender is, the message disappears from the screen. Poof.

My brain can't handle any more. I shut down.

CHAPTER 20

Dreams are so mysterious. Dagnabbit, if only I could unravel the arcane symbolism behind this one: *I'm on the ferry to Musqasset. I've just sold my parents' house, and the new owners are scheduled to move in later that day. I suddenly remember that I've left three dead bodies in the basement. I buried them years ago and forgot all about them. I need to get back to the house* now *and move the corpses before the new owners show up.*

I lurch from the mattress, gasping for air, my heart jackhammering.

Oddly, it isn't the dream itself that has awoken me at two forty-five, but rather a blast of mental urgency. Yes, I've woken myself up from an anxiety dream with an *even more* anxious waking concern. My brain is telling me there's something vital I need to remember from earlier in the evening.

I strip off my jeans and shirt—damp with sweat—as I try to think. What could it be?

It has something to do with an encounter that occurred in the village.

The encounter itself was seemingly insignificant. I stopped at the Mercantile on my way to Jeannie's, to buy the wine. As I approached the store, I noticed a trio of young men sitting on the covered porch of the closed gift shop next door, trying to stay dry.

"Excuse me, sir?" spoke the tallest of the three from under a hooded rain visor. "My friend T-Bone here is twenty-one," he said, pointing to one of his buddies, who flashed an insincere grin, all teeth. "Honest to God, but he left his I.D. on the ferry. Right, T? We wondered if you could possibly grab him a twelve-pack of Coors Light." He held out a twenty and said, "Keep the change?"

Tempted as I was to risk prosecution for a cool $4.71, I declined their business offer and wished them well. And that was that. Finis.

So why is this scene playing insistently in my head, driving me from sleep?

Finally, "Light dawns on Marblehead," as my mother used to say. Twenty-one!

The reason I can't remember buying that bottle of scotch for Miles all those years ago is that *I* didn't buy it. *I wasn't 21 yet.* In college, I was a year younger than my classmates, thanks to an accelerated academic program I was pressed into in high school. I didn't like to advertise my age difference, but when I graduated from Godwin, I was still only 20. Anytime I'd gone into a liquor store during my student years, I'd been with Miles or some other older friend.

I couldn't legally buy booze yet, and I couldn't ask Miles to buy that particular bottle for me, because it was a gift for him. So, I asked someone else to buy it for me.

With a shudder, I remember who that someone was.

✦✦✦

A knock on the door yanks me from the sleep of the dead. My phone shows five past eight. I must have crashed heavily when I finally fell asleep again.

"Who is it?" I ask, groping for my makeshift blackjack.

"Me." Miles.

I throw on last night's clothes, remove the security chair from beneath the doorknob, and open the door. Miles enters, holding two large coffees from Mary's Lunch. He sets them on our worktable and sits down as if ready to dig into another day at the office.

"I can't stay long," he explains. "Beth's on the war-path. Her folks are coming for an unplanned visit, as soon as they can get over, and she's freaking out." Right, *she's* freaking out. "I promised I'd help with the shop-ping and cooking and housecleaning."

"You and Beth do your own housecleaning?" Gasping, I pull back in silent-film horror.

"Our help's not on the island this weekend," he replies, straight as a board. The human tragedy of it all. "So, listen…" He slaps the table. "I talked to Jim."

"And?"

"He talked to the Mass police. He confirmed that the cops did find bottle fragments at the scene. Mostly in Goslin's car—the bottle punched through the wind-shield as it broke. There were fingerprints on a couple of the shards too"—a muscle in my neck tightens—"but no matches popped up in the database. But listen: the investigators *did* figure out the make of the scotch by piecing the label together."

"Holy crap." It's exactly what we deduced, but still I'm shocked to hear we were right.

"According to Jim, they tracked down three local sales of those 'special anniversary' decanter bottles of Glenmalloch. All three bottles, evidently, were bought with credit or debit cards. They were able to ID the buyers."

A current of chill hits my blood.

"Here's what's weird, though," he says. "You weren't one of them."

"Are you sure?" *I'm* sure, but I don't tip my hand.

"Yes, because they talked to all three buyers. Two of them still had the bottle on their shelves. The third guy said he had finished the booze and put the bottle out in the recycling bin the previous week. The police had no reason not to believe him. Plus, he had an alibi for the night of the accident, and his prints didn't match."

"Who was this person, this third buyer?"

"Jim didn't say. Anyway, the bottle angle dried up after that. But obviously the cops didn't know what we know."

"Which is...?"

"That at least one other bottle was sold. Somewhere nearby. The one *you* bought. I wonder why that one didn't get reported by any store owners."

I know one very good reason: because *I didn't buy it.* But I am not ready to tell Miles that detail just yet, or to remind him I wasn't 21 in the spring of '99. My mind is laser-focused on the almost certain identity of that third buyer and why he told the police the story he did.

"You still don't remember buying that bottle?" Miles asks.

"No," I say, which is the truth but not the whole truth. "Did Jim find out anything else?"

"He got some dirt on this Goslin character too. The guy's more than a sleazebag; he's an ex-con. Did time at Walpole. Runs with some seriously shady people. And apparently, he had alcohol in his system the night of the accident, but just below the legal limit. He'd also had a run-in with his wife—live-in girlfriend, whatever— twenty minutes before the accident. So, he may have been 'emotionally impaired' if not quite drunk enough to blow a point-oh-eight.

"They think he was speeding too," Miles continues. "And listen to this: the bottle didn't hit *him*; it hit the passenger side of the windshield and blew a hole. If he'd been sober and alert, he should have been able to pull the car safely into the breakdown lane. But instead, he freaked and started swerving. And that's when he smashed into the Abelsens."

I see what Miles is doing: trying to paint Goslin as partially, if not mostly, responsible for the accident himself. It's a touching gesture, meant to lessen my guilt. Little does he know, I'm not the one who needs the moral strokes.

"Oh, and something else," Miles says with an ominous note. "It seems Goslin's... *junk* was crushed in the accident. When the steering column got pushed in. That wasn't in the papers. I don't know how much repair work the surgeons were able to do, but..."

A wave of queasiness moves from my stomach to my groin.

Miles looks at his watch. "Oh, I've got to get going." He stands, grabs his coffee, and says, "Text me, call me, keep me in the loop. I'll be in touch later." And with that, Miles blows out like an island squall.

All-righty, then. Thanks, Miles. I'm surprised, considering what I heard in his recorded chat with Beth, that he is continuing to help me at all. He thinks I'm delusional, so why is he still invested in this thing, or even pretending to be? Maybe Jim's new info has swayed him?

Whatever his motivation, I wish he could have stuck around this morning. Two heads are better than one. When I work with Miles, all this stuff feels real to me. Like we're getting somewhere. When I work alone, I feel like a crazy person.

And I've just been given a fresh load of crazy-making material to digest here.

I open my coffee lid and fire up the laptop Miles has lent me. As I wait for it to boot, I think about Edgar Goslin. Considering what he lost in the accident, and the kind of guy he seems to be, it's easy to believe he would have a major ax to grind, even after all these years.

One thing's for sure, Goslin is the best "lead" we've turned up. I need to find out more about him, but I don't know if Web-surfing can help any further, even if the Wi-Fi cooperates.

Talk to him directly. Yes. *Call Goslin under some phony pretext. Try to push his buttons, see what he spills.*

To do that, though, I'd need his contact information.

Okay, so that's a place to start. Maybe I'll try one of those "people finder" services and see what I can turn up. If I can get on the Internet. Major if.

I give Safari a whirl on the laptop. Still no Wi-Fi. I try my phone's 3G network. Nothing but a spinning circle.

I lean my chair back, sipping my coffee and staring at the ceiling.

Sitting in my room at Harbor House—alone—is making me feel like a lobster in a trap, just waiting to get pulled up onto someone's boat. The feeling is more than poetic. I'm getting a strong sense of actually being watched.

I stand and pace around the room, trying to shake it off. No luck. Some people think it's hokum, this idea that you can *feel* when you're being spied on, but ask anyone in the surveillance trades: the sensation of eyes on you is palpable.

I walk over to the window. I feel framed and exposed, but there's not a soul to be seen in the storm-whipped village below, except a poncho-clad Dorna Caskie collecting bags of recycling from the shops in her electric cart. So why this under-a-lens feeling?

I return to my chair and lean back. That's when I notice it: a brand-new white plastic smoke detector on the ceiling.

CHAPTER 21

Was the smoke detector there when I checked in? I didn't notice it, but that doesn't mean much. Across the ceiling is another detector made of yellowed plastic. Why would there be two detectors in one room? One for heat and one for smoke? Nah.

Smoke detector: easiest place in the world to hide a webcam.

I glance again at the new detector and then casually look away. If there's a camera inside it, I don't want to betray my suspiciousness.

No question about it, I can feel eyes burning my skin, and I am sure there's a live camera on me. I need to get the hell out of here. Not just for an hour or two. For good. Relocate. But I don't want whoever's watching me to know that's my plan.

I stretch and yawn, then stand up and look offhandedly at my phone's clock. I react to the time in fake surprise. Pretending I'm late for something, I stuff Miles's laptop into my backpack. Luckily, most of my clothes and other belongings are still packed in there, but I deliberately leave a pair of socks on the floor and a tee-shirt draped over a chair, as if I intend to return. Then I throw on my raincoat, feeling for my homemade blackjack. Taking pains not to look up at the smoke detector, I exit the room.

Pellets of rain blast the upstairs hall window. That hurricane-like system is still parked out in the Atlantic, and the forecast is for more intermittent wind and rain and continued high seas. A craptastic Saturday-before-Labor-Day, in other words.

I'm tempted to go down to the front desk and ask JJ if he recently installed smoke detectors, but I decide to just get the hell out of Dodge. I exit by the fire escape on the third floor, then slip down the alley behind the island's mini-laundromat. The wind whistles through clapboards up and down Island Ave, creating steam-train sound effects.

I'd already planned on dropping in on a few old friends. That mission has now taken on urgency. I need a place to stay. Not someone's house—I can't ask anyone to take that risk—but maybe a tool shed or a guest cabin that's not being used this washed-out weekend.

Dennis and Billy's place is close by, so I head there first. I still haven't returned Billy's rain suit, but now I need to ask him for a bigger favor—the use of his storage locker as a hideout. I make my way to his door, on the bay side of the building. I need to time my way past the waves, which are now crashing into the base of the sandwich counter. No crab rolls today.

Dennis answers the door. He's holding a mop and looking frazzled. Seawater must be getting into the building. "Billy's in the shower right now," he declaims, unsmiling. The cold shoulder he showed me earlier has metastasized into third-degree frostbite.

No light is on in the bathroom, so I say, "Looks like he may be finished."

"He hasn't started yet."

"Well, can you tell him I came by, and I'll probably drop by again later?"

"He'll probably be in the shower later too."

Dennis doesn't quite *slam* the door, but he shuts it with feeling. Hi-ho, my friendship mission is off to a rollicking start. So, whom else can I hit up for shelter on this fine late-summer morn? Most of my other island friends live either in the Greyhook neighborhood or out on Studio Row—at least they did last I saw them.

I haven't been to Greyhook on this trip, so maybe I'll head over there first. As I start off in that direction, the wind is whipping so hard it feels like it'll lift me off my feet. Salt from storm-blown spindrift is mixing with the rain, stinging my eyes.

Greyhook occupies the eastern side of the bay all the way out to Seal Point. As I may have mentioned, Greyhook is where the working folk live—fishermen, dockhands, bartenders, shop clerks, and a number of "village artists."

There are three types of professional painter on the island, FYI. First you have the "rock stars" who own the large ocean-facing properties at the far end of Studio Row and whose work is represented by top galleries in New York, London, and Paris. Then you have the almost-famous Studio Rowers, who own the studio-galleries on—wait for it—Studio Row. Finally, you have the "village" artists. Like I was. These are painters who sell their work for three figures, occasionally four, in the village shops and coastal tourist galleries. Village artists are tradespeople, nothing more, nothing less. Like lobstermen and boat builders.

Many of my island friends are—or were—village artists. We had a loose club of sorts. We'd hang out together, doing *plein air* sessions around the island, then hoist a few at The Rusty Anchor or Pete's Lagoon at the end of the day. We kept each other sane and motivated.

The most diehard member of the gang was a guy named Enzo. I'll head for his place first.

I keep my head down, to cut through the wind and keep the saltwater out of my eyes.

Enzo is a crusty old socialist and conspiracy theorist who lives in a rundown Greyhook cottage near the point. He's a throwback to the days when liberals were the ones worried about secret government conspiracies. His paintings are sad, muddy-hued things layered with political symbolism. They don't sell, but Enzo doesn't care. Enzo was one of the earliest adopters of personal computers back in the Eighties. When he's not painting, you can usually find him at his high-end PC, blogging about men in black and warning people they're being spied on.

Not today, though. When I knock on his peeling, lockless door, only his dog Herbert Marcuse comes to check me out.

I poke my head inside, just in case Enzo's on the can, and shout, "Come on, Enzo, I'm dying out here."

His place boggles the mind. His state-of-the-art computer system and peripherals take up a whole wall, but the rest of the house looks like it's inhabited by a caveman. Dust bunnies the size of jackrabbits lurk in the corners. If anyone has Internet access during a storm, though, it's Enzo. But I can't use his equipment if he's not home. Can't ask him about a place to stay either.

Maybe later.

The tiny house next door is the extreme opposite of Enzo's. Meticulously painted in three tones and rimmed with lush window boxes, it is home to another village artist, Miranda. She's only fortyish, but she dresses like an old hippie and listens to Incredible String Band music from the Sixties. She's a good soul, though.

"Finny!" she shrieks, opening her arms for a hug. She invites me in for tea, which I gratefully accept. Miranda tells me that in the years since I left, the island has taken on bad juju. There is infighting, ill will, negative energy. Something about the *way* she's saying it, though, with her hand clamped on my wrist, feels more like a warning than an idle observation.

"All I can do is paint about it and hope my paintings heal," she says. Ah, Miranda, God bless her. I decide not to gum up her chakras with my housing woes.

Maybe the Bourbon triplets can help me: Matt, Zack, and Mike. They own a party fishing boat and one of the island's few apartment buildings, a four-unit affair. They're all painters too. They learned to paint because art is a sellable commodity on Musqasset. If they'd been born in Brooklyn, they'd have learned to make pickles.

But oddly—or maybe not—they're among the island's best painters. All three of them.

When Matt answers his door, his expression is more puzzlement than hostility. He looks around to see if anyone's watching. "Hey, Finn, kind of surprised to see you here." He lobs me a couple of polite catch-up questions from behind his screen door, but there's no "Come on in and dry off" or "Let me show you my latest work." Pulling teeth to keep the conversation going, I learn that his brother Zack got married last year and that Mike had a gallery showing in Boston. Matt's not expending one syllable more than required. Okay, fine. I was planning to ask him if any of his apartments were unoccupied, but clearly that would be fruitless.

I make my way through the eye-stinging rain to Pop's, the world's most inconvenient convenience store (opens at ten, closes at four). Pop's sells dairy products with adventurous expiration dates, and a baffling selection of overpriced canned goods. But it's the house *behind* Pop's I'm interested in today—a saltbox where Gerry and Ginny Harper live. They're a lobstering couple who also paint in oils. When Jeannie and I lived together, Gerry and Ginny were our best "couple" friends. Both of them are hilarious, both amazing cooks. I probably should have tried them first—they'll know a place I can stay, for sure.

Through their wavy old window glass, I can see Ginny moving about. But when I knock on the door, no one answers. I knock again, harder. Nope. They've been warned off. Tears rush to my eyes, melding with the salt spray.

As I march down rain-swept Camden Avenue, past the weathered homes and rooming houses that line the street, I feel as if I'm being watched from multiple angles. At one point, a curtain whips closed at my approach. Maybe I'm just being paranoid.

I decide to swing by The Rusty Anchor to dry off and see if anyone I know is hanging out there. Bad idea. The way Big Al eyes me from behind the bar makes me feel like a wanted man stepping into an old-West saloon. He cranks out an effortful smile and says, "Finn Carroll, in the flesh."

I ask him how he's been, and he replies, "Can't complain..."

"...since they closed the complaints department." It's an island moldy oldie.

I order a coffee—it's a bit early for a beer—and Big Al says, more out of compassion than animosity, "I'll get you the one, Finn, but then maybe it's best if you get rolling."

Wow, am I actually being kicked out of The Anchor? Normally you have to rip a urinal from the men's room wall to accomplish that feat. I take the coffee. Big Al waves off payment.

The place is nearly empty. Back in the day, there'd be a fair number of morning drinkers on a Saturday, but the weather is forcing folks to do their sorrow-drowning at home. The only patrons are a threesome of silent drinkers in hooded raincoats, none of whose faces I can make out, and, over in the corner, Enzo, the raving socialist painter, huddled over a breakfast tumbler of house red.

"Grizzled" doesn't begin to describe old Enzo; he looks as if the last tool he shaved with was made by Husqvarna. He gives me a surprised nod, which I take as an invitation to join him. Enzo cares not one jot what anyone thinks about him or the company he keeps.

Still, he does keep his voice down. "So, I take it you've been getting a heaping helping of island hospitality?" he says, as I sit at his table, pulling back my dripping rain hood.

"You might say that," I reply, matching his turned-down volume. After we trade pleasantries for a minute, I pursue the topic further. "I don't get it, Enzo. I mean, I know some people are pissed at me, but why am I being singled out for an Amish shunning?"

"*Homo sapiens* is a pack-hunting beast motivated by fear and self-interest and unmoved by reason... But to be fair to the beasts in question, you brought a lot of it on yourself, wouldn't you say?"

"Why? Because I spoke up for that development plan—in its early days, when it still had merit? So did a bunch of other people."

"You did a tad more than 'speak up' for it, *amico mio*."

"What? What did I do that was so terrible?"

He peers at me over the rim of his tumbler. "Are you asking that rhetorically or...?

"It's a real question, Enz."

"Come on, Finnian. Don't be coy. We're both too smart for that."

"What?" I really don't know what he means. "I introduced Miles Sutcliffe to a few people with bucks.

Big whoop. I talked some of the fishermen and selectmen into listening to his plan, but that's all I did—grease the wheels of conversation."

"You vouched for him, among other things."

"Because he was my friend. And because I thought his plan was exactly what the island needed—a way to rehab Fish Pier and also bring in some new tax and retail money. I didn't tell anyone how to think or vote, I just brought people together across tables."

"On this island, vouching for someone means something."

"Of course it does."

"And when the vouch*ee* lies and deceives, there are consequences for the vouch*er*."

"I get that, Enzo. But here's what I don't get. Miles struts around the island like he owns the place. No one seems to be shutting doors in *his* face. But he was the one—him and his partners—who *actually* tanked Fish Pier, not me."

"And the Romans were the ones who *actually* nailed a certain influential carpenter to a stick of lumber."

"What do you mean?"

He leans forward, closing the gap between us. "Whom does history blame for Calvary, Finnian? Not the people who did the literal stabbing and flogging and hammering."

I see where he's headed, but I allow him to make his point.

"There have always been, and always will be, Romans." He lowers his voice another notch. "People with power and money who seek to enforce their will at everyone else's expense. Romans are a given. A force of nature. Like weather. We don't take their actions personally. Miles Sutcliffe is a Roman. No one expected any better of him. You, on the other hand..."

"I may be many things, Enzo, but I'm no Judas. I didn't betray anybody."

"You might want to take an opinion poll on that, Buckaroo Banzai."

"I didn't know Miles's plan was going to change! I didn't know Fish Pier was going to be canned! Once that started happening, I washed my hands of the whole thing."

"Interesting choice of words."

"I was more upset than anyone when those plans started changing, Enz. I was the one who came up with the whole letter-writing idea and got all those letters to the developers."

Enzo leans back and appraises me with a hoised brow.

"What? Are you saying you don't believe me?"

"What I believe is unimportant. I'm not a member of—" He cuts himself off, looks around the barroom, and grumbles, "of a certain 'fraternity' that need not be named."

"What are you talking about?"

"You know exactly what I'm talking about."

Maybe I do, but I want to hear him say it. "Can I buy a vowel?"

The silent drinkers at the other table rise in tandem, sliding their chairs back.

Enzo flicks his eyes toward them and knocks on the table in a wrapping-up gesture. "The wine's done too much yapping already. ...Besides," he says in the tone of a strong suggestion, "you probably want to get on with your day."

The raincoat posse heads toward the door en masse. Enzo stares at the floor, waiting for them to leave. After they do, he pauses for a few seconds, then stands and zips his own raincoat to his chin. He tosses a scratch ticket on the table as a tip for Big Al and ambles to the exit. Before leaving, he surveys the street, then shoots a glance back at me that I take as a warning.

I stand and head toward the rear of the bar as if I'm going to use the men's room.

And duck out the back door.

CHAPTER 22

I make my way out of Greyhook, sticking to the back alleys. I haven't found roosting quarters yet, but right now the village seems a more welcoming place than Greyhook.

As I'm passing the row of old fishmonger shacks that divides the two "districts," I spot Jeannie, in a blue poncho, talking to someone behind a stack of lobster traps. My view of the second person is blocked by her body and filtered through the beat-up traps.

Jeannie notices me, and a "caught" look flashes across her face. She covers it with a smile then says something to the other person, who turns briskly in the opposite direction. I catch a flurry of motion behind the stacked traps as the figure stalks away.

Jeannie marches toward me. Before I can ask who her conversational partner was, she says, "Walk with me. I'm on my way to work. Let's take the scenic route."

We're only a minute from Pete's, but we take a detour loop around the small residential neighborhood north of Island Ave. Jean pulls down the visor of her rain poncho as if she doesn't want to be seen with me.

"I hear you've been snooping around Greyhook, looking for trouble," she says, aiming her voice at the ground.

"Can't a person take a dump on this island without CNN doing a Special Report?"

"It was on TMZ, actually. 'Carroll Takes Dump.' Hey listen, I'm sorry about the way I slammed the brakes on last night."

"It was late. I'd been blathering. It was time for me to leave."

"No. There was something I *wanted* to tell you. Something that might be important to you, but I couldn't. Not till I checked with someone first."

"And?"

"Well, I did that."

"And?"

"It's not something I can just blurt out in thirty seconds. It needs... context."

"Okay. What time do you get off work tonight?"

She tramps ahead for a few seconds before mumbling, "Ten."

Fine, I'll take that as a "date." We walk in silence for a bit. I want to know who she was talking to behind the traps—my gut is flashing warning signs—but she doesn't volunteer the information, and I don't feel it's my place to pry.

"Hey Jeannie, can I ask you a big favor? Say no if it makes you uncomfortable."

I ask her if she still has dial-up Internet at her house and if I can use it while she's at work. I expect some resistance, but she quickly answers, "Sure." I don't know if she's agreeing so fast because she wants to help me or because she wants to distract me from asking about her back-alley chitchat.

"I promise to respect your privacy. I'll just plug my computer in and work. I won't poke around or peek in drawers."

"You didn't have to say that, Finn. I trust you."

She hands me her key chain with the tiny stuffed Cthulhu doll on it—another old gift from me—and tells me where to find the logon instructions for the Internet. "Use the landline too, if you want, and help yourself to anything you need."

"Thanks. I *will* steal some of your underwear; I hope that's understood."

"Duh. It'd almost be creepy if you *didn't*."

We're approaching Pete's again but from the opposite direction. I say I'll meet her at ten. She doesn't argue. She's about to step inside when she says, "I'm worried about you, Finn."

"Why?" Like there aren't 57 varieties of reason to be.

"Just a vibe I'm picking up."

"Do you know something I don't? Have you heard something?"

She pauses pregnantly. "It's more what I'm *not* hearing. Something *not* being said to me. I don't know. But also—" She cuts herself off, her eyes darting toward the road behind me.

I turn around and see only a pair of fishermen strolling along, engaged in a friendly debate, arms waving in emphasis.

The door to Pete's closes.

After grabbing a donut at the post office (don't ask), I'm heading up Bristol Road toward Jeannie's when a figure appears in my vision, about fifty yards ahead. Wearing a hooded rain slicker—Davy's Grey in color—and sporting a high-on-the-cheek, black and white beard, the man is pacing around in an overgrown driveway two houses down from Jeannie's corner lot. He's talking to a shorter guy, lightly bearded. They seem to be watching the road for someone. Golly, I wonder who.

Acting on instinct, I zag behind a hedgerow and cut through a couple of yards to the rear side of The Barnacle. I recall that the restaurant has a high dining deck with one of those coin-op scenic viewers. I dash up the wooden steps, feed two quarters into the device, and adjust my eyes to the magnified view. Rotating the viewer, I locate Jean's house at the intersection of Bristol Road and Fishermen's Court. Then I pan down two lots.

There they are. Davy Grey has his back turned, but the shorter man's face gels into clear view.

Oh. It's the first time I've laid eyes on him since the inn trucks left the dock. E-cigarette guy, from the ferry.

This could be the break I've been hoping for. A chance to pivot from mouse to snake. These guys don't know I've spotted them. That means I can watch *them*, maybe figure out what they're up to and where they're operating from. I'm electrified.

Prowling like a cat burglar, I make my way down to Barbara DeCamp's house, across Bristol Road from Jeannie's. I duck behind her shed and peer through its windows. The men are still confabbing on the side of the road. The shorter guy points to the road itself, as if examining the very path I trod last night in the dark. These guys must have been part of the welcoming committee that followed me from Jeannie's. Which means they are almost certainly Trooper Dan and Chokehold. Their stakeout location tells me they're waiting for me to show up at Jean's again. How would they know I'm heading there? Only Jeannie and I know my plans. Same as last night.

An image in my mind tries to flag my attention: the person who was talking to Jeannie in the alley. Behind the lobster traps. No. I foul it off like a bad pitch. *Watch the men instead.*

The two guys finally turn and walk off in the direction of the village. Sick of waiting for me, I guess. Good. Now I can follow them. Here's where my knowledge of the island will pay dividends. I know how all the properties interconnect and where all the shortcuts are.

I watch them from a distance as they proceed toward the village. At one point, the smaller one crouches and studies a rain-eroded section of the road. It's the exact spot where I picked up my throwing stones, I believe. What are they looking for? They walk on, taking a right on Island Ave. I cut through a series of back yards and overgrown lots, then jog lightly down Thistle Path to pick up their trail as they reach the west end of Island.

The men turn down Town Road 1, the dirt lane that leads to the town barn.

The town barn, where Musqasset keeps its maintenance equipment, sits by itself in the wooded center of the island. I beat them there by taking a side path through a stand of birch.

I crouch behind a row of dripping beach-plum bushes and watch the men approach the rusty old Quonset-hut-style building with the peeling sign, "Musqasset Public Works." There's a walk-in door to the right of a large garage door. Trooper Dan—if it really is him—looks around, then jiggles his hand on the knob for several seconds, using either a badly cut key or a lock pick. The two men go inside.

So *this* is where these guys have been hiding out the last couple of days? Makes sense. With no town employees working over the long holiday weekend, the barn makes for a safe, out-of-the-way place to use as temporary headquarters.

There seems to be only one window on the building—to the left of the garage door. I want to peek in, but, of course, that would be imprudent. I'll creep around to the rear and see if there's any way to look in from the back.

Picking my way through the wet, untrimmed foliage, I'm careful not to jostle any branches that might scrape against the corrugated tin wall, giving away my presence.

I'm halfway to the rear of the building when a buzzer alarm goes off, making me literally jump off the ground. I spin around in panic, expecting to be gang-tackled by the men, but then I realize the sound is not a burglar alarm but the building's ancient motorized garage door. The sheet-metal walls are further amplifying the oil-thirsty, grinding-chain sound.

I dash back through the brush till I'm near the front of the building again. The unbelievably loud garage door is still on its glacial upward journey. I wait for it to finish. Blessed silence reigns at last. The door is wide open. I listen for the men inside. Nothing.

I wait a minute longer. Still no sounds. The men *must* be in there—where else could they have gone? From within the structure, I can hear the steady drip of water from a leaky roof onto a plastic tarp. All else seems still.

Maybe the place has an inner room the men have entered. I slink up to the building and crane my neck around the garage-door frame, taking in a small section of the interior. I gradually increase my angle till I'm looking fully into the open space. No signs of life.

A pickup truck is parked beside a big pile of road sand in the middle of a dirt floor. Arrayed around the room's perimeter is the typical assortment of landscaping tools and snow removal equipment you'd expect to find in any New England maintenance garage.

I spot an area in the far-left corner of the room that's set up like an office, with a desk, an old computer, and some file cabinets. Deserted.

Where could the men have gone?

Dare I risk stepping inside? If the men are staying this quiet, they probably know I followed them and are hiding in the shadows, waiting for me.

The blackjack is still in my pocket. I take it out and start swinging it around. Emboldened, I enter the large, open space, keeping my weapon in motion.

Still no sign of humans.

I'm about to shout, "Show yourselves"—that one works about as well as "Come back, thief"—but some vestigial trace of intelligence keeps my lips sealed.

I slink around the pickup truck and sand pile. No one lurking on the other side. Plenty of hiding spots, though, in amongst the plow attachments and road signs. I notice a lopper hanging on the wall, along with some other pruning tools. My throat goes dry, and my feet gain weight.

Taking a few steps closer to the "office" area, I catch sight of a back door—a small one sheathed in galvanized tin. Leading to where? It's all wild woodland out behind the barn, I think. Is that where the men went? Out back?

As I tiptoe closer to the door, its lever-style handle turns. Someone entering!

I dive for cover behind the desk. The back door opens, then closes again, and I hear two pairs of boot heels striding purposefully through the garage.

Muffled words are exchanged, and then that phenomenally loud grinding sound hammers down again, making me jump halfway out of my skin. The garage door descending.

As the big door rattles down—in calendar time—daylight is eclipsed, and the room is plunged into blackness. Beautiful. Now I'm locked *in* here with Davy Grey and company. I walked right into their trap. Somehow, I've pivoted back to being prey.

A minute passes in the dark. Two. Three.

Not a peep from anywhere.

Is it possible they didn't see me follow them inside and they've simply gone away, closing the garage door behind them on their way out? Did they take the pickup truck? Should I chance using my flashlight app?

My phone rings, shattering the silence. Shit!

I bolt toward where I *think* the back door is, about fifteen feet away. My hand fumbles for the door handle and finds it quickly. I thrust the door open and dive out into daylight.

I hit the ground rolling, in a patch of grassy gravel, and then spring to my feet, already at full speed. I think I hear running feet behind me. Yes? No?

I plunge through the wet brush, scratching my hands and face on thorny blackberry bushes as I run. My phone's still ringing, but I ignore it.

I run, run, run through the wild woods.

It takes me several long, hushed stops to conclude no one is pursuing me.

CHAPTER 23

I steal up on Jeannie's house from the woodland side.

I shouldn't have come here; it's too risky. For me, for Jeannie. But I need a place to dry off and use the Internet, and I don't know where else to go. It feels invasive to enter Jean's house alone, even though she gave me her key. Of course, it used to be *my* house too, but it no longer carries my energetic field.

After peering out the windows in all directions and closing the shades, the first thing I do is strip off my sopping-wet clothes and toss them into the dryer, then wrap a towel around my waist. Getting semi-naked in Jean's house feels a bit creepy, but that's the least of my concerns.

I need to get my business done as quickly as possible and get out of here.

For a minute I can't remember where the dialup modem is, and then I find it on the desk in the living room. I peek out a couple of windows again—no signs of company yet—then plug the modem cable into my borrowed laptop.

I'm about to try to get online when my phone rings again, flooding my nerves with panic juice. Angie. Ah, yes, it *is* past the crack of eleven. A popup notice on my phone tells me it was her who called while I was in the town barn, too. Thanks, sis. I slide the green Answer icon, and the call seems to come through, then disconnects. Here we go again. Cell service, still banjaxed.

I do need to talk to Angie, though. For reasons of my own. Might as well get it over with. Luckily, I have Jeannie's landline at my disposal. I dial Angie's number on it.

I need to handle this call carefully. My sister is acting bristly about my questioning, and now I have an even more bristle-inducing question to ask her.

"Jeannie?" answers Angie, hoarse-throated; her first vocalization of the day. Her caller ID must be showing Jeannie's number.

"No, it's Finn."

"Finn? What are you—I've been trying your cell. Hey, listen, did I call you last night? If so, forget it. It was nothing."

The Angie Saturday Morning Shuffle: who did I drunk-dial last night and what did I say? "Ange, I need to ask you a question, and it might seem weird."

A beat. "Does this have to do with all that skeevy nonsense you've been poking into? I told you, no more help with that till you tell me why you're so interested."

I flip the question on her. "Why do *you* care what my interest is? Why are you acting so touchy about this?" Silence. Dark energy is massing at the other end of the line. "Angie? Why?"

She finally blurts out, "Because you and I both know this is not a random, innocent line of questioning!"

Ah, here we go at last.

"Well, clearly it's not random to you," I say. "You seem to have something on your mind. Why don't you tell me what it is?

"No, no, no. I asked you first. Why are you poking into ancient history?"

"Why do you care?"

"Why the poking, Finn?"

"Why the concern?"

Stalemate.

She lets out a protracted sigh. "Just ask your damn question."

"When I left for California after my graduation..." Angie is three years younger than me. She was still living at home when I blew town for the West Coast. "Did the police ever come by and question Dad about anything?"

She doesn't answer right away. Her silence is a yes.

"Like what?" she asks at last.

"Like… a bottle of booze he might have bought with a credit card?"

More silence.

It was *my father*, you see, who bought that bottle of Glenmalloch for me before my graduation. I was a few months shy of 21, and he knew the bottle was a gift for Miles, who *was* 21, so it was hardly a shocker that he would consent to buy for me. What *is* surprising is that the police questioned him about it. And that he never told me.

"What did they ask him? What did he say?"

Again, her answer takes time. "I really would like to know what this is about."

"Angie, come on."

"Fine! They asked him if he bought some high-priced scotch, some Glen-my-bonnie-old-whore, or some such. He said he did. They asked him where the bottle was. 'It's off being recycled into a dozen aspirin bottles,' he said, 'which was exactly what I needed when I finished the scotch.'"

"Why would he say that?" I ask her.

"Um, because he was being Dad?"

"No, I mean, when did you ever know Dad to drink hundred-dollar-a-bottle scotch?"

"How do you know it was hund—"

"Because he bought that scotch for *me*, Ange. He didn't drink it."

She says nothing for a long count, then blows out a breath. "I know."

"Then why were you pretending you didn't? And why did Dad lie to the police?"

"For the obvious reason, I assume. You weren't twenty-one yet. Buying for you was illegal."

"Uh-huh. Does that sound like Dad to you? Lying to the cops about some minor legal infraction?"

More silence from Angie.

"Angie, does it? Does that sound like Dad?"

"You weren't here, Finn! That's what happened, and I don't want to talk about it!" Angie hangs up. A moment later my intuition whispers another question—seemingly out of left field—I should have asked her. But if I call her back now, she won't pick up. Angie often responds better to texts than calls. My cell isn't working for voice calls, but it might be working for texts. I type into the message box: *One last question: Did Edgar Goslin ever approach Dad?* I hit Send.

While awaiting a reply, I make another circuit of Jeannie's rooms, peeking out the window shades. Coast still clear, as far as I can tell.

A reply text from Ange comes through in screaming caps: *YOU OBVIOUSLY KNOW THE ANSWER SO WHY ARE YOU ASKING ME?!!!*

I *didn't* know, but now I do. Edgar Goslin did talk to my dad. Damn. So Goslin *does* know something that connects me to the accident. But how? And what did he say to my father?

My phone pings another text message.

Two dead fish emojis. And an exclamation point.

The "from" space at the top of the screen contains a random-looking mishmash of characters.

Once again, the message disappears from the screen as if it had never arrived.

CHAPTER 24

'm wearing dry clothes again and pacing Jeannie's floor like a tin shark in a shooting gallery. My brain is overheating, trying to make sense of all the information I've been bombarded with—about my father, Goslin, Angie, and the twisted tale of the scotch bottle—as well as the threatening emojis. It's all interconnected. But I can't see the invisible thread stitching it together.

I need to keep moving, keep swimming forward. Like a real shark, not a tin one. That's all I *can* do. That means trying to talk to Goslin, as I was planning to do earlier. In fact, my exchange with Angie has doubled my incentive to find out what Goslin knows.

Turning my attention to my borrowed laptop, I attempt to go online, using Jeannie's pre-Cambrian dialup. It's like traveling back in time to hear the phone modem kick to life and do that scratchy-sounding "handshake" that was the soundtrack of the Nineties.

I grow a full beard waiting for the linkup to happen. And then... hallelujah, connected. I navigate to Sure Search, a top-rated people-finding and background search site. It lets me do a trial search for Edgar Goslin of Wentworth, Massachusetts. The site tells me it has found some information on Goslin, but, of course, it won't part with that info till I cough up sixteen magical numerals and an expiration date. I purchase the Premium Passkey membership and wait.

And wait. And wait.

A web page appears, piecemeal—"Search Results for Edgar Goslin."

In the "Contact Info" section, I spot what I'm looking for: Goslin's phone number. I hope it's current. Under "Known Associates," a couple of other Goslins are listed, as well as a Sam Kubiak, a John Woodcock, a Frank Torrissi, a Gary Abelsen, a Theo Abelsen, and a Priscilla Begley. The Gary Abelsen connection snares my attention. Does this mean Goslin and Abelsen associated with one another after the accident, or is the software only linking their names because they've appeared in the same news articles?

As a Premium Passkey holder—yes, sir, that's me— I'm entitled to search as many people as I want. I type in Gary Abelsen. His address comes up as a place called Neighbors Village, which turns out to be an upscale assisted living program. I call the facility on Jean's landline and ask to speak to him. I expect to be given the privacy runaround, but they tell me he's living in the Memory Care unit. Gary Abelsen is an Alzheimer's patient. Another dead end.

Time to try calling Goslin. Of course, if he is involved in all this, he's not going to blurt out the truth to me. I need an angle. Wish I had Miles to bounce ideas off.

So, what do I know about Goslin anyway? Precious little. From what we've been able to gather, though, he seems like a real charmer. My gut says he'll react aggressively to any approach that smacks of prying or pressuring. Maybe, though, if I coddle his ego and offer *him* something of value…

I draft a basic talking script and pick up the phone. Not wanting Jeannie's landline to be identified, I key in the "block caller ID" code, then dial the number Sure Search provided.

Goslin's voicemail picks up. His "greeting" is a gruff "Goslin, leave a message," with no attempt to sound even remotely civil.

I've prepped myself in case of voicemail: "Hello, Mr. Goslin, sir, I'm calling on behalf of a group of… 'investors' who would be grateful for the opportunity to speak with you confidentially." I'm giving it the John Malkovich touch—genteel but quietly deadly. "We understand you may possess certain information regarding an incident that took place in 1999, information that has eluded the police. We believe this information might be valuable to us, and we may be willing to compensate you generously for it. Please call us back at your earliest convenience, sir. Ask for a Mr. Slade."

I can't leave Jeannie's number as the callback. I need to keep her out of this. I can't leave my cell number, either. My cell isn't working right—but also, if Goslin is involved in this, he might recognize my number. I have a work number that forwards to my cell, so I leave that as the callback. Then I take the steps to have calls to the work number forwarded to Jeannie's landline.

Barely a minute passes before Jeannie's phone rings.

"Hello?" I answer neutrally. It might be for Jeannie, after all.

A woman's voice—seasoned by ten thousand packs of Winstons—replies in a "Nawthshaw" Massachusetts accent, "Lemme talk to this 'Mr. Slade.'" She pronounces it "Swade" and says it in quotes as if she knows it's fake.

"Speaking, Madam."

"Yeah, so what do you need to talk to Edgar about?"

"We'd prefer to speak to Mr. Goslin directly."

"Yeah, well I'd prefer to be married to George Clooney"—says it *Jawdge Cwooney*—"but that ain't workin' out so good. I speak for Edgar when it comes to money."

"Well, Mrs. Goslin... *Is* it Mrs. Goslin?"

"It's Begley, and there's no 'Missus' involved." I think she mutters, "thank Christ."

According to Sure Search, Goslin co-owns his house with a Priscilla Begley. She must be the live-in girlfriend who's been mentioned.

"Well, Ms. Begley, we're not sure if this is a monetary situation or not. We'll need to speak to Mr. Goslin to determine that. If he does have the information we think he has, we could be talking about a substantial sum."

"You're damn right we could. You see, there may be a, ah, existing *marketplace* for this, ah, *commodity*, which you might not be, ah, *cognizant* of." She chuckles, proud of the verbal triple-Axel she has just landed.

"Has he talked to someone else?"

"You'll have to ask him that."

"May I do that, please?"

"He ain't here."

"When do you expect him back?"

"Can't say. He's off on one of his, what do you call, 'unscheduled junkets.' Why don't you tell me what kind of money we're talking, so I can know how many five-star hotels I should try ringing him at?"

"I'm not authorized to talk with anyone but—"

"Good luck with that."

She hangs up.

I can tell she's interested in the (fictitious) money, but she's wary, too. Wants me to show more of my cards. Hanging up on me is Negotiations 101 for Priscilla Begley.

Fine. I can play Negotiations 101 too.

I take a quick look out Jeannie's windows again, scanning for unwanted company, then call the number back. Begley answers with a "bored" sigh. "Yup?"

"Perhaps I wasn't clear, Ms. Begley. Our offer is time-sensitive. We're prepared to wire Mr. Goslin the money, but we need to know within the next twelve hours if he has the information we're looking for." I'm sounding more and more like a B-movie spy, but I can't seem to dial it back. "After that, our offer may no longer be on the table."

"Offer? What offer?" she replies. "I ain't heard no *offer*."

"We'll talk numbers with Mr. Goslin as soon as we—"

"Edgar ain't here. Are you deaf? I ain't seen him for days. But I know everything he knows, so you can—"

She stops herself short. "Hey, wait a second. I see your number, pal."

Damn. Forgot to block caller-ID when I called her back!

"You probably know where Edgar is better than I do," she says. "Who is this, really?"

"My name's David Slade and I—"

"Yeah, and my name's Katy Perry, and my tits are insured for fifty million bucks. Listen, you're going to tell me your real name and why you want to talk to Edgar, or this conversation's over."

"Mr. Goslin has twelve hours to—"

"Shove it, numbnuts."

The line goes dead.

I'm pacing like a shooting-gallery target again. I should be galvanized by what I've learned about Goslin and Begley—they *definitely* know something the police don't—but my mind wants to focus on one thing only: the way the conversation ended. Begley reacted to Jeannie's phone number as if she *recognized* it. How could that be?

The Begley-Goslins and Jeannie in communication with one another? I don't even want to consider the implications of such a thing. Too horrible.

Peering out the windows again, I think about the two times I was followed in the dark. In both cases, Jeannie and I had just parted company. I also recall Jeannie's secretive conversation with the person behind the lobster traps. A visual detail from that scene—one my mind has been diligently trying to Photoshop away—now insists upon revealing itself in blazing hi-def. When that person strode away from Jeannie, I saw a flash of color through the traps.

It was a tone we painters call Davy's Grey.

No, Jeannie, no.

I feel like the bottom is dropping out of my world yet again, and I'm tumbling through space. I'm starting to think Miles might be my only friend in this after all. I want to call him and tell him everything I've just learned, but the Miles/Beth situation is dicey.

I don't know what to do. But if I don't get out of Jeannie's house right this minute, I'm going to pop a blood vessel. I charge out the door.

As I'm locking up behind me, an idea strikes.

CHAPTER 25

"**M**r. Carroll! How's it going?"

I'm at the front door of Preston Davis, the young deckhand from the ferry.

Preston invites me in, and his mom and I exchange the requisite whatcha-been-uptas. I'm a minor hero in the Davis household because I took Preston under my wing when he was ten and gave him free art lessons. And now, I've just learned, he has a scholarship to study art in college. Wow—occasionally I fail to mangle people's lives despite my most valiant efforts.

The moment Mrs. Davis departs the room, Preston looks me hard in the eye. He can tell by my energy this is not a social call. "What's up, Mr. Carroll?"

Preston is a young man now, so I don't sugarcoat my answer. "Someone followed me to the island on the ferry, someone who wants to seriously hurt me, maybe kill me."

"Whoa, Mr. Carroll."

"Does Trombly Boat Tours keep records of passenger data?" I ask him point-blank. I hate to put him on the spot, but, fear not, I'll get over it.

"We collect a fair amount of data on passengers, actually," he says. "Contact information, especially. That's 'cause sometimes, like when we cancel a trip for bad weather, we have to get in touch with passengers at the last minute."

"What happens to all that data?"

"It's stored on a hard drive at the mainland office, but we also export some of it to a database our webmaster uses to send out ads, newsletters, other stuff."

"Who's your webmaster?"

"You're looking at his ridiculously handsome face."

"You're kidding."

"Well, they don't give me that official title, 'cause then they'd have to pay me in actual dollars, but yeah, I designed the site and do most of the—"

"You have access to that database?"

"'Course."

"Is there any way you could take a peek at it for me?"

"It's not the Pentagon Papers, Mr. Carroll. Even if it was, I'd do it for you."

"Do you keep records of who was on every trip?"

"The company does. But all the trip-ticketing stuff is done on an antique Dell system in the office. *That* data's only stored locally, not on the Cloud. Every few weeks, I export any new names and contact information it collects into the database I use."

"So there's no way for you to find out if a particular person was on a particular trip? Like on the same trip I came over on."

"I *could*, but I'd have to call someone at the mainland office and come up with a good excuse why I want that info. If you need it, though, I'll get it for you, Mr. Carroll."

"First things first. Can we check out *your* database?"

We go to the computer in his bedroom. He navigates to an Excel file and pulls it up.

"What's the person's name?"

"Edgar Goslin. G-o-s-l-i-n."

"You sunk my battleship. We got a hit. He's been a passenger."

He points to the screen. My heart does a little jig-step. Not only is there an Edgar Goslin on the spread-sheet, but there's a home phone number, a cell number, and an email address too. I recognize the home number from Sure Search, confirming it's *my* Edgar Goslin. The cell number and email address are new information. I hungrily jot them down.

"There's no way we can find out when he used the ferry?" I ask.

"I can't pin it down to an exact date from here, but there is something I *can* do." He clicks through his folders with a techno-speed unattainable by anyone over 22. "Every time I update the database, I create a new file. But I save the old versions. I can step back through them and see when his name shows up. Here's an old one I saved on August eighth."

Less than four weeks ago.

Preston opens the file and says, "Dude."

He tilts the screen toward me. There's a "Goski" and a "Gosselin," but, as of 8/8, no "Goslin" in between them. Aha, so Edgar Goslin was added to the database *only on its latest update*. That means his ferry trip has been *very* recent. That information, coupled with Priscilla Begley's news that her man is currently away on a multi-day trip, is all the proof I need that Goslin is indeed on Musqasset Island right now.

He *is* one of the guys who followed me here from Wentworth. He *is* Trooper Dan or Chokehold. Probably the latter.

Not only that, but I now have his cell phone number and email address. Holy crap.

Holy Sanctified, Consecrated, Beatified Crap on Toast.

I stand and take a deep breath, feeling something approaching exhilaration. For the first time since I did the floor-dive in my parents' kitchen, I have my hands on something real and actionable. Something I can base a strategy on.

Even better, I feel an emotional anvil lifting off my heart. Maybe Priscilla Begley didn't recognize Jeannie's *actual phone number.* Maybe she just recognized the *prefix*—the three numbers after Maine's 207 area code—as that of Musqasset. If she knows Edgar took the ferry here, then she would definitely react suspiciously to receiving a mystery call from the same obscure island thirteen miles off Maine's coast.

I give Preston a hug of thanks and head out. I have things to do.

Yes, I am a living, breathing man with *things to do.*

***

The moment I step back into Jeannie's house, the smell hits me like a tire iron. Rotten seafood. My nose leads me to her bedroom first. Someone has tucked a half-dozen spoiled mackerel into her bed. The kitchen and living-room floors and woodwork are smeared with fish guts and raw shellfish that smell like they've been sitting in a boat's hold for days, and a decaying jellyfish-looking creature has been mashed into the keyboard of Miles's laptop.

I make a dash through the whole place to ensure the perpetrators are no longer on site. I don't see anyone—but I'm not convinced I'm alone.

I throw open the cabinets and closet doors in every room, exactly as I promised Jeannie I wouldn't do, and open some windows to air the place out. If this stunt was designed to enrage me, it's working. On the bright side, this is proof that Jeannie is not involved in this. No way she would allow her home to be desecrated in this way. A voice in my head retorts, *On the other hand, what a perfect way to throw suspicion off herself.*

No. I can't allow myself to be eaten by this cancer of doubt. I need to trust Jeannie. Period. She let me into her home because she trusted *me.*

The cartoon demon on my left shoulder fires back, *But why were those guys waiting outside her house like they knew you'd be coming here?*

Maybe they saw me take her house keys, the angel on my right shoulder rebuts. Yes, of course. That would explain it. She handed me the keys right in front of Pete's.

There's one easy way to find out who Jeannie's been chatting with lately—by checking the call history on her landline. I know how to do that; I bought and installed the phone system when I lived here.

No. Again, no. Not only would that be breaking my word to her, but it would be breaking my fundamental trust in her. And once that dam breaks, it might never be rebuilt.

I grab a small garbage bag and some plastic gloves from under the sink and begin collecting animal corpses from around the house.

When that task is done, I step out the back door in my tee-shirt, checking for attackers. No one in sight. I look toward the green trash bin across the yard, beyond Bree's play castle. That's when I notice more "gifts" strewn about the tiny, overgrown yard: piles of rotting fish innards, oozing their juices into the muddy ground. The stink is ferocious, even though the wind is blowing the other way.

I march toward the trash bin, ready to blow a gasket. My shin catches on something unseen, and I go sprawling on the ground, my chest landing smack in a pile of fish guts.

I whip my head about to see what tripped me: a length of clear nylon fishing line strung bow-taut across the yard, eight inches above the ground, hidden by the tall grass. Hilarious. You guys are a major laff riot.

As I try to push myself out of the nasty bio-muck, something strikes my skull, rocking my head back. Stunned by the blow, it takes me a moment to realize I've been hit by a rock.

Next thing I know, I'm being *bombarded* with rocks from more than one direction. I dive for the ground again, using my arms to cover the sides of my face. Several lemon-sized rocks strike my back and side like hammer blows. Payback for *my* rock-throwing.

Another rock connects with my head, and I hear a sickening crack. For a moment, I think my skull has split open, but then I take a quick peek and notice the "rocks" are actually clams. Hard-shelled clams of cherrystone or quahog size, still in their closed shells.

After a couple more direct hits to my thighs and rear, the air assault stops, and I hear two sets of footsteps running away. By the time I get to my feet, my attackers are gone.

Once I determine I haven't suffered any serious injuries—perhaps a mild concussion, though—the first thought that crosses my mind is, "I am going to *get* Goslin."

My second thought is that I have a lot of work to do now. I can't go anywhere covered in this vile-smelling filth, and I can't leave Jeannie's home and bed befouled.

Before I start my cleanup project, though, I need to send a couple of text messages. The first is for Miles, to let him know what's been happening to me.

I go back inside the house, strip off my shirt and pants (again), toss them into the washer, scrub my hands, and grab my phone. For a moment, I forget why I grabbed it—maybe I *am* concussed. I shake my head clear and type the message: *Lots to talk about. Goslin is the man. He's here on the island right now. He just attacked me, but I'm okay. Can we meet somewhere?*

The second message is for Goslin. I find a dead fish emoji in my phone menus and select it as a text message for him. I would love to see his face when he receives this message from me to his personal cell number, which there's no way in the world I ought to know.

It's time for *me* to start messing with *his* head.

CHAPTER 26

I'm about to hit Send when an alien impulse—I think it's called wisdom—intercedes. If I text Goslin that emoji, I may gain a moment of smug satisfaction, but I'll also be playing his game. And tipping my hand in a way that doesn't serve me. I need to maximize my advantages.

What *are* my advantages, as things stand? One: I know who Goslin is, and he doesn't know I've figured that out. Two: I know he's on the island—*and* I have ways to contact him here. He doesn't know that either. Three, and this might be the biggie: I know he has anger management issues. That might be his Achilles heel; I can't afford to let it be mine.

Whatever my plan of attack will be, I need to exploit his weaknesses and leverage my advantages to the fullest. Yes.

First things first. I toss Jeannie's sheets into the washer with my clothes. Dressed in my rain jacket and some men's sweatpants (not mine, alas) I found in a closet, I grab some trash bags, a rake, and a snow shovel and go to work cleaning up the fish guts in the yard.

After double-bagging everything I can pick up, I hose away the residue from the grass. Wasting water is a capital offense on Musqasset, but I can't count on the rain to do this job. Next, I set to scrubbing the indoors clean.

The whole time I'm doing these tasks, my throbbing head is thinking about how to deal with Goslin—who may be watching me every moment. Employing the if/then logic of a game script, I realize my options hinge on one key variable: *if* I can find out where Goslin is staying on the island, *then* I can use a "first strike" strategy and make a move on him. If I *can't* find out his location, then I must lure him to me somehow, an entirely different strategy.

So, first and foremost, I must try to determine Goslin's whereabouts.

I have his cell number now. That's huge. I wonder: is there a way I can locate him based only on that number, via GPS? Or is that something only the police can do?

I don't know the answer to that, but I know someone who might.

The wash is finished drying, so I make Jeannie's bed and strike off into the storm again.

"Private property is an illusion," shouts a voice in response to my knock. I *think* that's Enzo's way of saying, "Come in, please."

I shake off the rain and step into his rattletrap house. He's working at his computer wall. After our last exchange, I'm not sure what Enzo's attitude toward me is, but I choose to believe our friendship means something.

I sit on a stack of old newspapers, and he surveys my bruised and nicked-up face. He doesn't ask how it happened, and I don't explain. "Hey Enzo, you're a pretty paranoid guy, right?"

"It's not paranoia..."

"If they're really out to get you. Tell me about it. What do you know about tracking someone's location by using their cellphone number?"

"What do you *need* to know?"

"Well, like... can it be done?"

He grunts. "Is this a hypothetical situation or...?"

"Call it quasi-hypothetical."

He laughs a bone-dry *heh-heh*. "Well, question number one is: do you have the person's permission to track them? If so, you just download an app. Your friends and family sign onto your list, like good little sheep, and then you can all find out who's sneakin' off to the no-tell motel when they're supposed to be in church praying to the Flying Spaghetti Monster."

"And if you don't have the other person's permission?"

"Then you need to get more creative. It all comes down to whether you can get your mitts on the person's phone. I mean physically. If so, there are GPS trackers you can plant that act like human LoJack systems. The software sits there completely invisible—the person has no idea it's on their phone. In fact..." He leans back in his chair and wiggles his brow. "If you can get hold of someone's phone, you can do a whole lot more than track their location."

"What do you mean?"

"There are programs you can install—not strictly legal, mind you—that'll let you turn that phone into a spying device J. Edgar Hoover would have soiled his tighty-whities for. You essentially gain complete control of the person's phone, remotely."

"Wow."

"Wow indeed."

Unfortunately, there's no way I can get my hands on Goslin's physical phone, so that route is moot. "What if you only have their number, not the phone itself?"

"Then you're S.O.L. If it's an emergency situation—a missing person or someone threatening to molest your cat—the cops can get a warrant and work with Lord Verizon to triangulate the person's location. But that option is generally unavailable to the merely curious private citizen."

He turns his back to me and cracks his knuckles. I take the hint and stand up to say goodbye. But then a thought occurs to me. "Hey Enz, can I ask you something else?"

He hears a note in my voice that makes him give me his full attention.

I skip the hypotheticals this time. "Some scary people planted a document—a letter—on my home computer. The letter claims I wrote it, but I didn't. But here's the crazy part: you would swear I did. It has my humor, my writing style, personal stuff about me. Even *I'm* half convinced I wrote it in some kind of fugue state. I can't figure it out."

"What type of scary people are we talking about? Criminal? Corporate scum? Government scum?"

"I think it's just a personal revenge thing, but I'm not a hundred percent sure."

"The reason I ask is... Well, let me back up a bit." He leans his chair back and thinks for a moment. "Do you know the main reason most scams and hoaxes fail? Lousy writing. I kid you not. Most people can't write and have no clue how to create letters and documents that are convincing. That's why you can usually spot an email scam; something's *off* about the wording and punctuation.

"But there *are* people out there who are good at this stuff," he continues. "Literary forgers. They're like art forgers but with words."

"Wasn't there a book out by someone who did that?"

"There was, but this is bigger than just writing fake Dorothy Parker letters for fun and profit. Government agencies and criminal enterprises—as if there's a difference—employ these folks too. They're talented writers, but they're also cunning linguists. Ha! I knew if I lived long enough, I'd find an excuse to say that! They can recognize any linguistic style and emulate it. And now they have technology on their side. If they can access your computer, they can run everything you've ever written—emails, Word docs, online posts—through an AI program that scans for all sorts of writing tendencies: frequently used words, sentence structure, literacy level, punctuation and formatting habits, common errors, even personality markers. With that kind of help, these forgers can write a letter even your wife or mother would believe you wrote."

Well, well, well, I am certainly getting an education from Enzo today. The coil of anxiety that has been tightening in my chest for the past week starts to loosen a little. Why? Well, now there is at least one plausible explanation for how that suicide note got written that doesn't involve my being batfish insane. It also would explain why Troop and company spent so much time on my computer that day.

It's hard to believe a guy like Goslin would go to the trouble and expense of hiring a "literary forger," though. But then again, if he runs in criminal circles, they might already have access to that kind of specialist. It's not so far-fetched, is it?

I thank Enzo for his help and get up to leave. As I'm heading out the door, he shouts in a movie-Amish accent, "You be careful out among them English."

CHAPTER 27

As soon as I leave Enzo's, I notice a reply from Miles to my earlier text. It reads, *Beth and I want to buy you dinner tonight. How about the Mermaid at 6:30?*

I recognize the purpose of the invite. Treating me to dinner at a restaurant will allow Miles and Beth to buy off some guilt about abandoning me, while still keeping me away from their home, their family, and their prying friends. Still, I suppose a decent meal wouldn't kill me. I text him: *Sounds good. Thx.*

Miles texts back: *Why don't I pick you up at 5? That'll give you and me time to talk about Goslin first. Then we'll meet Beth at the Merm.*

Good. Miles has managed to wangle some Beth-free time with me so we can strategize about how to handle the latest developments.

I have a few errands to run—buy a flashlight, some trail mix, and some first-aid supplies to treat my wounds.

I complete those tasks, and then it's time to start getting ready to meet Miles. I'm still a paid guest at Harbor House, so I decide to shower and change there. Anyway, I haven't found alternative lodgings yet.

There are no private bathrooms at HH, only a suite of shower and toilet stalls in the middle of the second floor. As I remove my clothes in front of one of the large mirrors, I find three quahog-sized bruises blossoming on my sides, and a couple of nice ones on my back. The right side of my forehead is cut and bruised from where a cherrystone struck it, and my lip is swollen—don't know how that happened. I have another cut on top of my head, with a lump under it. This new "fighting hobo" look will not play well with Beth.

Each encounter with Goslin and his goons has been more extreme than the last, and I have a pretty good idea what it's all leading up to. The torment they've been putting me through so far is just foreplay. Payback for the years of suffering Goslin believes I caused him. But the main event is yet to come.

I need to devise a plan *tonight* to deal with Goslin and, if possible, execute the plan tonight as well. Tomorrow morning at the latest. I don't want to wait around to find out what his next move will be. *I* need to make the next move. Somehow.

I sneak out of Harbor House by the fire escape to find Miles already waiting for me in his golf cart. He looks... tense. I slide into the cart beside him, and off we go.

It appears the rain may have finally stopped for good.

Miles waits till we're out of the village and then starts peppering me with questions. "Are you sure Goslin is one of the guys who attacked you?" "How do you know?" "Are you sure he's on the island?" "How do you *know* Goslin and Begley have inside info about the accident?"

As I feed him credible answers, he becomes increasingly agitated. Again, I find this odd. If he really thought I was nuts, he wouldn't be grilling me this way. And he wouldn't be getting so worked up about my answers.

I would love to believe his concern is solely for my safety, real or psychological, but I know Miles well enough to suspect there is more to it than that. He only gets *this* concerned about things that affect him personally.

As if to confirm my suspicions, Miles pulls the cart over, jumps out, and starts pacing in circles. "I'm screwed! Why does this have to be happening *right now*? Could the timing be any worse? Damn it to shit! Damn it to shit!"

"What is it, Miles?" He doesn't answer. "Does this have anything to do with the career moves you were telling me about?"

"Yes, damn it to shit!" He continues to pace a groove in the road.

"What's going on with all that?"

"I'm not supposed to talk about it."

I can tell he *wants* to talk about it, though, so I don't say a word. I just fold my arms and wait. It'll come.

It does. "Remember I told you there might be an opportunity coming up for me in Washington?"

"No, I forgot. Of course I remember."

"It's in the Senate, Finn. The U.S. Senate."

"Holy crap."

"Yeah. I don't know if you keep up with political news, but there have been rumors in the press about Pat Aldridge possibly resigning before his term is up." Aldridge is one of Maine's two U.S. Senators. "All pretty vague stuff, but my name has been tossed around in a couple of newspapers— very purposefully, by the way—as a possible replacement. Anyway, within the next week or so, Aldridge is going to announce he's stepping down. Turns out, he has terminal cancer and wants to spend his final months with his family. This isn't public information yet."

"And?"

"In the state of Maine, it's the governor who appoints an interim senator in a situation like this. And... it seems I might have an 'in' at the governor's office. Some kind of 'favor-owed' situation. Anyway, things have been heating up behind the scenes and now, well, it's..."

"Time to buy a ship-in-a-bottle for your new office on Capitol Hill?"

Deflecting my levity, he says, "This could become more than just a Senate seat too, Finn. A *lot* more, if a certain group of people have their way."

Is he saying what I think he's saying? "Wow, Miles. That's pretty freaking exciting."

"Try terrifying. If there was ever a time in my life when I had to be absolutely, positively, boiled-in-a-sterilizer clean, it's right now. I can't afford to have even the *whiff* of a scandal floating *anywhere near me*. Why does this stuff have to be surfacing *now*? Why?"

"Whoever is pursuing me, Miles—Goslin and his gang—has no knowledge of you being in that car."

At this, Miles's face flashes red and he stares hard at me for several seconds. He holds up his phone like an accusation, showing me a text message he's received:

Carlisle Road, Bridgefield, MA. 1:20 am, May 13, 1999.

My brain reels. Someone *does* know. "Who... Who sent this?" In the Sender box is a garble of random characters, like the one I saw on my phone when the dead fish messages came in. "When did you get it?"

Miles says nothing. His eyes bore into mine with almost physical force.

"This is impossible," I say. "There were no witnesses that night, and the bottle connects *me* to the scene, not you. The only person on Earth who can possibly put you in that car that night is..." I leave the unspoken "me" hanging heavily in the air.

A storm cloud passes over Miles's expression.

"Wait, come on, Miles. You don't think *I* sent this text... do you? You don't think *I'm* the one who's been—"

"No. Well, not... deliberately."

"Meaning what?"

"Meaning if you were... in ideal mental shape—the Finn I've always known—of course you would never..."

"Do you still think I'm delusional? Do you still think I made up that story about being attacked at my parents' house? That *I'm* the one stirring up all this old stuff? Even after what I've told you about Goslin? He's *on the island*, Miles, that's a fact." I lift my shirt and rotate my torso to show him the bruises on my sides and back. He gasps. "Do you think I did that to myself? Real events are happening here. With real people."

"I know. I know real events—*some* real events—are happening. But I also can't forget that you did just get out of a psychiatric hospital. I'm sorry, Finn, but I can't help but wonder how much of what's happening to you is—okay, I'll say it—your guilt *orchestrating* events so you somehow get punished for your misdeeds."

"God, Miles."

"People do that, Finn. I've seen it. They bring down upon themselves the punishment they think they deserve. And if that's what's happening here, then maybe part of you wants to make sure *I get punished too!*"

Ah, the nub of it. We face each other on the road like gunslingers, unmoving.

The *bloop* of a text message comes through on his phone. He checks it. His face turns the color of a cadaver's. He steps forward and shows me the new text. It's identical to the last one: *Carlisle Road, Bridgefield, MA. 1:20 am, May 13, 1999.*

And I sure as hell didn't send it.

✶✶✶

We drive around the island in silence. Miles is chewing his lower lip like it's calamari. Finally, some wobbly words escape him. "All right, assuming Edgar Goslin is on Musqasset right now—and that's still a big assumption in my mind..."

"He took the ferry here, Miles. Fact. Ask Preston Davis."

"...then where does that leave us?"

I tell him about acquiring Goslin's cellphone number from Preston. I also tell him about the money-for-information ploy I used on Priscilla Begley.

"That wasn't a terrible idea," he concedes, stopping the cart to think. "Actually, I don't see any reason it can't still work."

"Begley hung up on me. She knew I was playing her."

"No, I mean we approach Goslin directly. Leave Begley out of it."

"But he must have talked to her by now. I'm sure she told him about my call."

"So? What's to say we can't still reach out to him? We call his cell, tell him we know he's on the island, tell him that we're the interested party, that we're on the island too, and that we have cash for him *if* he can provide us certain information. Act like we're the ones with all the leverage. Play it coy, don't give him any details, just say we want to meet him. If I'm Goslin, I'm going to be curious enough, or suspicious enough, to show up."

"Maybe. But I'd be super-cautious too, if I were him. I'd definitely bring my goons along. And let's assume he bites. We'll need to find a stand-in to do the actual meeting for us. Goslin knows who I am."

"Right," Miles realizes. "And he might know who I am too." He looks at his watch, blows air out of his cheeks. "Beth's expecting us. Let's plan on doing something in the morning," he says. "Meanwhile, let's enjoy a..."

"Last supper?"

"Nice meal." He starts driving again. "Needless to say," he adds, needlessly, "don't tell Beth what we talked about."

Beth is a better actor than I remembered her to be. She orders a nice bottle of wine to get dinner rolling, makes lively conversation throughout the meal, and, in general, plays the perfect hostess. She even accepts, unchallenged, my obvious lie about slipping on some wet rocks at Mussel Cove as the explanation for my cuts and bruises.

The only time tension crosses her face is when I bring up her parents' upcoming visit. She covers immediately, though, saying how nice it will be for her kids to see their grandparents. At one point, I catch her flashing Miles an eye signal. Ten seconds later, she excuses herself to go to the bathroom.

"I'll walk with you," says Miles, who gets up and heads in the same direction. In the mirror over the bar, I see Beth walk right past the rest rooms. Miles follows her. They've gone into the back hallway to discuss something—probably how to ditch me now that the food-ingesting portion of the festivities is over.

Miles left his phone on the table. Dare I take a peek? Better not. It's probably locked anyway. But I remember him checking his email moments ago. Keeping my eyes on the bar mirror, I slide his phone onto my lap. His email app is still open; the phone is unlocked.

I tap my way to his text-message log and find half a dozen texts from random-looking sets of numbers—going back to yesterday. They're all the same message: *Carlisle Road, Bridgefield, MA. 1:20 am, May 13, 1999.* The first one came in yesterday at 10:22 a.m. That would have been shortly after I showed him the old newspaper article in the chapel.

Damn.

So *that* explains Miles's sudden change of attitude— when he showed up at Harbor House with his laptop, ready to work. And why he's been "helping" me with this whole thing. And hiding it from Beth. His concern is not for me. Never has been. His concern is for Miles. Why didn't I see that before?

Underneath his calm, "empathetic" exterior, Miles has been crapping cinder blocks since he got that first text yesterday. Because, to him, there are only two possible explanations: either *I'm* sending the texts because I'm a nutjob hellbent on seeing him get his karmic comeuppance, or else a third party, perhaps a political rival, really *has* tied him to that fatal accident. And even though Miles doesn't know he threw the bottle, just the fact that he was in the car with me, drunk, when people were killed, makes for the kind of story a state senator would hardly want anyone tweeting about. Especially a state senator with tall ambitions.

I slip his phone back onto the table, screen-side down.

As I'm walking down Island Avenue in the deepening darkness, wondering where I'm going to sleep tonight, my nose catches the scent of herb in the wind. I pass within ten feet of a trio of young men in raincoats standing under the eaves of a large woodshed. It's my three beer-buying buddies with the $4.71 business proposition. The alleged eldest of the trio flashes his toothy grin again, but it comes off as mildly threatening now.

My gut tingles, and I realize something is still bugging me about my earlier encounter with these guys and their whole "twenty-one" story. I can't put my finger on it, though.

I try to shake off the feeling as I walk on. I wonder if the lads are going to follow me.

My phone rings, startling me. Is my phone service working again, or will this be another dropped call?

I duck behind a rack of kayaks-for-rent, seemingly unfollowed by the lads. The number on the Caller ID does not warm my heart. It's Angie's. The sun is long past the yardarm, so *that* can't be good news. I slide the Answer button.

"Okay," says the gin-thickened voice at the other end. "You want to dig into this stuff, have it your way. Grab a bloody shovel."

CHAPTER 28

The words that tumble out of Angie's mouth over the next few minutes cause tectonic plates to shift in the psychological foundation of my life.

"He didn't think you were a bad person, Finn," she blurts, as if she's been holding her breath for two minutes. "He knew it was an accident. He was worried about it ruining *your* life."

"Who, Angie?" I know damn well who.

"You know damn well who."

Dad, of course.

"What are we talking about here?" I ask her.

"He knew, Finn."

I'm pretty sure I get what she's saying, but I need to hear the words aloud. In a voice that sounds hollow and distant to my own ears, I say, "Knew what?"

"Don't make me say it, Finn."

"Knew what, Ange?"

"That you caused that crash! The one that killed those people. That's why he lied to the police. Not to protect himself. To protect *you*. But you're not a bad person. You're not a bad—"

"Angie!" She is slipping into maudlin incoherence, a stage in her drunkenness progression from which there is no return. "I need you to stay focused."

"I can't promise anything," she slurs.

"How did he know? What made him come to that conclusion?"

"I told you. It was in the papers. That the cops suspected"—she mauls that word—"a bottle was thrown from that bridge. One day they showed up at our door with a credit card receipt. Asked Dad if he bought a bottle of that Glen-my-merry-ass stuff. Dad remembered the way you were acting the day after your graduation. He knew *something* had happened to you, but he didn't know what. When the cops started asking questions about the bottle, he put two and two together. Told 'em the bottle went out with the recycling."

I feel struck by a bottle myself. My whole "no one else could possibly have known about that night" theory has just flitted away like a bird escaping a cage. Dad knew. Which means Mom knew. Angie knew. And any of them could have told anyone, at any time. This changes everything.

"How long have you known what happened?" I ask my sister.

"Since the cops came that day. There was no hiding from it." Angie seems to sober up all at once. "Things got super-weird after you left, Finn. Dad started staying up late at night, drinking at the kitchen table. Scribbling notes about the Abelsens and Goslin. The whole thing was eating him alive, but there was no way he was going to turn his own son in."

Unreal. All of this was going on while I was learning how to make burritos in sunny Mission Beach, blissfully unaware anyone had even died that night.

"So *that's* when Dad started changing?" I say, as much to myself as to her. I remember when I came back from California, my dad was a different man. He looked twenty years older, and his eyes had a dark, pleading look. I'd always thought it was his mounting health problems that caused the depression of his later years, but now I see it was probably the other way around.

"Him and Mom were fighting too," says Ange. "The house was not a fun place to be, believe me. I started 'going out' every night just to get away from there."

Suddenly the whole Carroll-Family Holiday Tragicomedy Special sharpens into clear focus: To protect Miles's secret, I blew town and began steering my life into the breakdown lane. To protect *my* secret, Dad allowed guilt to consume him. Which, in turn, put the final nail in the coffin of his marriage to Mom. Which, in turn, caused Angie to start avoiding home like a communicable disease. Which, in turn, caused her to "fall in with the wrong crowd" and pick up her lifelong love of liquor, among other unhelpful tendencies.

It's an O. Henry tale on acid! An entire family brought down by the secrecy surrounding a single thoughtless act *none of us even committed*! I don't know whether to laugh or cry. But I do know this: if I start laughing, I will literally never stop. They will haul me off the island on a gurney, singing "Camptown Races" in a Daffy Duck voice.

It's my turn to deliver a blow to Angie. "I need to tell you something," I say to her, "and I need you to be sitting down." I give her a moment to steady herself. "Dad had it all wrong. The night of that accident, it wasn't me who—"

The phone connection cuts out as if I've hit End Call. I redial. The call goes through but then cuts out again. I try several more times. Same result—connect, disconnect. Angie calls *me* back, but when I try to answer, the line goes dead again. Thank you, oh Mighty Phone Gods of Musqasset, for your ever-impeccable timing.

I couldn't have left Angie dangling at a worse moment. By the time I reach her again later—*if* I manage to—she'll be too drunk to communicate.

Bloop. A text message comes through.

A knife emoji. A gun emoji. A coffin emoji.

Maybe I'm the one who needs a drink here. I make a beeline for Pete's Lagoon and plant myself at the corner of the bar. Jeannie looks at me as if I'm a suicide bomber with my finger on the detonator. She doesn't even ask how I'm doing; she simply fetches the bottle of Glenmalloch from the top shelf and pours me a finger.

Six seconds later, she pours me a refill. "Are we still on for ten o'clock?" she hazards.

I probe her eyes to see if there's some dark secret hiding in there I should be worried about. Not that I can see. I remind myself of my commitment to trust her.

I nod; yeah, we're still on.

I lie on my bed at Harbor House, warm from the good scotch but cold in my gut. My decision to return to my rented room was unplanned, reflexive. For the first time in days, my mind is empty of thoughts about men with loppers trying to kill me. Or about friends who think I'm psychotic. I am oblivious to email threats and to the fishy smoke detector hovering right over my face. I am even indifferent to the astonishing note I found under my door just now: "Hey, want to meet for a drink later and share codfish pie recipes? – Leah." It's been ages since a pretty woman courted my affections, but even lust can't set its hook in my mind.

All my thoughts are on my sad and twisted family.

I think about my father crawling into an early grave at the age of fifty-seven, believing himself partially responsible for the Abelsens' tragedy and believing his son to be an unredeemed killer. Lying to everyone *about a lie.* A falsehood. If only he had talked to me about it, just once, I could have lifted that burden from his shoulders. But of course, that would have broken the Carroll family code. The code of secrecy. In Dad's mind, keeping mum about my "crime" was the greatest gift of love a father could bestow on a son. That's how the Carrolls showed love, after all—by protecting one another's stories.

It becomes clear, for the first time in my life, exactly how septic we were as a family. A meal at the Carroll home was not an open-hearted gathering of loved ones. It was a weighty affair, filled with innuendo, in which each of us related to the others through a filter of secrets each alone was privy to. The layers of who-knew-what-about-whom and what-it-was-okay-to-talk-about were staggeringly complex, and power dynamics were always in play because each of us was holding private knowledge we could use to blow the others' lives apart.

My older sister Grace knew I sold illegal fireworks at school and also knew where I hid my porn stash. I knew she was using contraception and sneaking around with an older guy who liked to get rough. Angie knew I sometimes stole beer from Dad's private fridge. I knew she liked to cut her skin when she was alone. And so on and so on. Layer upon layer. But ultimately, we *kept* our secrets, at least the big ones, because that was how one behaved with honor—yes, honor—in the Carroll household.

I suddenly realize, as insane as it sounds, that I was actually seeking Jeannie's *approval*, on some level, when I looked the other way regarding her infidelities. I thought she would *credit* me for my discretion. Yep, I did.

God, what a rancid stew we Carrolls were steeped in.

And I'm still steeping in it. Look at Angie. She is a raging alcoholic, and I have never confronted her about it—have, in fact, covered for her on countless occasions. Look at my friendship with Miles. Ever since college, my value to him has derived from how well I could help him maintain his lie of being the perfect guy. The list goes on.

My whole life, I have sought to gain my power, my sense of worth, from lies. But—surprise!—there *is* no power in lies. Lying has sucked the life out of me for decades. But maybe the crisis I'm in is offering me a chance. A chance to explode this old pattern once and for all.

Maybe these terrible truths I've been learning about Dad, these memories I've been unlocking, are not here to condemn or shame me but to offer me clarity. I don't need to live the Carroll Way. I *can* reinvent myself.

I roll off the bed, fired up with fresh resolve. It *is* possible to change. Yes! I must believe that. Life has been holding that door open for me ever since I stumbled out of my parents' kitchen, clinging to a pulse, eight days ago. I will not toss that chance away.

I look at my cellphone clock. Nine fifty. Jeannie will be out of work in ten minutes.

Before I leave my room, I take the sweet note Leah left for me and write on the back, "Would love to exchange fish pie recipes with you, but, alas, I am a man in love. Next lifetime for sure. – Finn." I slip the note under her door as I walk past.

It's a small act of truthfulness, but it feels good.

CHAPTER 29

The Shipwreck see-saws on the edge of Table Rock. I'm surprised by how much integrity the hull still possesses. I'd have thought the ocean's ceaseless hammering would have broken it apart by now, but the old mailboat hangs stubbornly together—determined, it seems, to make its final voyage as the *K.C. Mokler*, not as a pile of anonymous sea shrapnel.

I was expecting Jeannie and me to go someplace quiet to talk, but the first thing she said when I met her at Pete's was, "It's *going*. Tonight, I can feel it." I knew what she meant—The Shipwreck. And I knew we had to be there to witness it. We borrowed Pete's ancient pickup truck and drove to Lighthouse Hill as fast as we could.

Now here we sit, looking down with flashlights at the wreck once again, waiting for one final monster wave to sweep it away. The rain has stopped, and the winds have calmed, but the sea is still pounding ferociously.

I've always been of the persuasion that places and objects hold onto "memories"—energetic traces—of emotionally charged events that take place in and around them. I think maybe that's what ghosts are. And so, when The Shipwreck lifts anchor tonight, I think it will be taking the ghosts of Jeannie and Finn's old love with it. Not just metaphorically but in some energetically real way. I believe that. I do. The idea lashes me in the heart like a stingray's barb. But then I recall all the lies, all the hurt silences, all the drunkenness-in-place-of-intimacy that took place in and around that old husk. The ghosts of *those* things will be going out to sea too.

Jeannie and I remain wordless for several minutes, and then at last I cast her a line. "So, you had something you wanted to tell me last night?"

Silence resumes as we watch the old wreck rock and groan on its great slate bed. I don't want Jeannie to speak until she's ready. Maybe I don't want her to speak at all.

"When you told me about Miles throwing that bottle," she finally says, "I was... surprised."

"What do you mean?"

"Angie told me about the accident, Finn."

"Jesus. When?"

"Years ago. When you and I were living together, here. She told me *you* had thrown that bottle—because, well, I guess that's what she believed. But she told it to me in confidence and made me swear I would never tell you."

"How did it come up?"

"You and I were having... issues. I used to talk to Angie about them sometimes. She knew you better than anyone else did. I just wanted to understand you." We watch another wave assault the wreck. Not the big one yet. "I always felt there were things... kinda major things... holding you back from being in a real relationship with me."

"Those things were called Stavros, Captain Jim, and Peter." I have never named her secret lovers aloud like this. It feels pretty good, actually.

She allows my remark to pass unchallenged and says, "I was on the phone with Angie one night and we were talking about it. She was drinking..."

"Do tell."

"...And she let it slip that you had this... burden you were carrying around that had been weighing on you for years. I asked what it was. I probably had no right to ask, and she probably had no right to tell me. But she did. On the condition I would *never* tell you."

"But you just did."

"I called her last night. After you left. Told her I might need to rescind my promise. I couldn't talk to *you* till I told her that."

So, Jeannie was the "everybody" Angie was ranting about in her drunken voicemail.

"This certainly puts a new face on things," I say. "Half the time we were living together, you thought I was a killer?"

"Not the 'malice aforethought' kind."

"But still... You've known about these deaths for years. And I've only known about them for—what?— three days. Things might have been different for us if you'd told me."

"I made a promise to Angie, Finn. To my credit, I did try to pry it out of you several times."

Thinking back, it's true, she did. She used to harp, to the point of genuine annoyance, on this theory that I was carrying some old secret that was dragging my life down like an anchor.

"I was actually a lot more surprised to learn you *didn't* throw that bottle," she says.

"Why?"

"Because I remember the bizarre way you were acting the day you said goodbye to me in '99 and left for California. And because it explained so much. I thought guilt was the whole reason you were so... What was the term I liked to use?"

"Insufficiently entitled."

"Right. I figured you were a textbook case of Catholic guilt. You believed you should have been caught and punished for your crime, but you weren't. Therefore, you didn't think you deserved to have good things happen to you. Therefore, you would never ask for anything you really wanted. Even if it walked into the room naked and gave you a lap dance."

"I don't think you were wrong about that part."

"I don't either. It's the *degree* of guilt I don't understand," says Jeannie. "Don't you think you're exaggerating your role in this thing? Miles threw that bottle. You didn't do anything."

"Exactly. I didn't do anything. I was the one—the only one—who had the power to act, but I didn't. Miles passed out. He had no idea he caused any harm."

"Neither did you. Not at the time."

"Because I *chose* not to know. I heard sounds that night, Jeannie. Sounds of glass and metal. After he threw that bottle. But I never followed up to find out what they were. In fact, I fled the freaking *state* so I'd never have to know for sure."

"And if you *had* known, that would have changed the outcome how? The only thing that would have been different if you'd come forward is that blame would have been placed on Miles. And you didn't want to see your friend's life ruined. I don't see how that makes you the devil. But I do see how it makes you an insanely loyal friend. You took on the moral burden that should have been his."

"Neither of us took on the moral burden. That's the point, Jeannie."

She emits the most rueful laugh in the history of rueful laughs. "Riiiight."

Thinking back on my life over the last eighteen years, I have to laugh too.

Part of me desperately wants to accept the shot at exoneration Jeannie is trying to offer me, but my con-science—that infallible inner calculator—tells me a debt is still owed. It seems Jeannie's inner ledger is coming up red too. Her downcast eyes tell me she hasn't said all she needs to say tonight.

"What is it, Jeannie?"

She stares at the wreck as if personally responsible for its ruin. "I kept my promise never to tell *you* what Angie said... but she never asked me not to tell *anyone*."

As I wait for her to complete this revelation, we turn our heads at the same moment. The horizon is rising eerily to meet the cloud-covered moon, and we both know what we are seeing. A mammoth wave is rolling in. We scramble up the cliff-side and watch it advance toward us, mesmerized.

I brace myself for the drama that will be unleashed when the killer wave breaks—the thunderclap of water, the bomb-blast of exploding spray, the shriek of hull-metal on rock... But the wave doesn't break. It arrives instead as a gigantic swell; dark water rising up the cliff-side by fifteen feet or more. The Shipwreck silently lifts off its stone berth, straddles the water's surface for a few seconds, and then sinks out of sight with a sigh of bubbles. The massive swell retreats to sea.

When Table Rock becomes visible again, it is a literal blank slate. The wreck is gone.

A tear runs down Jeannie's cheek. But I don't think it's for the *K.C. Mokler*, off on its final mail run. Jeannie squeezes my fingers as if she wants to break the bones.

✶✶✶

For reasons I can't quite fathom, it seems a foregone conclusion that Jeannie and I will sleep together tonight. This tacit understanding fills the cab of the truck like secret perfume as Jeannie drives to her house. It gels into certainty when, halfway there, the lights go out on Musqasset—eleven o'clock, lovers' hour—and Jeannie lays a finger on my hand, ever so lightly.

Why, oh why, is it that life only gives us the things we yearn for when we no longer yearn for them? Not that I don't want to sleep with Jeannie. I do. Oh, my good word, yes I do. But now I care about the reasons. I don't want it to be a one-and-done thing, an impulsive act committed for reckless or poetic causes. I don't want a farewell lay. I don't want a closure lay. I don't want a "two lost ships in a storm" lay. I don't want Jeannie sleeping with me out of abandon, pity, grief, desperation, existential loneliness, or even good ol' glorious randiness. Two days ago, I wouldn't have given two craps about the why. Now I do.

So I'll need to navigate these waters mindfully. The conditions, the *understandings*, must be right, or I won't be able to go through with it.

Jeannie parks Pete's truck in the woods behind Fishermen's Court. It's a token stab at privacy that will fool no one, but I salute the effort.

We approach her house, treading softly, and slip into its cinnamon-scented darkness. I still know by touch where the rechargeable lamp is located, but before I can turn it on, Jeannie presses me against the wall and kisses me. Her lips have a wet, silky warmth that dissolves all reason. I kiss her back without a *nanosecond's* hesitation. The idea that I was going to dictate the rules of this engagement—via a mutually agreed-upon set of emotional parameters, stamped in triplicate and signed by both parties—now seems as absurd as the idea that I could dictate the course of the ocean storm that has stranded me on Musqasset.

Before a coherent thought can form in my head, we are pulling at each other's clothes and lurching toward the nearest horizontal surface, which happens to be the living room rug.

I've always been a "lights on" kind of guy when it comes to lovemaking, especially with Jeannie. I never wanted to be robbed of the visual feast of her nakedness or the flush that comes over her face and neck when she's in the throes of lust. But tonight, darkness is the perfect milieu. It makes the tactile exploration of each other's bodies all the more pressing, the moments of touch-meeting-touch all the more mystically synchronized.

Every cliché ever written about making love applies here. Jeannie and I proceed to consume each other sexually with a hunger and ferocity I've never imagined even in my most debauched fantasies—and yet each urgent, darting movement is feathered by an exquisite gentleness of touch that turns it into art. Time disappears. Individuality disappears. There is only the act of love, performing itself, with Jeannie and me as the stunned and grateful witnesses. God enrapturing Godself and inviting us along for the party.

And stuff like that.

Somehow, we end up in her bed. And that may be the best part of all. Jeannie, naked, soft, and warm, wrapped around me like a blanket as sleep comes prowling for us in the dark. Still not a word spoken since we stepped from the truck.

A thought intrudes. What if the men are standing outside the house right now, watching, waiting? I don't even care. As long as they leave Jeannie and me alone right now, they can do whatever they want. Screw them.

But of course, my mind can't rest, now that I've thought about the danger. I slink out to the kitchen and fumble around in a drawer until I find a sharp knife. When I get back to bed, Jeannie is curled away from me on her side.

Screw them. Screw them and the ferry they rode in on.

✦✦✦

It's been years since anyone served me a hot breakfast without expecting a tip. I awaken to the smells of coffee brewing and eggs cooking in the rain-washed island air. For a moment I'm able to pretend life is just good. Here I am, with Jeannie, on a Sunday morning, in the home we once shared, my concept of lovemaking recalibrated to new heights—and now coffee and eggs await. A man can dream, can't he?

When I enter the kitchen, the dream evaporates like water on a hot griddle. Jeannie is sitting at the table, turned toward the window, her back to me. She doesn't turn to greet me. I know she has rowed away to her own private island, the one with no visitors' dock.

I grab a cup of coffee and sit behind the plate of toast and eggs she has made for me. If I detect even a whiff of regret from her over what happened between us, I will jam a fork into my neck.

"I'm not going to say last night was a mistake," she offers at last, still turned, "because clearly it wasn't *that*."

"Clearly." At least we agree on one thing. "But...?"

"But..." Here it comes. "I hope it hasn't raised any unrealistic expectations on your... on *either* of our parts."

"And by 'unrealistic expectations,' you mean..."

"Once the ferry is running, you need to be on it, and we both need to just... resume life as normal."

I need to chew on that. First of all, there is no "life as normal" for me. Not since a trio of assassins tried to boot me permanently from the good ship Lollipop. But that's beside the point. Do I have a right to ask Jeannie to change her life for me, based on one night of intimacy? Do I even want that myself? We have not remade enough ground with each other to be entertaining such thoughts. I haven't even met her daughter, for crying out loud. And yet, why close doors?

"I'm not going to make any awkward suggestions," I say. "Don't worry. But at the same time, I'm not going to pretend, for the sake of convenience, that last night was only a casual hookup. It wasn't. And I'm not going to lie and say it was. I'm done with lying."

"Finn, please, can we...?"

"That's all I'm going to say about it, Jeannie. The end. Let's just enjoy each other's company this morning. No demands. No promises. No heavy silences. You and I wasted enough of our time together that way."

That seems to mollify her, and she lightens up. We eat our breakfast and chat for a while, mostly about Bree, who's due back on the Tuesday morning ferry. I steer Jeannie onto the topic of writing and convince her to read me a short story she wrote. It's good. I mean real-deal, sock-knocking good. Jeannie has become a bona fide writer, with her own voice.

I ask what happened to the paintings I left behind. She leads me out to the storage shed I converted into a mini-studio, and I'm surprised to find it largely as I left it. My paintings are still here, and the place still looks like a studio. Even my inflatable motorboat that I would take on painting excursions is still sitting in the corner—deflated and packed onto its hand trailer. Just laziness on Jeannie's part or something else? I'm afraid to ask.

Looking at my paintings—both the finished ones and the eternally frozen works-in-progress—is like reading a forgotten diary. When you're a painter, stumbling upon your old paintings can release more stored memories than an electrode to the brain.

I point at a canvas of a dry-docked boat with a hole in its hull. "That was the week you had your breast cancer scare." No symbolism there, doc. Flipping through a rack of canvases, I find one of a Musqasset meadow blowing in the wind. It's good. Dang. Maybe I wasn't crazy to believe I had some genuine talent; maybe I was crazy to believe otherwise. Delusions of mediocrity, is that a thing?

It hits me like a gut-punch that I didn't leave just *one* lover behind when I walked away from my life on Musqasset. I feel a physical, almost sexual urge to hold a paintbrush in my hand again and spar with a canvas.

I notice Jeannie studying one of my pieces. She reluctantly angles it toward me. It is a nude. Of her. The one and only attempt I ever made to paint her, to bring my two lovers together. That was an experiment that didn't work out—for one embarrassingly simple reason: when she posed nude for me, I'd get all riled up. We had a lot of fun in the studio that week, but we more-or-less agreed it was not a workable long-term arrangement.

Jeannie must be having the same memories I am, because she drops the canvas and stares at me baldly.

Time elongates. She unbuttons the top button of her denim shirt, eyes never leaving mine. I stare back at her, transfixed as always, powerless before her beauty. But as I step toward her, she breaks eye contact and scuttles out the door.

CHAPTER 30

I find Jeannie sitting on a sawhorse in the wet grass, slump-shouldered. Whatever "moment" was about to happen—as the Viagra lady on TV would say—is now a fleeting memory.

"I didn't realize I still had a thing for you," she says. "Obviously my self-awareness needs some work in *that* department. But I need to act like a sober person now. For my daughter... and for myself. The bottom line is, you and I are not going to 'be together.' Na-ga happen. There are some... barriers to that, which we don't need to get into. But if I make love to you again, I'm going to talk myself into believing it actually *could* happen. And I'm going to make myself miserable. For months or years to come. So, we need to pull the plug right now. Cauterize the wound instead of making it deeper."

Somehow I knew she was going to say something like this.

"Maybe *I* can have a say in what's a 'barrier' and what isn't," I offer, edging myself onto the sawhorse beside her.

"No, you can't, because you don't know all the facts. If you did, you would turn your back and walk away without saying a word... again." A dig about the way I left last time.

"Facts about *what*, Jeannie? What could be so—"

"I did some unforgivable things, Finn. After you left."

"What kinds of things?" What could be worse than screwing Cliff the fisherman on the same sofa we watched *Breaking Bad* on?

"Things that... well, they're the reason I stopped drinking."

"Those things can remain your business, Jeannie. Forever."

"I thought I'd never see you again. And I was pissed at you and thinking *good riddance*. I never in a million years thought we would have another... chance with each other. Or that I'd want one. That doesn't make what I did right; it just explains my frame of mind."

"You don't need to explain anything."

"Yes, I do. I did things to hurt you and get back at you. I let my guard down and got involved with the wrong people."

"We both had reasons to hurt each other back then," I say. "But whatever you did after I left, it was only emotional acting-out. It didn't *actually* hurt me. I don't ever need to know about it, whatever it was. It has no power to affect me now."

"Yes, it does. There are... circumstances I have created that are... *ongoing*. And you *will* be hurt. Unless you leave the island on the first ferry run and stay away for good."

"What if I decide not to do that?"

"You need to."

"What if I decide I want to move back to Musqasset, start painting again, build a new life here, meet your daughter...?"

"Stop!" She jumps up off the sawhorse. "You need to go. Now. I have to get ready for work, and if you stay any longer I am going to say things that will..."—her voice loses its edge—"ruin a memory I want to hold onto. Please, Finn, go. ...Please."

She looks wrung out, flattened by a bus. I have no words for her. And yet I don't seem capable of locomotion.

My phone rings, breaking my paralysis. It's Miles. I text him, *Call u in a few.*

Jeannie leans over me, places her hands on my face, and gives me a lingering and delicious kiss. But it is deeply infused with "goodbye." When she stands up, I can feel the connection between us snap like a cut cord. She walks off into the house and into her private future.

✦✦✦

"Are you ready?" says Miles on the phone as I step out onto the road.

"For what?"

"*For what?* To flush out Mr. Edgar Goslin."

"Are we really going to do that?" My brain—not to mention other select portions of my anatomy—is locked into a Jeannie groove right now. I have trouble switching tracks to Goslin. I force my feet to commence the painful march away from Jeannie's house.

"We'd better be," replies phone-Miles. "I've recruited some helpers." He explains that a pair of young men who work at the new marina have agreed to serve as our "muscle" in the utterly insane event Goslin agrees to meet us in person.

"But we don't even have a plan," I point out.

"I've been working on that. Here's the deal. *If* we can get Goslin to agree to meet, we'll insist the meeting take place at the gazebo on the west common. My two guys are already staking it out, and I planted a webcam there. I've also thrown together some cash, which we can flash at Goslin to, you know, lubricate the gears of conversation."

"And then what?"

"Then we just... see what we can get him to say."

That's our plan? I'm glad my medical insurance is paid up.

Miles proposes that *he* make the initial call and conduct the actual face-to-face with Goslin. He's decided the situation is too delicate to use a stand-in—he's probably right—and so he will disguise his face with oversized sunglasses and Billy Staves' hooded rain suit with the super-high collar. Our two beefy young conscripts will stand guard nearby. In theory, there should be no real danger of violence. But in theory, bumblebees can't fly. We're messing with things we are eminently unqualified to deal with. As usual.

"I'll meet you at Harbor House in fifteen," says Miles, "and we can phone Goslin from your room."

I hit End Call and step up my pace. The weird clash of emotions I'm feeling—post-coital bliss, raw heartache, and mortal terror—is one I've never quite experienced before. I still feel oddly *vital*, though, in a way I haven't in years.

I'm feeling so jacked, in fact, that I barely break stride when I spot a dead crab lying in the middle of the road. Someone's dropped catch? Nope, it's been sawed cleanly in half. A second demi-crustacean greets me about twenty-five feet ahead. Another one after that. Intended for my eyes, no doubt. So, my buddies *did* stake me out at Jeannie's after all. Figures.

I march on, less fearful than I probably have any right to be.

As I'm about to pass a trailhead on my right, I see a dead mackerel nailed to the wooden trail sign, festering merrily in the morning air. *This is starting to feel a tad childish, guys.* I stop and look down the bush-lined trail. Three or four more rotting fish are nailed to trees, ten or twenty feet apart. Do my stalkers really think they're going to lure me into the woods by hammering dead fish to trees like trail-markers? How stupid do I look?

Wait, don't answer that.

I have no intention of walking into a trap, but I do jog down the trail a few yards to see how far ahead they've marked the path. Another fish has been nailed to a tree just beyond a fork in the trail, and another after that. I guess they want me to follow their trail toward the old orchard in the middle of the island. Right, guys. That'll happen. I turn around to head back to the main road.

The rustle of dead leaves sets my nerves ablaze. Two men grab my arms from behind. A third one yanks a stretchy headband over my eyes, forming an instant blindfold.

A fist slams into my side. I collapse to my knees.

One of the attackers ties a rag around my mouth to gag me as another one tries to pull my hands together behind my back. I thrash and squirm in resistance.

A shoe-heel whomps the side of my head with log-splitting force, and I see stars (yes, I've just discovered, that really happens). I give up the fight. They tie my hands.

The men carry me along, face down, my shoe-toes dragging in the dirt. They trot me across the road and through a patch of brush. They're moving in a half-run as if they want to get this thing handled quickly, whatever this thing is.

The men drag me for half a minute over rocky, brambly terrain. Then they lift me and toss me, not at all gently, into what feels like the bed of a pickup truck. My face hits the molded metal, and I yelp in pain, but my cry goes nowhere, thanks to the gag.

A motor starts and the truck drives off.

The truck bounces along a rough road and makes a series of sharp turns that have me slipping and sliding in every direction. Loose sand in the truck bed creates a gritty lubricant.

After a couple of minutes, the truck stops.

The men yank me from the bed and toss me onto the ground. The surface I land on feels and smells like a dirty carpet. The guys bind my legs together—thighs, knees, ankles—with a series of bungee cords.

Next, they roll me up inside the filthy-smelling carpet and wrap some more bungees around the roll. Then they hoist the roll, pallbearer-style, and carry me farther. Not a word has been spoken by any of them.

They toss me, rolled up in the rug, onto another hard surface. The rocking of the "floor" and the sloshing of surf tell me I'm in a small metal boat. A motor kicks over. That's when I realize how much trouble I'm in. How many benign reasons are there for hauling a person out to sea in a rolled-up carpet?

The boat starts off. The waves feel fence-high as we maneuver over them. We must be in the bay, though, because the water would be even rougher if we were in the open Atlantic.

It's hard to keep track of time, turns out, when you're rolled up in a carpet on your way to your own execution, but I estimate about ten minutes pass as the boat chugs and dips over the rolling waves, which grow steadily steeper as we go.

Finally, one of the men can no longer keep his mouth shut. He says to one of his cronies, in a voice meant for me to hear, "Should we toss him in here?"

Another voice—slightly familiar?—replies, "No," then adds a moment later, "Let's lower him in *gently*."

Both men laugh as if this is the grandest joke e'er told. The engine winds down.

I am edging toward panic. For the second time in just over a week, I am facing the near certainty that I'm about to die. And I still do not want to die.

Still do not, still do not, still do not.

The motor cuts out, and I hear a hollow thump that makes my heart leap with hope—the small boat has bumped up against what sounds like a larger boat. So maybe they're not going to dump me into the Gulf of Maine with weights attached. Not yet anyway.

The men stumble about as they attempt to tie the smaller boat to the bigger craft in the high-rolling surf. Footsteps clang up a metal ladder, and muffled voices engage in a debate. Seems they're trying to figure out how to maneuver me up into the larger boat. The rough water is making their job difficult. Good. Screw them—in case I haven't said that in a while. I hear the word "winch" being bandied about. Two of the men clamber back into the smaller boat and tie a couple of ropes around my carpet roll.

I feel myself being lifted out of the small boat via electric motor, my body sagging between the rope-holds.

The men release me from the winch boom, dropping me onto the higher deck of the bigger vessel. They undo the ropes and the outer bungee cords, and unroll me from the dirty rug, leaving me still blindfolded with my hands tied behind my back. My mouth is still gagged, and my legs are still bungeed together. The deck is pitching from the waves, but these guys seem to have seasoned sea legs.

They haul me roughly across the deck. One of them digs my phone and wallet out of my pockets. Another one throws open a heavy-sounding hatch, which thuds against the floor.

A horrific—nay, *apocalyptically* bad—stench is unleashed from the hold below. Rotting fish, many days old. A muscular guy (Chokehold?) grabs me around the torso, hoists me, and carries me down a steep, short set of stairs, grunting and panting. He heaves me, and I splash-land in a shallow pool of stinking liquid, amongst a clutch of slippery objects. Dead fish.

The man clangs back up the metal steps, escaping from the smell as fast as he can. I hear the clink of a string-operated light switch, and he shuts the hatch behind him.

It's me and the dead fish. Together in the dark.

CHAPTER 31

The blackness is vault-like.

A wave tips the boat, and the rotten-fish soup goes sloshing across the floor. It collects against the other side of the chamber, pooling in the canted angle between the wall and floor. My body tumbles with the fish, and I go plunging under the putrid liquid, face down.

My mind races toward panic. I'm going to drown in this stuff! My lungs burn to inhale.

No, I tell myself. *Hold your breath; the boat will shift back in a few seconds.* Those seconds stretch out into a thousand distinct microseconds, and then the liquid shifts back the other way, spreading thin again. My face breaks the surface. I pull in a mouthful of putrid air as I try to gain control of my rolling body. Oh God, that smell!

The awful broth splashes up against the other side and repeats its puddling effect. Again, I go underwater. Again, panic tries to rise.

The boat reverses angle again, the inner tide flows the other way, and I manage to gulp a little more O_2. I slide across the floor, blind as a cave eel, my mind grabbling to define the physical space I'm in. The hold is maybe seven or eight feet wide. The surface feels slick. Plastic-coated?

I mustn't go under again.

Keep your rear down and your face up, I command myself. That's my new life-purpose: rear down, face up. But which way is up?

Again the water pools, again I tumble. Ass over teakettle.

It's devilishly hard to control my body position, what with my limbs bound and the floor shifting like the tilty room in a Salisbury Beach funhouse. But somehow, when the nasty soup deepens again, I keep my face skyward. The rancid air feels thick and hot and almost viscous. I don't want to fill my lungs with it. But I must.

Breathe! Breathe! Breathe! Breath is life.

I force myself to take a full, deep mouth inhale, through the wet bandana-gag.

The tide heaves me again, and I roll like a rock.

My mind wants to run away from this insane reality, but I must stay grounded. I'm not dead yet. I'm alive. In this minute. And if I play my cards right, I can be alive in the next one.

A minute. I can shoot for that. One minute. Then maybe another one after that.

Mindfulness, Finn. Remember your old Zen practice: Release all judgments. Accept what is. *Suffering is resistance. Om Aranam Arada. Accept what is, do not resist it.*

I slosh across the floor again.

Stop resisting. Yes. I can do that.

This time, when the liquid pools, I allow it to *buoy* me instead of submerge me. My body relaxes into a back-float. Better, much better. Okay, that's the ticket: *ride* the tide, don't fight it. I'm sure there's a life-lesson in there somewhere.

Stop fighting. Float and breathe. Float and breathe.

Acceptance, not resistance, Grasshopper.

I'm breathing normally now. Staying afloat on my back. Good. Fine. Better.

My heart rate comes under control, even as my body keeps sliding back and forth in the dark. The danger of losing my mind begins to subside.

Okay, *now* what? What variable can I control?

The shifting of the liquid is out of my hands. But maybe I can find some way to anchor my body. That would be a step forward.

Anchor. Body.

If I can make it to the metal steps, maybe I can brace myself against them somehow. Or at least grab onto them. My wrists are tied behind my back, but my hands can still grasp.

Get to the metal steps, then. But how? As the liquid flows across the middle of the chamber, thinning out, I flip onto my side and try to inchworm my way toward where I think the steps are. No traction. And the flow of the inner tide is too strong to overcome. Is it my imagination or is this soup getting deeper?

Another idea strikes.

I ride the liquid—I swear it's deeper than it was when I landed in here—till it pools again on the other side. This time I hold my breath and deliberately go underwater. Flipping my tied legs like a dolphin's tail, I paddle in the direction of the stairs. When the water shifts again, my body slams full-force into the stair unit, cracking my elbow on the metal.

Damn, that hurts, but I manage to grab hold of the steel caging that blocks off the space under the stairs. My bound hands cling to it with an iron grip. Pumping my feet against the floor to create friction, I push myself to a sitting position, still gripping the caging behind me.

Hallelujah. I'm stable and anchored against the flow. For the moment. The fishy water goes sloshing past me. I'm a dock-post now, not driftwood.

I can hold on like this indefinitely, I think, if the stench doesn't kill me. Or can I? It suddenly becomes glaringly obvious: the water *is* getting deeper. Listening carefully, I pick up a sound I hadn't noticed before. The whooshing of water through a hose or pipe. Not a garden hose, either, but a big fat inch-and-a-halfer, by its sound.

The chamber is being pumped full of water.

The realization sends my body into panic. My legs thrash, and my throat makes terrible sounds.

Stop! Breathe. I need to get up the stairs, that's all. That's doable. Up the stairs.

Of course, even if I manage to do that, and then somehow, miraculously, open the hatch—with no hands, mind you—my buddies are still waiting for me topside.

But if I stay down here, I'm going to drown in the rising water. Up the steps it is, then.

One minute at a time. Just get through the next minute.

Inching my gripping hands along the cage-work behind me, I work my body around to the front of the stairs. Still can't see a thing. With much pumping and splashing of feet, I somehow push my butt up onto that first step. I rest and breathe through the wet gag, listening to the water rush in through the hose.

By sheer willpower, I push myself up two more steps. My head bumps up against the hatch with a thud.

Too loud!

I freeze, waiting to see if the sound has aroused any attention from above.

No footsteps approach.

The water is now covering my feet at all times—whichever way the boat is leaning. The hold is filling up fast. *Come on, Finn, do something.*

I push my head up against the hatch and am surprised to find it opens. Is gravity the only force holding it closed? I ease the heavy hatch back down into its frame and wait to see if my topside buddies have noticed the sound or motion. No reaction.

I push the hatch open with my head again, wider this time. I hungrily pull in some cool air through my ick-soaked gag, expecting my captors to come running. They don't.

I push myself up onto the next highest step, holding the hatch open, awkwardly, with my head. One more stair and I should be able to roll out onto the deck. It's going to hurt like the bejaysus because the heavy hatch cover is leaning all its weight on me.

And my kidnappers are probably standing around the hatch in a circle, grinning at each other, waiting for me to make my move. But I've got to do it. No choice.

In a fast, tumbling maneuver—which hurts as anticipated—I roll free of the hatch and onto the deck. The hatch slams shut.

I hold my breath in dread. No feet come running.

I can see again! My blindfold must have pulled free as I was rolling out.

I look around. The deck seems to be unoccupied. I pull in a few grateful breaths as I lie on my side, relishing the partial escape I've just pulled off. The relative dryness of the deck prevents me from sliding as the boat rocks in the waves.

It appears I'm on a mid-sized fishing vessel.

I wriggle my way to a tie-down cleat and use it to pry the bungee cord off my ankles. Over the next few minutes, I squirm free of all the leg bungees, using the cleat as an aid.

Next, I back up against the rusty corner edge of an old motor casing and saw through the rope binding my wrists. It takes a while, but at last my hands come apart.

I stand and stretch. I rip the wet gag off my mouth and fill my lungs with pure, unfiltered ocean air. It tastes more delicious than French champagne.

Now I'm able to walk around the deck, using the safety rail to steady myself against the pitching of the boat. It's a trawler I'm on. The smaller boat that brought me here has departed, and I seem to be alone on this vessel—anchored at the outer reach of the bay.

I spot a slop sink and rinse my face and hands with the running seawater, then make my way to the wheelhouse. It's a trashy little room containing the steering wheel, the boat controls, a two-way radio, and the fish-finding radar gadgetry—in addition to a dozen Mary's Lunch coffee cups serving as wet ashtrays, a plastic fryer-oil bucket stuffed with men's magazines, and several wall plaques bearing gems like, "It's almost beer-thirty," "S.S. Boobie Bouncer," and "I'm a drinker with a fishing problem."

The engine and electrical system are key-operated, like a car, but the key isn't in the ignition; why would it be? The radio won't operate without the key.

There's a metal catchall basket attached to the wall, and my confiscated wallet sits inside it. Underneath it is a plain white envelope, unsealed. I open it with a tingling of nerves. When I realize what I'm looking at, my feet turn into deep-sea-diver's weights.

The envelope contains printouts of three newspaper articles about the 1999 accident on Carlisle Road and the follow-up investigation.

Delusional my ass, Miles.

Keen to learn whose boat I'm on, I snoop further. A compartment in the piloting console contains the boat's paperwork. When I see the name of the owner, I tug in a breath. It should not surprise me, but it does. Clifford Treadwell.

Cliff. Jeannie's Cliff.

I collapse into the captain's seat to fight the rocking of the boat—and the rocking of my universe. Hold on, hold on. Does this mean Cliff Treadwell and Edgar Goslin *know* each other? Those two men—those two *worlds*—should not be connected in any way, except in my own mind and experience. And yet here they are, brashly intersecting with one another in reality.

What is the hidden root system connecting them?

A theory begins to assemble itself in the dark folds of my cerebrum. It makes my gut feel poisoned, and yet it would explain not only the link between Cliff and Goslin but also Jeannie's guilt and discomfort with me.

Wild hypothesis gels into near certainty.

Here are the facts whose logical connection I cannot ignore: Jeannie believed, for years, that I caused the accident in 1999. Jeannie was having an affair with Cliff when I left the island. Cliff hated me. Jeannie admits to having done something hurtful to me after I left. She even implies that she blabbed off to someone about the accident.

Conclusion—and really, you'd have to be a concussed sea cucumber not to see it: *Jeannie* told Cliff about me and the accident. Cliff, thrilled to have found a way to make my life miserable, did a little research, just as I did, and learned about Edgar Goslin. The two men, being birds of a dysfunctional feather, hit it off, and Bob's-your-uncle, a partnership was born. Why they waited so long to act against me remains unexplained, but one fact seems inescapable: Cliff and Goslin are working together, and their connection occurred through Jeannie.

The tectonic plates shift again as another supposition crumbles. I've assumed, from jump street, that my troubles began in my kitchen in Wentworth and followed me out to Musqasset. But what if that assumption has been ass backwards? What if, instead of *escaping from* my problems by coming to Musqasset, I was *running toward* them? What if, all along, Musqasset has been reaching out its tentacles and pulling me into its tooth-lined maw?

If so, then, weirdly enough, my father was the one who set it all in motion. After all, it was he who concluded, years ago, that I was guilty of manslaughter. Angie got her ideas about my guilt from him. Angie told Jeannie, then Jeannie told Cliff...

As I think about the cascading implications, I suddenly feel—strange as it sounds—drowsy. Maybe it's emotional fatigue, maybe it's adrenal burnout, maybe it's reluctance to face my fate, or maybe it's the ceaseless rocking of the boat like a damn cradle, but I drop off to sleep right there in Cliff's "captain's" chair.

✷✷✷

I awake to an urgent realization. My captors didn't leave me in the fish hold to die. If that was their intention, they would have done the job more cleanly. No, they left me there to break me. Which means they will be coming back to finish their business.

I must prepare for that event. How? For starters, I need to deal with the alarming odor clinging to my skin and clothes. It might betray me. I grab a canister of Boraxo from the sink, climb down the hull ladder, and jump into the heaving ocean. Keeping one hand on the ladder at all times, I peel off my clothes—now dyed a nasty reddish brown—and scrub them with the soap powder. Not an eco-friendly thing to do, but I'll plant a tree later.

Now that I'm in the water, I weigh the idea of swimming for shore. But the boat is anchored a fair distance out, and the seas are still rough. I *might* be able to make it, but is that my best move? Right now, I've gained a strategic advantage by escaping from the hold. My captors won't be expecting that. I'll have the element of surprise in my favor when they return.

I climb back on deck, wring out my newly laundered clothes, and put the wet duds back on my body. They're freezing cold, but I hardly notice. I embark on a weapons search and find a fish-skinning knife with a curved, four-inch blade that's all business. I lash it to my shin with a Velcro strap that I slice off a life vest.

Before I'm able to construct a real plan, I spy a small metal motorboat laboring over the rolling waves. It's the men, coming back.

CHAPTER 32

I f there was room in my psyche for fear, I'd be terrified, but there is room only for game-planning. The seeds of an idea start to form. It's one that will rely heavily on luck, but I don't have the time—or, oh right, the brains—to concoct something better.

I find a spool of heavy-gauge fishing line, cut a length of it with the knife, and shove it into my pocket. Then I return the envelope containing the news stories to its place in the catchall basket, wipe the captain's seat clean, and make sure the wheelhouse looks exactly as it did when I entered—i.e., like drunken dogshit.

Next, I creep across the deck, keeping a low profile. I gather up all the bungees I removed from my legs, shove them into my pockets, and search for more. Luckily, Cliff is a bungee-and-duct-tape kind of guy, and I find a bucket of the cords in a low cabinet. I hook a dozen of them onto my belt loops then quickly wipe up the bloody footprints and puddles I've created.

Gulping a lungful of fresh air, I descend into the foul-smelling hold, leaving the hatch open to allow daylight in. The stench hits me like the flat of a shovel as I get my first clear look at my former prison. As surmised, it's a smallish chamber, maybe seven by ten, five feet deep, lined with molded plastic. It's half full of murky, brownish water, with dozens of dead pollock floating in it. The flow of water through the hose seems to have stopped. The pump must have been on a timer, or else there's some kind of automatic shut-off valve.

Fortunately for my plan, the steps have a metal handrail on either side. Taking a page from my tormentors' book, I tie the length of the clear fishing line tightly across two support posts for the handrails, at shin height.

I climb back upstairs, shut the hatch after me, and hide under a tarp that's draped over a piece of deck equipment. I slip the knife out of its Velcro leg-strap and wait.

✶✶✶

I hear the engine of the smaller boat shut off and the men clamber up the hull ladder and onto the trawler's deck. From my low vantage point, I can see their rubber-booted feet moving about but not their full bodies.

There are three guys, as I more-or-less expected. Three is my lucky number. One of them says, "I'll check on Ass-Face," and throws open the hatch to the hold. I mentally cross my fingers as he starts down the steps. A muffled "Aaaagh!" rings out as he trips over the fishing line I tied there and plunges into the bloody fish-water with a splash.

"What happened?" shouts one of the guys on deck.

"I fell, that's what!" the muted voice from below shouts back. "Aww, shit! SHIT! Hey, where the hell is he?"

"Huh?" yells one of the deck guys, and then, in an act worthy of Yosemite Sam's dumber brother, he scampers down the steps too. Blammo. Just as the first guy is yelling, "Hey, watch out for the—," guy number two trips on the line and splashes into the goo, swearing his head off.

Amazing. A twofer. Now only one bozo remains topside. Peering out from under the tarp, I see he's a tallish dude. He is hovering near the hatch, looking down.

He's wearing a slicker. The color? Davy's Grey.

This is my chance. I've always wondered: if I needed to attack someone in cold blood to save my own skin or someone else's, could I do it? Time to find out.

I spring from beneath the tarp and charge across the deck, keeping my footfalls soft.

Just as Davy Grey reacts to the movement behind him, I hit the brakes and grab him by the neck, using the same chokehold that was used on me not long ago.

"Don't move." I place the point of the knife against his bearded cheek. "And don't make a sound." I step sideways, dragging him with me toward the open hatch. The boat is still rocking and rolling to a lively backbeat. Using my foot, I flip the bulky hatch closed, then drag the guy on top of the hatch cover with me, trapping the other two guys below.

Success. As of this moment, I have control over all three of these clowns. Aren't I awesome? Right. Well, I won't be able to maintain status quo for long. Law of entropy and all.

"Stand right there or I will stab you," I instruct the bearded guy. He nods, and I release him just long enough for me to dash over to a coiled chain nearby. Holding the knife in my teeth, I quickly drag the heavy coil onto the hatch. That should hold the men below, temporarily.

Wielding the knife again, I whip my attention back to Davy Grey. It's only now I get a good look at his face for the first time. His recently grown beard was throwing me off. It has more white in it than I'd have expected, but still the man is irritatingly handsome.

"Hello there, Cliff. Long time no see."

"Not long enough," he replies, flashing me a grin that somehow comes off as both shit-eating and menacing.

"You and I are going to chill for a while and shoot the breeze," I tell him. "So, I want you to walk over to the deck rail and sit with your back against that post."

"What if I'm not in the mood?"

"I WILL CUT YOUR FACE OFF!" I lunge at him with the knife, eyes wide and teeth bared.

He shoots his hands up in surrender, his face draining of color. Sometimes good ol' crazy is the only way to get a person's attention. He turns and marches docilely to the rail, as his buddies yell from the hold and pound against the hatch. The weight of the chain coil is holding them below, but not for long.

Cliff sits on the deck, facing me, as instructed. I order him to join his hands behind the post; he complies. I put the knife in my teeth again, and he permits me to reach through the rail and bind his hands together with a bungee. Next, I bungee his feet and legs together, then I wrap a couple of big cords around his torso and the rail post. He's not going anywhere.

Now: what to do about his buddies? I *could* pile more weight on the hatch cover and keep them trapped below deck, but I feel an urge to confront them all together, to get to the bottom of this thing once and for all. I crab-scuttle over to the hatch, drag the chain coil off it, then scuttle back to Cliff. Holding the knife against his neck, I wait till one of his buddies throws the hatch open and starts to emerge. He's a wiry guy with zero body fat who looks like he's spent a lifetime running around on fishing boats. He's painted head-to-toe with bloody water.

"I'm going to kill your friend," I say calmly while Wiry Guy is still on the steps. "Unless you do exactly what I tell you. ...Step out of the hatch."

He looks at us, wide-eyed and frozen. Cliff snaps, "Do what he says," and Wiry Guy complies.

I order the third guy out of the hold the same way. He's a gym-jacked dude who is probably Chokehold—and might be Goslin himself. Holding the knife-point against Cliff's neck, I order Wiry Guy to bungee Gym Bob to the railing post beside Cliff's. Both men cooperate. Next, I bungee Wiry Guy to the succeeding post.

Done.

Three little pirates all in a row, two of them wet and foul-smelling. I can't believe I've managed to pull this off. *Now what the hell do I do?*

Seizing a four-foot gaff hook from the wall to give me some added reach and authority, I march back and forth in front of my three prisoners, all tied helplessly to rail posts.

"So, who wants to start?" I say cheerily. "Okay, I'll go. You guys have been having some rip-roarin' fun at my expense, haven't you? Well, now it's my turn." Deliberately parroting the words Trooper Dan used in my kitchen, I say, "The way we work is this: I ask questions, you answer them without a moment's hesitation. Thus, you avoid the gaff. Are we clear on that?"

Moving the huge, needle-sharp hook back and forth between Gym Bob's and Wiry Guy's eyes, I say, "Which of you is Edgar Goslin?"

In their eyes I see only blank confusion.

I march over to Cliff and press the tip of the hook sideways against his neck.

"Which of these guys is Goslin?"

"What the hell are you talking about?" Cliff replies. Still with the cocky bit.

"I know Edgar Goslin is here on Musqasset," I tell him evenly. "And I know you're working together. If he's not one of these two morons, he must be the one I saw you with yesterday at the maintenance garage."

"Ronnie Milloy? The road guy? He works for the town. I was just borrowing his truck. I think you know why."

"Then which one of these losers was the owner of a 1987 El Camino that got a hole punched through its windshield by a scotch bottle eighteen years ago?"

Cliff rolls his eyes. "I *heard* you went off the deep end. Guess the rumors were true."

Boy, do I want an excuse to rip a blowhole in this guy's throat. "Don't even bother denying it, Cliff."

I march into the wheelhouse and grab the envelope I found in his catchall basket (and my wallet along with it). With the flair of a movie lawyer doing his big reveal, I whip out the news articles about the highway accident and dangle them in front of Cliff.

He does not break down and blurt out a courtroom confession. Instead, he laughs. "That? You think all this is about *that*?"

"You're going to claim it isn't?"

Cliff shakes his head as if in pity. "Jeannie told me you were the smartest guy she ever knew. Guess she didn't get around much." He pauses to reconsider his words. "Although you and me both know *that* ain't true."

I almost punch his clown-sphincter face. "I'm running out of patience here, Cliff. I know Jeannie told you about me and this car accident."

"So what if she did? You think *these* guys give a shit about that?" He tosses his head toward his compadres.

"Well, given that they tried to kill me in my own home," I say, my voice tightening, "and went to great lengths to write a convincing suicide note in which I confessed to the crime, then yeah, I'd say they give a LITTLE BIT OF A SHIT."

Wide-eyed, he backs into the steel post he's tied to. "Jesus," he says. It's not the "Jesus" of a man who's thinking, *Dang, I've been caught red-handed*, it's the "Jesus" of a man who realizes he's dealing with a truly unbalanced individual.

"Are you seriously going to tell me," I ask him, "that you don't know about what happened in my house in Wentworth?"

He looks me fully in the eye. "I. Have. No. Idea. What-you-are-talking-about."

Either he's a better actor than he has the brains to be or he's telling the truth. "Goslin didn't tell you?"

"WHO THE HELL IS GOSLIN?"

"Don't act like you don't know! I'm holding the evidence right in your face." I read aloud a sentence from one of the news articles in which Goslin's name is mentioned.

Cliff sighs and lets his head slump. "I didn't remember that was the guy's name," he says at last. "Honest. I barely even read those stories."

"Then why are you carrying them around on your boat?"

"A little added insurance, that's all. To make sure you got the message."

"Message?"

"The reason you're here on this boat, jagoff."

"Which is...?"

"Maybe I should let your friends explain that. No, not these guys here—your *old* friends. They'll be here any minute."

"Oh, right. The cavalry is on its way."

"Believe me, don't believe me, I don't care. But they'll be here. High noon. The appointed time of your sentencing."

"My sentencing?" I'm barely able to stifle a laugh. This guy has a flair for cheesy drama. "My *sentencing*?"

He looks at the deck for a long count, then raises his head with a sneer. "Fishermen's Court, asshole."

CHAPTER 33

*F*ishermen's Court is more than the name of the street
I once lived on.

If you've dwelt for a time on Musqasset—or certain other islands off the Maine coast where there is no
resident police force—you may have heard whispers of an
entity that goes by the same name. Fishermen's Court.
What is it? One learns not to ask.

A trawler captain finds his net cut to ribbons one
morning.

A lobsterman discovers that sugar in his gas tank has
ruined his boat's engine.

A heedless clammer gets his teeth knocked in after
leaving the Anchor one night.

In coffee joints and bars 'round the island, heads
nod darkly and someone mutters, "Fishermen's Court."
Conversation over.

There is a code of honor in Maine's seafood procure-
ment trades. You don't pull up someone else's trap. You
don't encroach on someone else's grounds. You don't
mess with another fisherman's livelihood. If you do so on
Musqasset, you will find your luck running thin. The pun-
ishments doled out are not usually lethal—though there

was a killing on Matinicus Island a few years back that made all the papers—but neither are they slaps on the wrist.

Fishermen's Court aims to send unambiguous messages.

But the first rule of Fishermen's Court is the first rule of Fight Club. Best not to chit-chat about it. Most people, in fact, believe it's just an island myth, a poetic way of saying fishermen watch out for one another; an eye for an eye.

But the old-timers and insiders aren't practitioners of poetry.

✶✶✶

"I don't see anyone else here but you and your nasty-smelling friends," I say to Cliff. "So why don't you explain what you're talking about."

"Not my place to say."

I drop the gaff and pull out the knife again. "*Make* it your place to say. What did you mean about Fishermen's Court?"

He beams defiance at me. "All you had to do was stay off the island. That's all you had to do. There wouldn't have *been* any more punishment."

"Punishment? For what?"

"The Court heard your case four years ago, asshole. And found you guilty."

"And what was my crime, exactly?"

"Treason," he says, without a hint of irony. "We were ready to give you your sentence at the time, but you skipped town. We figured you musta got wind of what was coming your way and took off. Fine, we said, let him go. That was all we wanted anyway." He thrusts his red-dened face at me. "But you had to come back, didn't you? *Didn't* you?"

The snarl of a boat engine carries in on the wind. Looking out toward shore, I see two small craft chugging in our direction. I get the sense that Cliff is telling the truth and that the approaching boats contain the other members of my tribunal.

"So now what?" I ask. The walls are closing in. "Now I'm supposed to receive my deferred sentencing and punishment? Let me take a wild guess: death by execution at sea."

Cliff says nothing. Which makes me believe my guess is correct. "Is that it, Cliff? Execution?" No answer. I lay the knife blade against his bearded cheek, unintention-ally drawing blood. Weird how comfortable I've become playing the demented heavy. "Are you guys planning to kill me? Answer!"

"What kind of psychos do you think we are?" he snaps back. "You *got* most of your punishment already. All we wanted to do was throw a scare in you for a couple of days, rough you up a little, break you down in the hold. Then, at the end, give you the fishermen's farewell."

"What the hell is that?"

"You know damn well what it is. Shit, maybe you don't. Each member of the Court gets a minute alone with you, to do whatever we want, short of killin' you— punch you in the gut, spit in your face, speak our piece.

Then we haul your ass back to the mainland and toss you out near Pemaquid Point. The end."

"And these?" I wave the printouts, still in my hand. "How do you explain these?"

"Those?" He coughs out a laugh. "Those were just a send-off, from me to you. A little reminder, so in case you were ever tempted to drag your sorry ass back to Musqasset or talk to anyone about what happened on this boat today, you would know *I* had something *I* could talk about too. And yeah, that something came to me courtesy of Jean Eileen Gallagher."

I don't think Cliff is capable of making this stuff up. The two small boats are drawing near, and they don't look like a Coast Guard rescue team, that's for sure.

"Can I ask you one last question, Cliff?" The macho has drained out of me.

He shrugs in a slap-worthy way.

"What were you and Jeannie talking about yesterday morning? Out behind that trap pile?"

He shakes his head, doing a world-weary bit. "You and me, pal, we're members of the same sad club. The Jeannie Left-Behinds. Miss Jeannie G., she's got a... situation goin' on, but it ain't with me, and it ain't what you think. One thing I can tell you, though—you got a world of hurt comin' your way."

Yeah, I'm starting to get that impression.

When the small boats draw up alongside Cliff's trawler, my heart deflates—more with sadness than fear. There are seven guys aboard the two vessels, and I know all of them: Billy Staves, my old Scrabble buddy; Matt and Mike, two of the three Bourbon triplets; Gerry Harper, husband of Ginny and frequent guest at my Musqasset home; and three other lobstermen/fishermen I shared an occasional table with at the Anchor.

As I stand at the rail looking down at them, a lump forms in my throat. When I'm sure I can talk without my voice cracking, I say to the small crowd, "I'm afraid Captain Kangaroo's Court has been canceled, folks. You'll have to take your lanterns and pitchforks elsewhere." I signal for Cliff to swivel his head so they can see his face, then I point the knife at him. "If anyone tries to board this boat, I will shove this knife into your friend's neck."

Seconds pass in silence.

"Like the one you shoved in us?" says Billy Staves with stone eyes.

"What are you talking about, Billy?"

I look out at the septet of men glaring at me from the boats. Their faces vary in age, race, and ethnicity, but they bear a single countenance: cold Yankee rectitude.

"Can someone please tell me what's going on?" I ask. "Because I don't get it. What did I do that was so unforgivable? Yes, I brought Miles Sutcliffe to the island. *Mea* fricking *culpa*. Yes, I asked you to break bread with him. That was a huge mistake. I know that now, but that's all it was: a *mistake*. I didn't mean harm to any of you. I think you know that."

My words are met with arctic silence. "I had no idea he was going to kill Fish Pier," I continue. "I tried to stop him. In fact, I tried to *help you fight him*."

"Oh, right," says Matt Bourbon. "That's rich, Finn."

"What? You know I did, Matt. Once Fish Pier was put on the chopping block, I started fighting the whole project. That letter-writing campaign was *my* idea. Or have you forgotten that? *I* was the one who proposed it and convinced you all to try it. *I* was the one who put a friendship on the line for it."

A few of the boat riders look at one another bemused. "I wouldn't brag about it if I were you," says Billy.

"I never promised you it would work. I just thought it was worth a try."

"So did we," says a lobsterman named Jean-Claude. "That's why we humbled ourselves to a bunch of money-grubbin' suits. Because you told us to. Because we trusted you."

"And I did everything I said I would."

"Like hell you did!" thunders Billy. "You blew town. You slunk off like a weasel when the henhouse light comes on. And we all know what happened next."

"No, we don't, Billy. *I* don't, that's for sure."

As I stare into the simmering eyes of those men across the short breach of water between us, I feel I'm staring across a vast gulf of understanding. Where does the disconnect lie?

✶✶✶

In the final days of my Musqasset tenancy, Miles's marina/ yacht club project was morphing into something unrecognizable. Miles had overcome many of the islanders' objections to the project by showing them what a boon it would be for Fish Pier and for all of Musqasset. Once the town had fallen in love with the idea of having its own police and fire department, a new schoolhouse, a tax surplus, and, oh yeah, a huge increase in the flow of retail dollars, the bait-and-switch started. Miles, speaking for his mainland partners, began to present amendments to the plan. The most drastic of these involved the scrapping of Fish Pier for a more "revenue-positive" idea.

At the town meeting when that amendment was presented, a hue and cry went up—mainly from the fishermen and artists. But you could feel the tide had already turned. The number of residents in favor of the new commercial development—no matter what changes it entailed—now far outweighed those who opposed it. There was still a vote to be taken, a few weeks hence, but we all knew how the vote would go.

The fishermen and their friends gathered at The Rusty Anchor to commiserate. Bo Baines, the guy who ran the Seafood Exchange, stood up on a chair, drunk, and shouted a bitter toast: "Fish Pier's dead! Long live the Mall of Musqasset!"

Saul Guptill chimed in, "Aye, there's nothin' can be done about it now."

Or was there? I was sitting alone in a corner of the bar, stewing. About Miles, to be specific. Did I fully trust him? During the whole proposal period, he alone had served as representative for his mainland partners. All information going back and forth between the island and the development group had traveled through him. Whenever I spoke to him, he would assure me he was fighting tooth and nail against his partners to preserve Fish Pier. But...

But what if that weren't true? *Maybe it was the Tullamore Dew talking, but I started to think maybe Miles wasn't fighting quite as hard for Fish Pier as he claimed to be. Maybe he wasn't presenting the full picture to his partners, or to us.*

I didn't want to voice my doubts to the fishermen; they were already mad enough at me for bringing Miles to the island. But I did stand up and say, "Listen to me for a minute, folks." *The place went quiet.* "These people—Miles Sutcliffe's partners—are human beings. Right?"

"Citation needed," *slurred Billy Staves.*

"Maybe we need to put a* human *face on the pier,*" I said. *"Maybe if the developers knew a bit more about what Fish Pier meant to each of you—not just money-wise but in your* lives, *in your* blood..." *Okay, the Dew was definitely weighing in.* "Maybe if they knew what it stood for, to you and your families, living and dead... Maybe if they heard your personal stories, they might revive the plan that* preserves *the pier instead of scrapping it. So why don't we tell them? Why don't we write to them? All of us. Tell 'em our stories."*

No one spoke for several seconds. "What you're talking about sounds like begging," *said Emmet DuPry, one of the old-timers.*

"Aye," *echoed Saul Guptill.*

Drinking recommenced.

But over the next few weeks, I hammered away at the fishermen. I worked with each of them to get their memories down on paper. Billy Staves, Matt Bourbon, and others rounded up old photos of their parents and grandparents on Fish Pier and wrote down the old folks' stories as well. Dorna Caskie dug up a children's book she had written about Fish Pier. I even saw a tear on the face of old Gawk Larson, the hardest and proudest of the lobstermen, when he scratched down his tale of seeing his father on the pier's end one night, singing "The Bells of Aberdovy" to the mermaids.

The letter-writing project took on a life of its own and became bigger than a tactic. It became an almost museum-worthy testimonial not only to a beloved physical landmark but also to a fading way of life and set of values. People were invested in it. Maybe overly so.

I didn't claim any role in the letter "campaign," and I didn't want any credit for it. I didn't even tell Jeannie I was doing it (our communication had gone down the curved pipe by that time anyway). But I did promise that when the collection of letters was ready to be delivered, I would handle it.

One fog-shrouded evening, I asked Miles to join me for a drink at Pete's. "There's no easy way to say this," I told him, "so I'll just spit it out. Some of us—myself mainly, but others too—are starting to have questions about the way you're presenting this development deal. On both sides of the water. We feel there are... aspects of the situation that maybe your partners aren't aware of. Because you're not telling them. The fishermen have written some personal letters about the pier, and we'd like to get them to your partners. We need you to deliver them."

Miles glowered as if I'd slapped him.

"If this is the last thing I ever ask of you, Miles, so be it. But I am asking this."

His face turned steamed-lobster red. "How DARE you question my word and try to do an end run around me," he said. "What gives you the RIGHT?"

"What gives you the right to deceive these fishermen, Miles? These people are my neighbors and friends."

"Is that so, Mr. Local Hero, savior of the ancient ways no one gives a crap about?"

"You *don't give a crap, that's for sure. You* never *intended to preserve Fish Pier, did you? You've been posturing about it since the get-go. Your plan since day one has been to—*"

"Oh, and what suddenly qualifies Finnian Carroll to analyze high-level real estate deals? Who promoted you from part-time bartender to grownup?"

"Gee, skip the foreplay and go right for the power tools."

"You like that, don't you? You love playing the poor martyr who gets screwed by The Man."

"And you love playing the pied piper who leads the happy lemmings off a cliff. You're so arrogant it doesn't even cross your mind that the 'lemmings' can see right through your lies."

"Oh yeah? Well, here's one for you, Finn: I really respect your opinion on this matter."

I rose from my seat and almost punched him. Things went downhill from there, each of us trying to wound the other with words—and very nearly with more than words.

Finally, after we both calmed a bit, he said, "If you absolutely insist on my doing this, Finnian, I will do it, I will deliver the letters. And I will suffer the blowback. But know one thing: *if you ask this of me, you are putting our friendship on the waiver wire.*"

"*You already* put *our friendship on the waiver wire. So many times, I've lost count.*" *I stood up from the table, handed him the folder bulging with papers, and said, "Deliver the package, Miles," then walked out. It was the last time Miles and I spoke before I left the island a few days later.*

★★★

And now as I face my accusers from the deck of Cliff's fishing boat, an inkling begins to arise as to the source of their anger. "So, tell me what happened," I say. "Give me the benefit of the doubt and pretend I don't know. Because I don't. I really don't."

"The next town meeting," says Jean-Claude, "when the vote was due, a bunch of your buddy-pal's golf-shirt-wearin' partners and lawyers showed up. Guess they wanted to be there when the deal went down. They started barreling ahead with the vote like nothing had changed, and Billy here stood up and asked the head one, the president guy, 'Sir, did you give our letters any thought?' Guy was like, 'What letters?'"

CHAPTER 34

"The worst part," says Jean-Claude, "was the guy turned out to be a decent fella. Said he wished he'd-a seen the letters, that he woulda took 'em into consideration."

"Bottom line," says Billy, "it was too late to make changes to the development plan by that time. The vote was held, and it passed. And now there's a freakin' cheese boutique where my boat used to dock. Bo Baines went out of business, and the hub fell out of our operation. Now we're all fending for ourselves, those that are still left. Anchoring out in the harbor, selling our catch on the mainland, working till dark every night, scraping by."

"I'm sorry, Billy," I say. "I never meant for this to happen." And now my voice does crack, and there's nothing I can do about it. "I cared about you. All of you guys. That's the only reason I got involved in the whole thing in the first place. I had nothing to gain from it."

"So say you," says Billy.

"Don't!" I snap at him, feeling my face burn. "Don't you dare suggest I got some kind of payback from this. If anyone wants to accuse me of that, you step up here on this deck and say it right to my face."

None of the men move, except with the rolling of the waves. For the first time, uncertainty registers on some of their faces.

"Here's the truth about Fish Pier that no one wants to remember," I say. "I loved the thing—painted it a dozen times—but it was a catastrophe. It was falling apart and sinking into the seabed. And all you guys used to do was bitch about it. Walk into Pete's or Mary's any time of the day and that's all you'd hear. People bitching about the pier—fighting over it, taking sides—but no one doing a damn thing. Yes, I put the bug in Miles Sutcliffe's ear about it. And when he came out with his first plan, the one that included money to rehab Fish Pier, I was all in. It wasn't a perfect plan, but it was going to help you guys, and that's all I wanted. And that's the honest truth."

It *is* the honest truth, so I'm pretty sure it rings that way to the men. But still they stare at me as if they've brought a noose along.

"I'm not a born islander," I go on. "I know that will always make me suspect in some of your eyes. But I actually *chose* this place. You know why? Because it's a working island, not some tourist trap from the cover of *Yankee* magazine. People just muck in together and get things done. I loved that, and I wanted to be part of it. Who was it that helped you put up your traps every winter, Billy? Who was it that sanded down your boat with you, Gerry, and helped you get your paintings in a gallery, Mike? Every time there was a trail that needed clearing or a fundraiser for the school, who was in there working elbow to elbow with you guys?"

"He did muck in a lot, give him that," says Billy to his peers.

"And no one questioned my loyalty then. But the first time something goes a little wonky, you're all ready to walk me from the nearest plank." Shame flashes in some of their eyes. "*Someone* lied to you about those letters, that's for sure. Maybe it was the president of the development group, maybe it was Miles Sutcliffe—or yeah, maybe it *was* me, but why would you assume that? Why wouldn't you give me the benefit of the doubt?"

"We got our reasons," tied-up Cliff replies.

"I busted my nuts to get you guys off your apathetic asses and write those letters. Why would I do that just to sell you out?"

"Payola," says Jean-Claude, but he says it at half-volume.

"Oh, right. Who believes that? Who really believes that? Come on, raise your hands." No hands go up. "The bunch of you make me sick."

Suddenly it's as if *I've* become Fishermen's Court and the fishermen have become the accused. The shift is palpable. It's Mike Bourbon who finally speaks to the others. "He's got a point. We should have talked to him first. Heard him out. We owed him that. We shouldn't have jumped to... *this*. I'm out."

No one says a word. Guilty silence reigns.

I untie Cliff and his two buddies, no longer fearing they will harm me—at least not here and now. "Which one of you has my phone?" I ask. Gym Bob hands it to me.

I climb over the deck rail and down the ladder into the metal boat that brought me here. Facing my accusers one last time, I say, "I find *you* all guilty of treason."

I start the engine. "I'm taking this boat. I'll leave it at the Greyhook launch."

I motor off toward the island. No one follows me.

The seas have calmed a bit. The storm is finally moving away.

✦✦✦

I haven't checked my phone since before my carnival-o'-laughs in the boat hold. Miles must be wondering what the hell happened to me. I'm so anxious to see my messages, the phone feels physically warm in my pocket, but right now my hands are full, operating this vessel. I'll check my phone as soon as I'm on terra firma.

I'm able to do some thinking as the boat putters along, though. It's only now that I start to untangle the Cliff-Goslin situation. I still find it mind-boggling that Cliff and Goslin aren't connected to each other. The idea that there have indeed been two separate parties trailing me is a preposterous notion I rejected early on. And yet Cliff seems to have been telling the truth. He had nothing to do with the forced suicide attempt at my parents' house. And he didn't follow me out to Musqasset. Those things were all Goslin.

The dead fish and the nighttime stalkings, those were Cliff and his buddies from Fishermen's Court. They had their own reason for pursuing me, which had nothing to do with some ancient highway accident. Cliff didn't care about that accident either, except to use it as ammo to keep me away from Musqasset. And from Jeannie.

Then what has Goslin been up to since he came to the island? Why hasn't he made any moves? Why has he been so quiet?

I wonder if Miles has taken any action on the Goslin front in my absence.

As soon as I've hauled the boat aground at the Greyhook landing, I dig out my warm phone. There are voicemails and missed calls from Miles, and texts from Preston Davis and Jeannie. I pull up Jeannie's message first. Considering what Cliff told me about her—and the warning she herself tried to give me—I open it with a dose of wariness.

Her text: *There's something I should have told you. About Cliff. He fell for me pretty hard back when he and I were... you know.* "Screwing on our Barcalounger," I mentally fill in. *It wasn't a casual thing for him. He was in love with me. Big-time. Still is. Won't let it go. Anyway, he's a pretty scary and super-insecure guy. (He must have asked me ten times how big your equipment was.)*

I have the urge to text her back, *How big was his?*

Just kidding.

Sort of.

After you left the island, her text goes on, *I got into badmouthing you with him. One night he filled me with my favorite truth serum. Patron Silver. And - I'm so sorry about this, Finn - I told him the whole story. About you, the bottle, the accident. Anyway, I think you ought to watch out for Cliff. He knows you're here and he might be trouble for you.*

Thanks, Jeannie. This information might have come in handy about three hours—or three days—ago. Our timing has always stunk. I am heartened to know, though, that she felt compelled to be honest with me and *try* to warn me.

Or maybe just she's covering her ass because she knows Cliff and I have already had our little *tete a tete.* Hmm.

There's one final chunk of text from her. It causes a hot flutter in my abdomen. *Last night was amazing, you jerk. Wish I could stop thinking about it.*

What Jeannie and I had last night was real. Right? I have to believe that, or truth no longer has a handhold.

The voicemails from Miles are of the worried type I was expecting: Where are you? Are you okay? What are we doing about Goslin? Call me, call me, call me.

I'll call him in a minute.

The text from Preston Davis is the one that sends my mind careening into crazyland for the ninetieth time this weekend: *Called the mainland office, asked about those passenger records. Edgar Goslin took one ferry trip to Musqasset, a little over two weeks ago. Stayed one night, then went back the next day. He's not on the island now. Hope that helps!*

Goslin, not on the island. What? So Goslin is *not* Trooper Dan or Chokehold—those guys definitely followed me out here; I recorded their voices. But Goslin's tied up in this thing for sure. My conversation with Priscilla Begley proves it. His trip to Musqasset proves it.

So where is Goslin now? Why has he gone below radar?

I'm about to call Miles, to share Preston's news with him, when my phone-finger freezes. Maybe it's because I've been revisiting all that Fish Pier drama—all the doubts I had about Miles back then, our confrontation—or maybe it's because I've learned those fishermen's letters never reached their intended recipients, but my trust in Miles is not at a high-water mark.

I'm wondering, in fact, if it's time to acknowledge the great blue whale that's been doing pushups in the middle of the room since this whole thing started: maybe Miles knows more about *everything* than he's been letting on.

My phone rings. Miles. I hesitate before picking up.

"Finn! Where the hell have you been? Are you okay? What happened?"

"There's a lot to tell."

"I want to hear all about it. But listen: Jim just dropped by. He learned something new about Edgar Goslin. You need to get over here."

"What about Beth? Won't she—"

"She's out. Having lunch with friends and doing some last-minute shopping. Her folks are coming in today."

"Today? But the ferry isn't running yet."

"They don't use the ferry," says Miles, a scoff in his voice. "Just get over here. Hurry."

"Goslin's dead," says Miles, meeting me at the door.

He turns and walks back inside, not commenting on my stained clothing, now air-dried.

Dazed, I follow him to his study, where he has two online newspaper articles open on his computer: "Missing Local Man Found Dead in Car" and "Police Find Week-Old Body in Car." Both articles were written yesterday.

The two articles report essentially the same facts. A car was found off Route 495 near the Wentworth-Bridgefield border in a densely wooded area. The driver, dead, was Edgar Goslin. His live-in girlfriend, Priscilla Begley, confirmed he went missing on August 22, nine days earlier, and had not been seen since. The vehicle evidently veered off the highway and remained hidden by foliage in a gully for over a week. Goslin, who was on blood-thinning medication, died of blood loss from a traumatic wound, the result of an apparent accident in his home workshop. Police believe he may have been driving himself to the hospital when he lost consciousness due to bleeding.

Miles stares at me wordlessly. I look at the date again. My stomach sours.

Goslin died on August 22. The home invaders came to my house on August 23.

Goslin was dead before any of my troubles began.

CHAPTER 35

All my previous conceptions about how and why I was targeted for extinction by a group of unknown killers have flown out the window.

"Did Jim have any inside information?" I ask Miles. "On Goslin's death?"

"As a matter of fact, he did. There were some details the cops didn't release because they're still investigating."

"And...?"

"Well, like the papers said, they think Goslin injured himself in the workshop behind his house. Priscilla Begley never looked in there, but when the cops checked it out, they found blood all over a worktable and an electric hedge cutter he was apparently trying to fix. They think the machine turned on unexpectedly."

"Yikes."

"Yeah. They found two of his fingers in the car."

My skin flushes hot as a couple of mental gears clink together almost audibly.

"They think he tried to call 911, but his phone was dead," Miles continues. "So he panicked, jumped in his car, carrying his fingers, then passed out en route to the ER"

I'm not listening anymore. I've planted myself in front of Miles's computer and am frantically googling Goslin. The articles about his death do not show a photograph. I need to see a picture.

A picture, come on, a picture...

I google "obituary Edgar Goslin," and a link pops up to the Sullivan Funeral Home in Wentworth. I click it, and a memorial page for Goslin—newly posted—opens. In the center of the screen is a photo of the man himself. It's probably fifteen years out of date, but the face is unmistakable.

It's the man in Trooper Dan's video, the man whose fingers Troop removed with the lopper.

"Goslin didn't die by accident," I say to Miles.

"What?"

"He was murdered. By the same guys who tried to murder me. They cut his fingers off, bled him out." Recalling the plastic bag that was wrapped around Goslin's hand to catch his blood, I add, "They staged it to look like an accident. Guess they didn't want him found right away, so they moved his car to a hard-to-spot location, planted the body in it, spread his blood around the workshop and the car."

I have trouble interpreting the just-punched look on Miles's face. Is he stunned by the information I'm giving him or by how deeply delusional I am?

I need to be alone for a minute. To think. To process. I excuse myself to that timeless temple of self-reflection, the bathroom.

I'm shaking like I'm in a walk-in freezer as I perch on the throne with the lid down. If Goslin was not my attempted murderer, then who was? Gary Abelsen? He's an Alzheimer's patient in an assisted-living community. Who else would have the motive to take such extreme measures? And why the eighteen-year delay?

Suddenly the great blue whale that was doing push-ups in the middle of the room stands up on its tailfin and starts Riverdancing. The fundamental assumption on which all my reasoning has been based is that I am the one and only person who has direct knowledge of the lethal events that took place in my car on my graduation night, 1999.

What if that weren't true?

What if *two* of us remember what happened?

Since the moment I heard—or *thought* I heard—crashing sounds on Carlisle Road on that blighted drive, I have unquestioningly believed that Miles passed out cold after tossing the bottle. And that he had no idea he threw it off the wrong bridge. After all, I had to take him to the damn ER. And no one could fake unconsciousness well enough to fool an ER staff. Right?

But then I realize—with a hollow laugh—that I myself, only nine days ago, played possum convincingly enough to fool a team of professional killers.

What if—my mind doesn't even want to go there—Miles *was* just faking? What if he heard the crashing sounds too? What if he knew full well what he did and just didn't want to deal with it? What if he left me to make the moral call and hold the moral bag, knowing, quite correctly, that I would latch onto it with a death grip?

Miles was an ambitious guy, even back in college, and highly protective of his blue-blood, Teflon-man image. Even back then, he figured someday he'd be living a big life in the public eye. In fact, I believe the reason he married Beth was that he saw her as his ticket to the show. Her family had money, his family had a Yankee pedigree. Together they could go to the moon and stars. But not if scandal derailed the dream.

What if Miles has always known people died at his hands that night? What if, for years, some part of him has been dreading the day the truth comes clawing out of the ground like a body buried alive in a horror movie? And what if emergent circumstances in his life—such as, oh, I don't know, winning a fast-track ticket to the U.S. Senate and beyond—were suddenly demanding he rid his closets of old skeletons, pronto?

And *if*, let's just say *if*, Miles wanted to clean up this *particular* closet, who would need to be permanently silenced? Who but the one person on Earth who knows exactly what happened in that car? Finnian T. Carroll at your service. And death by apparent suicide, with a signed confession to boot, would be the ideal way to dispense with said Mr. Carroll.

I think about the careful wording of "my" suicide note: *"Late in the evening, a close friend and I went outside to share a goodbye toast in private. Somehow, we'd gotten our hands on an expensive bottle of Glenmalloch single malt scotch. We passed it back and forth…"*

Why alter the fact that the bottle was a gift from me? Answer: because if my unnamed "close friend" had been the recipient of the gift (which he was), then *he* would have logically ended up with the bottle (which he did), not I. No good. Then why mention the friend at all, and why say we passed the bottle back and forth? Answer: in case Miles's fingerprints ever do get matched to the shards. That is still a possibility; the cops took prints from the glass, and those prints are still in the system. And if Miles's fingerprints were suddenly to be entered into the database—say, because he just joined the U.S. Senate and had to be fingerprinted for the federal job—a belated match might pop up. The mention in the note that my "friend" and I both handled the bottle offers a tidy explanation as to how his prints got on the glass, while still leaving me as the guilty party.

Hmm, in this scenario, who else would need to die? Answer: the only other person who seems to know something about what really happened that night— Edgar Goslin.

Maybe Goslin figured out somehow that Miles was in the car with me that night. Maybe—oh, crap—maybe he learned it from my own father. I know the two of them talked, Goslin and my dad. That's right! And my dad knew Miles was with me that night: *he bought me the scotch as a* gift *for Miles*. Maybe that's why Goslin came to Musqasset. To talk to Miles.

To blackmail him.

And maybe that's why Goslin is dead.

Damn. Once I get past my resistance to that single inconvenient idea—that Miles knows he killed those people that night—the dominoes just start toppling.

Whoa there, though, Jumpy Jumpington. Slow down. There's one major kink in this line of reasoning. That is, it hangs on a premise I simply cannot bring myself to believe—that Miles would be willing to kill me. That does not ring a true chord in my gut. Flawed as Miles is, I know he loves me. In fact, I believe he loves me more than he loves any other person alive, except maybe his children.

He knows I love him, too, as no one else does. And he *needs* that love. In fact, he gets something from me that goes even beyond love. I think, on some level, I give Miles his center. A big chunk of it anyway. Deep down, I don't think he knows who he is without me to reflect and affirm him. To kill me would be a terrifying act of self-annihilation, and that is something I *truly* don't think Miles is capable of.

And yet, the facts are pointing to him in a way you'd have to be insane to ignore.

An idea occurs to me. A possible way to put Miles to the test.

In light of the fact that Goslin was the man in Troop's video, there's one other person who might be involved in all of this. It's a name that's branded on my brain cells but that I have never spoken aloud. If I say the name to Miles and his eyes betray recognition, that would go a long way to telling me Miles is indeed hip-deep in this thing.

I exit the bathroom and return to the study.

Miles is waiting for me, arms folded, the photo of Goslin still staring belligerently from the computer screen. He gives me the perfect opening by asking, "What did you mean about Goslin being killed by the same people who tried to kill you?"

I describe to him the video Trooper Dan showed me when I was strapped into the chair. "It was Goslin in that video," I say. "They asked him who else knew what he knew. He didn't answer, so they cut off two of his fingers. He started screaming a name over and over." I watch Miles's eyes carefully as I say it: "Clarence Woodcock."

Damned if I don't see a flinch in his eyes. He tries to cover it, but it's too late. He knows the name. And he's thrown by it.

★★★

Miles is pacing back and forth in the study. He wants me to believe he's thinking about the Goslin situation, but what he's really thinking about—I know Miles—is that name. Clarence Woodcock. It's eating at him. He looks at his watch in a phony way.

"Listen, I've got to make a couple of phone calls," he says. "It might take me ten or fifteen minutes. Help yourself to a beer or a sandwich. Don't go anywhere, though, okay?"

He sprints upstairs.

What is he up to? Should I be worried about my safety? Probably. But fear of imminent grievous harm is a state I have become oddly accustomed to.

I turn to the computer and, just for the hell of it, type "Clarence Woodcock, Wentworth" into the search engine.

The top result is a *Wentworth Tribune* piece, "Former Wentworth Police Detective Found Dead." It's dated August 23. My heart does a swan dive into my belly.

John Clarence Woodcock, Jr., 62, was found dead in his Wentworth home this morning. Cause of death is under investigation but may have been an accidental fall on a staircase. Police believe death occurred sometime between 12 a.m. and 10 a.m. on Thursday, August 22.

Woodcock, known to friends and associates by his middle name Clarence, served as a detective on the Wentworth police force from 1982 until 1996, when he resigned and started a private investigation business. A widower, Woodcock had lived alone in his home at 4 Boxford Terrace for the past twelve years. His body was discovered by his daughter, Melissa Rodak, 39, who went to the home to check on him when he failed to answer his phone several times.

No further information has been released at this time.

Maybe I'll take that beer after all. I go to the kitchen, pour a third of a Sam Adams down my throat, and bite into an apple. I wonder if my sister Angie knows anything about this Woodcock guy. I thumb her name on my phone. Again, the call seems to go through but then disconnects. A second try, then a third, yield the same result.

If I had half a brain, I would run out of the house this minute, try to call the Maine state police, tell them everything I know, and hide in the woods until they arrive. If Miles is involved in all this, as the evidence screams, then I don't have to worry about protecting him anymore. I can come clean about the entire mess.

But evidently I am *not* the proud owner of half a brain, because I sit back down at the computer and retrieve the results of my Sure Search inquiry on Goslin. There it is, the name John Woodcock, among Goslin's known associates. I can't believe I didn't notice it earlier; must have been the "John" that threw me off. (There's another name I also overlooked before—Theo Abelsen— but I don't have time to think about it now.)

Another round of googling reveals that Woodcock was a well-liked cop in his day and a community advocate for the disabled. However, he "resigned" from the police force under a cloud of suspicion. Seems he was under investigation for taking payoffs from known criminals.

The timing of his death leaves no doubt that he was part of the purge that included Goslin and was meant to include me as well. A huge development, obviously. I don't know whether to share it with Miles or keep it to myself. Good sense tells me to play this card close to the vest.

What is Miles doing right now? I take my shoes off and tiptoe toward the staircase leading to the second floor. Only the soft hum of a printer meets my ears. I ascend the carpeted stairs. The kids' bedrooms are still and empty. I approach the room next to the master bedroom, the one Beth uses as her office and exercise room. Miles is seated at Beth's desk, moving a mouse around and staring at her computer screen, his jaw hanging open.

The printer near the door is churning out pages.

I step into the room, expecting Miles to react in surprise or guilt, but he doesn't. I reach into the printer tray and glance at one of the pages. A printout of a bank statement.

"What is this?" I ask Miles, not really expecting an answer.

"Beth's trust fund," he says numbly.

Ah, the one to which she gained access when she turned 21—and which, of course, played no role in Miles's decision to marry her.

I look more closely at the printout in my hand, then pick up a couple more sheets from the tray. Printed on the pages is a long series of check images, going back to the year 2000. All the checks are made out to the same party:

John Clarence Woodcock Agency, LLC.

CHAPTER 36

"I don't usually look at her private banking stuff," says Miles defensively, as if Beth's privacy were my main concern at this point. "But once in a while, like when we're doing our taxes... I remembered seeing that name."

He looks into my eyes, and I can tell he's feeling deeply bewildered, deeply betrayed. I feel sad for my friend. Questions, momentous questions, must be asked of Beth.

Maybe sooner rather than later: the bell jingles on the back door downstairs. We look at each other in mute paralysis. Beth's voice calls out, "They're here! Their boat came in! No more laughing, no more fun!" A beat passes. "Miles...?"

Miles seems powerless to use his voice, and it's certainly not my place to answer for him. I expect him to shut off Beth's computer and dash out of her room, but he doesn't.

Beth starts up the stairs. "Did you hear me? They're here. My parents. They're anchored outside the harbor because of the storm, but they want to have dinner with... Miles?" She is in the upstairs hall now. Her voice drops in pitch: "Miles?" She pokes her head around the doorframe. "What are you doing in my room?" She steps fully into the doorway. "Finn! What are *you* doing here?"

When neither of us replies, she marches to the computer. "Miles, what the *shit*? Why are you looking at my personal bank accounts, and why is *he* here?"

Miles says in a surprisingly neutral voice, "Who is Clarence Woodcock?"

A shock-tremor jitters Beth's face, but she banishes it with a mask of righteousness. "My private bank accounts are none of your business!"

"Why have you been writing him checks since the year after we graduated from college?" Miles points to the printer tray. He's either forgotten I'm in the room or doesn't care.

Beth fixes Miles with one of the iciest glares I have ever seen issue from human eyes. "You and I will discuss this in private," she says.

"Actually, Beth, I think—"

She cuts him off. "IN. PRIVATE." She snaps off the final "t" as if cracking a bone over her knee.

Miles caves. "You better scoot along, Finn, I'll talk to you later."

"I don't think I'll be doing any scooting right now, Miles. I think this is—"

"Go! Now!" He looks ready to blow steam out his ears. "Beth and I will deal with this privately, and I will call you later!"

"No," I say, raising *my* voice a bit now. "You don't get to exclude me from this. Not when I'm the person whose neck is on the chopping block, and you two seem to know—"

"Finnian! *I* will handle Beth! That's final!"

"It's not your call. Beth is a grownup, and she and I have business to discuss."

"Are we finally going to do that, Finn?" she says.

Her tone is stark and devoid of clemency.

For a moment, I don't know what she means, but then a light comes on in a long-darkened chamber of my mind. Beth transforms, right before my eyes, into her twenty-one-year-old self, complete with U2 tee-shirt and ill-advised Winona Ryder pixie cut. The doorway framing her dissolves into a hospital entrance. I am seeing her on graduation night, 1999.

"That night, when I took Miles to the ER..." I say, pausing to allow the old memory fragments to piece themselves together.

After Miles was brought in on a gurney and I gave the medical staff the redacted version of what happened in the car, I went to use the bathroom. When I came out, Beth was already arriving on the scene. I couldn't figure out how she had shown up so quickly, but I was happy to be off the hook. I slipped out the exit and went home, leaving Beth to handle the details.

"...how did you get to the hospital so fast, Beth?"

"BECAUSE I WAS IN THE DAMN CAR!" She regards our dumbstruck faces. "Graduation night! I was there! Lying under a blanket in the back seat. You two didn't even notice me—but that's nothing new. I heard everything that happened."

She waits for the aftershocks to bounce around the room a few times, then says, "I need a drink."

She stomps out of the room and down the stairs. Miles and I look at each other in open terror and follow her down into the study. She plants herself behind the mini-bar and pulls out a bottle. Will it shock anyone to learn it is the Glenmalloch?

She pours herself a hearty two fingers, takes a sailor's swig, and says, in a somewhat calmer but shaky voice, "I had a lot to drink that night. Who didn't, right?" Leaning on the bar to steady herself, she seems resigned to an unburdening. Relieved, almost. She swirls the scotch in the glass, gazing into the little vortex as if it were an eyehole into the past.

"By eleven o'clock I was wiped and ready to go home. I couldn't find either of you, so I figured you were off doing... whatever it is you two do when you're together. Finn, you had promised to drive us home, so I went to your car and lay down in the back seat. I figured that was the only way to be sure I didn't miss you guys. I fell asleep, passed out, whatever." She takes another swallow. "When I woke up, the car was moving. We were on the road. You two were talking about something private. I didn't want you to think I was listening in, so I didn't say anything. And then the longer it went on, the longer I just pretended..." No need to finish.

My brain has been harpooned. Is it really possible a third person was with us the entire drive home that night? It's hard to believe we wouldn't have noticed. But then again, Miles wouldn't have noticed *anything*, the shape he was in. And I was so focused on dealing with *him*... And she *was* under a blanket, lying down, in the dark...

It's not hard to believe at all.

"When that business with the bottle happened," Beth says, "I heard everything. I had this terrible feeling in my stomach all night, and the first thing I did when I woke up the next morning was turn on the news. There it was, a story about a highway accident in Bridgefield. I threw up for forty-five minutes straight.

"When you finally woke up, Miles—*came to*, I should say—I asked you some questions about the night before, and you obviously didn't remember a thing. I had a decision to make: destroy the life we were building together before it even got started—destroy *all* our lives, really; our careers, our dreams—or just keep my mouth shut and pretend I wasn't there." She stares at the bar top. "The decision made itself... as they often do."

"So, all these years you've known those people died that night?" says her husband.

"Don't you dare get self-righteous with me, Miles. Don't you dare!"

Miles backs down. "How does Clarence Woodcock factor into this?"

"Just let me talk!" She takes another swig of the ol' country, refills her glass, and says, "I felt horrible about not coming forward. Horrible. What sucked the most was that I had to deal with the guilt by myself. Miles, you knew nothing. Finn, you had vanished from the planet. I tried to..." She pauses and spins her wedding ring around her finger. "We got married that summer, Miles, and I tried to be happy. And I was. Sort of. But I couldn't forget what happened. I watched the newspapers obsessively for follow-up stories—about the accident, about Edgar Goslin and his rehabilitation.

"One of Goslin's friends started a website to collect donations for his rehab and to help him get back on his feet. It was kind of a new idea back then—a fundraising website. This was in the pre-GoFundMe days. I started making some donations—pretty big ones—from my trust fund. I had just gotten signing authority on it, and I was feeling my oats. The account wasn't titled in my name, and I didn't think my donations could be traced to me personally. Or *would* be, I should say. Young and stupid, right?"

She drinks again. "Well, no good deed, blah, blah. One day when you weren't home, Miles—this was a year or so after graduation—there was a knock at our door, and two not-very-country-club-looking guys were standing there. One of them was leaning on a walker. They introduced themselves as Clarence Woodcock and Edgar Goslin. I almost peed my pants. How the shit did Edgar Goslin find me?

"Well, he told me how. He started to get suspicious about those donations, he said. He figured—not stupidly, I must say—that when someone gifts that much money to a stranger, they might have more than a casual interest in his case. Maybe they're trying to buy off some guilt. So, he hired a private investigator to look into it. Woodcock."

She moves to the window and looks out at the ocean, swirling her booze again as she tries to assemble the story pieces for us. Miles and I wait.

"This Woodcock guy—red-faced creepo—tells me he traced the donation funds to me through my trust account. And then he started looking into *us*. You and me, Miles. He found out where we lived, where we *used* to live, who our friends and family were. 'How's your cousin Iris?' he says. 'Did she ever get that cyst removed?' He had my attention.

"Anyway, he goes on to tell me he has friends on the police force, and they told him they found pieces of the bottle that caused the accident. I knew that from reading the papers, but then he tells me something I didn't know. It was a rare scotch, he says, and the cops were able to track down three local people who'd bought a bottle of it. 'And that was kinda curious,' he says, getting all TV-detective on me, 'because one of the buyers was a guy name a' Carroll. Whaddya know, same last name as your husband's best pal.' He taps his head like he's some kind of special genius. 'Well, Edgar and me paid a visit to this Mr. Carroll,' he says, 'and, knowing what we knew, we were able to... *encourage* him to part with some information he'd lied to the cops about: that the scotch was bought as a gift for one Miles Sutcliffe.'"

So, my dad *did* supply the link to Miles. Good lord, what did they do to him to pry that information out of him? No wonder he was so stressed about the whole thing.

Beth proceeds. "I'm on the edge of panic at this point, and Woodcock knows it. He says, 'So I was starting to get the picture on why you made the donations. If only I had proof.' And next he tells me something I'm not sure if it was true or he was just making it up. At the time, I believed him, but later…" She tosses her shoulder in a stagy shrug. "He said, 'The cops had already turned Edgar's car inside-out for evidence, but just for the hell of it, I asked Ed what clothes he was wearing the night of the accident. Well, turns out the hospital returned those clothes to him when he was discharged a few weeks after the accident. The clothes were ruined, but Edgar kept them for some reason, and damned if they weren't still in their Patient's Belongings bag.' Woodcock tells me that when he opened the bag, lo and behold, a piece of glass dropped out, a good-sized one. Bottle glass, not windshield glass. Must have been lodged in a shoe or a pocket. Woodcock knew what he had.

"When he examined the glass, he said, he found a clean fingerprint on it. And it didn't belong to Finn Carroll. But he was able to find a match… in *our recycling bin.*

"'I've looked into you and your husband,' he says. 'I know you got a big life planned for yourselves—charity galas and museum boards— and I know who your daddy is, Sweetheart. So, here's what we're going to do.' It wasn't a discussion. 'You're going to… engage my services as a security consultant,' he says. 'I'm not going to do any work for you, but you're going to pay me a monthly retainer, commensurate with the value of my silence. In perpetuity.' Goslin started to grumble about the payment arrangement, I remember. Woodcock explained to him that the payments had to be in his agency's name—Woodcock's—to make them appear as a legitimate business expense but that he would give Goslin his cut every month.

"In case you're ever tempted to change your mind about our... agreement,' Woodcock says to me, 'I'll just be holding onto this.' And he pulls out a little plastic bag with a piece of bottle glass in it. And he laughs this smug little heh-heh-heh, and then—the arrogant bastard—he wiggles his eyebrows like he's actually coming on to me."

Beth dumps the rest of the drink down her throat and looks at Miles and me defiantly. "That's who Clarence *Satan* Woodcock is."

Miles is seething, though he's trying to contain his rage. Oddly enough, his anger seems aimed in my direction more than Beth's.

"Let me get this straight," he says to Beth. "All these years, you've been making extortion payments to some thug, living in fear, and putting our family at risk because of something *Finn Carroll* did on a drunken night twenty years ago."

"Finn?" says Beth, looking at him strangely. Then she turns to me and says, "You seriously haven't told him? Jeez, you really *must* be in love with him."

"What are you talking about?" Miles asks.

She spins toward her husband again. "Finn didn't throw the bottle that night, Roger Clemens. *You* did."

CHAPTER 37

Miles's eyes practically leap from their sockets, and his throat convulses in a series of gags. A dog-whimper sound leaks out of him. This is the Miles who, when backed into a corner, dissolves into a blubbering child.

"*I* threw the bottle?" he says, his eyes caroming around the room as if someone might be watching us. "What are you saying? You're saying *I* threw the bottle? *I* threw the bottle?" His voice is moving rapidly up the pitch scale. "No! This can't be happening to me!" To *him*. Ah, Milesy. "This can't be happening! Not now!" He paces back and forth like a leopard in a zoo, pressing his head with the heels of his hands. "Oh my God. No, no, no, no, NOOOO!"

He wheels on me and Beth with wild eyes and says, in a voice an octave above normal, "You've known this all along. Both of you. Why didn't you tell me? Why didn't you TELL ME?"

"Because I knew you'd get like *this*!" snaps Beth. "I knew the worry would burrow into your brain like a parasite and eat away at you, day after day, year after year. And somewhere along the line you'd blow it—you'd blurt something out, just to relieve your anxiety."

"Nice to know how highly you regard me."

"People are what they are, Miles. I did you a huge favor. I took the decision out of your hands. Like I always do when we face a really hard choice."

"You had no right to take anything out of my hands! Either of you. How dare you withhold this from me? I had a right to know about my own actions. I had a right to know!"

"So you could *what*, Miles?" I say, steadying my voice to lend ballast to his tottering ship. "Stand up and do the right thing? Step forward and claim responsibility? You and I both know that never would have happened. We saved you from twenty years of mental anguish and bad decision-making."

"It wasn't your place to save me from anything!"

"When it comes to the tough calls, Miles," says Beth, "the really tough calls... Well, that's not really your area of strength, is it? That's why Daddy's always been... slow to move forward with you. That's why he hasn't put you on a faster track."

"Oh God, your dad," Miles says. His face pales. He moves into a weird internal space and resumes his caged-leopard pacing. "Why is this happening to me *now*? Why *now*? Why *now*?" He stares wide-eyed at the Persian carpet, but he's not really seeing it. "I'm screwed, I'm screwed, I'm totally screwed. I'm screwed, I'm screwed, I'm totally screwed." He flashes us a pressured smile, then repeats the words in a sing-song way. "I'm screwed, I'm screwed, I'm totally screwed." Astonishingly, he starts dancing to the rhythm of the words—a miniature Irish jig. It is a deeply unsettling thing to behold.

"Miles!" I shout, but he seems not to hear me at all. "Miles!"

"I'm screwed, I'm screwed, I'm totally screwed. I'm screwed, I'm screwed, I'm totally screwed."

"Miles!" I bark, as if trying to call off a dog. "Stop!"

"Get a bloody grip!" shrieks Beth.

"I'm screwed, I'm screwed, I'm totally screwed." He's saying the words through an awful amalgam of laughter and tears. I am witnessing, perhaps for the first time in my life, a person truly "in hysterics."

I call his name a few more times. No response. He keeps laugh-sobbing the words, "I'm screwed, I'm screwed, I'm totally screwed."

I don't know how to get through to him. My eyes land on the bottle of Glenmalloch.

"Miles!" I holler one last time, to no effect.

I seize the bottle and, in an act the fates have been trying to place in my hands for eighteen years, I throw the Glenmalloch. It strikes the stone fireplace, smashing into flying splinters.

The sound gets through to Miles where words could not. He goes deathly silent. He looks at me with a *Where am I?* expression.

"Get hold of yourself," I say in a harsh whisper. He nods vacantly. He takes a silent minute to put himself together mentally.

Beth waits till he appears to be back in business, then wails, "What is *wrong* with you?" as if he has been coming unglued just to irritate her.

"What's wrong?" Miles's tone is now incongruously light. "Your father is here, that's what's wrong. And I'm a dead man." He goes to the bar and takes out a new bottle of scotch, the plebeian blended stuff. He pours a glass, sits, and tries to relax. No dice. He springs to his feet and starts pacing again. Something unsaid is still on his mind.

"Beth's dad is the one who has the 'in' with the governor," he spills at last. "He's the one who's been touting me for this Senate opening."

Ah. Now I see why Miles has been so guarded with me about the big career move. As I've said, he doesn't like me to know how tight a net Simon Fischer has around him.

"But it's grown even bigger than that," he adds. "Last time I saw him... he, he explained to me that there were these... people, these very... *elite* people he was making inroads with. These people were interested in backing someone for a run for... well, Pennsylvania Strap-It-On Avenue. Ha!" Beth knows all this, presumably, so he's laying it out for my benefit. "He recommended *me* as their man and—surprise—they agreed I might have just the set of attributes they're looking for. If your dad could do his part and get me that Senate seat, they would start their machinery up the day I took office. I would never meet these people directly, but they would remain extremely active in 'clearing the road' to the White House for me. They were only interested in backing a solid winner, though—someone they could count on to go all the way and to never, ever let them down."

Miles turns and faces Beth. "So then he looked at me, your dad did, and said, 'Son, before I put your ass in that Senate seat, I'm going to ask you a question."

This is a part of the story Beth doesn't seem to know yet. "It may be the most important question you will ever answer. I don't care if your response is yes or no. I only care if it's the truth." Miles pauses for effect. "'Do you have any bodies in shallow graves I need to know about?' I told him no. He patted me on the knee and said, 'That's good, son.' Then he gave me the patented Simon Fischer death-stare and said, 'Because if I find out otherwise, the fires of hell will rain down on you.' And now—*now*—all this old stuff decides to surface," Miles blubbers. "Goslin turns up dead..."

"Dead?" says Beth. "What? When?"

Miles ignores her. "*That's* going to get some people asking questions. And this Woodcock sleazebag, you can bet *he's* going to come crawling out of the woodwork..."

"You don't have to worry about him," I say.

Miles and Beth look at me in surprise. "What do you mean?" asks Miles. "Why not?"

"Why don't you ask your wife?"

Beth draws her head back in a show of affrontedness. "What the hell are you talking about, Finn?"

"You're seriously going to act like you don't know?"

"Don't know what?"

"Come on, Beth. Okay, I'll play along," Watching her face for a reaction, I say, "Woodcock's dead too."

Beth's eyes go blank and her jaw drops. If she's play-acting again, she's pretty good at it. "How? When? How do you know?"

"Google," I reply. I count off the names on two fingers: "Woodcock... Goslin... The two men who have been blackmailing you for years, Beth. Both dead from 'accidents' within the same twenty-four-hour period. Kind of a mammoth coincidence, wouldn't you say?"

"I certainly would," Beth allows. "But this is as big a shock to me as—"

"Now throw in the fact that someone tried to off *me* at the same time, and I'd say that moves it from coincidence to monkey-randomly-typing-*Lord of the Rings*."

"Why are you looking at me like that?" Beth says to me. "Finn, get serious. You and I have had our differences over the years—I've *wanted* to kill you a few times, God knows—but there's no way in hell you seriously think I'm capable of...?"

"Two hours ago, I wouldn't have thought so, Beth. But now...? The three people who have the dirt on your husband get killed—or almost killed—the same day? And, just to tie it all up with a ribbon, one of them conveniently pens a suicide note in which he confesses to causing the old accident himself."

"Okay, that's enough," says Miles, as if coming out of a fog. "I don't like where you're going with this."

"I didn't ask you, Miles." I continue to press Beth: "And all of this comes at a time when your husband is about to be thrust into the public eye in a very big way. Just like you've always wanted."

Beth stammers, "That's just so.... That's just so..." Her eyes roll from side to side like an overwound cat clock's.

"*Someone* is responsible for these killings and attempted killings, Beth, and who else on the face of the planet—"

"*Alleged* attempted killings," she says. "Alleged. Alleged. By you."

"Oh, that's right, Beth. No one really tried to kill me; that's just paranoid delusion. I'm clinically insane. A locked-ward psychotic. Right? Too dangerous to be around the kids."

"I never said that!"

"Oh really?" I hold up my phone. That gets her attention. And Miles's. "The other day, when I went to buy that wine for Jim, I left my phone recorder running on the desk. It captured everything you said."

Beth's face blanches again. She can't argue with a recording. "You did just get out of a psychiatric hospital," she attempts, weakly.

"Right, Beth. Painting me as crazy is also a mighty handy way for you to discredit everything I have to say. That way, nothing can land on you."

"It was my idea to invite you to the island! If I felt threatened by what you had to say, why would I do that?"

"Maybe to finish the job that didn't get done in Wentworth."

Her head jolts from the blow of what I'm suggesting.

"I won't say what I really want to say to you right now, Finn. Because *words have power*. But I am done with you. After twenty years, I am so thoroughly done." She slams her glass down and storms out of the room.

"When was the last time you saw Edgar Goslin?" I shout after her. She keeps walking. I follow her out to the kitchen where she punches her arms through the sleeves of her windbreaker. "When was the last time?"

"Last time?" she snaps. "I only saw that asshole once. The day he came to our door, back in 2000." She zips up the jacket and steps into her Muck rain shoes.

"That's a lie, Beth. You expect me to believe you're totally clean here, but you keep lying to me, so why should I?"

"I don't care what you believe, you freakin' headcase. You and Miles can stay here all day, working on your conspiracy theories. I'm going to round up the children so they can see their grandparents. Here in the real world."

Beth exits, slamming the door.

I pull it open and shout after her, "I know Edgar Goslin came to Musqasset a couple of weeks ago."

"And Bigfoot was on the grassy knoll with the second shooter!"

"Are you gonna try to tell me Goslin didn't contact you at all?"

She doesn't try to tell me anything.

By the time Miles and I find our shoes and make it out the door to follow her, she is out of sight. Miles runs down the walkway. I'm right at his heels. He looks both ways on the road, doesn't see her. Neither of us says a word. It's as if we are under a spell of silence that can't be broken until we find Beth and wring the final truth out of her.

Miles runs to the backyard and through a gap in the hedges that leads to a neighboring property. He bounds up to their porch. A woman answers the door and shakes her head no.

Miles runs back to his house and jumps into his golf cart. I follow him and jump in too. Thinking Beth may have taken the trail to the marina, he drives around to the high knoll where he and I parked the other day. Beth isn't anywhere to be seen. Miles drives off, crackling with nervous energy.

He heads through The Meadows on its winding main road, checking out all the properties. We spot Dylan shooting hoops in a driveway, but no Beth. Miles turns onto the road to Lighthouse Hill and drives to the top. I jump out of the cart before it's fully stopped and run to the path leading down to Table Rock. Miles comes up behind me.

There she is. Down below. Standing on the edge of Table Rock, in the slippery moss and seaweed. No waves are washing over the vacant slab of slate—the tide is out, and the storm has weakened—but still... One slip of the foot or errant wave will wash her out to sea.

We scramble down the steep, rocky path toward her. "Beth!" shouts Miles. "Move back!"

She takes a step *forward* as if to toss herself into the ocean, but then she turns and regards us, almost like strangers. She looks back at the sea one last time, then slumps her shoulders and shuffles toward higher ground.

By the time we reach her, she is sitting on a dry rock, well above sea level.

In a voice barely louder than a whisper, she says, "Edgar Goslin and Clarence Woodcock came to our house two weeks ago."

Miles and I wait for more.

"I let them in. What choice did I have? I didn't ask for this responsibility."

"Tell us what happened, Beth," I say in the tone of a friend. "Please."

She looks out into the vague distance and lets the scene form in her mind. "They sat at our kitchen table. Woodcock said to me, 'It might surprise you to know, we read the papers.' He threw down a newspaper with one of those op-ed pieces—the ones Daddy paid to have written—suggesting that you"—Miles—"might be a great choice for that Senate seat if Aldridge stepped down. Then he said, 'Now that your husband's career is about to get a shot of testosterone, this might be a good time to renegotiate our terms.' And he slipped me a piece of paper with his new and improved 'fee' on it.

"He was expecting me to be meek and compliant. I guess he just picked the wrong day to throw his fat, sweaty weight around. Something came over me. Maybe it was the fact that I've had seventeen years to build up hatred for these guys. Paying their hush money every month, knowing they had the power to sink our future anytime they chose. God! I've been seeing that smug red face of his in my sleep my whole adult life!"

She stares, unseeing, into the harsh Atlantic.

"Long story short, I told Woodcock to go to hell. ...He didn't see *that* coming. He says, 'You're forgetting what I have sitting in a plastic bag in my office, lady."

"'I'm not forgetting,' I said. 'A stupid piece of glass.'

"'With your husband's fingerprint on it,' he says.

"'So you claim,' I tell him back.

"'Oh, lady,' Goslin pipes up, 'You do not want to test us on that.'

"For some reason—impulse, really—I decided to call his bluff. 'Yes, that's exactly what I want to do,' I said. 'I don't believe that glass is from the accident, and I don't believe you have my husband's real fingerprint. And I don't want to deal with you anymore until I have proof.'

"Woodcock gets all sputtery and says, 'Even if it wasn't real, which it is, I've got records of you making payoffs to me going back seventeen years. Deal with *that*.'

"'Records cut both ways,' I said. 'Extortion is a crime. Now get the hell out of my house and don't ever, ever come near my door again.'

"He stands up, gets in my face, and says, 'I better see that new fee show up on the fifteenth. Or dire consequences will follow. Dire.'

"'You'll be lucky to see the old fee,' I told him. And then..." She lowers her face into her hands—a bit melodramatically for my taste. "I wasn't planning to say it; it just came out. I said, 'If you ever do one thing to threaten me or my family again, I will send people to *your* home who will kill you, for real.'"

Miles and I wait, in frozen suspense, for the final shoe to drop. "Those were literally the last words I said to them before they left." She hangs her head as if finished.

Miles grants her a moment, then says, "So... what did you do next?"

"Do? I didn't *do* anything. I was bluffing. I don't know any 'people'; you know that. But those were the last words I said to two human beings before they turned up dead in *just the way I spoke*. Don't you think that means something?"

Means something? Yes, I thought it meant she was about to confess to the killings.

"Wait, wait, wait," I say, trying to wrap my head around what's going on here. "Are you actually saying— and I need your honest answer here, Beth, for once in our godforsaken lives—that you had nothing to do with the deaths of those men or with what happened to me?"

"Not directly. I didn't make a phone call or hire some hit men. But clearly, *words have power.* Look what happened to those men! They're both dead!"

What? You've got to be kidding me. She actually thinks she's cosmically guilty of killing these guys because she *wished it on them with her words.* And she says *I'm* the crazy one?

Given the facts that have come to light, it is almost impossible to believe she had nothing to do with Goslin's and Woodcock's deaths, but, looking at her drained face and sunken eyes, it is equally impossible to believe she is lying. I had no idea this woman was such a nutjob.

Beth stands up, and we all regard one another mutely.

My phone rings, nearly jolting me off the rock I'm standing on. The caller ID shows Pete Dooley, the proprietor of Pete's Lagoon. I step up to a higher rock to answer the call.

"Hey, Finn," says Pete, "JJ gave me your number. Have you seen Jeannie?"

"Not since this morning. Why?"

"She's gone. Disappeared. In the middle of her shift. Went out back to get a keg, and no one's seen her since."

CHAPTER 38

Miles flips me his golf-cart keys. I run up the steep trail and jump behind the wheel, pulling for breaths. I'm at Pete's Lagoon within minutes, praying Jeannie will have turned up.

Prayer denied. Pete is standing behind the bar in her place, ineptly drawing a pint of Guinness. "She's never done anything like this," he says. "All these years, never." *Until you showed up again* is the obvious subtext.

"Did she take her stuff with her?" I ask him.

He points to a shelf in a back area. Her rain jacket is folded there with her shoulder bag on top of it. It's a sight that scares my mind white.

"Has anyone checked the grounds, the bathrooms? She might have fallen and hurt herself."

"Franca took a look around. Anya too."

I charge off to do my own search of the place. Pete doesn't stop me. I check the bathrooms, the dark corners of the storeroom. I check Pete's office. A coat rack has been tipped over and the rug is rumpled. From someone else's search or…?

I run outside and check the pilings under the building, then the bushes and undergrowth around the restaurant. No Jean. No floating bodies visible in the bay.

Panic rises, and I have the impulse to run the length of the island screaming Jeannie's name. Before I can execute on that innovative strategy, it occurs to me to try the police again. Now that the storm has abated and the sea is settling, maybe our roving part-time officer can make it over from Monhegan.

I find the police number in my contacts list. The call goes through, or seems to. But then, just as with my calls to Angie, it disconnects as someone picks up. I try twice more. Same result. I try the state police too. No luck.

Bloody Musqasset cellphone service—an evil god with a mind of its own.

I've got to do something. I "speed" over to Jeannie's house in Miles's cart. I know she won't be there, but I need to check anyway.

Predictably, she does not answer her door. The raven sculpture in the garden still hides her spare key, though. I tear through the house, calling her name and looking in nonsensical places, like the fridge, even though her absence is obvious.

I jump back into the cart, drive around the corner to Studio Row, and run up and down the footpaths, knocking on doors, shouting in windows, asking everyone if they've seen Jeannie. No joy.

I floor it back to the village, wringing every watt of anemic horsepower from the electric cart. I need to talk to anyone and everyone who knows Jeannie. That includes my fisherman "friends." I start toward Billy Staves' place when Billy himself looms into view, standing on Island Ave, talking to Gerry Harper. I hate these two guys with a burning fever right now, but finding Jeannie is my sole concern.

I stop the cart and jump out. The men go silent.

"Jeannie's missing."

"Missing?" says Gerry. "How do you mean?"

I give them the seven-second version, and Gerry starts off, breaking into a jog. "I'll get some people together, we'll turn the town inside out," he calls as he goes. "Don't worry, man, we'll find her."

"Dennis and I will take the boat," says Billy. "Circle the island. See what we can see from offshore."

"Thanks, Billy." Words I never expected to escape my mouth again.

I run back toward Miles's cart. "Finn," shouts Billy from behind. "I need to say something to you. Real quick."

"Another time, Billy. After we find Jeannie."

"This'll only take a sec."

I stop to listen, but my mind is racing ahead to next steps.

"Mike Bourbon was right, out there today. We rushed to judgment. I'm sorry for that. You deserve your say. We owe you that. And I, for one, am ready to hear your side whenever you're ready to talk."

"That's mighty big of you, Billy." I don't have time for this conversation. "But if my friendship meant so little to you, I'm not sure I really *want* to win it back."

"Fair enough. Friends ought to be loyal. In that case, you might want to talk to your own friend."

"What do you mean?"

"I mean Miles Sutcliffe was the one who flipped us all against you." I'm itching to run, but instinct tells me I need to hear this. I lock eyes with my old Scrabble partner. What dazzling word combo is he about to play?

"We did trust you, Finn," Billy says. "We all figured it was Sutcliffe who deep-sixed those letters of ours. So, one night, a day or two after the vote, Fishermen's Court took him out on the pier to have a little 'heart to heart.' But when we questioned him, he swore blue-faced that he'd passed the letters on to his partners. One of the guys suggested we perform a 'buccaneer's baptism,' just to be sure. He and another fella tackled Sutcliffe and grabbed him by the ankles, like they were going to dunk him in the bay, and he started bawling like a five-year-old. 'Okay, it was Finn!' he says. 'I'm sorry! I was just trying to protect him. He's my friend! Don't hurt him!' He finally told us you never gave *him* the letters. The story he heard, says him, was that one of his development partners, the one who was in for the biggest wedge of the pie, got wind of your little campaign. He was afraid some of the other partners might be swayed by a bunch of sob stories, so he paid you off to lose the letters, leave the island, and never come back."

"*Miles told you this?*" My brain is ready to blow a valve.

"We practically had to beat it out of him, but yeah." He adds with a mildly sheepish note, "You did disappear from the island, Finn, and you didn't come back."

"I left the island because I broke up with Jeannie and because my mother was dying and needed care. I told you that. Why did you believe him over me?"

"Guess it was the *way* he told it, the way we had to wring it out of him, the way he begged us to spare *you*, not him. I mean, you'd have to be an Olympic gold-medal liar to play that the way he did."

"Yes, Billy," I say. "Yes, you would."

I run off.

✶✶✶

The story Billy just told me is gnawing at my belly like an ulcer, but I need to focus on Jeannie's safety. I'm trying to decide where to search for her next when a text comes in on my phone. From her!

They have me.

Blood pounds in my ears. I type, *Who has you? Where?*

The reply comes flying back: *Can't.*

I assume that means she can't answer right now, but I try anyway:

Jeannie, who has you? Where did they take you? No reply.

I type, *Jeannie?* and hit Send again.

I pace back and forth in the middle of Island Avenue, *willing* a reply to come in. Nothing.

Something feels wrong about Jeannie's texts, but I can't put my finger on it. I close my eyes and try to let it come to me. An image pops into my head. Jean's phone. Damn.

I run the stone's-throw distance back to Pete's, fling the door open, and race up to the bar. There it is, sitting in the outside pocket of Jeannie's purse: her phone in its kelly-green case. She doesn't have it with her. So how did those texts...?

I charge behind the bar and grab her phone. The Messages screen is open. Our most recent text exchange is on display. Wait, what?

"Pete, who's been back here?" I ask.

"No one but the ghost of Captain Bradish." An old bar yarn.

"You sure?"

"Oh wait, the Patriots were back here doing team sprints a while ago; I forgot. Hell yeah, I'm sure. I've been standing right here."

I consider taking Jeannie's phone with me but slip it back into her purse. I barrel full-speed out of the bar, bouncing off L.L.Bean dad as he's entering, almost knocking him off his feet. He looks at me as if I'm clinically insane. He might be on to something.

As I'm about to jump into Miles's cart, I freeze. I realize Pete, and Pete alone, had access to Jeannie's phone the whole time the text exchange was going on. I recall the disordered state of his office—signs of a struggle? I turn around and march back into the bar.

My phone pings another text. One word. From "Jeannie": *Help.*

Pete hasn't budged from his place at the register. Jeannie's phone hasn't moved either.

WTF? How could text messages be issuing from her phone without anyone typing them?

Have I mentioned I'm a giant freaking idiot?

The answer slams me in the head like a falling air conditioner. I recall the way my own phone has been misbehaving. Dropping calls in an odd way, feeling warm to the touch when I'm not actively using it, popping in and out of service at key moments. I've been chalking it all up to the Musqasset cellphone gods. But now: Jeannie's phone sending phantom texts?

How could I have been stupid enough not to think of this?

I run to Miles's cart and floor it to Enzo's.

Before approaching his door, I ditch my phone outside in an empty flowerpot. If my new theory is correct, such precautions have become essential.

Enzo spots me before I knock and lets me in. I quickly fill him in on Jeannie's disappearance and then say, "Remember those spy programs you were telling me about? Is there any way to tell if someone has planted one on your phone?"

"Has your phone been acting funny?"

I list the myriad ways it has. "I thought it was just Musqasset cell service in a storm."

"You have an Apple, right?" he asks. I nod. "Like I told you earlier, someone would need to have access to your physical phone, and they would need to jailbreak it."

I nod as if I have an embryonic clue what jailbreaking a phone means.

"Has your phone been out of your physical possession?" he asks.

"It has." It was sitting in my parents' house the whole time I was in the hospital. I've left it in my room a few times on Musqasset too.

"The only way to know for sure if you're infected is to dig directly into the phone's root file system. That's tricky to do with most phones; they don't have the tools built in. But you don't want to do that anyway—if you're really being spied on, you'd tip off your spies that you're on to them. Remember, they can see everything you do on your phone."

"There's no way to look into the files remotely?"

Enzo's eyes twinkle. "Well, look at you, getting all tech savvy. That's sort of the *only* way to do it." He leads me to his computer wall. "All the files on your phone are probably backed up remotely on the Cloud."

If you say so, Enzo.

We figure out how to log into my Cloud account from his iMac, and, sure enough, we find the backup of my phone's files. Using the basic file-search tools available on the computer but not on the phone, Enzo is able to dig into the phone's file system. He pulls in a breath when he finds a file with the harmless-seeming name, K20.

"Holy crap, I've read about this one," he says, duly gobsmacked. "High-level, pro-grade stuff. Illegal as hell. It's not just spyware, it's a full phone hijacker. There's a tiny chip that goes into the phone when you install it. The hardware/software combo enables you to remotely turn the person's phone on and off, track their location even when the phone's off, listen in on phone conversations, read their texts and emails, *send* texts and emails, delete files, track their online activity, even turn the mic and camera on and off."

Translation: someone's been tracking my every move, my every word—probably since I left the hospital. Manipulating my calls and files too. Like that recording from the ferry that suddenly vanished. I tell Enzo about the "ghost" texts I'm getting from Jeannie's phone, and he concludes her phone may be infected too.

"You're being seriously watched, my friend, by some serious people."

Not good news but good to know.

At this point, my spies don't know I've discovered their spyware, so I may be able to use that to my advantage. But from now on I will have to censor everything I say and do. Obviously, I should have been doing that all along.

"You'll need a burner phone," says Enzo, "in case you want to talk confidentially." He digs in a drawer where he has several old phones. He finds a wiped smartphone, a few years out of date, with a new phone number assigned to it. Thank you, Enzo's paranoia.

He quickly figures out how to import my Contacts list from the Cloud onto the burner so I'll have all my important numbers, including his, then hands me the burner.

"Let me look for a charger for that."

"No time." I'm already out the door.

"Go find her, man," Enzo shouts after me. "I'll do what I can from my end."

I retrieve my regular phone from the flowerpot outside—no new texts from "Jeannie" yet—and then I'm off in Miles's speedmobile.

CHAPTER 39

I drive a frantic circuit around Greyhook, asking everyone I know, friend or frenemy, if they've seen Jeannie. Along the way, I send several texts to fake Jeannie, such as: "Where r u?" "Are u safe?" "I'm worried!" I know she's not really seeing my texts and that if a response comes back, it will be from her captors, not her. But I need to play dumb. Not a stretch for me.

I run into The Rusty Anchor. The fishermen stop talking at once and stare at me, but when I shout, "Jeannie's gone missing!" they jump out of their seats, buzzing with questions, their drinks forgotten. As I'm heading back out the door, a sign on the wall hooks my attention—"Be 21 or Be Gone."

My unconscious mind starts sending up flares again. *That's* why my first encounter with the three young beer hunters has continued to needle me. The eldest of the trio claimed to be 21: the age one would be today if one had been three years old in 1999—as the Abelsens' surviving child was. From the get-go, Miles and I have been asking, *Why would someone wait eighteen years to seek payback?* Could the answer be as simple as *because he needed to grow up first?*

As I jog toward Miles's cart, I replay the meeting with the wannabe beer-buyers. The name of the oldest one—the toothy smile guy—was spoken aloud by his wheeler-dealer friend. What was it? I'm trying to drag the name from memory when a text comes in from "Jeannie."

Instantly I forget about the beer boys. The first text bubble reads, *In cave at robs head*; the second, *No come 2 dangerous*. Then nothing.

Rob's Head. I know where that is. Okay, so by telling me, as Jeannie, *No come 2 dangerous*, her captors are obviously baiting me *to* come. They know I won't be able to resist. And, of course, they're right. They probably have a host of fun surprises in store for me when I arrive. And it's doubtful Jeannie is even in this "cave"—they just want to lure me there.

✷✷✷

Rob's Head is a protruding cliff face on the north side of the island. Through past explorations, I know of several small caves where gulls nest but not a cave large enough to house adult humans. It's possible such a cave exists, though, in an area I never explored.

Now... if I were possessed of intelligence, which clearly I am not, what I would do at this juncture is throw together a posse and march en masse to Rob's Head.

What I do instead is run off into the woods, alone, armed only with the fish-skinning knife still strapped to my shin. The quickest route to the north side is via the inland trails.

I know I can't storm the enemy's lair single-handed—I'm not quite *that* stupid—but I'm hoping maybe I can get close enough to the cave in question to assess the threat level, then call in reinforcements, as needed, on the burner.

I make good time crossing the island's central wilds. By the time I reach the trailhead to Rob's Head Trail, though, my lungs are stinging. I stop and take a breather, hands on knees.

"Old dudes, so pathetic," comes a voice to my right. Leah steps out of the woods with a lopsided grin and a pair of binoculars. The Beans of Maine, it seems, are birdwatchers. Reading my anxiety level, she looks sharply into my eyes. "What's going on, Finn?"

For some crazy reason, I trust Leah, though she's practically a stranger. "Someone I care about is in trouble with some very scary people."

"Would this be the love interest you passed up a roll in the hay with a gorgeous twenty-three-year-old for?"

"It would."

"How can I help?"

It's an earnest offer, and I'm in no position to refuse it. "I'm looking for a cave at Rob's Head, one big enough for people to hide out in."

"I think I might know of one." Without ado, she dashes off down Rob's Head Trail. My breath restored, I run after her.

Within a few minutes, we're drawing near the head. Leah slows her pace and starts down a muddy trail that leads around to the cliff-face and the water's edge. "The cave I'm thinking of is around this way. Hope you brought your climbing shoes, 'cause it's about twenty feet up the cliff-face."

"The people we're talking about are dangerous, Leah. We can't just stroll into their hideout holding a three-bean salad."

She stalks ahead undaunted. I hesitate a moment, then step forward to follow her.

A cloth sack comes down over my head.

I feel the same rock-muscled arm around my neck that held me in its pipe-like embrace nine days ago. The voice of Chokehold says, "Miss me, Finnian?"

✭✭✭

After a short jaunt across choppy waters in what feels like a skiff, and then a blind ascent up a tall boat ladder, my feet land on a building-solid deck. My hands are bound in front of me with nylon cuffs. Chokehold marches me along a carpeted corridor, then down a set of stairs into a lower room. He shoves me onto a padded bench where I land awkwardly, my skull smashing into a wooden wall.

T-Bone! The name pops into my mind as if jarred loose by the blow. That was the name of the eldest beer-buying kid, the one with the creepy smile. T-Bone, T for short. T as in Theo? Theo Abelsen, heir to the Abelsen estate?

The bag/blindfold is yanked from my head. I'm in a sparsely appointed, sunken room with slatted wood walls and a series of portholes looking out to sea. The only furnishings are a couple of bolted-down table-and-chair units and the wall bench I'm sitting on. Still, it's clear that the vessel I'm on is a luxury yacht, a massive one. Are the Abelsens yacht-wealthy?

When I see the trio sitting around the table in front of me, my brain seizes up in incomprehension: the entire L.L.Bean family—Mr., Mrs., and daughter Leah.

"Good afternoon, Mr. Carroll," says Mrs. Bean with her mouthful of small, even teeth. The tone and cadence are instantly familiar. Trooper Dan. That voice, which was in the high-talker range for a man, and which I thought sounded a tad prissy, is completely normal for a woman, turns out. Strange I didn't pick up on that. The fake beard she apparently wore that day at my parent's house—and yes, her violent cruelty—flipped my mental switch to assuming she was a man. I think they call it premature cognitive commitment.

"Our instructions are to treat you civilly," she says. "So, we will remove the handcuffs... If you can assure us there won't be any idiocy." I nod. Chokehold, aka *Mister* Bean, cuts the polymer restraints with a razor tool.

"Take a moment to get your bearings," says the missus.

Looking left and right, I see that someone's sitting on the bench beside me.

Jeannie. Arms folded, wearing an inscrutable expression.

A sickening realization dawns. Both Cliff and Jeannie herself have tried to warn me that Jeannie is involved in something that will hurt me. Till now I've taken that to mean *emotional* hurt, but evidently the meaning was more literal. There are no "captors" in this drama after all. Jeannie is in cahoots with these guys.

Oddly enough, I feel a rush of relief—at least her life's not in danger.

Relief vaporizes when I notice the animal terror in her eyes. No, she's not in with them. She's a prisoner too. She and I exchange a silent, guarded look. Chit-chat isn't exactly appropriate, given the circumstances, but I try to project calmness toward her.

An urgent thought stabs at me, one that might make the difference between life and death. The captors are most certainly going to body-search me. I'm surprised they haven't done so already. When they do, they will find my knife and my burner phone. I must not allow that to happen. Those items might be Jeannie's and my only hope. These wankers are well aware of my regular phone—they've been using it to spy on me for days—but the burner must be kept from their knowledge. The knife too.

I survey the room and once again call on my gamer mind. *Another puzzle to be solved, Game Boy. Solve it. Fast.*

The room is bare; few objects for me to employ.

Shifting my butt, I notice the bench padding slides a bit on the wood surface. It is not glued down to the bench but is attached in sections by ties.

A rough idea hatches in my skull, and a plan begins to assemble itself. Well, "plan" is an ambitious word. But three distinct steps must occur in sequence. If I can pull off those three steps, I will gain a potentially critical edge. Easier thought than done.

I'll need Jeannie's help. Working in our favor is the fact that Jeannie and I can communicate complex messages nonverbally. I meet her gaze and, with a nano-shift of my irises, signal her to get up and walk to the nearest porthole. Amazingly, she picks up on my cue. She stands, stretches, and strolls toward the window. The three captors' heads turn and goggle at her; she's clearly not supposed to be wandering around freestyle.

I seize the distraction to slip the knife out of its shinstrap and slide it under the seat cushion of the bench, below my rear.

Mrs. Bean clears her throat at Jeannie, who turns with a *Who, me?* look.

"You didn't tie us up," says Jeannie, "so I assumed we were free to move about the cabin."

"You assumed incorrectly." Mrs. B. juts her jaw toward the bench.

Jeannie returns to her seat, but her brief exchange with Mrs. B. has bought me enough time to slip the burner phone, too, under the seat cushion. Both items are thin. I pray they won't make a telltale lump in the cushion when it's time to stand.

Step One complete. Objects hidden. Now for Step Two.

I want them to search me. I want them to find my main phone, my wallet, and the Velcro strap on my shin, and conclude I am carrying nothing of threat or consequence. Once they've searched me, I see no reason they'll want to do so a second time. That is my hope.

The Beans are in no hurry to do anything. They seem to be awaiting word from someone.

I need to engage them, get them talking. Try to make something happen.

I address the trio. "So, did you bring your lopper along today or will you be resorting to the fine selection of *nautical* torture devices available to today's enterprising and psychologically disturbed hit-person?"

Does Mrs. Bean crack a tiny smile? "I guess that's for us to know and you to find out, Mr. Carroll," she replies in a not-unfriendly tone.

"I hear three-hooked fishing lures can be used in a number of inventive ways."

"Is that so?"

She seems to have let her guard down a bit. Good. I'll press on.

"I hate to admit it," I say, "but I bought your dude impersonation. The beard worked. Was it super-realistic or was I just too dense to notice it came from Halloween City?"

"The mind believes what it is cued and predisposed to believe. Gender stereotypes tend to work in my favor."

"Yeah, most chicks wouldn't lay into the lopper work the way you do." I'm deliberately being dickish, just to ignite some sparks. "Anyway, the beard sure fooled me."

"It wasn't designed to fool *you*, Mr. Carroll. It was a simple precautionary measure necessitated by the risks of my trade."

"Which is what, exactly?"

No answer.

"So let me guess the pecking order here," I say to Mrs. Bean. "You're the crew foreman and chief enforcer." I project my voice toward Mr. Bean: "You're the muscle and mop-up guy, right? Do you get paid for the hours you spend on the Bowflex?"

Jeannie shoots me a warning look. *Why are you antagonizing these people?*

"Which one of you is the computer hacker-slash-'literary forger'?" Trotting out the term Enzo used doesn't trigger any overt reactions. "I'm guessing that's you, Leah, or whatever your name is. Kudos on that suicide note. That was some top-notch writing work. Natural talent alone or did you have some software help?"

At this, "Leah" does look a bit surprised. "You're not quite as dumb as you let on."

"Close but not quaahhht," I reply in a cartoon hill-billy voice. "But I thaink I done figgered out what all-y'all been up to since the day you like-to kilt me." I drop the shtick, disappointing no one. "Once you realized you'd messed up and I was in the hospital, not the morgue, you came back to my house. You deleted the suicide note from my computer, tidied up the mess. Things were more complicated now, though. You didn't know whether I'd seen the note or talked to anyone about it. So, you couldn't just try to kill me again. You needed to find out what I knew, who I might be talking to, what I was planning to do."

Trooper Danielle raises her brow in a show of amused tolerance. I go on. I'm piecing this together as I go, but it feels right. "You went to work on my phone. You planted a file called K20 and a microchip on it." Both women's eyes flash surprise at this. "I know you've been tracking my location since I left my house in Wentworth, listening to my conversations, reading my texts and emails, deleting files, blocking phone calls. You obviously sent those fake texts from Jeannie."

They're letting me ramble; they must want to know how much I've figured out. As for me, I hope I'm not getting too cute for my own good when I say, "Here's the thing, though. You don't know how long I've been aware my phone was hijacked. You don't know how long I've just been feeding you what *I want* you to hear, while conducting my real business—like talking to the police—on a burner phone."

Trooper Danielle sighs through her teeth. It's an annoyed sigh that says, *You're bluffing but, fine, you've forced my hand.* She catches Choke's eye and head-nods toward me.

Choke approaches me. "You, up," he orders.

I obey. He starts the pat-down I've been angling for. He finds my regular phone immediately and tosses it to Leah, who starts examining it. "Oh, and here's hers," he says, taking Jeannie's phone from his pocket and lobbing it, too, to Leah. "I went back to the bar and got it."

The accent: Brooklyn definitely, not Boston.

Continuing his body-search of me, Choke finds my wallet and takes it. Patting down my leg, he finds the Velcro strap around my shin. "What's this?"

"I had a knife. ...Past tense."

He removes the strap from my leg.

"Or maybe," I tease, "that was where I hid my burner."

"Okay, asshole, you asked for it." He commences another pat-down of my body, only this time it's more of a smack-down. Each slap is designed to inflict pain. He takes special relish in slamming my gonads with the heel of his hand.

"Easy," warns Mrs. B.—a reminder that, for some reason, I'm not to be treated too roughly.

He shoves me into my seat and pulls off my shoes, searching them as well.

Good. This is precisely the kind of body search I was hoping for. Minus the gonad-slamming thing. I want them to believe I'm cleaner than a Mormon sit-com. I don't want them to have any reason to check me again.

Step Two down. Search complete.

Now, for Step Three. Can I somehow sneak the items back into my clothing?

A text message comes through on Mrs. Bean's phone. "All right, time to move you two lovebirds upstairs," she says.

Shit.

CHAPTER 40

Troop and company rise and gather their things. They look expectantly at Jeannie and me, waiting for us to stand and accompany them out of the room. It appears I have no choice but to leave the knife and burner phone behind.

Jeannie seems to intuit my predicament. She stares at Troop, wide-eyed, and says, "Are you going to kill us now?"

Choke gestures impatiently, *come on, stand up, let's go.*

Jeannie repeats, "Are you going to kill us? ...That's what's happening, isn't it? You're taking us somewhere to kill us! WHY? What have I done? Why am I even here?"

"Enough of the theatrics, Ms. Gallagher," says Madam Troop. "Let's move it along."

"No!" Jeannie shouts, a quaver of panic in her voice. "I don't want to die!" I *think* she's creating a distraction for my benefit, but I'm not positive she isn't freaking out for real. Maybe it's some of both. "Please, no! I'm not ready to die! I have a daughter. She needs me. Please!"

Choke grabs her by the shirtsleeve, yanks her to her feet. "Come on, lady, let's go."

Jeannie jerks her arm from him with a sharp "NO!" She starts backing toward the far end of the room, away from the stairs. The three captors close in on her as she shrieks, "NO! NO! NO!" in authentic-sounding terror.

I seize the distraction. I grab the phone from under the cushion and slip it into my left pants pocket, lightning fast, then grab the knife. Choke took my leg strap, so the knife will have to go into my right pocket. It's hard to angle it into my pants while sitting down, but I don't dare stand up and draw anyone's gaze. I slide it in, blade first. Crap, it doesn't fit. The handle sticks out of the pocket.

Jeannie is kneeling on the floor now, wailing, "I don't want to die!" like John Turturro in that haunting woodland scene in *Miller's Crossing*. It is a terrifying spectacle.

I try to jab the point of the knife through the bottom of my pocket, but it snags. Won't poke through. What are these pants made of, woven titanium?

Jeannie shouts, "NO! NO! NO!"

"SHUT UP," Choke orders, standing over her. He produces a black oblong object from his pocket. "Do you know what this is, lady?" I do. A stun gun. "Do you want me to use it?"

"I don't want to die!" screams Jeannie in reply.

"*Do you want me to use it?*" he repeats, moving the weapon closer to her.

Jeannie "comes to her senses," shouts, "No!" and thrusts her hands up in surrender. She lets Choke jerk her to her feet. He turns her body toward the stairs.

The knife, the knife. Why won't it poke through?

I give it a hard shove and the blade finally pops through the fabric with an audible *fup*. It slices my skin as it shoots down the inside of my pant leg and then stops at the handle. Damn, that hurt. Well, at least the knife is hidden, for the moment.

Troop and company surround Jeannie and march her toward a doorway to the right of the steps. Choke gestures for me to follow.

I comply. I don't know how badly I've cut myself. It's not the injury that worries me; I'll live. It's the blood. If a red stain starts blossoming on my pants, I'm in deep guano.

I place my palms on my thighs as if doing the hands-down perp walk, but I'm really trying to hold the wound closed and hide any blood that might appear.

We are led down a corridor, past a pair of staterooms as nice as five-star hotel rooms. We come to a T-junction. Chokehold ushers me down a short corridor to the left; the two women escort Jeannie to the right. Choke points to a doorway. I step through it.

It's a bathroom, the most outlandishly elegant one I've ever set foot in. The floor, tub, toilet, bidet, shower chamber ("stall" doesn't do it justice), and sink are dark green marble—you'd swear they were cut from a single piece. The fixtures are polished brass, the cabinetry cherry wood buffed to a gemstone finish.

"Get out of those filthy clothes and take a shower," orders Choke. "Then get dressed." He points to the cherry wardrobe wherein clean clothes presumably reside.

This is not what I foresaw happening next, I must say. I guess it's thoughtful that they want me tidied up for my own execution, but really, they shouldn't have.

Chokehold stands near the door, hands on hips. He's waiting for me to disrobe, maybe even to hand him my clothes. Big nope there.

"I have a thing about undressing in front of other dudes." I say, still shielding my wounded thigh from view. "Traumatic gym class experience."

Choke doesn't appreciate my humor. "Boo-hoo." But he doesn't fight me on the issue. He points to a tasseled gold rope dangling from a brass eye in the wall and says, "Ring when you're done," then leaves the room. Yes, you can actually ring for service on the S.S. Ostentatious. With a gold bleeping rope, no less.

Hoping there are no hidden cameras in the room, I take the knife and phone out of my pockets and stash them in a drawer. I strip off my clothes—there is indeed a bloodstain on the pants—and toss them into the trash. Don't want anyone seeing them.

The knife-cut on my leg is three inches long; can't tell how deep. Steady stream of blood, though.

After I shower in the outrageously soft water, the cut is still bleeding. I press several layers of toilet paper onto it, hoping that will stanch the blood-flow for now.

In the cherry-wood wardrobe I find some new men's underwear, a folded pair of chino-style pants, a blue Oxford shirt, and a pair of boat moccasins, which I guess I'm supposed to wear sans socks, as is custom for the island-hopping set.

I don the clothes. Luckily, the chinos are loose-fitting. Recovering my stashed items from the drawer, I stab the knife-blade through the bottom of the right pocket, hiding the handle. Now seems to be the right time to turn the burner on. Its battery power is at about sixty percent. I'll just have to hope that's enough.

Enough for what, I have no bloody clue.

I silence all the phone's sounds, then scroll through the contacts list and select a name. I send a text: *Call coming from me. Not a butt dial. Don't speak. Leave phone on. Might be long.* I then push Call and wait for the phone to be answered on the other end.

Before I can confirm that the call has gone through, there's a rap at the door. Darn, I didn't even get to pull the gold rope and ring for Lurch.

I slide the phone into my left pocket, mic facing outward, and hope for the best.

"Come in."

I didn't think my brain had any room left for surprise, but clearly I was mistaken. It's not Lurch—i.e., Chokehold—who enters the bathroom. Nope, it's a waiter in a short tuxedo jacket and bow tie. A slim Korean-American man, he says, "The pleasure of your company is requested for dinner. Would you please follow me?"

Sure, why the hell not?

I follow the waiter down a corridor with a glass wall showing a stunning vista of the rocky northern side of Musqasset, then up a set of stairs. We pass a private dining room with a table made up for dinner and enter a small side room. It features a couple of tables and a little bar. A cocktail lounge. Quaint. The waiter seats me.

"May I start you with a refreshment? Mr. Fischer will be joining you for dinner shortly."

Mr. Fischer. The name comes as a blow, but then again, not really. Simon Fischer. Who else's boat could this really be, after all? The Abelsen theory goes flying out the porthole.

"Water will be fine," I reply to the waiter. I sit in silence on my brocaded chair as he fills a glass with ice water.

He scampers off. A few minutes later he returns, ushering Jeannie into the room. She's wearing a simple black dress, presumably provided by "management." Her eyes bug with terror.

The waiter pours her some water, then leaves us alone.

And so, here we are, Jeannie and I, dressed for dinner on a fine yacht at anchor in the Gulf of Maine. If we didn't know we'd both been kidnapped and dragged here against our will, this might be the start of a lovely evening. Alas, we do know.

"Are you okay?" I throat-whisper.

"No permanent damage."

"Nice work back there."

"You too. What were you trying to hide? I couldn't quite see." I shake my head, don't want to say the words aloud.

"You know whose boat this is, right?" she whispers. A confirmation, not a question.

"Beth's dad's."

"So do you have any idea what in the Jumping Jack Crap is going on here?"

"I wish I didn't, but... Jeannie, I think Simon Fischer had some people killed, and I think he's the one who tried to have me killed too."

She filters this information. She must have endless questions, but she asks only one. "Do you think...

don't lie to protect my feelings... they're going to kill *us*? Tonight?"

"I don't see what other path they have."

"No! Bree! What am I going to do about Bree? How is she going to—"

"Shh. That may be *their* path, but it doesn't have to be ours."

"What are you saying?"

"I'm saying I have no intention of letting them go through with it."

"What can *you* do about it?

I don't much care for the way she says that.

"I don't know yet," I reply, "but I do know one thing: I'm done with accepting whatever cards I'm dealt. I'm playing this thing out all the way. To win. So be ready."

"Don't do anything stupid and heroic. Not on my behalf. I don't want to live in a world that has no Finn Carroll—"

"Shh. Listen, Jeannie, I don't know how much time we have alone here. It might be just a minute, so I need to say something to you." I grasp her hand. "I love you. Remember that, no matter what happens. I love you so much it literally hurts."

She squeezes my hand, but her eyes retreat like a hermit crab backing into its shell.

"I wish I hadn't let you go the first time," I continue. "I wish I had made you the center of my universe the second time around. I wish I had told you I never wanted you to touch another man and that I wanted every bit of you."

She's fighting tears and losing the battle. "Why couldn't you have said this to me years ago, when it would have mattered?"

"Because I was damaged goods, Jeannie. Still am. But I'm ready to be whole. I am so, so ready. And that means owning the fact that I love you. I always have."

"Oh God, Finn, our timing. Our pathetic, miserable timing."

"When we get out of this thing, Jeannie—and I'm saying *when*, not *if*—I want to meet your daughter. And if meeting me doesn't make her puke, I want to start spending some time with the two of you. And if that goes well, I want—"

"Stop! Finn. Please. You need to stop. I've told you over and over, that can't happen. I have made some choices that cannot be undone. I didn't want to tell you. I wanted to spare your feelings and—yes, okay—to enjoy the brief fantasy that you and I could be together again... But that's all it was. A fantasy. There's something you need to know, and it—"

"Jean! Finnian!" booms a growling baritone from a few yards away. Simon Fischer enters the lounge with his arms out in welcome, as if greeting two long-lost friends. Barrel-chested and bald as Mr. Clean, he exudes the absolute confidence of a man accustomed to having his way in all things. "Please. Join me. Let's have some wine and a bite d'eat."

CHAPTER 41

"**M**r. Fischer, not to be an ungrateful 'guest' or anything," I say, glued to my seat, "but I think you have some explaining to do."

"Pleasure before business. Come. Everyone needs food." Fischer tends to speak in short, bark-like bursts. Punctuated by brief silences. Which somehow gives his words. Added weight. Whether they deserve. It. Or not.

"Seriously, Fischer, what the hell?"

"Call me Simon."

He looks mildly peeved that I'm not jumping at his offer of hospitality. What planet does this guy live on? I already know the answer to that: Rich-Guy Earth, a parallel dimension to mine with an entirely different set of rules.

"Look. If there was any unpleasantness," he says. "In the way you were brought here. I'm sorry. I told my crew to go easy on that stuff."

Oh. Okay. Guess all is forgiven, then. Kumbaya.

"Come, come." He beckons with both hands. "A little wine, a little yip-yap. No reason we can't be civilized here."

"With all due respect"—I almost say "sir," but I won't give him that—"being overdosed, left for dead, spied on, assaulted, and kidnapped could be construed as reasons."

"Don't test a man's generosity, Finnian. Come. Eat."

When I fail to budge, his shoulders slump in dismay, and he casts an eye toward Chokehold, whom I hadn't noticed in the background. Point taken. I don't feel a crying need to be manhandled by Chokehold again. I rise from my seat. Jeannie follows my cue.

The long formal dining table is set for five, with all the place settings grouped at one end. Simon Fischer moves to the head of the table and gestures for Jeannie and me to take the two seats to his right. The waiter appears out of thin air and pulls Jeannie's seat out for her.

"Hoon," Fischer says, addressing the man, "bring us a bottle of the Margaux. The twenty-ten should be fine."

"Yes, sir. Right away."

We're all seated. Fischer rubs his hands together.

"So... Finnian... I think the last time I saw you was on Dylan's seventh. Beth and Miles had that big do. Whatcha been up to since you left Musqasset?"

He's really going to do this? The cozy chit-chat thing? "Living in a dump, getting drunk, and trying to commit suicide," I reply.

He barks a laugh.

"You, Simon?"

"Little this, little that. Trying to keep the books in the black. And the ass in the pink. Jean, you're looking stunning. I see what all the blather's about. How's life treating you?"

"Can you please tell us what's going on here, Mr. Fischer?" she says.

"Relax. You're among friends. No more hostilities." Hoon arrives with the bottle. "Let go of the past. Don't sweat the future. Embrace the present. Isn't that what Eckhart Tolle says? I love that guy. Let's just enjoy some nice wine in a lovely setting."

"I don't drink," Jeannie says.

"Shame. Oh well, more for us, right? Hoon, get the lady a sparkling water." Hoon scampers off. "Nervous fella. Must be genetic. So, Finnian... Been enjoying your stay on Musqasset?"

"It's been a pip."

"That so?"

"Ayuh."

Before the crackling wit of our dialog can put Aaron Sorkin any further to shame, an even more uncomfortable development occurs. The other two guests arrive. Miles and Beth.

Upon seeing us, the Sutcliffes feign pleasant surprise, a titanically inappropriate response, given the circumstances.

"Sit, sit," says Simon Fischer after kissing Beth on the cheek. "Your mother won't be joining us this evening. Migraine. She sends her regrets."

Hoon appears with San Pellegrino for Jeannie and fills the other glasses with thousand-dollar-a-bottle Bordeaux.

I note that Troop and company have moved to the periphery of the room. "No, they don't sit at the table,"

Fischer explains to me, though I didn't ask. Read: there's only one alpha hound in *this* room, sonny boy.

Once everyone is seated, Fischer cracks his knuckles, stretches his lips in a parody of a smile, and says, "So..." He drums his fingers on the tabletop, chuckles to himself at some inner amusement, then takes out his phone. He reads something on it. He swipes to another screen, chuckles again, makes a little "hmm" sound. This behavior goes on for a solid minute as the rest of us sit there in silence. I look across at Miles and Beth. Neither of them wants to make eye contact with Jeannie or me.

Simon Fischer puts his phone away, looks at each of us in turn for three beats, then says, "I had the weirdest damn dream last night." He leaves the statement dangling in air.

Neither Jeannie nor I is in the mood to take the bait. Miles looks as if he just wants to shrink into his Sperry Top-Siders, tap-dance out of the room, and fling himself into the ocean. Beth is steaming, her arms folded—I guess she knows this routine.

And so, the silence goes on. And on.

At last Beth hisses, through clamped teeth, "What was the dream about, Daddy?"

"I forget," he replies. He looks at us all again for a beat or two, then starts laughing uproariously. He fixes his gaze on Miles until Miles has no choice but to join in. As soon as Miles's laughter gains momentum, Fischer silences himself, leaving Miles laughing alone.

Miles awkwardly kills his laugh.

Fischer continues to stare at him with hooded eyes. "What's the matter, son? Feeling uncomfortable?"

"No, sir, not real—"

"Don't lie to me!"

"Yes, sir, I'm feeling uncomfortable."

"Good. I *want* you to feel uncomfortable. Do you know why? Because you have put *me* in an uncomfortable position." Long, silent stare. "The last time I sat down with you... I asked you a very simple question. And demanded a truthful answer. I asked if you had any buried bodies. That I needed to know about. I thought I was being... what's the word? Metaphysical? Meta*phor*ical. Ha."

He takes a slow sip of wine, relishes the taste. It *is* good damn wine, but I need to stay clearheaded.

"I explained to you," Fischer goes on, "that I was in the process of joining a... *fellowship* of sorts. With some extremely influential people. International people. With a keen interest in U.S. politics. The kind of people you absolutely do not cross. I told you I had taken a huge risk on your behalf. Recommended *you* as a potential candidate. For their backing and support. Do you think I did that because you're my son-in-law?"

"No, sir."

"Do you think I did that because I *like* you?"

"No, sir."

"Do you think I did that because you're handsome and make the ladies warm in their woolies?"

"No, sir."

"You're damn right I didn't! I did it because it was good business. I'm handing you the keys to the universe here. And I expect the world in return."

"Yes, sir."

"Anyway... these potential... 'partners' of mine. They liked what they saw in you. For whatever reason. Liked your 'fight for the cause' image. Liked the way you come across for the mics and cameras. Your ja-na-say-kwah." He takes another slow sip of wine. "The one thing I told you... was that if they were going to consider 'backing' you... they wanted no baggage. None. Not even a shaving kit. So, you can imagine how... *perturbed* I was. When I learned you had lied to me. Not on just one major count. But two."

Miles's eyes bulge out of his head as he stares at the table.

"Lies of omission, the filthiest kind." Fischer makes a fist with one hand and rubs it with the other, as if polishing it. "What upsets me... is not that you lied. Be clear on that. In the career path you have chosen, you will lie on a daily basis. An hourly basis. Lying will be your bread and butter. And you'd better do it well. No, what upsets me is not that you lied. But that you lied to *me*. I am THE MAN YOU DO NOT LIE TO."

He glares at Miles with the wattage of an inquisitor's lamp. Miles stares equally intensely at the table.

"Did you really think I would take you at your word? I can find out anything I want about you. Like *that*." He snaps his fingers. "What you eat for breakfast. Which websites you linger on. Which hotels you visit and with who. When I asked if you had any secrets, I wasn't looking for *information*. I was looking for fealty. And you let me down."

Miles and Beth look as if they'd rather be facing a firing squad than sitting at this table. It has become clear to me that the reason Jeannie and I are here is to bear witness to Miles's humiliation. And once we've served our purpose, we will be dispensable.

"Let's look at your lies of omission. One by one. Shall we?"

"Sir, can we please do this in private?" pleads Miles.

"No! We cannot. Let's start with Lie Number Two." Simon Fischer turns to the rest of us and, in an almost playful voice, says, "Quick quiz. Who can tell me what *filia nothus* means?" I think Miles, the lawyer, probably knows, because he winces in dread. "No one? Oh well. Don't be embarrassed. I had to look it up myself. It's an antiquated term. Hint. It has to do with a situation. Amongst your little foursome. Two of you know about it. Two of you don't. But you all deserve to be on the same page. Miles, you're among the cognoscenti. Why don't you start?"

Miles doesn't speak, just continues to stare lasers at the table.

"Courage. That's what you lack, son. That's what frightens me most about you. Come on, tell them what you've done. Say the words."

Miles says nothing.

"Come on, Miles. Okay, let me get you started. Repeat after me: I..." Fischer pauses. "Stuck my... meat-pole..." Another pause. "In... my... best... friend's..."

"Filia nothus," shouts Jeannie, slamming her fist on the table, jangling the tableware. She waits till everyone's attention is fixed on her. "Means bastard daughter. Miles is my daughter's father."

A knife blade slips into my soul and twists.

"I'm sorry, Finn," Jean says. "This is what I've been struggling to tell you."

Silence descends. Seconds pass like big, heavy objects.

Jeannie picks up a butter knife, twirls it slowly in her fingers. She stares at her eyes in the blade's reflection. "After you left, I wanted to punish you in some way," she says, to me alone, "and I... That's no excuse. I'm sorry—so, so sorry. That's all I can say."

Something vital slithers out of me. I long for my parents' worn-out sofa, a bowl of cereal, and an evening of watching Animal Planet alone. Bring back the dead life.

"B-Beth," stammers Miles, "I was going to tell you. I—"

"Enough!" thunders Fischer. "When you lie to my daughter, you lie to me." He turns to Beth and says, "See? While you were paying hush money... to hide *one* of your husband's indiscretions... He was busy creating a second one. *That's* who you married. *That's* who you've given me to work with. Which brings us to Lie Number One..."

His attention suddenly swings toward the kitchen. "Hold on," he says. "Dinner is served." Hoon wheels in a table containing five covered plates and a basket of steaming focaccia bread. "I took the liberty of ordering for all of you," says Fischer. "The stripers are running right now."

Hoon serves and uncovers the plates. In a high, delicate voice, he says, "Pan roasted sea bass with a light drizzle of fennel aioli."

"Whatever the hell aioli is," blares Fischer. "Ha! I don't like to over-season fish. When it's fresh, let it speak for itself. Am I right?"

"The sides are a roasted okra with bacon and heirloom tomatoes," continues Hoon, his light voice trembling slightly, "and a popover shell with fig and chestnut stuffing."

"Me, I prefer french fries," says Fischer. "But whatever. Dig in."

He's going to have us eat dinner under the weight of the steel girder he just dropped on us. Creating human discomfort is a recreational sport for this guy.

I'm glad to have the food to concentrate on, though. I can't look at Miles. Can't look at Jeannie. Beth's not really an option either, never has been. Judging from the torpid pace of the silverware clinks around me, no one seems to have an appetite but Simon Fischer.

"I've always been aware of your payments to Clarence Woodcock, Elizabeth," says Fischer, picking up his former conversational thread. "I have access to your trust account. Did you imagine I didn't? I'm the one who set it up. And funded it. I'm still an accountholder." He chews his food for a moment. "I knew Woodcock was a private eye. I figured you had him on your payroll to keep tabs on Mr. Itchy Zipper over here. Your business. And probably a wise idea. Considering.

"But over the past few weeks... With this new 'political opportunity' shaping up... I needed to take a closer look at everything. Due diligence. So, I had my crew..." He angles his head toward Troop and company. "...turn up their eyes and ears. If this Woodcock *had* anything on hubby dearest—hotel room videos, whatever—I needed to know about it. We learned that Woodcock had booked a ferry trip to Musqasset. Noteworthy, given the timing. …I know he came to your house, Elizabeth. Along with this Edgar Goslin joker. I know everything that was said."

"You were spying on me, Daddy?" says Beth, petulantly, like a teenager.

"Spying *for* you, Sweetheart. I found out this Woodcock was putting the squeeze on you. But not over some hotel-room photos. No. Over something I didn't understand. So, we decided to put the squeeze on *him*. And Goslin. And what did we find out? That your husband did a very bad thing. One night a very long time ago."

"It was an accident, sir, I didn't even know about it," says Miles. "I wasn't hiding anything from you."

"Quiet! So now these people, Goslin and Woodcock, they had to be... made into a non-liability. Which, of course, creates additional risk. For me. My crew handled it efficiently. I'm sure. Exactly how, I don't know. And I don't *want* to know. And I don't have to. Do you know why, Miles? Because when you attain my position in life... you can pay others to live with that kind of knowledge. So you can sleep at night. But—and here's what you need to understand—YOU HAVE NOT EARNED THAT PRIVILEGE YET!"

"*No one* earns that privilege, Mr. Fischer," I break in. "Not you, not me, not anyone. Your 'crew' murdered Clarence Woodcock by pushing him down his stairs. Your crew murdered Edgar Goslin by bleeding him out and then staging it to look like he died in his car. Your crew *tried* to murder me by forcing me to swallow some booze and pills. But they screwed up. Didn't get the job done. Hence, here I am. Hope that didn't ruin your night's sleep."

Fischer laughs sourly. "You make a lot of assumptions, you little shit."

"Is that so, Mr. Fischer?"

"For instance, you assume I *wanted* you to die in your kitchen. You assume I didn't realize you were the best source of information I had. About the 'incident' in 1999. You assume we didn't just give you..." He looks to Trooper Danielle.

"...some sugar pills and enough Rohypnol to lay you out like deli meat," she supplies.

"You assume we didn't *want* you to find that suicide note," says Fischer. "You assume we didn't *want* you to go into a panic after you'd read it. Wondering who could possibly know such facts about you. You assume we didn't just tap your phone, sit back and watch. To see what you'd do. Who you'd call. Who you'd email. What you'd google. What you'd write. Who do you think sent those 'mystery messages' to Miles? 'Carlisle Road, Bridgefield, Mass. May 13, 1999.' And why do you suppose we sent them?"

I don't reply.

"Same damn reason," he says. "To stir the pot. See what bubbled up."

CHAPTER 42

"You're claiming you *faked* my overdose?" I say to Simon Fischer. "And you've been spying on me this whole time, just to find out who knew what about Miles?

"All I'm 'claiming,'" says Fischer, "is that for such a wise-ass, you make a lot of assumptions. Eat your food. You're skin and bones."

I think he's lying. He can't stand the fact that I "beat" him by surviving his attack. I forced him to go to Plan B, and now he must make it seem like Plan B was Plan A all along. Either way, lying or not, this guy is in serious need of a hand grenade up his descending colon.

"You're not as clever as you think," I say to Fischer and friends. "I know you planted that fake smoke detector in my room. And those disappearing emojis were a dead giveaway that you were tapping my phone." They weren't, of course, because I'm mentally deficient. "You think I didn't notice you blocking my calls to the police and my sister?"

"Maybe the emojis were a warning," Leah replies. "A courtesy. Maybe if someone blocked a few calls to your sister, they were doing you a kindness."

"A *kindness*?"

"Your sister Angie still thinks it was you who threw that bottle. If you had been permitted to correct her on that point..."

Angie would have had to join the ranks of Goslin and Woodcock. Maybe Leah does have the remnants of a soul.

"That's enough!" bellows Simon Fischer. "All of you. I've heard way more than I want to. The point I'm trying to make, Miles... is that things have gotten messy. Very messy. For me. Because of you."

Fischer chews his food and his thoughts. "I'm a powerful man, son. More powerful than you will ever be. Even if you one day hold the highest public office in the land. But there are men more powerful than me. Pass the salt, would you? Even the gods have greater gods, eh? *Ad infinitum*, so it seems.

"Let me tell you something about these people I've been cozying up to. I'll never tell you everything... but let me tell you *something*. These people aren't the PACs or the Super PACs. They're not the LLCs or the five-o-one-c-four political charities. These are the people *beyond* the Super PACs. These are the people with the resources to make things happen... directly. Need a senior congressman to get caught in a bathroom stall with a teenage kid? Need the stock market to get the jitters before a vote on the hill? Need a truckload of military weapons to fall into the wrong hands? That's what these people do. They influence things. In the real world.

"This business of ours. Yours and mine. Getting you that Senate seat. That was meant to be... a 'test.' For me as much as for you."

He chews some more.

"The governor of our fine state, you see... we golf, him and me. We schmooze. Visit each other's summer homes. And as you know... in the state of Maine... when a U.S. Senator resigns mid-term... it's the governor who names their replacement. So, when I heard about Aldridge getting a visit from ol' Johnny Carcinoma... And with you getting some good press. And that state Senate seat. The stars were aligning. I saw an opportunity. I suggested to my pal. The governor. That you'd make a fine member of Congress's upper chamber. When Aldridge threw in the towel. But it turned out Governor Rick had his own guy in mind. Shame.

"I turned to my... document specialist here." He indicates Leah. "She'd already helped me in a couple of... business situations. I knew the quality of her work. With my access and her skills, we were able to plant some... *things* on Governor Rick's computer. Written, anyone would think, in his own words. Then 'leak' them to me. Through an 'anonymous source.' I won't tell you what those *things* were, but... Devastating. Take a bow, Leah. Fine work, fine work."

Leah *is* her real name, then. She responds with a tiny nod.

The fact that Simon Fischer is letting Jeannie and me hear all this stuff is not an auspicious development for either of us.

"Anyway, the governor is now enthusiastically on board. But we still need a rock-solid 'product' to launch." He wipes his mouth, fires his napkin at the table. "What I'm trying to tell you is... I have been stepping out on the slippery ledge for you, Miles. And what have you been doing in return? PUTTING MY NUTS IN A VISE!"

"I didn't lie about that accident, sir," pleads Miles. "I didn't *know* about it. I was drunk that night. I passed out. I had to be taken to the ER." He looks to Beth, but she's not going to bail him out—no siree, not this time. "I only found out about it this weekend!"

"This weekend? Even if I believed such grass-fed horseshit... you lied to me about the *filia nothus*. Therefore, I must assume you lied to me about other things. So be it. Accept what *is*. Right? That's what Eckhart says. But before the book is closed on this day... we *will* clean up our messes, you and me. All of them."

"What are you planning to do, sir?" asks Miles, a cringe in his voice.

"Me?" says Fischer. He stands and gazes at the sinking sun through the huge dining room window, stretches his arms, then locks eyes with Miles. "*I'm* going to take a nap. I don't need to redeem *my*self. I don't need to prove *my*self. You, on the other hand..."

"What? What do you want me to do, sir?" says Miles in a little-boy voice that makes me pity him despite the circumstances.

"Handle the situation."

"How?"

"By making a decision and acting on it, that's how. Prove to me you are worthy of my absolute trust and confidence."

"I've proven that to you over and over, sir. With the Camden situation, with the golf course at Belgrade Lakes, with Fish Pier..."

"Fish Pier was nothing. You just followed my orders. I told you what I wanted to happen. And you carried out my wishes."

Damn. So *Simon Fischer* was the silent money— the big money—behind the marina development on Musqasset. Of course he was. Of course he was. Why didn't I see that?

"What I'm talking about here, my boy," says Fischer, "is an *executive* decision. *You* evaluate the situation. *You* decide on a course of action. *You* ensure that it's carried out to completion. That's what needs to happen. And then we will reassess."

On that note, Simon Fischer departs.

✶✶✶

Several minutes later, no one has spoken yet. Miles is pacing the floor, grabbing at his hair as if he literally wants to tear it out. "What should I do?" he asks Beth at last.

"You're on your own," she says, "and I mean that in every possible way." She pushes her chair away from the table and walks out of the room, slamming the carved mahogany door.

Quiet resumes as Miles paces back and forth.

At last he stops, a decision apparently made. He turns to Chokehold. "You," he says, "stay here and guard them"— meaning Jeannie and me.

"I take orders from Mr. Fischer," says Choke. "Not you."

"Well, I'm giving orders on Mr. Fischer's behalf. If you want to verify that, you can go blow up his nap and ask him."

Choke waves his hand in concession.

"You two," says Miles, pointing to Leah and Trooper Danielle. "Come with me. You're my consulting team."

Miles exits the room, muttering, "Sorry, Finn," as if a twelve-ounce sinker is jammed in his throat. Leah and Danielle follow him out.

Jeannie and I are left alone, with Chokehold standing guard. An eternity seems to pass, Jeannie and me sitting side by side, not looking at each other. I want to say something, but my vocal cords refuse to budge.

Jeannie finally ventures, "Miles had been... 'expressing an interest' in me since college. I never reciprocated. Never. Until..." She chews on her inner cheek, stares abstractedly ahead. "We only hooked up a few times, and then I came to my senses. ...I said I did it to punish you, but that's not really true. I did it to punish myself. You were the only person in the world whose opinion I cared about."

I feel an urge to point out she had a funny way of showing it, but my tongue clings to muteness.

"I figured you already thought I was... well, maggot slime," she goes on. "Worse. So, I asked myself, what can I do to really *earn* the feeling that I'm worthy of your contempt? Miles started hitting on me the moment you left the island. I said to myself, 'That'll do the trick.'"

"All right, that's enough, you two," says Chokehold. "Save it for Maury."

"That was hitting bottom for me," continues Jeannie, undeterred. "That's when I quit drinking. That's when I started examining my life and making some changes." She takes a long, shuddery breath. "After a month of sobriety, I was already seeing things more clearly. I decided I would go to the mainland, track you down, tell you I loved you, try to win you back. And that was when I found out I was..." Pregnant. "And that was the end of that."

"Ah, Jeannie," I say, finding my voice. "Jeannie, Jeannie, Jeannie."

"Because I *do*, you know," she says in a papery voice. "Love you. So much. I don't know why I could never convince you of that. You've always been the one. Ever since I laid eyes on you in that Abnormal Psych class. No one else ever had my heart. No one."

"I mean it, you two," says Choke. "Shut up. You're giving me a toothache. In fact... you"—he points at me—"in there." He nods toward a nearby men's room.

✶✶✶

The bathroom is tiny, just a toilet and a sink.

Chokehold shuts the door on me. Good. This may even play into my hands.

What I just learned about Jeannie and Miles has knocked the wind out of me, but still, I must keep my wits about me. I slide the burner phone from my pocket and check it. The call I placed earlier seems to have connected and is still live. But the battery power is down to about twenty percent. I might be stuck in here a while. I need to conserve what little juice the phone has left. I whisper, "I'll call back," into the mic and shut off the phone. I'll have to reboot it and place the call again later. That might not be easy to pull off, though.

After a good chunk of time has passed—at least an hour—I hear the big dining-room door open and footsteps cross the larger room. Words are exchanged, and the footsteps depart. Listening against my small door, I hear Choke sigh, crack his knuckles and say, "Showtime, princess." Okay, time to roll.

I slide my butt back toward the middle of the bathroom floor and press the "on" button on the burner phone. Time to power up.

Choke slides his chair away from the table.

I stare at the burner, willing it to boot up faster. It is taking its sweet time. I'm not familiar with this model—even though the volume is turned off, it might make an electronic jingle of some kind when it boots. If it does, I'm toast.

Choke's heels clack in my direction. He's about fifteen feet away.

The phone shows only *black screen with logo, black screen with logo, black screen with logo.* Come on, turn on, you piece of junk. Come on, come on!

Finally, the phone lights up, in blessed silence, and is running again, with its small reserve of battery power. Choke stops at the bathroom door.

I frantically navigate to the Recent Calls list and redial the earlier number—Enzo's—then slip the phone back into my left pocket, mic facing outward, just as Choke opens the door.

He enters, wielding his stun gun. My hand is still in my pocket. I ease it out, hoping the glow of the phone screen doesn't show through the fabric of my pants.

Choke orders me to stand up and jerks me out into the dining room. Jeannie is still waiting there.

Outside the yacht's massive windows, the sun has set, and darkness is rapidly descending. The decks are tastefully lighted for nighttime.

To Jeannie's surprise and mine, Choke hands us both back our confiscated phones. He also returns my wallet to me. Why, I can't guess. He then gives me a knowing grin, reaches over and pulls open the top of my left pants pocket—the one with the burner in it.

My heart sinks.

He stares at me for a long moment, waiting for me to surrender the burner voluntarily.

I start to say, "Take it," but then he reaches into his own shirt and pulls out an item: a folded-up piece of paper in a sealed Ziploc sandwich bag. Odd.

He slips it into my pants pocket. As his fingers slide down into my chinos, I'm sure they're going to touch the burner, but they miss it by a hair's breadth. He pulls his hand away.

"Leave that there," he says, referring to the ziplocked paper in my pocket, then gives Jeannie and me a shove and tells us to get moving. To where, who knows?

As we march along, my regular phone—the one Choke just returned to my hand—pings a text-sent signal. Jeannie's phone pings a text-received tone. I look down at my phone screen and see a Sent text from me to Jeannie. Ah, so Leah has taken control of our phones again. The text from "me" reads, *I just wanted to say I'm sorry... I've been thinking a lot about what you said... And, of course, you're right.*

A few seconds later, another text exchange pings. This time it's Jeannie's hijacked phone replying to mine. *It doesn't mean I don't love you,* texts phantom Jeannie. The real Jeannie hasn't touched her phone's screen. Jeannie and I exchange WTF looks.

Choke marches us down a set of stairs to a lower deck, and we head toward the stern. If there's going to be an opportunity to use the knife in my pocket, it will have to happen soon.

My phone pings Jeannie's phone again: *I know. I get it. I was thinking with my 'little head'... I know we can't have a life together... And I know that doesn't mean you don't love me.*

Jeannie's phone to mine: *Glad you see it that way. Sorry.*

My phone to hers: *I'll be heading out on the ferry in the morning, if it's running... But hey, before I go, want to see something amazing?*

Jeannie's phone to mine: *Not if it's an anatomical feature! Haha. What?*

Choke leads us down a final staircase to an exterior deck at the stern, a few feet above water level. It's an open area where people can sunbathe and around which small craft can moor.

Tied to the rear of this lower deck is a yellow inflatable boat with an outboard motor—mine, the one I left in Jeannie's shed. Moored beside it is a motorized skiff with a squared-off bow and stern—probably the same one that carried me to this yacht. Both boats are accessible by a single short ladder.

My phone sends another text to Jeannie's: *Turns out our shipwreck didn't go far out to sea...* Clever, Leah is, bringing The Shipwreck into this text exchange, knowing it had special meaning to Jeannie and me. *It's 50 yds offshore, underwater... And it's doing something incredible...*

Jeannie's phone: *Doing? What do u mean?*

My phone: *I can't explain. You have to see it... Can you meet me at the dock in, like, 15? We'll take my inflatable.*

Jeannie's: *K bye.*

Ah. I'm starting to piece together what's going on here. A chain of evidence is being established whereby I'm inviting Jeannie to my boat and we're going to take a ride on the still-choppy waters. I have a feeling we're going to have an "accident at sea."

Miles cannot seriously be in on this.

No sooner does this thought occur than the man himself appears on the deck above us in the lambent lighting. He's talking with Trooper Danielle and Leah and looking out at the water.

"Miles, you've got to be kidding me!" I shout up at him. His face looks ten years older than it did two hours ago. "I know what you're planning to do here. Murder Jeannie and me. Are you out of your mind?" He flinches as my words hit him, but he refuses to look at me.

"Seriously, Miles? Seriously? Murder?"

Miles nods to Choke: time to get things moving. I've never seen such a miserable, drained expression on my friend's face. The stress of this decision must have stripped something elemental from his soul.

"All right, you two, into the boat," Chokehold orders Jeannie and me.

"Snap out of it, Miles!" I shout at the upper deck. "If you do this, it can never be undone. You think what happened with that scotch bottle was bad, try living with murder on your conscience. For the rest of your life!"

Miles is staring at his phone to avoid making eye contact with me. He's trying to appear focused and in-command.

Suddenly a voice rings out from the interior of the upper deck. "What the hell is going on here, will someone please tell me?" It's Beth, in her bathrobe, trotting out to see what the commotion is. Thank God. Beth and I have never been besties, but she won't condone *this*.

"Beth!" I shout up at her. "Miles has lost it! He's trying to have us killed!

"Miles, what are you doing?" she demands, eyes popping with disbelief.

"Beth, go back inside!" shouts Miles.

"Miles, answer me!" she says.

"Go back inside, Beth! I am handling this."

Beth trots down the stairs to the lower rear deck where Jeannie and I and Chokehold are standing. She inserts herself between Choke and me, arms folded, awaiting my explanation.

"They're going to take us out on the water and kill us," I tell her. "They planted fake texts on our phones to make it look like I'm the one who's orchestrating it."

Beth grabs my phone from my hand and studies the recent text exchange. "Did *you* write this?" she shouts up at Miles, incredulous.

"The three of us did," says Miles defensively, indicating Leah and Trooper D. "It's what needs to be done, Beth. Stay out of it!"

"I'm in shock," she responds, staring up at him with her head cocked back. "It's actually pretty good." She wipes her prints off the phone and places it back in my hand.

"Let me know when it's over," she says to her husband and starts back up the stairs.

CHAPTER 43

"Beth, no!" I yell after her, my voice going high with panic. "You're the only sane one here. I need your help. As a friend."

"Friend?" She freezes on the stairs and spins her head toward me. "Is that what you said?" She turns and walks back down a couple of steps. "You're not my friend, Finnian Carroll, don't you know that? I *hate* you. Ever since that night in the car, I've wished you were dead."

"I didn't throw that bottle, Beth. All I did was—"

"I'm not talking about the bottle, jagoff. That was an accident. I'm talking about before. When Miles had his meltdown. When he was thrashing on the ground and saying he was jealous of you and what you had with *her*." She points to Jeannie with her head. "Do you remember what you said to him? *I* do. 'You don't love Beth,' you said. 'And if you marry her, you will be profoundly unhappy for the rest of your life.' Well, those words crawled under his skin and laid eggs. And those eggs hatched in *our home* and *our bedroom*. And now every night it's like *you're* lying between the sheets with us. You and your judgments about me.

"Who does he call whenever he's having doubts about our marriage? Who does he visit whenever he needs time away from the ol' ball and chain? Who does he *claim* to visit whenever he slips away for a Hilton Weekend Special with the intern of the month? Finn Carroll, his blood brother in Beth hatred. *Help* you? *Help* you? I can't wait till fish are eating your dead eyes."

"If you believe *I* planted those doubts in his head, Beth," I say, "you are delusional to a degree even I didn't imagine. If Miles really loved you, you wouldn't have to—"

"Enough!" shouts Miles. "Don't say another word. It's time for you to go. Get on the damn boat."

"Are we really going to do this, Miles?"

"Get on the *boooooat*." He looks as if he's about to cry.

Choke steps closer to Jeannie and me, nudging us toward my yellow inflatable.

A seed of a strategy is germinating in my mind. I eye-signal Jeannie to go first, then, with a tiny gesture of my hand, mime the act of starting the boat motor. I hope she reads me. Jeannie knows her way around boats, big and small.

My plan won't help me, but it might help her.

She descends the short ladder leading down to the tied-up inflatable.

I start down the ladder after her. The moment my lower half is out of view from above, I slip the knife out of my pocket.

I grab the rope that's mooring my boat and whisper to Jeannie, "Start the engine." I slice the rope with a brisk swipe of the blade. The engine starts on the first pull. I give the boat a big kick-shove away from the yacht's stern. Then I turn and take a step back *up* the ladder.

"Go! Go! Go!" I shout behind me at Jeannie in the small boat.

The reason I didn't climb into the boat with her? Because I know my rubber inflatable can't outrun a skiff. But if I can buy Jeannie enough time to escape alone, she might be able to make it to shore—it's only a few hundred yards away. I stand on the ladder, prepared to defend it against all comers.

"I'm not leaving you here, Finn!" Jeannie shouts.

"Go! No time to argue!"

"Jump on board," Jeannie pleads, refusing to go without me.

"No! You have a daughter, don't screw around!"

Those words get through to her. She shifts the prop into forward and gives the small engine some gas.

Chokehold steps toward the ladder I'm standing on, stun gun in hand. For that weapon to work, it will need to make good contact with me. I don't plan to let that happen. Before Choke can reach the ladder, I lash out with the knife, swiping the blade from side to side.

I don't intend to let him get close enough to stun me or climb down into the skiff.

"This doesn't mean I'm leaving you!" shouts Jeannie as she aims my boat toward land, maxing the throttle. She's saying she'll be back with help. The truth is, I was hoping help would have arrived by now. But I guess my little burner phone ploy didn't work. It was a long shot anyway.

The good news is that, for the first time in days, the waters are reasonably safe for small craft. Jeannie ought to be able to make it to land in decent time if I can buy her a head start. I swing the knife back and forth, allowing her to progress toward shore in the rubber boat.

Suddenly I'm blinded by a light from an upper deck, and an unfamiliar voice shouts, "Drop the knife!" The light-beam shifts its angle to show me that the holder of the high-intensity flashlight has a pistol in his other hand. Then the light strikes my face again. A second beam of white light hits Jeannie, as another unknown voice shouts at her, "Freeze! Stop the boat!"

Jeannie hasn't traveled far enough to be safely out of pistol range. She stops the boat and lifts her hands in surrender. I drop the knife and do the same.

It never occurred to me that Simon Fischer might have armed bodyguards. But of course, why wouldn't he? Troop and company are mission specialists; they're not around him 24/7. A guy like Fischer would naturally have round-the-clock protection.

"Bring that boat back, NOW!" shouts one of the upper-deck guards. Jeannie circles back toward the yacht.

✶✶✶

I stand on the rear deck with Chokehold and the pair of armed bodyguards, my hands held aloft. Jeannie waits in my boat at the bottom of the ladder, a gun trained on her.

Miles descends the stairs from above, carrying himself with an erect, shoulders-back posture meant to look commanding, presidential even. He sells it pretty convincingly, if you don't know him too well. As he approaches me, he and I can't avoid brief eye contact. He casts a glance up at the second deck for my benefit.

I look up to see Simon Fischer and Beth, side by side, leaning on the upper rail and looking down on all of us like the Lannisters watching a deathmatch.

Guess I'm supposed to forgive Miles for his actions because he'll be in hot water with the in-laws if he backs down. Get a grip, Miles.

"Into the boat," Miles orders me, his voice cracking slightly.

I have no choice but to obey. I climb down into the inflatable craft, eyeing Miles every step of the way. He evades my glance.

"You two," Miles says to Chokehold and one of the bodyguards, "into the skiff." Choke and Bodyguard clamber down into the larger of the two small craft.

I know Miles so well I can watch his thoughts play out on his face. He's still thinking he can delegate this whole operation. But then he looks up at Simon Fischer, and awareness dawns. Miles realizes this is a test. Of his mettle. Of his hands-on leadership and decision-making. Delegating won't do.

He climbs down into the rectangular skiff and takes the wheel, a general with his two lieutenants. He orders Choke out of the skiff and into the rubber boat with Jeannie and me. Damn, I was hoping he'd leave Jeannie and me in our own vessel.

It's tight quarters on the inflatable with Choke aboard. He's a sizable dude.

Jeannie is left to helm the tiller while Choke watches over both of us.

"Go," Miles orders, pointing eastward.

We strike off toward the black horizon. The full dark of night is upon us now, and the moon is only a high sliver in an oddly starless sky. The island lies to our starboard side. In a few minutes we'll be clear of land and heading into the depths of the open Atlantic.

Miles follows us in the skiff without any lights. I can hear his motor but can barely see his boat, so dark is the night.

Why are we going east? The way the fake texts were written, I thought we were supposed to have our "accident" near Table Rock, on the northwestern edge of the island. Guess he wants us farther out to sea, where our screams can't reach any ears.

The only bits of light we can see are from the scattered homes on the northern side of the island. Soon the last of the lighted world will be behind us.

I am heading into blackness, never to return, it seems. How strange. A mere nine days ago, I was living a marginal existence in my parents' decaying home, wallowing in melancholy and despair, failing to savor the life that was mine for the grabbing. Then I was given the gift of attempted murder. Yes, *gift*, because it made me hunger for life again. The past several days have been terrifying, exhausting, and more stressful than anything I've ever endured, but they've been electrifying too. I've tasted true love again and had my heart flayed to the core. I've made love as only the angels can. I've pushed my mind and body to new levels. And I've discovered that when my back is against the wall, I'm not a coward. These are life-changing revelations.

Alas, there is little life left for the changing. It will all be over soon. My crazy hope was that, even if I couldn't figure out a way to escape this mess, help would arrive. That's why I called Enzo on the burner phone and let the line stay open all through dinner and beyond. I was hoping he would listen in on what was happening and send in the troops. Maybe fetch our policeman from Monhegan or figure something else out.

But no. Maybe my call didn't really go through, maybe Enzo wasn't listening, maybe he couldn't make out what was being said, or maybe he just didn't give a crap.

I still can't believe Miles, my best friend, intends for Jeannie and me to die out here, but that seems the course he's committed to.

Ahead on the right lies the green boat signal at Mussel Cove. That's the last light we'll pass on the eastern end of the island. Then it's nothing but blackness till Ballyconneely Bay in County Galway, my ancestral home.

I look behind me at the western horizon. It's still showing some faint luminescence from the recently set sun. If any rescuers were following us in the distance, even with their lights off, I'd see their silhouettes. But I don't. We're all alone out here.

If I'm going to die on the black ocean, though, I refuse to die in servitude to Miles's lies. I refuse to make this easy for him. I still have a few things that need saying. And I want to ensure that on the off-chance Enzo is still listening and my burner phone still has power, there is a record of what is about to go down. But the hitch is, if we go much farther, we'll lose cellphone reception. That means I need to stop this boat somehow. Force the endgame to happen close to shore. Make it harder for Miles to pull off his crime unwitnessed.

Time is running out.

"I wonder how much gas this thing has," I say to Jeannie, lading my words with meaning I hope she will unpack: *Can you make the engine quit somehow?*

"Shut up," orders Chokehold. Silver-tongued rogue.

We putter along for a minute or two, followed by the skiff. We steer around the Mussel Cove light and its protruding apron of rocks. Now the last sites we'll pass are Seal Point on the right and George's Knob on the left. George's Knob is not as obscene as it sounds—it's just a rounded rock formation lying off the northeastern shore. Once we get through the channel between George's Knob and Seal Point, it's H_2O as far as the eye can see.

The engine starts to cough and sputter. *Yes! Good work, Jeannie. Whatever you did.*

"What's going on?" says Chokehold. "Did you pull the choke out? Push it back in, lady."

The engine dies. Chokehold whips out his phone and hits the flashlight app, illuminating Jeannie. One of her hands is holding the engine tiller, the other is holding a now-empty bottle of spring water. She grins. Bless her pirate soul. The cap of the gas tank is off and the boat's emergency kit is open, revealing the source of the water bottle.

"Did you just dump water in the gas tank?" Choke asks Jeannie, aghast.

"Sure did, asshole," replies Jeannie.

CHAPTER 44

"All right, everyone calm down!" shouts Miles, the least calm person on the high seas tonight. He has drawn the skiff up beside the crippled inflatable. "I need to think."

"Yes, you really should do that," I say, turning on my phone's flashlight and shining it in his face. I need to engage his attention before his actions become irreversible. "Think about what you're about to do, Miles. Do you really want to murder— *murder*—your best friend and the mother of your child?"

"I don't *want* to do any of this! Things are out of control! Things have been set in motion. And now what needs to happen needs to happen."

"You're not thinking clearly. You're in panic mode, and your lizard brain has taken over. Step back and take a deep breath. You still have options."

"Like what?"

"Speak the truth. Come clean. About everything. About the accident. About Fish Pier. About Bree. About this sleazy political puppet show your father-in-law is trying to orchestrate. Hold your head up, take accountability for whatever you've done, and then push the restart button on a new life. A better life, a freer life."

"Ha."

"You haven't done anything unredeemable yet. You won't go to jail for those highway deaths. It was an accident. There'll be consequences, but you can handle them."

"That's easy for you to say, Finn. You don't know what it's like to stand in my shoes."

"Ah, there it is."

"There *what* is?"

"The premise of our friendship, in black and white." Part of me is trying to stall, buy some time, but part of me is also saying what needs to be said.

"I have no idea what you're talking about."

"You know exactly what I'm talking about. You just said it yourself."

Now he shines *his* phone-beam on *me*. "Enlighten me, Finn. What premise?"

"That Miles Sutcliffe, scion of the Old Greenwich, Connecticut Sutcliffes, carrier of destiny's torch, has more to lose than crooked-toothed, working-class Finnian Carroll from Wentworth, Massachusetts."

"That's ridiculous. That's your low self-esteem talking, not me."

"It's been our story since day one, Miles. When you got pulled over for that DUI and begged me to switch places with you, why did we both agree to that? Because I could afford to have an arrest record, you couldn't. Same with the cheating thing on our philosophy final. When you got caught with that townie girl in senior year, I said she was with me. Why? Because you were about to get married and couldn't afford to screw *that* up." I'm surprised he's letting me carry on like this. Maybe *he's* trying to stall the inevitable too. "We never talked about the underlying premise, but we both understood it."

"Maybe *you* did. I sure the hell didn't. I don't even *remember* this stuff. It's gone. It has no foothold in my mind."

"What about Fish Pier? Does that have a foothold in your mind? I know what happened the night Fishermen's Court paid you a visit. You threw me under the bus. Again."

"You're delusional."

"You told them I never gave you their letters."

"I said no such thing!" he fumes with overblown indignation.

"You promised me you would pass those letters on to your partners. Those letters were important, Miles. They had people's *lives* bound up in them. Their pride, their hopes, their stories."

"Those letters were a joke. They weren't going to do a damn bit of good. Simon Fischer had already decided the pier had to go. And Simon Fischer always gets his way."

"That's not the point. Those letters mattered *to the fishermen who wrote them*. They mattered a lot. And you told those guys *I* sold them out!"

Miles's eyeballs lose focus and start dancing from side to side. I know the look. "You had left the island," he says, "and you weren't coming back. I still had a home here. I had to *live* with these people."

"That makes it okay? Expediency trumps truth? These people were my friends. And for the past four years they've hated me, all because of a lie you told them."

"Those letters were a stupid idea. *Your* stupid idea. All they did was create false hope. You *deserve* to take the blame for that."

Time has frozen, and no one exists but the two of us. We're going to finish this thing—despite the insane circumstances—and nothing is going to stop us now.

"Go to hell," I say. "Ever since the day I made the mistake of inviting you here, you have taken the one thing of worth I ever built for myself—my life on this island—and pissed all over it. And all because of that one lifelong belief."

"Which is?"

"That your life is more valuable than mine. That you *matter more than I do*!"

"You're wrong, Finn." Miles laughs glumly and shines his light in my eyes. "That's what *you* believe. That's the *real* story of our friendship."

His light feels painfully bright.

"From the first time you met me," he says, "you thought I had a big life, and you wanted in. But you didn't think you were *enough*. On your own merits. You thought you had to *buy* your way in. *Serve* me in some way, provide a value-add."

I detest this guy. I detest Miles Sutcliffe.

"*You* held yourself lower than me," he continues. "I never asked that of you."

"Come on, Miles, you know you never saw me as equal to your preppy friends and your Sugar Loaf friends and your Greenwich friends." Something raw and primitive is being exposed in me, and I hate it. "I was a sociology experiment for you: can people from different social castes be friends? But when you were with your real peers, I embarrassed you."

"You did embarrass me. Not because of your cheap shoes or your crooked teeth, but because you tried so freaking hard. *You* felt you didn't belong, so you were always *auditioning*—with your humor, with your intellectual gymnastics, with your willingness to play the fall guy— trying to win a spot on the varsity squad."

He shines his light up and down my body, as if taking stock of the totality of me.

"I'm going to let you in on a little secret, Finn. The reason the rich get richer isn't because the privileged have the key to some special club. It's because life gives us what we *expect*. That's why I have a house in The Meadows and another one in Cape Elizabeth, and you're living in your parents' house in Wentworth. You *expect* squat, and you *get* squat."

"You have two homes on the ocean because you married money. You were too scared to follow your dreams. Don't give me that 'great expectations' bullshit."

"You've always been cleverer than me, Finn, but you've always eaten my table scraps. Why? Because you don't think you belong at the table. Every bad thing that happens to you, you see it as confirmation of your essential worthlessness, punishment for the sin of being you."

"Drop dead, Miles."

"Whereas I view setbacks as speed bumps, aberrations. That's why I can't even *remember* those stupid incidents you mentioned. I don't cling to that kind of stuff, I let it go."

"That's because you're never the one who pays the price!"

"That's because *you* pay the price for things that aren't even yours to pay for! Look at this scotch-bottle mess. You've been letting it eat at you for eighteen years, and you didn't even throw the stupid thing. Me, I took one look at those news stories, saw there was nothing that could be done to change the outcome, and purged it from my mind."

"Wait. What?" It takes me a moment to process what I've just heard. "Are you telling me you *knew* you caused that accident? That you've known all along?"

His eyeballs start the dance routine again.

"Those are two different questions," he says. "With different answers. But all right, yes, I'll admit, the night of the accident, I heard the crash sounds. I didn't know what to do, so I just... shut down. Pulled the plug, checked out. The next day, I turned on the news. Saw what had gone down. But I asked myself a simple question: will my taking the blame change anything for the victims? The answer was no. So I pushed 'delete file.'"

"And what, just erased it from your memory? Click, gone?"

"Absolutely. I had a lot to think about—the wedding, law school, finding a house. I literally never gave that night another thought, never fed it another watt of mental energy. Not one. For eighteen years. Even when you came back here and started rehashing the whole thing, I honestly didn't remember throwing the bottle. ...It was only today, when Beth said it was me who did it, that the actual memory bubbled up. And it threw me for a hot minute, I'll admit. But let me ask you something, Finn—and this is the point I'm making: who's been better off for the last eighteen years, you or me?"

I lose it. Animal rage takes over. I launch myself off the inflatable, across a patch of black water, and onto Miles's skiff.

I take him down like a linebacker courting a penalty flag.

The second he hits the floor of the boat, I am on top of him, hammering his face and torso with my fists. I punch him for my father. I punch him for my sister. I punch him for Beth. I punch him for Jeannie and Bree and for his betrayal of our friendship. I punch him for Edgar Goslin. Most of all, I punch him for the Abelsens, an innocent family whose lives he stole with a careless act he decided he was never going to own. I've never struck Miles in my life before, but it feels so bloody good.

A hollow cylinder presses against my temple.

"Enough," orders Bodyguard. Am I wrong or has he taken his sweet time intervening?

"Get him out of here!" Miles shrieks at the guard in a shaky voice. "Get him back on the other boat!"

Bodyguard presses the gun barrel to my ribs, forcing me to maneuver back into the inflatable.

"What are you going to do now?" I shout at Miles from my boat. "Murder Jeannie and me? Then what? Click—delete file? On with your blissfully ignorant life?"

"No, asswad, *you're* going to do it."

The hair goes up on my neck and arms.

"What do you mean?" I shine my phone-light on him. His eyes are wild with the fury of a wounded child. His nose is oozing blood.

"The News at Nine team will call it a 'tragic murder-suicide.' You've explained it all in the note you wrote. The one we stuck in your pocket, in a waterproof bag. Leah outdid herself this time, I must say. The note spells out how you've been living a tortured life, wracked with depression, ever since you killed that family on route 495. But how things were looking up lately. You hooked up with your old flame again, and life was good. You trusted her so much, you even confessed to her what you'd done all those years ago. Whoops, major turn-off. She shut down the love train, and now she's insisting you go to the police and admit what you did.

"She had to be dealt with, the meddlesome cow," he goes on. "So, you lured her to your boat, as your phone texts will show, and now it's time to do the dark deed. Just like in that old folk song you used to sing..."

And then, most bizarrely, he begins to sing. *"Polly, pretty Polly, come go along with me."*

The flat look in his eyes tells me the Miles I've always known has left the building.

"Polly, pretty Polly, come go along with me." He reaches under the seat of the skiff and drags out a heavy object. It's an anchor, of navy design, with a curved bottom and two up-posts. A rope is attached to it. My God, he's really thought this through.

"Before we get married, some pleasure to see..."

He lugs the anchor to the edge of the skiff, then heaves it across the gap onto the inflatable, where it lands with a thud. It must be a twenty-pounder.

"Tie the anchor rope around her ankles," Miles orders me, no longer singing.

"No, I'm not going to do that, Miles," I say, lighting his face with my beam.

"Tie. The rope. To. Her. FEET."

"No."

Miles, seething, shines his light on Choke and says, "Then *you* do it."

Choke grabs the anchor rope and tries to tie it around Jeannie's ankles.

"Don't touch me!" Jeannie screams, kicking at him with both feet. Choke reaches for the stun gun in his back pocket. I time *my* kick perfectly—my shoe strikes the device and sends it flying into the coal-black water.

Before Choke and I can come to blows, a voice from the skiff shouts, "Freeze! Or I will shoot." Bodyguard shines his light on me.

I shine my light back on him. He is aiming his pistol at me. As soon as Jeannie sees this, she stops kicking and goes perfectly still.

"Now, let him tie your feet," shouts Miles at Jeannie. And then, as his next words—"YOU MISERABLE BITCH"—spew from his mouth, something inexplicable happens.

His words boom across the water at ten times their normal volume, crackly and distorted, with an echoey time delay—as if broadcasting from an electronic speaker of some kind.

"WHAT IS HAPPENING?" cries Miles. Again, his voice is unexplainably amplified. "WHAT THE HELL IS HAPPENING?"

Suddenly we are all bathed in light, beaming from multiple sources. Intense light, bright as day. From both sides of the channel. Searchlights, spotlights, heavy-duty flashlights.

"Put the gun down!" shouts a voice from the unseen loudspeaker.

A dozen boat engines turn over in unison, like giant cats growling. What the hell *is* happening?

CHAPTER 45

S hielding my eyes against the spotlight assault, I see two rows of fishing boats closing in on us, one from the north, one from the south. They've been sitting there, lining the channel in the dark, their silhouettes subsumed by the larger silhouettes of Seal Point and George's Knob.

As the two rows of boats churn closer, the searchlights and flashlights are lowered from our faces, but the whole area remains awash with light, from the boats' headlights and the crisscrossing beams. Familiar faces man the wheels of the boats, other familiar faces dot the deck-rails. Even Cliff Treadwell is here with his trawler. Some of the fishermen hold rifles and harpoons. Some hold phone cameras, recording everything that's going down.

The two rows of boats stop, hemming us into the center.

My eyes are drawn to the Bourbons' party fishing boat. It's equipped with a loudspeaker by which the captain talks to the passengers. Matt Bourbon stands at the wheel on the upper deck, and Enzo stands beside him, holding his cellphone up to the boat's microphone. The burner in my pocket is still beaming live to his phone! That's how Enzo has been blasting Miles's voice across the water.

Standing on the lower deck of the Bourbons' boat is Jim, the statie, now wearing his badge and holding his gun. This has become official police business.

"Drop your weapon and put your hands where I can see them," Jim shouts at Bodyguard. "That's a police order."

Bodyguard drops his weapon.

"Miles, you're under arrest. And so are you two." Jim points his gun at Bodyguard and Chokehold. "All of you, aboard this vessel."

The fishermen toss out lines to our two small boats. I grab one of the ropes, and Jeanie and I start pulling the inflatable toward the larger boat. Miles tries to lift his hands in surrender, but he is spotlighted from all directions by searchlights and flashlights. He covers his face to block the unforgiving beams.

A man's voice issues from a loudspeaker on another boat. "Miles Sutcliffe," it announces in a formal tone that defies challenge, "Fishermen's Court finds you guilty of treason."

A woman's voice—might be Dorna Caskie's—shouts from a megaphone on yet another boat, "Leave this island and don't come back. If we ever see your face again, your sentencing will commence. And it *will* be harsh."

I expect Jim to make some sort of pronouncement about how there'll be no vigilante justice here, yada-ya. But he says no such thing.

He's a cop, but he's an islander first.

I stand on the high bridge of the Bourbons' boat with Matt and Enzo, as Matt steers around Seal Point toward the harbor on the south side. Jim is holding Miles, Bodyguard, and Chokehold—his real name turns out to be Bela Negrescu—below on the first deck. Jeannie sits alone in a passenger seat at the rear of the upper deck.

"How did you find us in the pitch dark?" I ask Enzo.

"GPS. On your burner. We figured you had to come through the channel."

It was a total shot in the dark that he'd receive my call and figure out what was happening, but if anyone could do it, it would be Enzo.

"Keeping the line open was smart," he says. "I'm just glad your mic was decent and the battery held up. I recorded everything."

"Must have been a lot of work for you to pull all this together," I say to him.

"Nah. Once I put the word out, everyone mucked in." He winks.

"Whoa. What have we here?" says Matt, looking out a distance beyond his bow.

Simon Fischer's yacht is chugging around the island from the opposite direction. Two smaller craft flank it on its starboard side—they're "herding" it into the harbor. I can't read the lettering on the escort boats, but both have blue lights. Police. The smaller one, I'm guessing, is Kelvin, our part-time peace officer. The bigger one must be the Maine Marine Patrol or State Police. Kidnapping, murder, and conspiracy to commit murder are evidently frowned upon in these waters. I'd still love to shove a grenade into Fischer's anatomy with a plunger, but watching him get hauled away in handcuffs will have to do.

I turn to Matt Bourbon and say, "I was surprised to see the whole gang show up tonight. Especially after... today. I thought Fishermen's Court only looked out for its own."

"We do," says Matt. He doesn't look me in the eye but reaches out stiffly and squeezes my arm. "We do."

I want to say something, but nothing comes. I have no idea how to feel about Fishermen's Court right now, and maybe I never will. But I am happy, so bloody happy, to be alive.

I wander toward the back of the upper deck. Jeannie is standing now, looking out over the deck rail. Not at the parade of fishing boats churning up the brine behind us but across the Gulf, toward the mainland. I stand beside her and look out too.

"Going back on the ferry tomorrow?" she asks. "Back to Wentworth?"

"Ferry, yeah. Wentworth, nah. Just long enough to pack my stuff and settle things up with the house. Angie can take it. It should have been hers all along."

"Uh-huh. And your long-range plans?"

I make my way over to the opposite rail so that I'm facing the island. Jeannie moves with me. "I already told you those."

She shoots me a questioning glance.

"I'd like to meet your daughter. And if meeting me doesn't make her puke, I'd like to start spending time with the two of you. And if that goes well..."

"Shh, Finn," says Jeannie. "Please." But there's no anger or acrimony in her voice.

Fine. I'm good with silence. I gaze across the short stretch of water, locking my sights on Musqasset's town dock. Jeannie studies my face as if to see whether any trace of falseness is showing in my eyes. Then she settles her gaze on the town dock alongside mine.

After a few silent moments, her hand sneaks tentatively toward me and grasps the loose fabric of my shirt with two fingers. This is an old, old move of hers, going back to college. Whenever she wanted to feel close to me but wasn't quite sure where we stood, she would lightly clasp my shirt between her first two fingers and wait to see how I responded. It was a gesture I found irrationally endearing.

I reach my arms around her and pull her to my chest, pressing her head to my heart. And I hold her there, hard. This is not a move I would typically make— it smacks of possessiveness, territoriality, dominance. But right now, I don't much care what it smacks of. And neither, it seems, does Jeannie.

I feel her warm tears soaking my shirt, but they are good tears, cleansing tears, tears we have earned together. She wraps her arms around me and clutches me like a life preserver.

I look back at the line of fishing boats urging us onward from behind, then at the harbor pulling us forward with ever-widening arms, and I feel peace. For the first time I can remember. I don't know what tomorrow will bring. I don't have a plan. I don't have a goal. As of this moment, I know only three things with certainty.

This is my love.

This is my island.

This is my life.

THE END

Thank you for reading, and we sincerely hope you enjoyed *Wreckage*. As independently published authors, we rely on you, the reader, to spread the word. So if you enjoyed the book, please tell your friends and family, and if it isn't too much trouble, we would appreciate a brief review on Amazon. Thanks again. Our best to you and yours.

—J.D. & Andy

ACKNOWLEDGEMENTS

Thanks to my wife and soul-partner Karen for insisting I was a novelist despite my well-constructed arguments to the contrary. Thanks also to my late parents, Bob and Irene, and to my sisters, Carol, Diane, and Maureen (who left us in 2023), for their endless celebration of the English language over the years—and to my daughters, Phelan and Quinn, for continuing the word party. Together, you've been my writer's institute.

Immense gratitude to friends and family—Ken L., Ken M., Sean, Matt, Chase—who read various beta versions of the book and gave me appreciated comments. Ken L., your friendship, feedback, and encouragement are treasures in my life.

I also greatly appreciate the early support of the book by Jill Marsal of Marsal-Lyon Literary Agency and Reagan Rothe of Black Rose Writing.

Many thanks, too, to Dylan Pratt. We've had a fruitful and fun collaboration on two novels so far, and I hope there are many more.

ABOUT THE AUTHORS

J.D. Pratt is a moniker created to represent work published by the Pratt family after the passing of author Scott Pratt. Under this name, we'll continue telling compelling stories featuring colorful characters that stay true to the Scott Pratt literary legacy.

Jdprattfiction.com

Andy is the ghostwriter of over seventy fiction and non-fiction books, some for New York Times bestselling authors. He ghostwrote the #1 Amazon bestseller *Last Resort* in 2023. He has written/designed over twenty-five computer and video games, including many children's "classics" from the '90s and '00s, such as *Darby the Dragon,* several Magic Tales titles, *3D Dinosaur Adventure*, and *M&M's The Lost Formulas*. Andy is the author of the well-reviewed thrillers, *Fishermen's Court* and *The Treatment Plan*, and the award-winning children's book, *The Girl from Glocken's Glen*. He has also written an award-winning stage play, *Empties*, and done scriptwriting work for Disney, Blizzard Entertainment, Titanium Comics, and other entertainment companies. He is a member of International Thriller Writers.

Andywolfendon.com

ALSO BY J.D. PRATT

Last Resort (Joe Dillard Book #10)
Untitled Scott Pratt Biography – Releasing Fall, 2024
Jack Dillard Book #1 – Releasing Winter, 2024
Leon Bates Book #1 – Releasing Fall, 2025

LAST RESORT

BY

SCOTT PRATT

&

J.D. PRATT

ACKNOWLEDGEMENTS

Thank you to Dan Pratt and Andrew Wolfendon for helping me bring this manuscript to life. Also, thank you to Captain Andrew Ford for helping us get an authentic feel for a day in the life of an inmate in Washington County.
To Mom and Dad – Save me a seat by the lake and have a Bud Light waiting on me if it isn't too much trouble. In a bottle. I'll find you when the time is right.
I loved you both before I was born and I'll love you both after I'm long gone.
—Dylan Pratt

*This book, along with every book I've written and
every book I'll write, is dedicated to my darling
Kristy, to her unconquerable spirit and to her
inspirational courage. I loved her before I was born
and I'll love her after I'm long gone.*
                    —Scott Pratt

I have long feared that my sins would return to visit me, and the cost is more than I can bear.
—Benjamin Martin (character), *The Patriot*

PROLOGUE

The Summer Before

"Steeee..." called the umpire, lifting his fist to half-mast. Eleven-year-old Abby Pruitt stepped out of the batter's box and shot a look back at him, not because she disagreed with the call—it was low and outside, sure—but because the ump seemed bored. He couldn't even bother saying the whole word: steee-rike.

Doesn't he know this is the city championship! So why does he sound like he's about to take a nap? Abby didn't usually have a problem with the old guy. He had umped tons of her games and had a decent eye. He walked with a limp and didn't say much, but there was a game earlier in the season where he had yelled, "Go Abby!" after she got a hit.

Abby had shot up three inches in the last six months—all of it in her legs—and her uniform didn't hang on her the same way it used to. She no longer felt like "one of the boys." And she was just fine with that.

Anything that gave her an edge.

She stepped out of the batter's box and stretched the bat high over her head, playing the moment for all its drama. It was the bottom of the sixth—the final inning in Little League—and Abby's team, the Detrick Funeral Home Tigers, was down to its last out and behind by one.

The small bleacher-style stands at the Church Street ballpark in Elizabethton, Tennessee were filled on this cool Saturday morning. Full or empty, the ballpark was Abby's favorite place to be. It was the only place where things made sense to her. The only place where she never got that twisty feeling in her chest—that thing her mom called "The Anxiety."

Abby stepped back into the box and dug in for the next pitch. The crowd quieted.

"Forget about the strike zone," she heard Coach Jack say in her mind. "If it's a pitch you know you can hit, take a swing. I trust you."

I trust you. No one had ever said that to her before. Not once. This was Abby's second year playing baseball, and she had already learned so much from Coach Jack Dillard. Abby was one of only three girls in the local league. At first Coach didn't seem to know how to handle her and bent over backwards to pretend he didn't notice she was a girl. But once he saw the way she played, he started taking a special interest. Until last year, Abby had never felt like she was good at anything or belonged anywhere. She and her mom, Verna, had moved around a lot, living in Hampton, Erwin, and Mountain City before ending up in a rental trailer here in Elizabethton. Abby loved her mom, who worked as a clerk at Food City, but it always seemed to Abby that if Verna didn't have a kid, she might be happier.

But here, in *this* place, with *this* coach, Abby felt a sense of belonging.

The ball whipped past her, smacking the catcher's glove. "Steeee…" said the umpire, slightly louder this time. Abby was down in the count, one and two. She looked up at the opposing pitcher in his blue and white Dodgers' uniform. He was huge and looked like he was already shaving. No way this kid was 12.

Time to notch it up. She gave the pitcher a crooked smile, wriggled her torso, and hunkered down for the next pitch. Abby was pretty, and she knew it. She wasn't above using her "charms" to try to distract an opposing pitcher—or an opposing batter if she was on the mound. It was as if she had suddenly developed some new brand of voodoo. All she had to do was flash her eyes and toss her head a certain way and boys—*guys* too—would smile and do things for her. She thought maybe that was even why her daddy had started coming around a bit more often.

The pitcher set himself and stared at her. Someone yelled at him from the stands, "Come on, Jordan, you got this. She's just a girl."

Just a girl. The magic words. The words that brought out the killer inside. Coach Jack had told her she had the purest swing he'd ever seen—and he'd been a bigshot player in high school and college, had even made the Minors. She might not be able to drive the ball into the parking lot like some of the boys, but she could slow the pitch down with her eyes and she could *connect.* Same thing with her pitching. She'd probably never numb a catcher's glove-hand, but she made up for it with control and deception. At age 11, she already had a bankable curveball and a filthy sinker. And she was *always* around the zone.

Control. That's what Abby had in spades. Control.

As she tapped her bat on the plate and adjusted her hips, she heard a voice yell, "See the ball, Hawk!" It was Coach Jack. He called her Hawkeye, Hawk for short. "Slow it down. Breathe."

Abby squinted her eyes against the sun and waited to see what kind of pitch was coming. She watched the ball come straight down the pipe to her favorite spot, a little high and outside, and she slapped it over the first baseman's head. She tossed the bat and flew past Coach Jack, who was waving her on from the first base coach's box. "Take second!" he yelled, and Abby slid in even though she'd beaten the throw by a week.

The crowd cheered, and Abby looked over at Coach. His face lit up with a smile. As she dusted her pants off, she glanced back at the right-fielder who'd made the throw to second. That's when she saw him. Greg. Her dad. Sitting on the tailgate of an old blue truck with a guy who had the biggest beard she'd ever seen. They had cans of beer in their hands and a red-and-white plastic cooler between them. "Hells yeah!" Greg yelled. "That's my kid!"

Abby felt blood rush to her face, and her mind began to race. *How long has* he *been here?* A jumble of feelings assailed her. Yes, she was glad her dad had showed up for a change. But a bigger part of her was cringing inside. You never knew how he was going to act. Why did he have to be here now? During the most important game of her life. In front of the person she most wanted to impress. Coach Jack. *Oh well, game should be over in a minute.*

"She took you to school, lard ass!" Greg shouted at the pitcher. Abby's face flushed as the kid on the mound turned to see who was yelling. Greg's bearded buddy roared with laughter. "That all you got, fattie?" Abby wished she had a hole to crawl into.

The next kid up to bat was Jeff, a decent hitter. As he strode out toward the plate, half the parents and guests stood and cheered for him. *If Jeff gets a hit and I score, we tie it*, Abby told herself. *We can win this. We really can.*

"Come on, throw some more of that garbage so my kid can score!" Greg Pruitt shouted. The pitcher looked pleadingly at his coach. "Just ignore him," the Dodgers' coach yelled. "Some grownups don't know how to act." Abby thought she saw the glint of a tear in the pitcher's eye as he glanced back to see how far off second base she was.

The first pitch to Jeff was way over the catcher's head. Abby took off for third. She held up there as the catcher rushed back to the plate, ball in hand.

The Dodgers' coach marched out to the mound to talk to his pitcher. "Yeah, give the little baby his bottle!" yelled Greg. Abby glanced at Coach Jack and saw rage flash in his eyes. *Does Coach know that loudmouth jerk is my father? God, I hope not.*

The Dodgers' coach patted his pitcher on the head and returned to the dugout.

"You got this, Jordan," a parent shouted.

"He don't got shit," yelled Greg. "He's a fat little momma's boy."

The pitcher no longer looked like a grownup to Abby. He looked like a fragile kid. She knew the feeling. Greg's words had the power to shrink people.

The instant the ball left the pitcher's hand, Abby knew she was going to tie the game. She started moving before she even heard the ping of the aluminum bat. The ball hit the dirt and skipped toward the shortstop, who fielded it cleanly and drew his arm back.

The throw to home would be close, for sure.

It wasn't. The ball sailed high, and the catcher had to step back and reach for it. Abby slid into home on one leg and was safe by a Tennessee mile.

"Yer out!" the umpire called.

Abby's world imploded.

Out? What just happened here? She *knew* she was safe, but the ump had said out. Which meant the game was over. Her Tigers had lost. *How?*

Parents jumped up, shouting and booing. Abby took a step back as Coach Jack strode toward the umpire to have a chat. And then suddenly, Greg Pruitt was right in the middle of things. Shouting and cursing at the old ump. Spit flying out of his mouth, eyes flashing like a crazy dog's. Coach Jack held his arm out like a traffic cop's, trying to calm Greg down. Abby rushed in to tell her dad to stop, but Coach blocked her and told her to go wait in the dugout.

That was when Greg made a move on the ump. Shoved him. Hard. In the chest. The old guy hit the ground with a loud "oooof" and a puff of dust. A collective gasp went up as parents rushed in to make sure the ump was okay.

Abby froze as Coach Jack stepped up to Greg and the two men stood face to face. Coach Jack Dillard had never looked so big before, and her father had never looked so small. "Leave. Now," Coach said, his voice calm but tight, "or I will *remove* you. Your choice."

A hush came over the bystanders as the two men faced off. Greg pumped himself two inches taller and leaned into Jack's face. "Oh, you the big man now? Coach Wonderful? You gonna be my kid's new daddy now, that it?"

"I mean it, Pruitt. You have three seconds." Abby's heart pounded. "…Two."

For a moment, Abby was sure her father was going to take a swing. But he just smiled, poked his finger into Coach's chest, and said, "You're gonna regret this…" And then he turned and walked off with the bearded guy, adding over his shoulder, "*Counselor.*"

PART I

CHAPTER 1

Tuesday, April 12

It was my fiftieth birthday, and I was celebrating the occasion by steeping in the aromas of human waste and industrial floor cleaner in the visitors' room of the Washington County Detention Center. My name is Joe Dillard, and it was rare for me to interview clients in jail these days. After more than twenty years in criminal defense, I now spent most of my work hours, which were down to about ten a week, in a largely advisory role at our small firm in Jonesborough, Tennessee. My son, Jack, and his fiancée, Charlie—Charleston Story, an auburn-haired beauty who reminded me of my wife, Caroline—carried the bulk of the caseload nowadays, and our legal secretary, Beverly, ran the office.

On this fine spring morning, however, Jack and Charlie had an appointment to tour a wedding venue called Millstone Manor, down near Greeneville. Thus was I "volun-told" by Beverly that I would inherit the honor and privilege of interviewing a court-appointed defendant by the name of Clovis "Badger" Daley.

According to his records, Badger was a semi-regular guest at the "Washington County Hyatt," though never for anything too serious. Until now. The door buzzed open and a deputy with a sagging, regret-filled face marched Badger in like he was a truck dolly and parked him on the other side of the table from where I sat. Badger was short, densely packed, and muscular—like his animal namesake. His dark-brown mutton-chop sideburns and heavy eyebrows, in tandem with the widow's peak tattooed on his forehead, told me the nickname was one he courted proudly. Maybe it's just me, but I've always believed that the day a man gets his first facial tattoo is the day he pretty much kicks the corporate ladder into the woodchipper.

Badger had been arrested on a second-degree murder charge, and my son Jack had caught the case, courtesy of one Judge Cora Mae Talbot. The DA's office had minced no words about its intention to press for the maximum sentence, and, frankly, I'd have done the same, back when I was DA. All evidence pointed toward a cataclysmically guilty client.

As the deputy left the room, the orange-clad Badger folded his arms, sat back, and grinned widely, unveiling a corncob of yellow teeth. He smelled like spoiled laundry and sweat.

"Hot damn. You's my lawyer?"

"For the moment. Are you Clovis Daley?"

"Badger. Ain't nobody calls me Clovis 'cept my Mamaw, and she been dead six years now. Say, ain't you the *famous* Dillard, the one I seen on TV a few times? I thought I'd be gettin' your kiddo, not the man hisself!"

For a man staring down the barrel of a murder charge, he seemed downright perky.

"Jack couldn't be here today, so I agreed to do your initial interview, Mr. Da… Badger."

"Well, butter my butt and call me a biscuit." He slapped his thigh with glee. "Looks like I'm in good hands. Like them ol' Allstate commercials. Think you can git me off?"

My mouth replied, "My son Jack will give you the best defense possible, I'm sure," but my brain was already thinking, *No way on God's green Earth.*

From what Jack had told me, Badger was found by police, sitting on the tailgate of his truck with a literal smoking gun in his hand, five yards from the murdered man, waiting to be taken into custody.

"Badger, I'm a little fuzzy on the details. Why don't you tell me what happened? I'm on my son's legal team, so anything you say to me is protected by attorney-client privilege."

"I shot that peckerwood Eddie Braun stone-cold dead with a Rock Island M-two-aught-six. You're welcome."

I had to admit, his candor was refreshing. Most inmates shout their innocence from the rooftops even when they've been caught dead to rights. Badger not only admitted his guilt, he seemed proud of it.

According to the report I'd read, the police had received a call the previous Thursday from a woman in Limestone, a sleepy community southwest of Jonesborough that ran along the railroad track. Mrs. Arnita Matthews told the duty officer she "might have found a dead man" on her property. When police arrived and looked behind her storage shed, they were puzzled by her equivocation: a male body was found, face down and covered with flies, rotting away in a pool of dried-black blood. Matthews reported having smelled what she thought was a dead animal for a week before finally taking a peek behind the cinder-block structure.

The ground behind the woman's shed was peppered with the short, sharp stumps of invasive bamboo stalks that had been cut off near the ground, and it appeared the man had fallen, impaled himself on several of the stumps, and bled out. The body, identified by the contents of the wallet in his pocket, was that of Clayton Daley. Badger's brother.

"Did you tell the police you shot Mr. Braun?" I asked.

"Do I look like an id'jit?"

I refrained from answering the question.

"Naw," he said. "All I told the boys in blue was that I done nothin' wrong. And that ain't no word of a lie."

"Explain, Mr. Daley. Er, Badger."

"I done the *right* thing by killin' that egg-suckin' dawg."

I sighed. "Why don't we start at the beginning?"

Badger surveyed my face with a crunched brow, took a deep breath, leaned back, and let his gaze drift into the middle distance.

"'Bout a month ago, Clay went missin'. ...*Again*."

"That would be your brother Clayton? He went missing often?"

"More 'n never. Clay had a problem with booze and hillbilly heroin." Local slang for Oxycontin. Oxy was a major player in the opioid addiction crisis that had been sweeping the Appalachians like wildfire for years.

"He'd been gone pert' near a month when that lady found him a few days ago. They had me come down to the morgue to make sure it was him. 'Bout broke poor Momma's heart."

"I'm sorry about your brother, Badger, but the police ruled his death an accident. What does that have to do with Mr. Braun?"

"Weren't no accident. Braun killed my brother sure as I killed Braun. He's killed *lots* of folks, I reckon, peddlin' that poison of his to anyone who could rub two nickels together. That stuff's what done my brother in. 'Bout time somebody did somethin'."

"Help me understand."

"Clay couldn't kick the oxy. A few months back, he lost his license on account of takin' that poison, and he started drivin' one of them scooters." Small gas-powered scooters were the transportation mode of choice for those who had lost their driving privileges in the great state of Tennessee.

"Last Fri-dee around lunchtime I'm down't the Marathon station on 321, on my way to work, when this kid pulls in next to me on Clay's scooter. I recognize the decals. I as't the kid where he got it, and he says from Braun. So that night, when I get offa work, I head out to Braun's place to have us a parlay, and he tells me Clay sold him the scooter a few weeks ago to buy some more pills. 'Dumbass just took the pills and wandered off through them trees over there,' he says to me." Badger lifted his eyes to mine, redness rising in his face. "So, you see, Mr. Joe, when my brother turned up in that morgue a couple days later, I knew exactly who done it to him."

The report said the police received a call Sunday evening at 7:16 p.m. from the same woman who had found the Clayton Daley kabob behind her storage shed and who happened to live next door to Eddie Braun's single-wide. She told them she'd heard gunshots from the direction of the Braun residence. Twenty minutes later, a deputy arrived at the trailer to find Edmund Braun sitting in a lawn chair on his front porch, three bullet holes in his chest and belly, and Badger Daley sitting on the tailgate of his truck, a gun in his lap and an open bag of Brim's barbecue pork rinds in his hands.

I'd read the report, but I wanted to hear it from Daley. "So, what happened next, Badger?"

"I went back to see Braun and canceled his birth certificate."

"You shot him."

"No sense lyin' to a famous lawyer."

Badger was quiet for a minute as I took some notes. When I looked up, he was staring at me with tears in his eyes.

"I know Clay weren't no saint, Mr. Joe. He made his choices. But Braun just kept feeding him that poison, and Clay just couldn't kick it. *Couldn't.* You ever had someone do a thing like that to a person you love, Mr. Joe?"

I thought of my sister Sarah. When I was a boy, I walked in on my uncle Raymond sexually assaulting her. It was an incident that set off endless ripple effects in my life, not to mention Sarah's. None of them good. I was too young to do anything about it at the time, but I think if I'd had access to a gun, I'd have killed my uncle Raymond on the spot.

When I reached adulthood, I wasn't so powerless anymore, and I must confess there have been many times over the years that my anger has driven me to step outside the lines to protect someone I love. Even if they didn't strictly need protecting. It was only by sheer good fortune that I hadn't found myself on the other side of this table.

"Yeah, Badger. I've been there."

"Then you know, Mr. Dillard. Family's all they' is."

CHAPTER 2

After my meeting with Badger, I ambled out to the parking lot in the sweet-smelling Jonesborough air. The mountains of East Tennessee can be a bit oppressive, climate-wise, in the throes of summer, but most days in fall and spring made you forget all that. Today was sunny, just north of seventy degrees, you could practically hear the trees and flowers kicking up their heels in celebration. Part of me wanted to join them, but a rock of heaviness sat in my chest.

As I drove home in my truck, I felt the weight of the conversation I needed to have with Caroline and the kids pressing down on me. I had planned to talk to them on the drive back from the university hospital last Friday but couldn't muster the courage. How does one utter such terrible syllables?

So instead, I'd spent the weekend enjoying my family. Milking every drop of life out of every precious interaction. Trying to feel gratitude for what we still had.

Gratitude for my blessings was not my customary response to awful news. Historically, when life dealt me a blow I perceived as unfair, I went straight for anger. These last few days had felt different, though. And now, as I drove out along the Boones Creek Highway, heading toward Johnson City, I felt an almost *sweet* sadness. I noticed I was driving below the speed limit. How many times in my life had that ever happened?

As a younger man, I sped through everything, always in a big damn hurry to get to… who knows what. I crammed in a lot of living, but I also missed a lot. I wondered if today's slower pace stemmed from my talk with Dr. Seals or from turning fifty. Or both.

I crossed Kingsport Highway and drove out along Pickens Bridge Road, toward Boone Lake, where I had raised my family and where I still lived.

Fifty years. Damn. They'd been pretty good ones, though, hadn't they? Sure, there had been some tough times, some *really* tough ones, but, still, I'd been ridiculously fortunate. I thought of every precious day I'd spent with my wife, Caroline. I was still as crazy in love with her as I'd been in high school. Who gets to say that at fifty? I thought of how proud I was of our son Jack and the man he had become. Of our daughter Lilly and how much like her mother she was. I thought of everything I'd done to try to make a difference in this world, and, for perhaps the first time in my life, the old cliché rang true: I wouldn't change a thing.

Scratch that, I thought, pulling my truck into the garage. There was one *very large thing* I would change in a nanosecond. Caroline's cancer. I hated it to my core.

I felt the old anger rising again as I walked toward the house. I took a deep breath before entering, stopping on the porch to rub Rio's head. When my old German Shepherd was younger, he'd be so happy to see me he'd pee all over my shoe. These days, he just lay on his doggy bed and thumped his tail a few times. Guess I wasn't the only one who'd slowed down.

"Do anything exciting this morning, ol' boy?"

One tail-thump. No pee.

"Yeah… me either."

I stepped in the door and made my way to the kitchen, dropping my keys and briefcase on the table and draping my jacket over a chair.

"Just me," I announced.

My daughter, Lilly, poked her head out of the main bedroom.

"Back already?" she said, padding up to give me a hug and kiss.

"Amazing how fast things go when clients actually tell the truth." I nodded toward the bedroom. "How is she?"

"Same."

Last Friday, Caroline, Jack and I had taken yet another trip to Vanderbilt University Medical Center in Nashville to meet with Caroline's doctors. Lilly flew in from Boston, where her husband was doing his residency, and met us at Vandy. She rode back to East Tennessee with us and was scheduled to return to Boston in the morning.

That meant no more deferrals. Today was the day "the talk" needed to happen.

When Caroline had first been diagnosed with breast cancer almost nine years ago, there was never any question: we would beat it. And we had. Many times. Caroline was the strongest, most determined person I knew. But cancer doesn't care. Cancer is like the monster from that movie *The Thing*. No matter how many times we knocked it down, it always came back. In some new form. Over the years, we had ridden the roller coaster of hope and heartache till we were flat worn out: A period of relative health, then more cancer. More treatments. More hope. Then a period of stasis or remission. Then more cancer. More tears. More pain.

At this point, she was sleeping at least sixteen hours a day. Which was a mercy, really. The pain she endured when lucid was so intense, Oxycontin was like baby aspirin. And when the oxy didn't cut it, it was on to the morphine.

There was no "next level" of pain medication.

"Is she asleep?"

Lilly nodded. "You going in to the office today?"

I shook my head no.

My self-imposed retirement was partly due to sheer weariness—hell, I'd been weary ten years earlier when I made my first attempt to get out of the legal profession. Lying clients, manipulative law enforcement officers, petty politics, and arrogant judges had taken a toll on my passion for the law. But it wasn't weariness that kept me home these days. It was Caroline. She needed a lot of hands-on care and couldn't be left alone for long. The real reason I spent so much time at home, though, was a selfish one: I didn't want to miss a minute with her.

When we took the trip to Nashville last week, I'd known things weren't good, but we'd been down that road before. And we'd always toughed it out, somehow. From time to time, some well-meaning doctor would mention "end-of-life care." That conversation never went well. We weren't going to give up. Ever. From the beginning, we had agreed that the moment we lost hope was the moment cancer won. Not an option for the Dillards.

This meeting at Vanderbilt had been different. The cancer, which had long ago metastasized to her bones, was adapting and becoming more aggressive. Over the past few months, the tumors had moved into the soft tissue. We were now monitoring several small spots on her liver, as well as a particularly sinister tumor that had drilled its way through her skull and was threatening to infiltrate the meningeal fluid around her brain. Once cancer cells start showing up in that fluid, it's game over.

After about thirty minutes of the usual examinations and questions, the lead oncologist, Dr. Janet Seals, asked me to step outside to sign some insurance papers.

There were no papers to sign.

"We're out of options, Joe." Janet had become more than a doctor to us over the years. She was a friend—kind and brilliant, unafraid to try something aggressive if she thought it would help. She read my eyes before I could even respond and said, "I know what you're thinking. You and Caroline have been abundantly clear that you will never throw in the towel, but Joe… there's nothing left that we can do."

"Quitting is not on the table."

"I knew you'd say that." She sighed. "And I *can* prescribe something if you want: a very old, very potent chemo drug that may extend her life by a few days…"

"We'll take it. We'll take whatever days we can get."

"…but they won't be good days, Joe. Not at all."

The rage flared up again. It is the curse of cancer medications that they are, for all intents and purposes, poison. Poison that's meant to kill cancer cells but invariably destroys a lot more than that. But I didn't even need to ask Caroline to know her answer—she'd want to try it. She'd want to keep fighting. Even if it meant her final days would be hell on earth.

"I'm sorry, Joe. Take her home. Be together. Tell me your decision when you're ready, but just know this: stopping isn't quitting." Her voice began to shake. "Quitting is when you don't try, and I have never, in all my years of oncology, seen anyone try as hard as Caroline Dillard. But sometimes, stopping treatment is… the right thing to do."

I'm not sure how long I stood there after Dr. Seals left, but eventually I went back into the room where Caroline and the kids were waiting. Caroline had nodded off but she half-opened her eyes and looked at me.

"Anything new?" she croaked.

"More of the same. It's going to take some time."

She raised her eyebrows. "You're pissed, I can tell. Why?"

"I was just hoping for… more progress."

The ride back to East Tennessee was painfully quiet. It was as if a ghost had moved into the car with us. On the way *to* Nashville that morning, Jack and I had talked about work and baseball—the Little League team he coached had made the finals last year, and he was excited about this year's prospects, especially a girl player named Abby Pruitt—while Caroline slept in the back seat.

On the long ride home, no one spoke.

We hadn't discussed the trip since.

CHAPTER 3

"This is our famous stone bridge," said the slight man in the seersucker suit and straw fedora. Ernesto was the events coordinator for Millstone Manor, a ten-acre indoor/outdoor wedding venue outside of Greeneville. Jack and Charlie followed him onto the gray stone bridge that arched over a babbling creek. "And everyone—I mean *everyone*—wants to do their formal shots here. You can see why."

Jack could indeed. The moss-covered bridge looked like it was plucked from a fairytale. Jack Dillard and Charlie Story looked out over the meandering stream and across a field of butterweed toward the stone manor, nestled against the tree line. They shot a knowing glance at each other. This was exactly the kind of venue they were looking for. Their plan was to host a simple but elegant wedding—outdoors, if possible—for a small group of family and friends. They didn't want to spend house-down-payment money on one day of pageantry; they were saving the money they earned at the law practice to build a future together. But still, they wanted their wedding day to be memorable. Millstone Manor offered a nice blend of elegance and affordability.

Jack wished he felt less distracted, though. He pressed his hand against the phone in his pocket for the tenth time, as if expecting it to vibrate any second.

Ernesto spun on his heels and led them back toward the manor, his uplifted palms saying *feast your eyes on these gardens and walkways.* Ernesto wore rose-rimmed sunglasses and a manscaped beard and looked like a three-quarter-sized version of a Hollywood actor. "From what you've told me," he said, "you'd probably be interested in our Intimate Gatherings package, for groups of fifty or less. That includes up to fifty chairs for the ceremony itself and another fifty for the reception. The beauty of the IG package is that we can switch from an outdoor to an indoor setting at a moment's notice, if the Tennessee weather gods decide not to cooperate. The Garden Chapel is a great sunny-day choice, but we can always…"

Jack tuned out. Part of him was thrilled to be making actual wedding plans with Charlie, the woman he loved, but part of him felt deeply unsettled. Ever since the trip to Nashville with his mother, a cloak of heaviness had sat on his shoulders. He felt like he was waiting for a shoe to drop. He placed his hand on his phone again.

"…And our award-winning chef has just released some to-die-for new menu options," Ernesto continued as he led the couple into his office at the rear of the manor. Jack tripped on the door jamb, snapping himself back to awareness. Ernesto sat at his desk and waved Jack and Charlie into the guest chairs. "Unfortunately…" Ernesto clicked a mouse and brought his computer to life. "We're booked *pretty* solid through December. We do have one opening at the end of June—the couple got into a fight over a pet tortoise and called the whole thing off—and then nothing till early October."

Jack and Charlie did a silent eye consultation. Ernesto took the cue. "Well, I'll leave you two lovebirds alone to talk. Can I bring you back some coffee? It's *good*."

The couple nodded graciously, and Ernesto departed, leaving them alone.

"I love this place," Charlie said, eyes wide. "It's just what we were hoping for."

"It is," Jack concurred, but his enthusiasm level hit only a 7 out of 10.

"But...?"

"There's no but."

"Then why am I hearing one in your voice? Come on, Jack, what are you thinking about? Your mom, right?" Charlie herself had no family considerations. Her mother had abandoned her as a child, and her father had spent most of her life in prison. A few years back, he had been killed just before his release. Except for her horse, her dog, and Jack, Charlie was alone in the world. "You're worried about how she's going to—"

"This wedding is super important to her, Charlie. In fact, I think it's the one thing she's still looking forward to in her life."

"That's why we're here, making plans, instead of waiting. But if you don't think she'll like this place, we can..."

"No, no, it's not that."

"Then what?"

"It's more about... the timing."

"How so?"

"I don't know, Charlie. That trip to Nashville was..." He shook his head, looking down at the floor. "And you saw her on Sunday. She barely made it out of bed. The only time she came to life was when you showed her the venue brochures. And then she became *Mom* again. There was a light in her eyes and... I mean, it's almost as if..."

"You can say it, Jack: It's almost as if she's keeping herself alive *for* the wedding."

"People do that. They stick around for important events. Did you know that in China, the mortality rate among old folks goes down in the weeks before Chinese New Year? People stay alive for the holiday."

"And now you feel like we're holding your mom's fate in our hands?"

"Maybe we are," Jack said. "To some extent." He craned his head to look out the door for Ernesto, then lowered his voice. "I mean, I hope she's around for five more years. Ten. But what if her timetable is... shorter? In that case, the date we pick could be critical."

Charlie took Jack's hand and looked him in the eye. "Part of you thinks we should grab that June date, to be sure your mom..."

"Makes it," Jack whispered. His hand unconsciously groped for his phone again. No calls or messages. "On the other hand," he went on, "maybe if we go with the October date, we give her motivation to... stick around longer."

"That's possible. But it's also possible that if we wait *too* long..."

"Exactly."

Charlie took Jack's hand, cradled it in hers. "Jack, can I just say? You're overthinking this. And giving us too much power in the matter. Your mom will be here on this planet until exactly such time as she—and her Maker—decide. It's not on us. And besides, I don't think turning our wedding day into a death sentence for your mom is a super-great way to launch a marriage, do you?"

"No, but still. Choosing the date feels… significant." Jack's phone vibrated. The call he'd been half-expecting all day? He slipped his phone out of his pocket. A text. From his dad. Joe Dillard was not a texter—a text from him meant business. *"Can you come to the house before the b'day dinner?"* the message read. The whole Dillard clan was planning to go out to dinner together that evening—to celebrate Joe's fiftieth birthday and to get Caroline out of the house. *"I want to talk to you kids about something."* Oh, God. The last time Jack's dad had asked to talk to "you kids" was after his mother had received her initial cancer diagnosis.

Jack pulled in a shuddery breath. "Let's go with the June date."

CHAPTER 4

Caroline managed to look luminous as we strolled into Café Luna—despite her rail-thinness. She wore a sparkling violet top and a light-catching set of dangling earrings I'd bought her in the Caymans during a magical trip we took there years ago, along with her "good wig," which was combed to a sheen. But most of the sparkle emanated from her. It was hard to believe this was the same person I'd spent the last few days and weeks with; the person who barely got out of bed except to use the toilet. Maybe it was my birthday that was giving her the energy boost—if so, I would have a birthday every day—or maybe it was the prospect of dining at one of her favorite restaurants with her whole family around her.

I'd switched our reservation to Café Luna in Johnson City at the last minute, not only because Caroline loved it here but also because it had a private back room. I'd had "the talk" with the kids back at the house while Caroline was still asleep, and we'd discussed the terrible options before us. I had also given them their marching orders: tonight was for celebrating only.

So, we were all on the same page. But still, raw emotion was apt to rear its head. And if it did, I wanted us to have some privacy.

A young woman in a white shirt and black bowtie signaled to Caroline and me. "This way, Mr. and Mrs. Dillard."

Caroline's face lit up with a smile of recognition. I'd specifically requested Ashley as our server. She was a former dance student of Caroline's. For over two decades, Caroline had run a dance studio in Johnson City and had taught hundreds of local girls, many of them now women, how to chassé and pirouette. Her work had probably done more to uplift the collective spirit of East Tennessee than that of any ten therapists or priests.

Ashley led us to the table, set for seven, chatting with Caroline as we walked. We were the first to arrive, but the kids showed up a minute later. They'd come in a separate car: Jack and Charlie, my legal "protégés," and Lilly. Lilly was carrying a guitar case, which she quietly ditched in a corner of the room, and they all wore smiles that were a little too bright. Everyone told Caroline how incredible she looked as we made small talk and pretended to read our menus. The cuisine was not my personal favorite—tapas, which I think is Spanish for "not enough food." But tonight wasn't about the dining. It was about family.

Sarah, my sister, came in a few minutes later, carrying a wrapped present, her eight-year-old daughter Grace in tow. She handed me the gift, saying, "This is a giant scam, by the way, this whole fiftieth birthday thing. Because if you were really fifty, that would make *me* fifty-one. Which literally *can't* be true, can we all agree on that?" Everyone laughed.

Sarah and I had traveled a rocky road together over the years. There'd been the time she'd stolen Lilly's car and wrecked it, drunk, and I'd had her arrested; the time she'd driven drunk with Grace in the car and I'd forced her to enter rehab; the drugs; the bad choices in men... It was all fallout from the trauma she had suffered as a kid, of course, but that didn't make it easier to live with. For the last six years, though, she'd been doing amazingly well. Clean, sober, and running her own restaurant in Jonesborough. And somehow managing to look years younger than her kid brother.

At Sarah's bidding, Ashley brought champagne to the table, along with a split of the non-alcoholic stuff for Sarah. My sister hadn't been briefed on the latest news about Caroline, though, and so her energy level was at a higher pitch than the rest of ours.

Playing unofficial host, Sarah clinked a fork on her glass of faux champagne. "I'd like to propose a birthday toast," she said, hoisting her glass. "But first... I believe Lilly has a musical surprise in store for us."

Lilly, a dancer like her mother, had been teaching herself guitar lately, as she stayed home to care for our grandson, Joseph. Rumor had it—okay, Jack spilled the beans—she had written a song for my fiftieth birthday. A humorous set of lyrics set to Dylan's *The Times They Are a-Changin'*. But right now, she looked like she would rather perform a tap dance in a minefield. "The talk" had shaken her to the roots.

"Maybe Lilly would rather save the song for later," I suggested.

Lilly beamed her gratitude at me, and Sarah took note of the somber undercurrent beneath our celebratory exteriors. An awkward silence descended. It was broken by a clinking sound to my right. Caroline, tapping *her* champagne glass.

"Actually, *I* have a toast," my wife announced, "and a bit of an announcement." Announcement? What was this? "But if I'm going to do this…" She raised her finger, catching Ashley the server's eye. "Could I get a Bud Light instead? No glass."

Everyone cheered as Ashley dashed off to fill the order. Bud Light was Caroline's go-to celebration drink. And she liked to drink it from the bottle, which never failed to delight me.

When Caroline had her Bud firmly in hand, she lifted it with her bone-thin fingers and said, "First, the toast. I'd like to wish a happy eight hundredth birthday to…" She paused and looked at me. "The kindest, strongest, handsomest, and just plain *good*-est man I've ever met."

"Aw, did you have to bring your boyfriend along?" I quipped. "It's my birthday."

My joke garnered more laughs than it merited, and then Caroline continued. "Seriously, Joe. In addition to things I can't say at a, ahem, family gathering, you've been my friend, my partner, my knight, my caretaker—which I never wanted you to be—and my rock. If I say any more than that, I'll cry. And I don't want to do that. Not tonight. Tonight is an unexpected gift. I didn't know if I'd ever sit around a table like this again with my favorite people on Earth."

"There'll be many more occasions like this," said Sarah, lifting her glass. "Many more."

The rest of us raised our glasses and echoed, "Many more! Many more! Many more!"

Caroline waited politely for the chorus to peter out to silence. "I appreciate the sentiment," she said, then shifted to a somber gear, "but we all know it isn't true."

The quiet of the room deepened to a well-like silence. Jack opened his mouth to protest, but Caroline shushed him with her hand. "I don't mean to be maudlin or self-pitying, just honest. And honesty is something I think we all need right now…" Glances shot around the table in anticipation of her next words. "Sarah, you might not want Grace here for this part."

Sarah wrapped her arm around her daughter, signaling Grace was fine to stay.

"I'm dying," Caroline said. A heartbeat passed. Then another. "I haven't spoken those words aloud before—refused to even consider them—but I'm saying them now. I'm dying."

The temperature dropped in my gut. If this was what honesty felt like, give me deceit.

"Stop it, Mom," said Jack, an edge of real anger in his voice. "I don't want to hear that kind of talk from you. None of us do."

"I'm sorry, Jack," Caroline replied. "I'm not thrilled to be saying it either. But it's true. I'm dying, and it's time we all accept it."

"Come on, babe," I said, attempting lightness. "We can talk about this later. Let's just enjoy our drinks and order some extremely tiny plates of food."

"Stop it, Joe. We need to do this first." She looked around the table, fierceness beaming from her eyes. "Do you really think I don't know what went down at Vandy last Friday?" she said to us all. "Joe, it was written all over your face. Do you seriously think I didn't call Janet Seals the moment I got home?"

That was exactly what I thought. Fool that I am.

"I know what my options are. Or rather, my lack of options. And I've made a decision. I'm not taking that last-resort chemo drug. Or any other horrific Hail Marys they may try to throw my way."

"What are you saying?" Jack snapped at her, almost shouting. "You're waving the white flag? Giving up? That's not my mother talking." Jack pushed his chair away from the table and stood up as if to leave. "I don't want to listen to this anymore. When you're ready to—"

"Jack! Sit!" Caroline thundered. Where was this resurgence of power coming from? Jack obeyed his mother, sheepishly. "Listen to me, all of you." She paused. "Life ends. At some point, life ends. Death—it's time we used the 'd' word—is not a defeat, it's a fact. I hate to break it to you, but none of us are getting out of this thing alive. My time is up. Sooner than we hoped, but it *is* up. Soon. And I have only one question for you. Do you want to help me? Or not?"

"You know we do, Mom," Lilly said. "Don't even ask that. But how can we help you if you're not even going to help your—"

"Lilly! You're not hearing me. Do you *really* want to help me? If so, I need you to be *with* me on this, not against me. I need you to accept my choice. I need you to accept reality. That means no more fighting this thing. No more shaking our fists at God. I'm dying, and I'm scared, and I need my family with me. On this final leg. What I don't need is you punching walls or covering your ears in denial because *you're* too scared to talk about it."

She looked around the table, locking eyes with each of us. Charlie met her gaze more fully than the rest of us and reached out to take her hand. Jack and Lilly nodded, looking down at the table. I squeezed my wife from the side and kissed her head.

"All right, then," she said. "This morning I called Nolichucky Hospice Care. I want to start hospice services tomorrow."

The air left the room at the word *hospice*. Hospice meant the end of all curative treatment and the start of purely palliative care. Make the patient comfortable and help them with their transition. Hospice was one-way only. And we all knew it.

But none of us protested.

"Accepting death doesn't mean we can't appreciate life," Caroline said. "In fact, it means we can appreciate it ten times more. Tonight, we're celebrating. Celebrating Joe's birthday. Celebrating my amazing, wonderful family. And I, for one, intend to enjoy the hell out of it." She seized the menu with wide eyes and a ravenous growl. "Let's order! I'm starving."

That was when it hit me: the burst of vigor she was exhibiting tonight was not because of my birthday or even because of the gathering of the clan. It was the energy one acquires when one has made an unshakable life decision.

CHAPTER 5

Five Days Later

The 911 call came in at 6:05 a.m.

DISPATCHER: 911, what is your emergency, please?

CALLER: It's my girl! My little girl! I can't find her anywhere. She plumb disappeared.

DISPATCHER: What is the address where the emergency is occurring, ma'am?

CALLER: I don't know where the emergency is occurring! I don't know where she is! Someone took her. I'm calling from the Baptist church out on Willow Springs. But that ain't where we live, me and my girl. We's over on Possum Hollow. They shut my phone off, so I had to come down here.

DISPATCHER: Your name, please?

CALLER: Verna. Verna Roy. R-o-y.

DISPATCHER: Are you able to stay where you are until an officer arrives? Can you do that, ma'am?

CALLER: Yes! The Holston Mountain Baptist Church.

DISPATCHER: We have the address. Can you tell me exactly what happened?

CALLER: I slept hard last night. Took a extra one of my pills, 'cause my thoughts was racin'. Mighta had a drink or two, I don't remember. But when my alarm went off for work, she was gone! No note, nothin', no cereal bowl in the sink. She never leaves this early. And she *never* leaves without writin' a note. Ever since we had that trouble last summer with that pervo prowlin' around these parts, she knows better. She's in trouble, I know it. You gotta find her!

DISPATCHER: Have you checked the places she usually frequents? Called her friends?

CALLER: My car ain't workin', and I told you, my phone's shut off. That's why she'd never leave without tellin' me. Somethin' bad happened. A mother knows. She can feel it in her belly, in her baby place. Besides, her bike's still at the house. Oh, I forgot to say that! Her bike's still at the house! She don't go nowhere without her bike. Somethin' bad happened!

DISPATCHER: What is your daughter's name?

CALLER: Abigail. Abigail Pruitt. We call her Abby. She kept her daddy's last name because he said he'd stop sendin' the checks if we changed it. Not that he sends 'em anyway.

DISPATCHER: The girl's father doesn't live with you? Is that correct?

CALLER: That's *damn* correct.

DISPATCHER: Can you tell me his name and address?

CALLER: His name's Gregory Pruitt. And his address is Somewhere in the Butt-Crack of Unicoi County. I'd tell you to check him out, but I know *he* didn't take her, because that would mean takin' some 'sponsibility for her. Which he ain't done since she was three.

DISPATCHER: Can you give me a physical description of the child?

CALLER: About five-two, tall for her age. Close to my height. Sandy hair, down to her shoulders. Pretty young thing. Prettier'n her mama. And don't she know it? Struttin' around, shakin' her hair and peekin' out from behind it, all coy-like. I keep tellin' her, you gotta watch that stuff. You don't know yet 'cause you're only eleven. That stuff's like gunpowder. If you ain't careful, it can get you into a world of hurt. Maybe it already done happened.

✶✶✶

"And can you show us her bicycle, please, ma'am?"

Elizabethton Police Officer James T. Grandy was not having a grand morning. He'd slept the night on the old couch in the basement after arguing till twelve thirty with his wife, then polishing off a half pint of Fireball. The morning sun felt like a searchlight in his eyes, and his mouth tasted like burnt cotton as he followed Verna Roy from the house to the back shed. He and his partner, Officer Melissa Price, had met the distraught mother at the Baptist church where she made the 911 call. After questioning her there, they'd driven her home in the cruiser.

Home was a sixty-year-old house trailer on the side of a wooded hill about three-quarters of a mile from the church. The trailer's sun-faded, mustard-colored metal siding was dented all around, at shoulder height, as if someone had punched the place a thousand times. Its overgrown lot was strewn with abandoned objects: a bottomless rowboat, a car engine, two refrigerators, a stack of old bed springs.

Verna, clad in micro-shorts and a lacy gray baby-doll tank top that looked like underwear to Grandy, pointed into the doorless toolshed. A pink Huffy bicycle leaned against the rusty sheet-metal wall.

"This the only bike she owns?" Grandy asked.

"We look like the Kardashians to you?" Verna lit a cigarette with shaking hands. Grandy had trouble pegging her age. She could have been 40 or a hard-living 27. Good looks still in evidence but fading fast. Furtive-eyed and skittish.

"And does she ever walk anywhere from here?"

"There's nowhere *to* walk. Look around you."

"Just so you know, ma'am, the vast majority of children reported missing turn up in a familiar place."

"I'm telling you, there's no familiar place she can *get* to without her bike or gettin' a ride. She don't run in the woods like some kids. Coons and salamanders ain't her thing."

"You said she plays on a Little League team in town," Officer Price chimed in.

"Not at five a.m. in the morning she don't."

Grandy noted her eyeballs jittering from side to side. Chemically induced, he surmised. "How does she get to practices and games?"

"Sometimes by bike. Sometimes her coach picks her up. I think he got some kind of notion Abby needs rescuin' or takin' care of. She don't. I'm a good mom. They won't be makin' no Disney movies about me, that's for sure, but we do okay, Abby and me."

"What about the father? You said he lives over in Unicoi County. How often does your daughter see him?"

Verna raised her voice. "You gonna ask questions all day or are you gonna look for my daughter?"

"The only way we'll know where to look is by asking questions," said Price. "How often does she see the father?"

"Whenever 'the father' feels like showin' up. Which is usually about once in a blue frickin' moon. And then he's gone, fast as he came. Though lately..." Verna trailed off.

"Lately what, ma'am?" Price asked.

"Lately, I don't know... Seems he been comin' round more often. Maybe lingering a bit longer. Making noise about carin' about her."

"You're saying the father has taken a sudden interest in the girl?"

"I guess you could call it that." Verna folded her arms and looked at the ground. "I'm hopin' the reason's what I *think* it is, not... somethin' else."

"Ma'am?" asked Price, a note of wariness creeping into her voice.

"My daughter Abby, she's a heck of a ballplayer, officer. Last year her team went sixteen and two, made the finals, mostly on account a' her. And she's about to start a new season. I heard from someone I work with, over at the Food City, that her daddy was takin' bets on her games last year with all his no-'count drinkin' buddies. Makin' himself a lot more'n beer money, from what I heard. He denies it, a-course, but..."

"But what, ma'am?"

"...But I hope that's the reason it seems like he's been tryin' to —what's the word—'gratiate' himself with her these days."

"You *hope* the girl's father is taking bets on her Little League games?" said Grandy.

"Better *that* than..." Verna trailed off.

"Than what, ma'am?" Grandy prodded. He was not in the mood for Twenty Questions. "Than what?"

"You seen a picture of my daughter, officers?"

"We were hoping you'd provide one."

Verna Roy pulled a six-year-old smartphone out of her skin-tight back pocket. Its screen was cracked and cloudy, but the picture shone through clearly enough: a ten-year-old girl with twin bows in her hair, a huge grin on her face, and a missing canine tooth.

"That was Abby last summer," Verna said to the police. She swiped the screen a few times and brought up a new image: Abby, at age eleven, hair swept across her face, baby fat gone, a worldly glint in her eye. Pretty in a whole new way. "That's Abby last Tuesday, not even a year later."

Price turned her head to the radio on her shoulder. "This is unit seven. We're going to need to talk with the sheriff's department over in Unicoi. Make that a 10-18."

If you enjoyed the beginning of *Last Resort*, you can purchase here via Amazon:

Last Resort

Again, thank you for reading!
Scott